YAMA

CLASSICS OF RUSSIAN LITERATURE

ALEXANDRE KUPRIN

YAMA [THE PIT] A NOVEL IN THREE PARTS ❦ Translated from the Russian by Bernard Guilbert Guerney

*"All the horror is in just this,
that there is no horror...."*

HYPERION PRESS, INC.
Westport, Connecticut

Privately printed in New York, 1922
Copyright 1922 by A. Koren
Hyperion reprint edition 1977
Library of Congress Catalog Number 76-23883
ISBN 0-88355-493-3 (cloth ed.)
ISBN 0-88355-494-1 (paper ed.)
Printed in the United States of America

Library of Congress Cataloging in Publication Data

Kuprin, Aleksandr Ivanovich, 1870-1938.
   Yama = The pit.

   (Classics of Russian literature) (The Hyperion
library of world literature)
   Reprint of a priv. print. ed., New York.
   I. Title. II. Title: The pit.
PZ3.K965 Yam10   [PG3467.K8]   891.7'3'3   76-23883
ISBN 0-88355-493-5
ISBN 0-88355-494-1 pbk.

158383

AUTHOR'S DEDICATION

I know that many will find this novel immoral and indecent; nevertheless, I dedicate it with all my heart to MOTHERS AND YOUTHS—A. K.

TRANSLATOR'S DEDICATION

I dedicate the labour of translation, in all humility and sincerity, to
K. ANDRAE.—B. G. G.

INTRODUCTION

"With us, you see," Kuprin makes the reporter Platonov, his mouthpiece, say in *Yama*, "they write about
detectives, about lawyers, about inspectors of the revenue,
about pedagogues, about attorneys, about the police,
about officers, about sensual ladies, about engineers, about
baritones—and really, by God, altogether well—cleverly,
with finesse and talent. But, after all, all these people are
rubbish, and their life is not life, but some sort of conjured
up, spectral, unnecessary delirium of world culture. But
there are two singular realities—ancient as humanity
itself: the prostitute and the moujik. And about them we
know nothing, save some tinsel, gingerbread, debauched
depictions in literature..."

Tinsel, gingerbread, debauched depictions...Let us
consider some of the ways in which this monstrous reality
has been approached by various writers. There is, first,
the purely sentimental: Prevost's *Manon Lescaut*. Then
there is the slobberingly sentimental: Dumas' *Dame aux
Camelias*. A third is the necrophilically romantic: Louys'
Aphrodite. The fertile Balzac has given us no less than
two: the purely romantic, in his fascinating portraits of the
Fair Imperia; and the romantically realistic, in his *Splen-
deurs et Miseres des Courtisanes*. Reade's *Peg Woffington*
may be called the literary parallel of the costume drama;
Defoe's *Moll Flanders* is honestly realistic; Zola's *Nana* is
rabidly so.

There is one singular fact that must be noted in connection with the vast majority of such depictions. Punk or
bona roba, *lorette* or drab—put her before an artist in
letters, and, lo and behold ye! such is the strange allure

emanating from the hussy, that the resultant portrait is either that of a martyred Magdalene, or, at the very least, has all the enigmatic piquancy of a Monna Lisa... Not a slut, but what is a hetæra; and not a hetæra but what is well-nigh Kypris herself! I know of but one depiction in all literature that possesses the splendour of implacable veracity as well as undiminished artistry; where the portrait is that of a prostitute, despite all her tirings and trappings; a depiction truly deserving to be designated a portrait: the portrait supreme of the harlot eternal—Shakespeare's Cleopatra.

Furthermore, it will be observed that such depictions, for the most part, are primarily portraits of prostitutes, and not pictures of prostitution. It is also a singular fact that war, another scourge, has met with similar treatment. We have the pretty, spotless grenadiers and cuirassiers of Meissonier in plenty; Vereshchagin is still alone in the grim starkness of his wind-swept, snow-covered battle-fields, with black crows wheeling over the crumpled masses of gray...

And, curiously enough, it is another great Russian, Kuprin, who is supreme—if not unique—as a painter of the universal scourge of prostitution, *per se*; and not as an incidental background for portraits. True, he may not have entirely escaped the strange allure, aforementioned, of the femininity he paints; for femininity—even though fallen, corrupt, abased, is still femininity, one of the miracles of life, to Kuprin, the lover of life. But, even if he may be said to have used too much of the oil of sentimentality in mixing his colours for the portraits, his portraits are subordinate to the background; and there his eye is true and keen, his hand steady and unflinching, his colours and brushwork unimpeachable. Whether, like his own Platonov—who may be called to some extent an autobiographical figure, and many of whose experiences are Kuprin's own—"came upon the brothel" and gathered his material unconsciously, "without any ulterior thoughts of writing", we do not know, nor need we rummage in his dirty linen, as he puts it. Suffice it to say here—to cite but two instances—that almost anyone acquainted with Russia will tell you the full name of the rich, gay, southern port city of K—; that any Odessite will tell you that Treppel's is merely transplanted, for fictional reasons, from his own city to K—...

Alexandre I. Kuprin was born in 1870; 1909 marked the twenty-fifth anniversary of his literary activity. He attained his fame only upon the publication of his amazing, epical novel, *The Duel*—which, just like *Yama*, is an arraignment; an arraignment of militaristic corruption. Russian criticism has styled him the poet of life. If Chekhov was the *Wunderkind* of Russian letters, Kuprin is its *enfant terrible*. His range of subjects is enormous; his power of observation and his versatility extraordinary. *Gambrinus* alone would justify his place among the literary giants of Europe. Some of his picaresques, *The Insult*, *Horse-Thieves*, and *Off The Street*—the last in the form of a monologue—are sheer *tours de force*. *Olessiya* is possessed of a weird, unearthly beauty; *The Shulamite* is a prose-poem of antiquity. He deals with the life of the moujik in *Back-woods* and *The Swamp*; of the Jews, in *The Jewess* and *The Coward*; of the soldiers, in *The Cadets*, *The Interrogation*, *The Night Watch*, *Delirium*; of the actors, in *How I Was an Actor* and *In Retirement*. We have circus life in "*Allez!*", *In The Circus*, *Lolly*, *The Clown*—the last a one-act playlet; factory life, in *Moloch*; provincial life, in *Small Fry*; bohemian life, in *Captain Ribnicov* and *The River of Life*—which no one but Kuprin could have written. There are animal stories and flower stories; stories for children—and for neuropaths; one story is dedicated to a jockey; another to a circus clown; a third, if I remember rightly, to a race-horse... *Yama* created an enormous sensation upon the publication of the first part in volume three of the *Sbornik Zemliya*—*The Earth Anthology*—in 1909; the second part appeared in volume fifteen, in 1914; the third, in volume sixteen, in 1915. Both the original parts and the last revised edition have been followed in this translation.

The greater part of the stories listed above are available in translations, under various titles; the list, of course, is merely a handful from the vast bulk of the fecund Kuprin's writings, nor is any group of titles exhaustive of its kind. *The Star of Solomon*, his latest collection of stories, bears the imprint of Helsingfors, 1920.

It must not be thought, despite its *locale*, that Kuprin's *Yama* is a picture of Russian prostitution solely; it is intrinsically universal. All that is necessary is to change the kopecks into cents, pennies, sous or pfennings; compute the versts into miles or metres; Jennka may be Eugenie or Jeannette; and for Yama, simply read Whitechapel, Montmartre, or the Barbary Coast. That is why *Yama* is a "tremendous, staggering, and truthful book— a terrific book." It has been called notorious, lurid— even oleographic. So are, perhaps, the picaresques of Murillo, the pictorial satires of Hogarth, the bizarreries of Goya...

The best introduction to *Yama*, however, can be given in Kuprin's own words, as uttered by the reporter Platonov. "They do write," he says, "...but it is all either a lie, or theatrical effects for children of tender years, or else a cunning symbolism, comprehensible only to the sages of the future. But the life itself no one as yet has touched...

"But the material here is in reality tremendous, downright crushing, terrible... And not at all terrible are the loud phrases about the traffic in women's flesh, about the white slaves, about prostitution being a corroding fester of large cities, and so on, and so on...an old hurdy-gurdy of which all have tired! No, horrible are the everyday, accustomed trifles; these business-like, daily, commercial reckonings; this thousand yearold science of amatory practice; this prosaic usage, determined by the ages. In these unnoticeable nothings are completely dissolved such feelings as resentment, humiliation, shame. There remains a dry profession, a contract, an agreement, a well-nigh honest petty trade, no better, no worse than, say, the trade in groceries. Do you understand, gentlemen, that all the horror is in just this—that there is no horror! Bourgeois work days—and that is all...

"More awful than all awful words, a hundredfold more awful—is some such little prosaic stroke or other as will suddenly knock you all in a heap, like a blow on the forehead..."

It is in such little prosaic strokes; everyday, accustomed, characteristic trifles; minute particles of life, that Kuprin excels. The detailism which crowds his pages is like the stippling of Whistler; or the enumerations of the Bible; or the chiselling of Rodin, that endows the back of the *Thinker* with meaning.

"We all pass by these characteristic trifles indifferently, like the blind, as though not seeing them scattered about under our feet. But an artist will come, and he will look over them carefully, and he will pick them up. And suddenly he will so skillfully turn in the sun a minute particle of life, that we shall all cry out: 'Oh, my God! But I myself—myself!—have seen this with my own eyes. Only it simply did not enter my head to turn my close attention upon it.' But our Russian artists of the word—the most conscientious and sincere artists in the whole world—for some reason have up to this time passed over prostitution and the brothel. Why? Really, it is difficult for me to answer that. Perhaps because of squeamishness, perhaps out of pusillanimity, out of fear of being signalized as a pornographic writer; finally from the apprehension that our gossipping criticism will identify the artistic work of the writer with his personal life and will start rummaging in his dirty linen. Or perhaps they can find neither the time, nor the self-denial, nor the self-possession to plunge in head first into this life and to watch it right up close, without prejudice, without sonorous phrases, without a sheepish pity, in all its monstrous simplicity and everyday activity... That material...is truly unencompassable in its significance and weightiness... The words of others do not suffice—even though they be the most exact— even observations, made with a little note-book and a bit of pencil, do not suffice.   One must grow accustomed to this life, without being cunningly wise..."

"I believe, that not now, not soon—after fifty years or so—but there will come a writer of genius, and precisely a Russian one, who will absorb within himself all the burdens and all the abominations of this life and will cast them forth to us in the form of simple, fine, and deathlessly-caustic images. And we shall all say: 'Why, now, we ourselves have seen and known all this, but we could not even suppose that this is so horrible!' In this coming artist I believe with all my heart."

Kuprin is too sincere, too big, to have written this with himself in mind; yet no reader of the scathing, searing arraignment called *Yama*, will question that the great, the gigantic Kuprin has shown "the burdens and abominations" of prostitution, in "simple, fine, and deathlessly-caustic images"; has shown that "all the horror is in just this—that there is no horror..." For it is as a pitiless reflection of a "singular", sinister reality that *Yama* stands unsurpassed.

B. G. GUERNEY.

New York City,
 January, 1922

TRANSLATOR'S NOTE.

A word must be said of Kuprin's style. He is by no means a purist; his pages bristle with neologisms and foreign— or, rather outlandish—words; nor has he any hesitancy in adapting and Russianizing such words. He coins words; he is, at times, actually Borrowesque, and not only does he re- sort to colloquialisms and slang, but to dialect, cant, and even actual argot. Therein is his glory—and, perhaps, his weak- ness. Therefore, an attempt has been made, wherever cor- ruptions, slang, and so forth, appear in the original, to render them through the nearest English equivalents. While this has its obvious dubeities and disadvantages, any other course would have smacked of prettification—a fate which such a book as Yama surely does not deserve.

PART ONE

CHAPTER I.

A long, long time ago, long before the railroads, the stage-drivers—both government and private—used to live, from generation to generation, at the very farthest confine of a large southern city. And that is why the entire region was called the Yamskaya Sloboda—the Stage-drivers' Borough; or simply Yamskaya, or Yamkas —Little Ditches, or, shorter still, Yama—The Pit. In the course of time, when hauling by steam killed off transportation by horses, the mettlesome tribe of the stage-drivers little by little lost its boisterous ways and its brave customs, went over into other occupations, fell apart and scattered. But for many years—even up to this time— a shady renown has remained to Yama, as of a place exceedingly gay, tipsy, brawling, and in the night-time not without danger.

Somehow it came about of itself, that on the ruins of those ancient, long-warmed nests, where of yore the rosy-cheeked, sprightly wives of the soldiery and the plump widows of Yama, with their black eyebrows, had secretly traded in vodka and free love, there began to spring up wide-open brothels, permitted by the authorities, regulated by official supervision and subject to express, strict rules. Towards the end of the nineteenth century both streets of Yama—Great Yamskaya and Little Yamskaya—proved to be entirely occupied, on one side of the street as well as the other, exclusively with houses of ill-fame.* Of the private houses no more than five or six were left, but even they were taken up by public houses, beer halls, and general stores, catering to the needs of Yama prostitution.

---

*"Houses of Suffrance"—i. e., Houses of the Necessary Evil.—*Trans.*

The course of life, the manners and customs, are almost identical in all the thirty-odd establishments; the difference is only in the charges exacted for the briefly-timed love, and consequently in certain external minutiæ as well: in the assortment of more or less handsome women, in the comparative smartness of the costumes, in the magnificence of the premises and the luxuriousness of the furnishings.

The most *chic* establishment is that of Treppel, the first house to the left upon entering Great Yamskaya. This is an old firm. Its present owner bears an entirely different name, and fills the post of an elector in the city council and is even a member of the city board. The house is of two stories, green and white, built in the debauched pseudo-Russian style, *à la* Ropetovsky, with little horses, carved facings, roosters, and wooden towels bordered with lace—also of wood; a carpet with a white runner on the stairs; in the front hall a stuffed bear, holding a wooden platter for visiting cards in his outstretched paws; a parquet floor in the ballroom, heavy raspberry silk curtains and tulle on the windows, along the walls white and gold chairs and mirrors with gilt frames; there are two private cabinets with carpets, divans, and soft satin puffs; in the bedrooms blue and rose lanterns, blankets of raw silk stuff and clean pillows; the inmates are clad in low-cut ball gowns, bordered with fur, or in expensive masquerade costumes of hussars, pages, fisher lasses, school-girls; and the majority of them are Germans from the Baltic provinces—large, handsome women, white of body and with ample breasts. At Treppel's three roubles are taken for a visit, and for the whole night, ten.

Three of the two-rouble establishments — Sophie Vassilievna's, *The Old Kiev*, and Anna Markovna's— are somewhat worse, somewhat poorer. The remaining houses on Great Yamskaya are rouble ones; they are furnished still worse. While on Little Yamskaya, which is frequented by soldiers, petty thieves, artisans, and drab folk in general, and where fifty kopecks or less are taken for time, things are altogether filthy and poor—the floor in the parlor is crooked, warped, and full of splinters, the windows are hung with pieces of red fustian; the bedrooms, just like stalls, are separated by thin partitions, which do not reach to the ceiling, and on the beds, on top of the shaken down hay-mattresses, are scattered torn, spotted bed-sheets and flannel blankets, dark from time, crumpled any old way, full of holes; the air is sour and full of fumes, with a mixture of alcohol vapours and the smell of human emanations; the women, dressed in rags of coloured printed calico or in sailor costumes, are for the greater part hoarse or snuffling, with noses half fallen through, with faces preserving traces of yesterday's blows and scratches and naively bepainted with the aid of a red cigarette box moistened with spit.

All the year round, every evening—with the exception of the last three days of Holy Week and the night before Annunciation, when no bird builds its nest and a shorn wench does not plait her braid—when it barely grows dark out of doors, hanging red lanterns are lit before every house, above the tented, carved street doors. It is just like a holiday out on the street—like Easter. All the windows are brightly lit up, the gay music of violins and pianos floats out through the panes, cabmen drive up and drive off without cease. In all the houses the entrance doors are opened wide, and through them one may see from the street a steep staircase with a narrow corridor on top, and the white flashing of the many-facetted reflector of the lamp, and the green walls of the front hall, painted over with Swiss landscapes. Till the very morning hundreds and thousands of men ascend and descend these staircases. Here everybody frequents: half-shattered, slavering ancients, seeking artificial excitements, and boys—military cadets and high-school lads—almost children; bearded paterfamiliases; honourable pillars of society, in golden spectacles; and newly-weds, and enamoured bridegrooms, and honourable professors with renowned names; and thieves, and murderers, and liberal lawyers; and strict guardians of morals—pedagogues, and foremost writers—the authors of fervent, impassioned articles on the equal rights of women; and catchpoles, and spies, and escaped convicts, and officers, and students, and Social Democrats, and hired patriots; the timid and the brazen, the sick and the well, those knowing woman for the first time, and old libertines frayed by all species of vice; clear-eyed, handsome fellows and monsters maliciously distorted by nature, deaf-mutes, blind men, men without noses, with flabby, pendulous bodies, with malodorous breath, bald, trembling, covered with parasites—pot-bellied, hemorrhoidal apes. They come freely and simply, as to a restaurant or a depot; they sit, smoke, drink, convulsively pretend to be merry; they dance, executing abominable movements of the body imitative of the act of sexual love. At times attentively and long, at times with gross haste, they choose any woman they like and know beforehand that they will never meet refusal. Impatiently they pay their money in advance, and on the public bed, not yet grown cold after the body of their predecessor, aimlessly commit the very greatest and most beautiful of all universal mysteries—the mystery of the conception of new life. And the women with indifferent readiness, with uniform words, with practiced professional movements, satisfy their desires, like machines—only to receive, right after them, during the same night, with the very same words, smiles and gestures, the third, the fourth, the tenth man, not infrequently already biding his turn in the waiting room.

So passes the entire night. Towards daybreak Yama little by little grows quiet, and the bright morning finds it depopulated, spacious, plunged into sleep, with doors shut tightly, with shutters fixed on the windows. But toward evening the women awaken and get ready for the following night.

And so without end, day after day, for months and years, they live a strange, incredible life in their public harems, outcast by society, accursed by the family, victims of the social temperament, cloacas for the excess of the city's sensuality, the guardians of the honour of the family—four hundred foolish, lazy, hysterical, barren women.

CHAPTER II.

Two in the afternoon. In the second-rate, two-rouble establishment of Anna Markovna everything is plunged in sleep. The large square parlor with mirrors in gilt frames, with a score of plush chairs placed decorously along the walls, with oleograph pictures of Makovsky's *Feast of the Russian Noblemen*, and *Bathing*, with a crystal lustre in the middle, is also sleeping, and in the quiet and semi-darkness it seems unwontedly pensive, austere, strangely sad. Yesterday here, as on every evening, lights burned, the most rollicking of music rang out, blue tobacco smoke swirled, men and women careered in couples, shaking their hips and throwing their legs on high. And the entire street shone on the outside with the red lanterns over the street doors and with the light from the windows, and it seethed with people and carriages until morning.

Now the street is empty. It is glowing triumphantly and joyously in the glare of the summer sun. But in the parlor all the window curtains are lowered, and for that reason it is dark within, cool, and as peculiarly uninviting as the interiors of empty theatres, riding academies and court buildings usually are in the middle of the day.

The pianoforte glimmers dully with its black, bent, glossy side; the yellow, old, time-eaten, broken, gap-toothed keys glisten faintly. The stagnant, motionless air still retains yesterday's odour; it smells of perfumes, tobacco, the sour dampness of a large uninhabited room, the perspiration of unclean and unhealthy feminine flesh, face-powder, boracic-thymol soap, and the dust of the yellow mastic with which the parquet floor had been polished yesterday. And with a strange charm the smell of withering swamp grass is blended with these smells.

To-day is Trinity. In accordance with an olden custom, the chambermaids of the establishment, while their ladies were still sleeping, had bought a whole waggon of sedge on the market, and had strewn its long, thick blades, that crunch underfoot, everywhere about—in the corridors, in the private cabinets, in the drawing room. They, also, had lit the lamps before all the images. The girls, by tradition, dare not do this with their hands, which have been defiled during the night.

And the house-porter has adorned the house-entrance, which is carved in the Russian style, with two little felled birch-trees. And so with all the houses—the thin white trunks with their scant dying verdure adorn the exterior near the stoops, bannisters and doors.

The entire house is quiet, empty and drowsy. The chopping of cutlets for dinner can be heard from the kitchen. Liubka, one of the girls, barefooted, in her shift, with bare arms, not good-looking, freckled, but strong and fresh of body, has come out into the inner court. Yesterday she had had but six guests on time, but no one had remained for the night with her, and because of that she had slept her fill—splendidly, delightfully, all alone, upon a wide bed. She had risen early, at ten o'clock, and had with pleasure helped the cook scrub the floor and the tables in the kitchen. Now she is feeding the chained dog Amour with the sinews and cuttings of the meat. The big, rusty hound, with long glistening hair and black muzzle, jumps up on the girl with his front paws, stretching the chain tightly and rattling in the throat from shortness of breath, then, with back and tail undulating all over, bends his head down to the ground, wrinkles his nose, smiles, whines and sneezes from the excitement. But she, teasing him with the meat, shouts at him with pretended severity:

"There, you—stupid! I'll—I'll give it to you! How dare you?"

But she rejoices with all her soul over the tumult and caresses of Amour and her momentary power over the

dog, and because she had slept her fill, and passed the
night without a man, and because of the Trinity, according to dim recollections of her childhood, and because
of the sparkling sunny day, which it so seldom befalls
her to see.

All the night guests have already gone their ways.
The most business-like, quiet and workaday hour is
coming on.

They are drinking coffee in the room of the proprietress.
The company consists of five people. The proprietress
herself, in whose name the house is registered, is Anna
Markovna. She is about sixty. She is very small of
stature, but dumpy: she may be visualized by imagin-
ing, from the bottom up, three soft, gelatinous globes—
large, medium and small, pressed into each other without
any interstices; this—her skirt, torso and head. Strange,
her eyes are a faded blue, girlish, even childish, but the
mouth is that of an old person, with a moist lower lip of
a raspberry colour, impotently hanging down. Her
husband—Isaiah Savvich—is also small, a grayish, quiet,
silent little old man. He is under his wife's thumb;
he was doorkeeper in this very house even at the time
when Anna Markovna served here as housekeeper. In
order to be useful in some way, he has learned, through
self-instruction, to play the fiddle, and now at night plays
dance tunes, as well as a funeral march for shopmen far
gone on a spree and craving some maudlin tears.

Then, there are the two housekeepers—senior and
junior. The senior is Emma Edwardovna. She is a tall,
full woman of forty-six, with chestnut hair, and a fat
goitre of three chins. Her eyes are encircled with black
rings of hemorrhoidal origin. The face broadens out
like a pear from the forehead down to the cheeks, and is
of an earthen colour; the eyes are small, black; the nose
humped, the lips sternly pursed; the expression of the
face calmly authoritative. It is no mystery to anyone
in the house that in a year or two Anna Markovna will
go into retirement, and sell her the establishment with

all its rights and furnishings, when she will receive part in cash, and part on terms—by promissory note. Because of this the girls honour her equally with the proprietress and fear her somewhat. Those who fall into error she beats with her own hands, beats cruelly, coolly, and calculatingly, without changing the calm expression of her face. Among the girls there is always a favourite of hers, whom she tortures with her exacting love and fantastic jealousy. And this is far harder than her beatings.

The other one is called Zociya. She has just struggled out of the ranks of the common girls. The girls, as yet, call her impersonally, flatteringly and familiarly, "little housekeeper." She is spare, spry, just a trifle squinting, with a rosy complexion, and hair dressed in a little curly pompadour; she adores actors—preferably stout comedians. Toward Emma Edwardovna she is ingratiating.

The fifth person, finally, is the local district inspector, Kerbesh. This is an athletic man; he is kind of bald, has a red beard like a fan, vividly blue slumbrous eyes, and a thin, slightly hoarse, pleasant voice. Everybody knows that he formerly served in the secret service division and was the terror of crooks, thanks to his terrible physical strength and cruelty in interrogations.

He has several shady transactions on his conscience. The whole town knows, that two years back he married a rich old woman of seventy, and that last year he strangled her; however, he was somehow successful in hushing up this affair. But for that matter, the remaining four have also seen a thing or two in their chequered life. But, just as the *bretteurs* of old felt no twinges of conscience at the recollection of their victims, even so do these people regard the dark and bloody things in their past, as the unavoidable little unpleasantnesses of their professions.

They are drinking coffee with rich, boiled cream—the inspector with Benedictine. But he, strictly speaking, is not drinking, but merely conveying the impression that he is doing it to oblige.

"Well, what is it to be, Phoma Phomich?" asks the proprietress searchingly. "This business isn't worth an empty eggshell, now. . . Why, you have only to say a word. . ."

Kerbesh slowly draws in half a wine-glass of liqueur, works the oily, strong, pungent liquid slightly with his tongue over the roof of his mouth, swallows it, chases it down, without hurrying, with coffee, and then passes the ring finger of his left hand over his moustaches, to the right and left.

"Think it over for yourself, Madam Shoibes," he says, looking down at the table, spreading out his hands and screwing up his eyes. "Think of the risk to which I'm exposed! The girl through means of deception was enticed into this . . . what-you-may-call-it. . . well, in a word, into a house of ill-fame, to express it in lofty style. Now the parents are searching for her through the police. Ve-ery well. She gets into one place after another, from the fifth into the tenth. . . Finally the trail is picked up with you, and most important of all—think of it!—in my district! What can I do?"

"Mr. Kerbesh, but she is of age," says the proprietress.

"They are of age," confirms Isaiah Savvich. "They gave an acknowledgment, that it was of their own will . . ."

Emma Edwardovna pronounces in a bass, with cool assurance:

"Honest to God, she's the same here as an own daughter."

"But that's not what I am talking about," the inspector frowns in vexation. "Just consider my position . . . Why, this is duty. Lord, there's no end of unpleasantnesses without that!"

The proprietress suddenly arises, shuffles in her slippers to the door, and says, winking to the inspector with a sleepy, expressionless eye of faded blue:

"Mr. Kerbesh, I would ask you to have a look at our alterations. We want to enlarge the place a bit."

"A-ah! With pleasure. . ."

After ten minutes both return, without looking at each other. Kerbesh's hand is crunching a brand-new hundred rouble note in his pocket. The conversation about the seduced girl is not renewed. The inspector, hastily finishing his Benedictine, complains of the present decline in manners.

"I have a son, now, a schoolboy—Paul. He comes to me, the scoundrel, and declares: 'Papa, the pupils swear at me, because you are a policeman, and because you serve on Yamskaya, and because you take bribes from brothels.' Well, tell me, for God's sake, Madam Shoibes, if that isn't effrontery?"

"Ai, ai, ai! . . And what bribes can there be? Now with me . . ."

"I say to him: 'Go, you good-for-nothing, and let the principal know, that there should be no more of this, otherwise papa will inform on all of you to the governor.' And what do you think? He comes to me and says: 'I am no longer a son to you—seek another son for yourself.' What an argument! Well, I gave him enough to last till the first of the month! Oho-ho! Now he doesn't want to speak with me. Well, I'll show him yet!"

"Ah, you don't have to tell us," sighs Anna Markovna, letting her lower, raspberry-coloured lip hang down and with a mist coming over her faded eyes. "We keep our Birdie—she is in Fleisher's high school—we purposely keep her in town, in a respectable family. You understand, it is awkward, after all. And all of a sudden she brings such words and expressions from the high school that I just simply turned all red."

"Honest to God, Annochka turned all red," confirms Isaiah Savvich.

"You'll turn red, all right!" warmly agrees the inspector. "Yes, yes, yes, I understand you fully. But, my God, where are we going! Where are we only going? I ask you, what are these revolutionaries and all these various students, or . . . what-you-may-call-'ems? . . trying to attain? And let them put the blame on none but themselves. Corruption is everywhere, morality is falling, there is no respect for parents. They ought to be shot."

"Well, now, the day before yesterday we had a case," Zociya mixes in bustlingly. "A certain guest came, a stout man . . ."

"Drop it!" Emma Edwardovna, who was listening to the inspector, piously nodding with her head bowed to one side, cuts her short in the jargon of the brothels. "You'd better go and see about breakfast for the young ladies."

"And not a single person can be relied upon," continues the proprietress grumblingly. "Not a servant but what she's a stiff, a faker. And all the girls ever think about is their lovers. Just so's they may have their own pleasure. But about their duties they don't even think."

There is an awkward silence. Some one knocks on the door. A thin, feminine voice speaks on the other side of the door:

"Housekeeper, dear, take the money and be kind enough to give me the stamps. Pete's gone."

The inspector gets up and adjusts his sabre.

"Well, it's time I was going to work. Best regards, Anna Markovna. Best wishes, Isaiah Savvich."

"Perhaps you'll have one more little glass for a stirrup cup?" the nearly blind Isaiah Savvich thrusts himself over the table.

"Tha-ank you. I can't. Full to the gills. Honoured, I'm sure! . ."

"Thanks for your company. Drop in some time."

"Always glad to be your guest, sir. *Au revoir!*"

But in the doorway he stops for a minute and says significantly:

"But still, my advice to you is—you'd better pass this girl on to some place or other in good time. Of course, it's your affair, but as a good friend of yours I give you warning."

He goes away. When his steps are abating on the stairs and the front door bangs to behind him, Emma

Edwardovna snorts through her nose and says contemptuously:

"Stool-pigeon! He wants to take money both here and there . . ."

Little by little they all crawl apart out of the room. It is dark in the house. It smells sweetly of the half-withered sedge. Quiet reigns.

CHAPTER III.

Until dinner, which is served at six in the evening, the time drags endlessly long and with intolerable monotony. And, in general, this daily interval is the heaviest and emptiest in the life of the house. It remotely resembles in its moods those slothful, empty hours which are lived through during the great holidays in scholastic institutes and other private institutions for females, when all the friends have dispersed, when there is much leisure and much indolence, and a radiant, agreeable tedium reigns the whole day. In only their petticoats and white shifts, with bare arms, sometimes barefooted, the women aimlessly ramble from room to room, all of them unwashed, uncombed; lazily strike the keys of the old pianoforte with the index finger, lazily lay out cards to tell their fortune, lazily exchange curses, and with a languishing irritation await the evening.

Liubka, after breakfast, had carried out the leavings of bread and the cuttings of ham to Amour, but the dog had soon palled upon her. Together with Niura she had bought some barberry bon-bons and sunflower seeds, and now both are standing behind the fence separating the house from the street, gnawing the seeds, the shells of which remain on their chins and bosoms, and speculate indifferently about those who pass on the street: about the lamp-lighter, pouring kerosene into the street lamps, about the policeman with the daily registry book under his arm, about the housekeeper from somebody else's establishment, running across the road to the general store.

Niura is a small girl, with goggle-eyes of blue; she has white, flaxen hair and little blue veins on her temples. In her face there is something stolid and innocent, reminiscent of a white sugar lamb on a Paschal cake. She is lively, bustling, curious, puts her nose into everything, agrees with everybody, is the first to know the news, and, when she speaks, she speaks so much and so rapidly that spray flies out of her mouth and bubbles effervesce on the red lips, as in children.

Opposite, out of the dram-shop, a servant pops out for a minute—a curly, besotted young fellow with a cast in his eye—and runs into the neighbouring public house.

"Prokhor Ivanovich, oh Prokhor Ivanovich," shouts Niura, "don't you want some?—I'll treat you to some sunflower seeds?"

"Come on in and pay us a visit," Liubka chimes in.

Niura snorts and adds through the laughter which suffocates her:

"Warm your feet for a while!"

But the front door opens; in it appears the formidable and stern figure of the senior housekeeper.

"*Pfui!** What sort of indecency is this!" she cries commandingly. "How many times must it be repeated to you, that you must not jump out on the street during the day, and also—*pfui!*—only in your underwear. I can't understand how you have no conscience yourselves. Decent girls, who respect themselves, must not demean themselves that way in public. It seems, thank God, that you are not in an establishment catering to soldiers, but in a respectable house. Not in Little Yamskaya."

The girls return into the house, get into the kitchen, and for a long time sit there on tabourets, contemplating the angry cook Prascoviya, swinging their legs and silently gnawing the sunflower seeds.

In the room of Little Manka, who is also called Manka the Scandaliste and Little White Manka, a whole party has gathered. Sitting on the edge of the bed, she and another girl—Zoe, a tall handsome girl, with arched eyebrows, with grey, somewhat bulging eyes, with the most typical, white, kind face of the Russian prostitute—

---

*A German exclamation of disgust or contempt, corresponding to the English *fie.—Trans.*

are playing at cards, playing at "sixty-six." Little Manka's closest friend, Jennie, is lying behind their backs on the bed, prone on her back, reading a tattered book, *The Queen's Necklace*, the work of Monsieur Dumas, and smoking. In the entire establishment she is the only lover of reading and reads intoxicatingly and without discrimination. But, contrary to expectation, the forced reading of novels of adventure has not at all made her sentimental and has not vitiated her imagination. Above all, she likes in novels a long intrigue, cunningly thought out and deftly disentangled; magnificent duels, before which the viscount unties the laces of his shoes to signify that he does not intend to retreat even a step from his position,* and after which the marquis, having spitted the count through, apologizes for having made an opening in his splendid new waistcoat; purses, filled to the full with gold, carelessly strewn to the left and right by the chief heroes; the love adventures and witticisms of Henry IV—in a word, all this spiced heroism, in gold and lace, of the past centuries of French history. In everyday life, on the contrary, she is sober of mind, jeering, practical and cynically malicious. In her relation to the other girls of the establishment she occupies the same place that in private educational institutions is accorded to the first strong man, the man spending a second year in the same grade, the first beauty in the class—tyrannizing and adored. She is a tall, thin brunette, with beautiful hazel eyes, a small proud mouth, a little moustache on the upper lip and with a swarthy, unhealthy pink on her cheeks.

Without letting the cigarette out of her mouth and screwing up her eyes from the smoke, all she does is to turn the pages constantly with a moistened finger. Her legs are bare to the knees; the enormous balls of the feet are of the most vulgar form; below the big toes stand out pointed, ugly, irregular tumours.

---

*Probably a sly dig at Gautier's *Captain Fracasse.—Trans.*

Here also, with her legs crossed, slightly bent, with some sewing, sits Tamara—a quiet, comfortable, pretty girl, slightly reddish, with that dark and shining tint of hair which is to be found on the back of a fox in winter. Her real name is Glycera, or Lukeria, as the common folk say it. But it is already an ancient usage of the houses of ill-fame to replace the uncouth names of the Matrenas, Agathas, Cyclitinias with sonorous, preferably exotic names. Tamara had at one time been a nun, or, perhaps, merely a novice in a convent, and to this day there have been preserved on her face timidity and a pale puffiness—a modest and sly expression, which is peculiar to young nuns. She holds herself aloof in the house, does not chum with any one, does not initiate any one into her past life. But in her case there must have been many more adventures besides having been a nun: there is something mysterious, taciturn and criminal in her unhurried speech, in the evasive glance of her deep and dark-gold eyes from under the long, lowered eyelashes, in her manners, her sly smiles and intonations of a modest but wanton would-be saint. There was one occurrence when the girls, with well-nigh reverent awe, heard that Tamara could talk fluently in French and German. She has within her some sort of an inner, restrained power. Notwithstanding her outward meekness and complaisance, all in the establishment treat her with respect and circumspection—the proprietress, and her mates, and both housekeepers, and even the doorkeeper, that veritable sultan of the house of ill-fame, that general terror and hero.

"I've covered it," says Zoe and turns over the trump which had been lying under the pack, wrong side up. "I'm going with forty, going with an ace of spades—a ten-spot, Mannechka, if you please. I'm through. Fifty-seven, eleven, sixty-eight. How much have you?"

"Thirty," says Manka in an offended tone, pouting her lips; "oh, it's all very well for you—you remember all the plays. Deal . . . Well, what's after that, Tamarochka?" she turns to her friend. "You talk on—I'm listening."

Zoe shuffles the old, black, greasy cards, allows Manya to cut, then deals, having first spat upon her fingers.

Tamara in the meanwhile is narrating to Manya in a quiet voice, without dropping her sewing.

"We embroidered with gold, in flat embroidery—altar covers, palls, bishops' vestments. . . With little grasses, with flowers, little crosses. In winter, you'd be sitting near a casement; the panes are small, with gratings, there isn't much light, it smells of lamp oil, incense, cypress; you mustn't talk—the mother superior was strict. Some one from weariness would begin droning a pre-Lenten first verse of a hymn . . . 'When I consider thy heavens . . .' We sang fine, beautifully, and it was such a quiet life, and the smell was so fine; you could see the flaky snow out the windows—well, now, just like in a dream . . ."

Jennie puts the tattered novel down on her stomach, throws the cigarette over Zoe's head, and says mockingly:

"We know all about your quiet life. You chucked the infants into toilets. The Evil One is always snooping around your holy places."

"I call forty. I had forty-six. Finished!" Little Manka exclaims excitedly and claps her palms. "I open with three."

Tamara, smiling at Jennie's words, answers with a scarcely perceptible smile, which barely distends her lips, but makes little, sly, ambiguous depressions at their corners, altogether as with Monna Lisa in the portrait by Leonardo da Vinci.

"Lay folk say a lot of things about nuns . . . Well, even if there had been sin once in a while . . ."

"If you don't sin—you don't repent," Zoe puts in seriously, and wets her finger in her mouth.

"You sit and sew, the gold eddies before your eyes, while from standing in the morning at prayer your back just aches, and your legs ache. And at evening there is service again. You knock at the door of the mother superior's cell: 'Through prayers of Thy saints, oh Lord, our Father, have mercy upon us.' And the mother superior would answer from the cell, in a little bass-like 'A-men.'"

Jennie looks at her intently for some time, shakes her head and says with great significance:

"You're a queer girl, Tamara. Here I'm looking at you and wondering. Well, now, I can understand how these fools, on the manner of Sonka, play at love. That's what they're fools for. But you, it seems, have been roasted on all sorts of embers, have been washed in all sorts of lye, and yet you allow yourself foolishness of that sort. What are you embroidering that shirt for?"

Tamara, without haste, with a pin refastens the fabric more conveniently on her knee, smooths the seam down with the thimble, and speaks, without raising the narrowed eyes, her head bent just a trifle to one side:

"One's got to be doing something. It's wearisome just so. I don't play at cards, and I don't like them."

Jennie continues to shake her head.

"No, you're a queer girl, really you are. You always have more from the guests than all of us get. You fool, instead of saving money, what do you spend it on? You buy perfumes at seven roubles the bottle. Who needs it? And now you have bought fifteen roubles' worth of silk. Isn't this for your Senka, now?"

"Of course, for Sennechka."

"What a treasure you've found, to be sure! A miserable thief. He rides up to this establishment like some general. How is it he doesn't beat you yet? The thieves—they like that. And he plucks you, have no fear?"

"More than I want to, I won't give," meekly answers Tamara and bites the thread in two.

"Now that is just what I wonder at. With your mind, your beauty, I would put such rings-around-a-rosie about a guest like that, that he'd take me and set me up. I'd have horses of my own, and diamonds."

"Everyone to his tastes, Jennechka. You too, now, are a very pretty and darling girl, and your character is so independent and brave, and yet you and I have gotten stuck in Anna Markovna's."

Jennie flares up and answers with unsimulated bitterness:

"Yes! Why not! All things come your way!.. You have all the very best guests. You do what you want with them, but with me it's always either old men or suckling babies. I have no luck. The ones are snotty, the others have yellow around the mouth. More than anything else, now, I dislike the little boys. He comes, the little varmint; he's cowardly, he hurries, he trembles, but having done the business, he doesn't know what to do with his eyes for shame. He's all squirming from disgust. I just feel like giving him one in the snout. Before giving you the rouble, he holds it in his pocket in his fist, and that rouble's all hot, even sweaty. The milksop! His mother gives him a ten kopeck piece for a French roll with sausage, but he's economized out of that for a wench. I had one little cadet in the last few days. So just on purpose, to spite him, I say: 'Here, my dearie, here's a little caramel for you on your way; when you're going back to your corps, you'll suck on it.' So at first he got offended, but afterwards took it. Later I looked from the stoop, on purpose; just as soon as he walked out, he looked around, and right away into his mouth with the caramel. The little swine!"

"But with old men it's still worse," says Little Manka in a tender voice, and slyly looks at Zoe. "What do you think, Zoinka?"

Zoe, who had already finished playing, and was just about to yawn, now cannot in any way give rein to her yawns. She does not know whether she wants to be angry or to laugh. She has a steady visitor, some little

old man in a high station, with perverted erotic habits.
The entire establishment makes fun of his visits to her.

Zoe at last succeeds in yawning.

"To the devil's dam with all of you," she says, with
her voice hoarse after the yawn; "may he be damned,
the old anathema!"

"But still, the worst of all," Jennie continues to discourse, "worse than your director, Zoinka, worse than
my cadet, the worst of all—are your lovers. What can
there be joyous in this: he comes drunk, poses, makes
sport of you, wants to pretend there's something in him—
only nothing comes of it all. Wha-at a lad-die, to be
sure! The scummiest of the scum, dirty, beaten-up,
stinking, his whole body in scars, there's only one glory
about him: the silk shirt which Tamarka will embroider
for him. He curses one's mother, the son of a bitch,
always aching for a fight. Ugh! No!" she suddenly
exclaimed in a merry provoking voice, "The one I love
truly and surely, for ever and ever, is my Mannechka,
Manka the white, little Manka, my Manka-Scandalis-
tochka."

And unexpectedly, having embraced Manya by the
shoulders and bosom, she drew her toward herself, threw
her down on the bed, and began to kiss deeply and vigorously her hair, eyes, lips. Manka with difficulty tore
herself away from her, with dishevelled, bright, fine,
downy hair, all rosy from the resistance, and with eyes
downcast and moist from shame and laughter.

"Leave off, Jennechka, leave off. Well, now, what are
you doing? Let me go!"

Little Manya is the meekest and quietest girl in the
entire establishment. She is kind, yielding, can never
refuse anybody's request, and involuntarily everybody
treats her with great gentleness. She blushes over every
trifle, and at such a time becomes especially attractive;
as only very tender blondes with a sensitive skin can be
attractive. But it is sufficient for her to drink three or
four glasses of Liqueur Benedictine, of which she is very

fond, for her to become unrecognizable and to create
brawls, such, that there is always required the intervention of the housekeepers, the porter, at times even the
police. It is nothing for her to hit a guest in the face or
to throw in his face a glass filled with wine, to overturn
the lamp, to curse out the proprietress. Jennie treats her
with some strange, tender patronage and rough adoration.

"Ladies, to dinner! To dinner, ladies!" calls Zociya
the housekeeper, running along the corridor. On the run
she opens the door into Manya's room and drops hurriedly:

"To dinner, to dinner, ladies!"

They go again to the kitchen, all still in their underwear, all unwashed, in slippers and barefoot. A tasty
vegetable soup of pork rinds and tomatoes, cutlets, and
pastry—cream rolls—are served. But no one has any
appetite, thanks to the sedentary life and irregular sleep,
and also because the majority of the girls, just like school-
girls on a holiday, had already managed during the day
to send to the store for *halvah*, nuts, *rakhat loukoum*
(Turkish Delight), dill-pickles and molasses candy, and had
through this spoiled their appetites. Only Nina alone—
a small, pug-nosed, snuffling country girl, seduced only
two months ago by a travelling salesman, and (also by
him) sold into a brothel—eats for four. The inordinate,
provident appetite of a woman of the common people has
not yet disappeared in her.

Jennie, who has only picked fastidiously at her cutlet
and eaten half her cream roll, speaks to her in a tone of
hypocritical solicitude:

"Really, Pheclusha, you might just as well eat my
cutlet, too. Eat, my dear, eat; don't be bashful—you
ought to be gaining in health. But do you know what
I'll tell you, ladies?" she turns to her mates, "Why,
our Pheclusha has a tape-worm, and when a person has
a tape-worm, he always eats for two: half for himself,
half for the worm."

Nina sniffs angrily and answers in a bass which comes as a surprise from one of her stature, and through her nose:

"There are no tape-worms in me. It's you that has the tape-worms, that's why you are so skinny."

And she imperturbably continues to eat, and after dinner feels herself sleepy, like a boa constrictor, eructs loudly, drinks water, hiccups, and, by stealth, if no one sees her, makes the sign of the cross over her mouth, through an old habit.

But already the ringing voice of Zociya can be heard through the corridors and rooms:

"Get dressed, ladies, get dressed. There's no use in sitting around ... To work..."

After a few minutes in all the rooms of the establishment there are smells of singed hair, boric-thymol soap, cheap *eau-de-cologne*. The girls are dressing for the evening.

CHAPTER IV.

The late twilight came on, and after it the warm dark night, but for long, until very midnight, did the deep crimson glow of the sky still smoulder. Simeon, the porter of the establishment, has lit all the lamps along the walls of the drawing room and the lustre, as well as the red lantern over the stoop. Simeon was a spare, stocky, taciturn and harsh man, with straight, broad shoulders, dark-haired, pock-marked, with little bald spots on his eye-brows and moustaches from small-pox, and with black, dull, insolent eyes. By day he was free and slept, while at night he sat without absenting himself in the front hall under the reflector, in order to help the guests with their coats and to be ready in case of any disorder.

The pianist came—a tall, elegant young man, with white eyebrows and eyelashes, and a cataract in his right eye. The while there were no guests, he and Isaiah Savvich quietly rehearsed *Pas d'Espagne*, at that time coming into fashion. For every dance ordered by the guests, they received thirty kopecks for an easy dance, and a half a rouble for a quadrille. But one-half of this price was taken out by the proprietress, Anna Markovna; the other, however, the musicians divided evenly. In this manner the pianist received only a quarter of the general earnings, which, of course, was unjust, since Isaiah Savvich played as one self-taught and was distinguished for having no more ear for music than a piece of wood. The pianist was constantly compelled to drag him on to new tunes, to correct and cover his mistakes with loud chords. The girls said of their pianist to the guests, with a certain pride, that he had been in the conservatory and always ranked as the first pupil, but since he is a Jew, and in addition to that his eyes had begun to trouble him, he had not succeeded in completing the course. They all treated him carefully and considerately, with some sort of solicitous, somewhat mawkish, commiseration, which chimes so well with the inner, backstage customs of houses of ill-fame, where underneath the outer coarseness and the flaunting of obscene words dwells the same sweetish, hysterical sentimentality as in female boarding schools, and, so they say, in penal institutions.

In the house of Anna Markovna everybody was already dressed and ready for the reception of the guests, and languishing from inaction and expectation. Despite the fact that the majority of the women experienced toward men—with the exception of their lovers—a complete, even somewhat squeamish, indifference, before every evening dim hopes came to life and stirred within their souls; it was unknown who would choose them, whether something unusual, funny and alluring might not happen, whether a guest would not astonish with his generosity, whether there would not be some miracle which would overturn the whole life... In these presentiments and hopes was something akin to those emotions which the accustomed gamester experiences when counting his ready money before starting out for his club. Besides that, despite their asexuality, they still had not lost the chiefest instinctive aspiration of women—to please.

And, in truth, altogether curious personages came into the house at times and ludicrous, motley events arose. The police would appear suddenly together with disguised detectives and arrest some seemingly respectable, irreproachable gentlemen and lead them off, pushing them along with blows in the neck. At times brawls would spring up between the drunken, trouble-making company and the porters of all the establishments, who had gathered on the run for the relief of a fellow porter—a brawl, during which the window-panes and the decks of grand-pianos were broken, when the legs of the plush chairs were wrenched out for weapons, blood ran over the parquet floor of the drawing room and the steps of the stairs, and people with pierced sides and broken heads fell down into the dirt near the street entrance, to the feral, avid delight of Jennka, who, with burning eyes, with happy laughter, went into the thickest of the melee, slapped herself on the hips, swore and sicked them on, while her mates were squealing from fear and hiding under the beds.

There were occurrences when there would arrive, with a pack of parasites, some member of a workingmen's association or a cashier, long since far gone in an embezzlement of many thousands through gambling at cards and hideous orgies, and now, in a drunken, senseless delirium, tossing the last money after the other, before suicide or the prisoner's box. Then the doors and windows of the house would be tightly closed, and for two days and nights at a stretch a Russian orgy would go on—nightmarish, tedious, savage, with screams and tears, with revilement over the body of woman; paradisaical nights were gotten up, during which naked, drunken, bow-legged, hairy, pot-bellied men, and women with flabby, yellow, pendulous thin bodies hideously grimaced to the music; they drank and guzzled like swine, on the beds and on the floor, amidst the stifling atmosphere, permeated with spirits, befouled with human respiration and the exhalations of unclean skins.

Occasionally, there would appear a circus athlete, creating in the low-ceiled quarters a strangely cumbersome impression, somewhat like that of a horse led into a room; a Chinaman in a blue blouse, white stockings, and with a queue; a negro from a cabaret, in a tuxedo coat and checked pantaloons, with a flower in his button-hole, and with starched linen, which, to the amazement of the girls, not only did not soil from the black skin, but appeared still more dazzlingly white.

These rare people fomented the satiated imagination of the prostitutes, excited their exhausted sensuality and professional curiosity, and all of them, almost enamoured, would walk in their steps, jealous and bickering with one another.

There was one incident when Simeon had let into the room an elderly man, dressed like a bourgeois. There was nothing exceptional about him; he had a stern, thin face, with bony, evil-looking cheek-bones, protruding like tumours, a low forehead, a beard like a wedge, bushy eyebrows, one eye perceptibly higher than the other. Having entered, he raised his fingers, folded for the sign of the cross, to his forehead, but having searched the corners with his eyes and finding no image, he did not in the least grow confused, put down his hand, and at once with a business-like air walked up to the fattest girl in the establishment—Kitty.

"Let's go!" he commanded curtly, and with determination nodded his head in the direction of the door.

During the entire period of her absence the omniscious Simeon, with a mysterious, and even somewhat proud air, managed to inform Niura, at that time his mistress, while she, in a whisper, with horror in her rounded eyes, told her mates, in secret, that the name of the bourgeois was Dyadchenko, and that last fall he had volunteered, owing to the absence of the hangman, to carry out the execution of eleven rioters, and with his own hands had hung them in two mornings. And—monstrous as it may be—at that hour there was not in the establishment a single girl who did not feel envy toward the fat Kitty, and did not experience a painful, keen, vertiginous curiosity. When Dyadchenko was going away half an hour later with his sedate and stern air, all the women speechlessly, with their mouths gaping, escorted him to the street door and afterwards watched him from the windows as he walked along the street. Then they rushed into the room of the dressing Kitty and overwhelmed her with interrogations. They looked with a new feeling, almost with astonishment, at her bare, red, thick arms, at the bed, still crumpled, at the old, greasy, paper rouble, which Kitty showed them, having taken it out of her stocking. Kitty could tell them nothing. "A man like any man, like all men," she said with a calm incomprehension; but when she found out who her visitor had been, she suddenly burst into tears, without herself knowing why.

This man, the outcast of outcasts, fallen as low as the fancy of man can picture, this voluntary headsman, had treated her without rudeness, but with such absence of even a hint at endearment, with such disdain and wooden indifference, as no human being is treated; not even a dog or a horse, and not even an umbrella, overcoat or hat, but like some dirty, unclean object, for which a momentary, unavoidable need arises, but which, at the passing of its needfulness, becomes foreign, useless, and disgusting. The entire horror of this thought the fat Kate could not embrace with her brain of a fattened turkey hen, and because of that cried—as it seemed even to her—without cause and reason.

There were also other happenings, which stirred up the turbid, foul life of these poor, sick, silly, unfortunate women. There were cases of savage, unbridled jealousy with pistol shots and poisoning; occasionally, very rarely, a tender, flaming and pure love would blossom out upon this dung; occasionally the women even abandoned an establishment with the help of the loved man, but almost always came back. Two or three times it happened that a woman from a brothel would suddenly prove pregnant— and this always seemed, on the face of it, laughable and disgraceful, but touching in the profundity of the event.

And no matter what may have happened, every evening brought with it such an irritating, strained, spicy expectation of adventures that every other life, after that in a house of ill-fame, would have seemed flat and humdrum to these lazy women of no will power.

CHAPTER V.

The windows are opened wide to the fragrant darkness of the evening, and the tulle curtains stir faintly back and forth from the imperceptible movement of the air. It smells of dewy grass from the consumptive little garden in front of the house, and just the least wee bit of lilac and the withering birch leaves of the little trees placed near the entrance because of the Trinity. Liuba, in a blue velvet blouse with low cut bosom, and Niura, dressed as a "baby", in a pink, wide sacque to the knees, with her bright hair loose and with little curls on her forehead, are lying embraced on the window-sill, and are singing in a low voice a song about the hospital, which song is the rage of the day and exceedingly well known among prostitutes. Niura, through her nose, leads in a high voice, Liuba seconds her with a stifled alto:

> "Monday now is come again,
> They're supposed to get me out;
> Doctor Krasov won't let me out...."

In all the houses the windows are brightly lit, while hanging lanterns are burning before the entrances. To both girls the interior in the establishment of Sophia Vasilievna, which is directly opposite, is distinctly visible— the shining yellow parquet, draperies of a dark cherry colour on the doors, caught up with cords, the end of a black grand piano, a pier glass in a gilt frame, and the figures of women in gorgeous dresses, now flashing at the windows, now disappearing, and their reflections in the mirrors. The carved stoop of Treppel, to the right, is brightly illuminated by a bluish electric light from a big frosted globe.

45

The evening is calm and warm. Somewhere far, far away, beyond the line of the railroad, beyond some black roofs and the thin black trunks of trees, down low over the dark earth in which the eye does not see but as though senses the mighty green tone of spring, reddens with a scarlet gold the narrow, long streak of the sunset glow, which has pierced the dove-coloured mist. And in this indistinct, distant light, in the caressing air, in the scents of the oncoming night, was some secret, sweet, conscious mournfulness, which usually is so gentle in the evenings between spring and summer. The indistinct noise of the city floated in, the dolorous, snuffling air of an accordeon, the mooing of cows could be heard; somebody's soles were scraping dryly and a ferruled cane rapped resoundingly on the flags of the pavement; lazily and irregularly the wheels of a cabman's victoria, rolling at a pace through Yama, would rumble by, and all these sounds mingled with a beauty and softness in the pensive drowsiness of the evening. And the whistles of the locomotives on the line of the railroad, which was marked out in the darkness with green and red lights, sounded with a quiet, singing caution.

> "Now the nurse is co-oming in,
> Bringing sugar and a roll,
> Bringing sugar and a roll,
> Deals them equally to all."

"Prokhor Ivanich!" Niura suddenly calls after the curly waiter from the dram-shop, who, a light black silhouette, is running across the road. "Oh, Prokhor Ivanich!"

"Oh, bother you!" the other snarls hoarsely. "What now?"

"A friend of yours sent you his regards. I saw him today."

"What sort of friend?"

"Such a little good-looker! An attractive little

brunet . . . No, but you'd better ask—where did I see him?"

"Well, where?" Prokhor Ivanovich comes to a stop for a minute."

"And here's where: nailed over there, on the fifth shelf with old hats, where we keep all dead cats."

"Scat! You darn fool!"

Niura laughs shrilly over all Yama, and throws herself down on the sill, kicking her legs in high black stockings. Afterward, having ceased laughing, she all of a sudden makes round astonished eyes and says in a whisper:

"But do you know, girlie—why, he cut a woman's throat the year before last—that same Prokhor. Honest to God!"

"Is that so? Did she die?"

"No, she didn't. She got by," says Niura, as though with regret. "But just the same she lay for two months in the Alexandrovskaya Hospital. The doctors said, that if it were only this teeny-weeny bit higher—then it would have been all over. Bye–bye!"

"Well, what did he do that to her for?"

"How should I know? Maybe she hid money from him or wasn't true to him. He was her lover—her pimp."

"Well, and what did he get for it?"

"Why, nothing. There was no evidence of any kind. There had been a free-for-all mix-up. About a hundred people were fighting. She also told the police that she had no suspicions of any sort. But Prokhor himself boasted afterwards: 'I,' says he, 'didn't do for Dunka that time, but I'll finish her off another time. She,' says he, 'won't get by my hands. It's going to be bye-bye for her.'"

A shiver runs all the way down Liuba's back.

"They're desperate fellows, these pimps!" she pronounces quietly, with horror in her voice.

"Something terrible! I, you know, played at love with our Simeon for a whole year. Such a Herod, the skunk! I didn't have a whole spot on me. I always went about in black and blue marks. And it wasn't for any reason at all, but just simply so—he'd go in the morning into a room with me, lock himself in, and start in to torture me. He'd wrench my arms, pinch my breasts, grab my throat and begin to strangle me. Or else he'd be kissing, kissing, and then he'd bite the lips so that the blood would just spurt out... I'd start crying—but that's all he was looking for. Then he'd just pounce on me like a beast—simply shivering all over. And he'd take all my money away—well, now, to the very last little copper. There wasn't anything to buy ten cigarettes with. He's stingy, this here Simeon, that's what, always into the bank-book with it, always putting it away into the bank-book... Says when he gets a thousand roubles together—he'll go into a monastery."

"Go on?"

"Honest to God. You look into his little room: the twenty-four hours round, day and night, the little holy lamp burns before the images. He's very strong for God... Only I think that he's that way because there's heavy sins upon him. He's a murderer."

"What are you saying?"

"Oh, let's drop talking about him, Liubochka. Well, let's go on further:

"I'll go to the drug store, buy me some poison,
    And I will poison then meself,"

Niura starts off in a very high, thin voice.

Jennie walks back and forth in the room, with arms akimbo, swaying as she walks, and looking at herself in all the mirrors. She has on a short orange satin dress, with straight deep pleats in the skirt, which vacillates evenly to the left and right from the movement of her hips. Little Manka, a passionate lover of card games, ready to play from morning to morning, without stopping, is playing away at "sixty-six" with Pasha, during which both women, for convenience in dealing, have left an empty chair between them, while they gather their tricks into their skirts, spread out between their knees. Manka has on a brown, very modest dress, with black apron and pleated black bib; this dress is very becoming to her dainty, fair little head and small stature; it makes her younger and gives her the appearance of a high-school undergraduate.

Her partner Pasha is a very queer and unhappy girl. She should have been, long ago, not in a house of ill-fame, but in a psychiatric ward, because of an excruciating nervous malady, which compels her to give herself up, frenziedly, with an unwholesome avidity, to any man whatsoever who may choose her, even the most repulsive. Her mates make sport of her and despise her somewhat for this vice, just as though for some treason to their corporate enmity toward men. Niura, with very great versimilitude, mimics her sighs, groans, outcries and passionate words, from which she can never refrain in the moments of ecstasy and which are to be heard in the neighbouring rooms through two or three partitions. There is a rumour afloat about Pasha, that she got into a brothel not at all through necessity or temptation or deception, but had gone into it her own self, voluntarily, following her horrible, insatiable instinct. But the proprietress of the house and both the housekeepers indulge Pasha in every way and encourage her insane weakness, because, thanks to it, Pasha is in constant demand and earns four, five times as much as any one of the remaining girls—earns so much, that on busy gala days she is not brought out to the more drab guests at all, or else refused them under the pretext of Pasha's illness, because the steady, paying guests are offended if they are told that the girl they know is busy with another. And of such steady guests Pasha has a multitude; many are with perfect sincerity, even though bestially, in love with her, and even not so long ago two, almost at the same time, offered to set her up: a Georgian—a clerk in a store of Cakhetine wines, and some railroad agent, a very proud and very poor nobleman, with shirt cuffs the colour of a cabbage rose, and with an eye which had been replaced by a black circle on an elastic. Pasha, passive in everything save her impersonal sensuality, would go with anybody who might call her, but the administration of the house vigilantly guards its interests in her. A near insanity already flits over her lovely face, in her half-closed eyes, always smiling with some heady, blissful, meek, bashful and unseemly smile, in her languorous, softened, moist lips, which she is constantly licking; in her short, quiet laugh—the laugh of an idiot. Yet at the same time she—this veritable victim of the social temperament—in everyday life is very good-natured, yielding, entirely uncovetous and is very much ashamed of her inordinate passion. Toward her mates she is tender, likes very much to kiss and embrace them and sleep in the same bed with them, but still everybody has a little aversion for her, it would seem.

"Mannechka, sweetie, dearie," says Pasha lightly touching Manya's hand with emotion, "tell my fortune, my precious little child."

"We—ell," Manya pouts her lips just like a child, "let's play a little more."

"Mannechka, my little beauty, you little good-looker, my precious, my own, my dear..."

Manya gives in and lays out the pack on her knees. A suit of hearts comes out, a small monetary interest and a meeting in the suit of spades with a large company in the king of clubs.

Pasha claps her hands joyously:

"Ah, it's my Levanchik! Well, yes, he promised to come to-day. Of course, it's Levanchik."

"That's your Georgian!"

"Yes, yes, my little Georgian. Oh, now nice he is. I'd just love never to let him go away from me. Do you know what he told me the last time? 'If you'll go on living in a sporting house, then I'll make both you dead, and make me dead.' And he flashed his eyes at me so!"

Jennie, who had stopped near, listens to her words and asks haughtily:

"Who was it said that?"

"Why, my little Georgian, Levan. 'Both for you death and for me death.'"

"Fool! He isn't any little Georgian at all, but simply a common Armenian. You're a crazy fool."

"Oh no, he isn't—he's a Georgian. And it is quite strange on your part...."

"I'm telling you—a common Armenian. I can tell better. Fool!"

"What are you cursing for, Jennie? I didn't start cursing you first off, did I?"

"You just try and be the first to start cursing! Fool! Isn't it all the same to you what he is? Are you in love with him, or what?"

"Well, I am in love with him!"

"Well, and you're a fool. And the one with the badge in his cap, the lame one—are you in love with him too?"

"Well, what of it? I respect him very much. He is very respectable."

"And with Nicky the Book-keeper? And with the contractor? And with Antoshka-Kartoshka?* And with the fat actor? Oo–ooh, you shameless creature!" Jennie suddenly cries out. "I can't look at you without disgust. You're a bitch! In your place, if I was such a miserable thing, I'd rather lay hands on myself, strangle myself with a cord from my corset. You vermin!"

Pasha silently lowers her eyelashes over her tear-filled eyes. Manya tries to defend her.

"Really, what are you carrying on like that for, Jenchka? What are you down on her like that for...."

"Eh, all of you are fine!" Jennie sharply cuts her short. "No self-respect of any sort! Some scum comes along, buys you like a piece of meat, hires you like a cabby, at a fixed rate, for love for an hour, but you go all to pieces: 'Ah, my little lover! Ah, what unearthly passion!' Ugh!" she spat in disgust.

She wrathfully turns her back upon them and con-

*Tony the Potato.—*Trans.*

158383

tinues to promenade on a diagonal through the roor
swinging her hips and blinking at herself in every mirrc

During this time Isaac Davidovich, the piano playe
is still struggling with the refractory violinist.

"Not that way, not that way, Isaiah Savvich. Yc
throw the fiddle away for one little minute. Listen
little to me. Here is the tune."

He plays with one finger and hums in that horrib
goatish voice that all musical directors—for which callir
he had been at one time preparing—possess.

"*Ess–tam, ess–tam, ess–tiam–tiam.* Well, now, repe
after me the first part, first time off...... Well...
ein, zwei..."

Their rehearsal is being attentively watched by the gre
eyed, round-faced, arch-browed Zoe, mercilessly bedaub
with cheap rouges and whiteners, leaning with her elbov
on the pianoforte, and the slight Vera, with drink-ravag
face, in the costume of a jockey—in a round little c
with straight brim, in a little silk jacket, striped blue ar
white, in tightly stretched trunks and in little pate
leather boots with yellow facings. And really, Vera do
resemble a jockey, with her narrow face, in which t
exceedingly sparkling blue eyes, under a smart bob cor
ing down on the forehead, are set too near the humpe
nervous, very handsome nose. When, at last, after lo
efforts the musicians agree, the somewhat small Verl
walks up to the large Zoe, in that mincing, tethered wal
the hind part sticking out, and elbows spread as though
flight, with which only women in male costume can wal
and makes a comical masculine bow to her, spreading h
arms wide and lowering them. And, with great enjo
ment, they begin careering over the room.

The nimble Niura, always the first to announce all t
news, suddenly jumps down from the window sill, a
calls out, spluttering from the excitement and hurry:

"A swell carriage... has driven up... to Treppel.
with electricity... Oi, goils... may I die on the spot.
there's electricity on the shafts."

All the girls, save the proud Jennie, thrust themselves out of the windows. A driver with a fine carriage is indeed standing near the Treppel entrance. His brand-new, dashing victoria glistens with new lacquer; at the ends of the shafts two tiny electric lights burn with a yellow light; the tall white horse, with a bare pink spot on the septum of its nose, shakes its handsome head, shifts its feet on the same spot, and pricks up its thin ears; the bearded, stout driver himself sits on the coach-box like a carven image, his arms stretched out straight along his knees.

"Oh, for a ride!" squeals Niura. "Oh, uncle! Oh you swell coachman!" she cries out, hanging over the window sill, "Give a poor little girlie a ride... Give us a ride for love."

But the swell coachman laughs, makes a scarcely notice-able movement with his fingers, and immediately the white horse, as though it had been waiting just for that, starts from its place at a goodly trot, handsomely turns around and with measured speed floats away into the darkness together with the victoria and the broad back of the coachman.

"*Pfui!* What indecency!" the indignant voice of Emma Edwardovna sounds in the room. "Well, where did you see that respectable girls should allow themselves to climb out of the windows and holler all over the street. O, scandal! And it's all Niura, and it's always this horrible Niura!"

She is majestic in her black dress, with her yellow flabby face, with the dark pouches under her eyes, with the three pendulous, quivering chins. The girls, like boarding school misses, staidly seat themselves on the chairs along the walls, except Jennie, who continues to contemplate herself in all the mirrors. Two more cabbies drive up opposite, to the house of Sophia Vasilievna. Yama is beginning to liven up. At last one more victoria rattles along the paved road and its noise is cut short abruptly at the entrance to Anna Markovna's.

The porter Simeon helps someone take off his things in the front hall. Jennie looks in there, holding on with both hands to the door jambs, but immediately turns back, and as she walks shrugs her shoulders and shakes her head negatively.

"Don't know him, someone who's an entire stranger," she says in a low voice. "He has never been in our place. Some daddy or other, fat, in gold eye-glasses and a uniform."

Emma Edwardovna commands in a voice which sounds like a summoning cavalry trumpet:

"Ladies, into the drawing room! Into the drawing room, ladies!"

One after the other, with haughty gaits, into the drawing room enter: Tamara, with bare white arms and bared neck, wound with a string of artificial pearls; fat Kitty with her fleshy, quadrangular face and low forehead—she, too, is in *decollete*, but her skin is red and in goose-pimples; Nina, the very newest one, pug-nosed and clumsy, in a dress the colour of a green parrot; another Manka—Big Manka, or Manka the Crocodile, as they call her, and—the last—Sonka the Rudder, a Jewess, with an ugly dark face and an extraordinarily large nose, precisely for which she has received her nickname, but with such magnificent large eyes, at the same time meek and sad, burning and humid, as, among the women of all the terrestrial globe, are to be found only among the Jewesses.

CHAPTER VI.

The elderly guest in the uniform of the Department of Charity walked in with slow, undecided steps, at each step bending his body a little forward and rubbing his palms with a circular motion, as though washing them. Since all the women were pompously silent, as though not noticing him, he traversed the drawing room and let himself down on a chair alongside of Liuba, who, in accordance with etiquette, only gathered up her skirt a little, preserving the abstracted and independent air of a girl from a respectable house.

"How do you do, miss?" he said.

"How do you do?" answered Liuba abruptly.

"How are you getting along?"

"Thanks—thank you. Treat me to a smoke."

"Pardon me—I don't smoke."

"So that's how. A man—and he doesn't smoke, just like that. Well, then, treat me to some Lafitte with lemonade. I am terribly fond of Lafitte with lemonade."

He let that pass in silence.

"Ooh, what a stingy daddy! Where do you work, now? Are you one of the government clerks?"

"No, I'm a teacher. I teach the German language."

"But I have seen you somewhere, daddy. Your physiognomy is familiar to me. Where have I met you before?"

"Well, now, I don't know, really. Unless it was on the street."

"It might have been on the street, likely as not... You ought to treat me to an orange, at least. May I ask for an orange?"

He again grew quiet, looking about him. His face began to glisten and the pimples on his forehead became red. He was mentally appraising all the women, choosing a likely one for himself, and was at the same time embarrassed by his silence. There was nothing at all to talk about; besides thát the indifferent importunity of Liuba irritated him. Fat Katie pleased him with her large, bovine body, but she must be—he decided in his mind—very frigid in love, like all stout women, and in addition to that not handsome of face. Vera also excited him, with her appearance of a little boy, and her firm thighs, closely enveloped by the white tights; and Little White Manya, looking so like an innocent school-girl; and Jennie with her energetic, swarthy, handsome face. For one minute he was all ready to stop at Jennie, but only started in his chair and did not venture—by her easy, inaccessible and negligent air, and because she in all sincerity did not pay him the least attention, he surmised that she was the most spoilt of all the girls in the establishment, accustomed to having the visitors spend more money on her than on the others. But the pedagogue was a calculating man, burthened with a large family and an exhausted wife, destroyed by his masculine demands and suffering from a multiplicity of female ills. Teaching in a female high school and in an institute, he lived constantly in a sort of secret sensual delirium, and only his German training, stinginess and cowardice helped him to hold his constantly aroused desires in check. But two or three times a year, with incredible privations, he would cut five or ten roubles out of his beggarly budget, denying himself in his beloved evening mug of beer and contriving to save on the street cars, which necessitated his making enormous distances on foot through the town. This money he set aside for women and spent it slowly, with gusto, trying to prolong and cheapen down the enjoyment as much as possible. And for his money he wanted a very great deal, almost the impossible; his German sentimental soul dimly thirsted after innocence, timidity, poesy, in the flaxen image of Gretchen; but as a man he dreamt, desired, and demanded that his caresses should bring a woman into rapture and palpitation and into a sweet exhaustion.

However, all the men strove for the very same thing—even the most wretched, monstrous, misshapen and impotent of them—and ancient experience had long ago taught the women to imitate with voice and movements the most flaming passion, retaining in the most tempestuous minutes the fullest *sang froid*.

"You might at least order the musicians to play a polka. Let the girls dance a little." asked Liuba grumblingly.

That suited him. Under cover of the music, amid the jostling of the dances, it was far more convenient to get up courage, arise, and lead one of the girls out of the drawing room, than to do it amid the general silence and the finical immobility.

"And how much does that cost?" he asked cautiously.

"A quadrille is half a rouble; but ordinary dances are thirty kopecks. Is it all right then?"

"Well, of course...if you please... I don't begrudge it," he agreed, pretending to be generous... "Whom do you speak to?"

"Why, over there—to the musicians."

"Why not?.. I'll do it with pleasure... Mister musician, something in the light dances, if you please," he said, laying down his silver on the pianoforte.

"What will you order?" asked Isaiah Savvich, putting the money away in his pocket. "Waltz, polka, polka-mazourka?"

"Well... Something sort of..."

"A waltz, a waltz!" Vera, a great lover of dancing, shouted from her place.

"No, a polka!.. A waltz!.. A vengerka!.. A waltz!" demanded others.

"Let them play a polka," decided Liuba in a capricious tone. "Isaiah Savvich, play a little polka please. This is my husband, and he is ordering for me," she added, embracing the pedagogue by the neck. "Isn't that true, daddy?"

But he freed himself from under her arm, drawing his head in like a turtle, and she without the least offence went to dance with Niura. Three other couples were also whirling about. In the dances all the girls tried to hold the waist as straight as possible, and the head as immobile as possible, with a complete unconcern in their faces, which constituted one of the conditions of the good taste of the establishment. Under cover of the slight noise the teacher walked up to Little Manka.

"Let's go?" he said, offering her his bent arm.

"Let's go," answered she, laughing.

She brought him into her room, gotten up with all the coquettishness of a bedroom in a brothel of the medium sort, with a bureau, covered with a knit scarf, and upon it a mirror, a bouquet of paper flowers, a few empty bonbonierres, a powder box, a faded photograph of a young man with white eyebrows and eyelashes and a haughtily astonished face, as well as several visiting cards. Above the bed, which is covered with a pink pique blanket, along the wall, is nailed up a rug with a representation of a Turkish sultan luxuriating in his harem, a *narghili* in his mouth; on the walls, several more photographs of dashing men of the waiter and actor type; a pink lantern hangs down from the ceiling by chains; there are also a round table under a carpet cover, three vienna chairs, and an enameled bowl with a pitcher of the same sort in the corner on a tabouret, behind the bed.

"Darling, treat me to Lafitte with lemonade," in accordance with established usage asked Little Manka, unbuttoning her corsage.

"Afterwards," austerely answered the pedagogue. "It will all depend upon yourself. And then—what sort of Lafitte can you have here? Some muddy brew or other."

"We have good Lafitte," contradicted the girl touchily.

"Two roubles a bottle. But if you are so stingy, then buy me beer at least. All right?"

"Well, beer is all right..."

"And for me lemonade and oranges. Yes?"

"A bottle of lemonade, yes; but oranges, no. Later, maybe, I will treat you to champagne even. It will all depend on you. If you'll exert yourself."

"Then, daddy, I'll ask for four bottles of beer and two bottles of lemonade? Yes? And for me just a little cake of chocolate. All right? Yes?"

"Two bottles of beer, a bottle of lemonade, and nothing more. I don't like when I'm bargained with. If need be, I'll order myself."

"And may I invite a friend of mine?"

"No, let it be without any friends, if you please."

Manka leaned out of the door into the corridor and called out resoundingly:

"Housekeeper, dear! Two bottles of beer and a bottle of lemonade for me."

Simeon came with a tray and began with an accustomed rapidity to uncork the bottles. Following him came Zociya, the housekeeper.

"There, now, how well you've made yourself at home here. Here's to your lawful marriage!" she congratulated them.

"Daddy, treat the little housekeeper with beer," begged Manka. "Drink, housekeeper dear."

"Well, in that case here's to your health, mister. Somehow, your face seems kind of familiar to me?"

The German drank his beer, sucking and licking his moustache, and impatiently waiting for the housekeeper to go away. But she, having put down her glass and thanked him, said:

"Let me get the money coming from you, mister. As much as is coming for the beer and the time. That's both better for you and more convenient for us."

The demand for the money went against the grain of the teacher, because it completely destroyed the sentimental part of his intentions. He became angry:

"What sort of boorishness is this, anyway! It doesn't look as if I were preparing to run away from here. And besides, can't you discriminate between people at all? You can see that a man of respectability, in a uniform, has come to you, and not some tramp. What sort of importunity is this!"

The housekeeper gave in a little.

"Now, don't get offended, mister. Of course, you'll pay the young lady yourself for the visit. I don't think you will do her any wrong, she's a fine girl among us. But I must trouble you to pay for the beer and lemonade. I, too, have to give an account to the proprietress. Two bottles at fifty is a rouble and the lemonade thirty—a rouble thirty."

"Good Lord, a bottle of beer fifty kopecks!" the German waxed indignant. "Why, I will get it in any beer-shop for twelve kopecks."

"Well, then, go to a beer-shop if it's cheaper there," Zociya became offended. "But if you've come to a respectable establishment, the regular price is half a rouble. We don't take anything extra. There, that's better. Twenty kopecks change coming to you?"

"Yes, change, *without fail*," firmly emphasized the German teacher. "And I would request of you that nobody else should enter."

"No, no, no, what are you saying," Zociya began to bustle near the door. "Dispose yourself as you please, to your heart's content. A pleasant appetite to you."

Manka locked the door on a hook after her and sat down on the German's knee, embracing him with her bare arm.

"Are you here long?" he asked, sipping his beer. He felt dimly that that imitation of love which must immediately take place demanded some sort of psychic propinquity, a more intimate acquaintance, and on that

count, despite his impatience, began the usual conver-
tion, which is carried on by almost all men when alone
th prostitutes, and which compels the latter to lie
most mechanically, to lie without mortification, enthu-
sm or malice, according to a single, very ancient
ncil.

"Not long, only the third month."

"And how old are you?"

"Sixteen," fibbed Little Manka, taking five years off
r age.

"O, such a young one!" the German wondered, and
gan, bending down and grunting, to take off his boots.
hen how did you get here?"

"Well, a certain officer deprived me of my innocence
re... near his birthplace. And it's terrible how
ict my mamma is. If she was to find out, she'd strangle
with her own hands. Well, so then I ran away from
me and got in here..."

"And did you love that same officer, the one who was
first one, now?"

"If I hadn't loved him, I wouldn't have gone to him.
promised to marry me, the scoundrel, but then man-
d to get what he was after, and abandoned me."

"Well, and were you ashamed the first time?"

"Of course, you'd be ashamed... How do you like
daddy, with light or without light? I'll turn down
lantern a little. All right?"

"Well, and aren't you bored here? What do they call
?"

"Manya. To be sure I'm bored. What sort of a life
urs!"

he German kissed her hard on her lips and again asked:
"And do you love the men? Are there men who please
? Who afford you pleasure?"

How shouldn't there be?" Manka started laughing.
ve the ones like you especially, such nice little fatties."
You love them? Eh? Why do you love them?"
Oh, I love them just so. You're nice, too."

The German meditated for a few seconds, pensive
sipping away at his beer. Then he said that whi
every man tells a prostitute in these moments precedi
the casual possession of her body:

"Do you know, Marichen, you also please me ve
much. I would willingly take you and set you up

"You're married," the girl objected, touching his rir

"Yes, but, you understand, I don't live with my wi
she isn't well, she can't fulfill her conjugal duties."

"The poor thing! If she were to find out where y
go, daddy, she would cry for sure."

"Let's drop that. So, you know, Mary, I am alwa
looking out for such a girl as you for myself, so mod
and pretty. I am a man of means, I would find a f
with board for you, with fuel and light. And for
roubles a month pin money. Would you go?"

"Why not go—I'd go."

He kissed her violently, but a secret apprehensi
glided swiftly through his cowardly heart.

"But are you healthy?" he asked in an inimical, quav
ing voice.

"Why, yes, I am healthy. There's a doctor's inspect
every Saturday in our place."

After five minutes she went away from him, as s
walked putting away in her stocking the earned mon
on which, as on the first handsel, she had first spat, af
a superstitious custom. There had been no further spe
either about maintenance or natural liking. The Germ
was left unsatisfied with the frigidity of Manka a
ordered the housekeeper to be summoned to him.

"Housekeeper dear, my husband demands your pr
ence!" said Manya, coming into the drawing room a
fixing her hair before a mirror.

Zociya went away, then returned afterwards and cal
Pasha out into the corridor. Later she came back i
the drawing room, but alone.

"How is it, Manka, that you haven't pleased y
cavalier?" she asked with laughter. "He complains ab

you: 'This,' he says, 'is no woman, but some log of wood, a piece of ice.' I sent him Pashka.''

"Eh, what a disgusting man!" Manka puckered up her face and spat aside. "Butts in with his conversations. Asks: 'Do you feel when I kiss you? Do you feel a pleasant excitement?' An old hound. 'I'll take you,' he says, 'and set you up!' ''

"They all say that," remarked Zoe indifferently.

But Jennie, who since morning has been in an evil mood, suddenly flared up.

"Oh, the sneak, the big miserable sneak that he is!" she exclaimed, turning red and energetically putting her hands to her sides. "Why, I would take him, the old, dirty little beast, by the ear, then lead him up to the mirror and show him his disgusting snout. What? Good-looking, aren't you? And how much better you'll be when the spit will be running out of your mouth, and you'll cross your eyes, and begin to choke and rattle in the throat, and to snort right in the face of the woman. And for your damned rouble you want me to go all to pieces before you like a pancake, and that from your nasty love my eyes should pop out onto my forehead? Why, hit him in the snout, the skunk, in the snout! Until there's blood!"

"O, Jennie! Stop it now! *Pfui!*" the susceptible Emma Edwardovna, made indignant by her tone, stopped her.

"I won't stop!" she cut her short abruptly. But she grew quiet by herself and wrathfully walked away with distending nostrils and with fire in the darkened, handsome eyes.

CHAPTER VII.

Little by little the drawing room was filling. There came Roly-Poly, long known to all Yama—a tall, thin, red-nosed, gray old man, in the uniform of a forest ranger, in high boots, with a wooden yard-stick always sticking out of his side-pocket. He passed whole days and evenings as a habitue of the billiard parlor in the tavern, always half-tipsy, shedding his little jokes, jingles and little sayings, acting familiarly with the porters, with the housekeepers and the girls. In the houses everybody—from the proprietress to the chamber-maids—treated him with a bit of derision—careless, a trifle contemptuous, but without malice. At times he was even not without use: he could transmit notes from the girls to their lovers, and run over to the market or to the drug-store. Not infrequently, thanks to his loosely hung tongue and long extinguished self respect, he would worm himself into a gathering of strangers and increase its expenditures, while the money taken as a loan during this, he did not carry away somewhere else, but spent it right here for women—unless, indeed, he left himself some change for cigarettes. And, out of habit, he was good-naturedly tolerated.

"And here's Roly-Poly arrived," announced Niura, when he, having already managed to shake hands amicably with Simeon the porter, stopped in the doorway of the drawing room, lanky, in a uniform cap knocked at a brave slant over one side of his head. "Well, now, Roly-Poly, fire away!"

"I have the honour to present myself," Roly-Poly immediately commenced to grimace, putting his hand up to his brim in military fashion, "a right honourable privy frequenter of the local agreeable establishments, Prince Bottlekin, Count Liquorkin, Baron Whoatinke-

vich-Giddapkovski—Mister Beethoven! Mister Chopin!"
he greeted the musicians. "Play me something from
the opera *The Brave and Charming General Anisimov, or,
A Hubbub in the Coolidor.* My regards to the little
political economist Zociya.* A-ha! Then you kiss only
at Easter? We shall write that down. Ooh-you, my
Tomalachka, my pitty-itty tootsicums!"

And so with jests and with pinches he went the round
of all the girls and at last sat down alongside of the fat
Katie, who put her fat leg upon his, leant with her elbow
upon her knee, while upon the palm she laid her chin,
and began to watch indifferently and closely the surveyor
rolling a cigarette for himself.

"And how is it that you don't ever get tired of it,
Roly-Poly? You're forever rolling a coffin nail."

Roly-Poly at once commenced to move his eyebrows and the skin of his scalp and began to speak
in verse:

> "Dear cigarette, my secret mate,
> How can I help loving thee?
> Not through mere whim, prompted by fate,
> All have started smoking thee."

"Why, Roly-Poly, but you are going to croak soon,"
said Kitty indifferently.

"And a very simple matter, that."

"Roly-Poly, say something still funnier, in verse,"
begged Verka.

And at once, obediently, having placed himself in a
funny pose, he began to declaim:

> "Many stars are in the bright sky,
> But to count them there's no way.
> Yes, the wind whispers there can be,
> But there really is no way.
> Blossoming now are burdocks,
> Now sing out the birds called cocks."

---

*An untranslatable pun on *Economochka*, a diminutive for
"housekeeper."—*Trans.*

Playing the tom-fool in this manner, Roly-Poly would sit whole evenings and nights through in the drawing rooms of the establishments. And through some strange psychic fellow feeling the girls counted him almost as one of their own; occasionally rendered him little temporary services and even bought him beer and vodka at their expense.

Some time after Roly-Poly a large company of hair-dressers, who were that day free from work, tumbled in. They were noisy, gay, but even here, in a brothel, did not cease their petty reckonings and conversations about closed and open theatrical benefits, about the bosses, about the wives of the bosses. All these were people corrupt to a sufficient degree, liars, with great hopes for the future—such as, for example, entering the service of some countess as a kept lover. They wanted to utilize to the widest possible extent their rather hard-earned money, and on that account decided to make a review of absolutely all the houses of Yama; only Treppel's they could not resolve to enter, as that was too swell for them. But at Anna Markovna's they at once ordered a quadrille and danced it, especially the fifth figure, where the gents execute a solo, perfectly, like real Parisians, even putting their thumbs in the arm holes of their vests. But they did not want to remain with the girls; instead, they promised to come later, when they had wound up the complete review of the brothels.

And there also came and went government clerks of some sort; crisp young people in patent leather boots; several students; several officers, who were horribly afraid of losing their dignity in the eyes of the proprietress and the guests of the brothel. Little by little in the drawing room was created such a noisy, fumy setting that no one there any longer felt ill at ease. There came a steady visitor, the lover of Sonka the Rudder, who came almost every day and sat whole hours through near his beloved, gazed upon her with languishing oriental eyes, sighed, grew faint and created scenes for her because she lives in a brothel, because she sins against the Sabbath, because she eats meat not prepared in the orthodox Hebrew manner, and because she has strayed from the family and the great Hebrew church.

As a usual thing—and this happened often—Zociya the housekeeper would walk up to him under cover of the hubbub and would say, twisting her lips:

"Well, what are you sitting there for, mister? Warming your behind? You might go and pass the time with the young lady."

Both of them, the Jew and the Jewess, were by birth from Homel, and must have been created by God himself for a tender, passionate, mutual love; but many circumstances—as, for example, the pogrom which took place in their town, impoverishment, a complete confusion, fright—had for a time parted them. However, love was so great that the junior drug clerk Neiman, with great difficulty, efforts, and humiliations, contrived to find for himself the place of a junior in one of the local pharmacies, and had searched out the girl he loved. He was a real, orthodox Hebrew, almost fanatical. He knew that Sonka had been sold by her very mother to one of the buyers-up of live merchandise, knew many humiliating, hideous particulars of how she had been resold from hand to hand, and his pious, fastidious, truly Hebraic soul writhed and shuddered at these thoughts, but nevertheless love was above all. And every evening he would appear in the drawing room of Anna Markovna. If he was successful, at an enormous deprivation, in cutting out of his beggarly income some chance rouble, he would take Sonka into her room, but this was not at all a joy either for him or for her: after a momentary happiness—the physical possession of each other—they cried, reproached each other, quarreled with characteristic, Hebraic, theatrical gestures, and always after these visits Sonka the Rudder would return into the drawing room with swollen, reddened eyelids.

But most frequently of all he had no money, and would sit whole evenings through near his mistress, patiently and jealously awaiting her when Sonka through chance was taken by some guest. And when she would return and sit down beside him, he would, without being perceived, overwhelm her with reproaches, trying not to turn the general attention upon himself and without turning his head in her direction. And in her splendid, humid, Hebraic eyes during these conversations there was always a martyr-like but meek expression.

There arrived a large company of Germans, employed in an optical shop; there also arrived a party of clerks from the fish and gastronomical store of Kereshkovsky, and two young people very well known in the Yamas—both bald, with sparse, soft, delicate hairs around the bald spots: Nicky the Book-keeper and Mishka the Singer—so were they both called in the houses. They also were met very cordially, just like Karl Karlovich of the optical shop and Volodka of the fish store—with raptures, cries and kisses, flattering to their self-esteem. The spry Niurka would jump out into the foyer, and, having informed herself as to who had come, would report excitedly, after her wont:

"Jennka, your husband has come!"

Or:

"Little Manka, your lover has come!"

And Mishka the Singer, who was no singer at all, but the owner of a drug warehouse, at once, upon entering, sang out in a vibrating, quavering, goatish voice:

> "They fe-e-e-l the tru-u-u-u-uth!
> Come thou daw-aw-aw-aw-ning. . ."

which he perpetrated at every visit of his to Anna Markovna.

Almost incessantly they played the quadrille, waltz, polka, and danced. There also arrived Senka—the lover of Tamara—but, contrary to his wont, he did not put on airs, did not go in for "ruination", did not order a funeral march from Isaiah Savvich, and did not treat the girls to chocolate... For some reason he was gloomy, limped on his right leg, and sought to attract as little attention as possible—probably his professional affairs were at this time in a bad way. With a single motion of his head, while walking, he called Tamara out of the drawing room and vanished with her into her room. And there also arrived Egmont-Lavretzki the actor, clean-shaven, tall, resembling a court flunky with his vulgar and insolently contemptuous face.

The clerks from the gastronomical store danced with all the ardour of youth and with all the decorum recommended by Herman Hoppe, the self-instructor of good manners. In this regard the girls also responded to their intentions. Both with these and with the others it was accounted especially decorous and well-bred to dance as rigidly as possible, keeping the arms hanging down, while the heads were raised high and inclined to one side with a certain proud, and, at the same time, tired and enervated air. In the intermissions, between the figures of the dance, it was necessary to fan one's self with a handkerchief, with a bored and negligent air... In a word, they all made believe that they belonged to the choicest society, and that if they do dance, they only do it out of condescension, as a little comradely turn. But still they danced so ardently that the perspiration rolled down in streams from the clerks of Kereshkovsky.

Two or three rows had already happened in different houses. Some man, all in blood, whose face in the pale light of the moon's crescent seemed black from the blood, was running around in the street, cursing, and, without paying the least attention to his wounds, was searching for his cap which had been lost in the brawl. On Little Yamskaya some government scribes had had a fight with a ship's company. The tired pianists and musicians played as in a delirium, in a doze, through mechanical habit. This was towards the waning of the night.

Altogether unexpectedly, seven students, a sub-professor, and a local reporter walked into the establishment of Anna Markovna.

CHAPTER VIII.

They had all, except the reporter, passed the whole day together, from the very morning, celebrating May Day with some young women of their acquaintance. They had rowed in boats on the Dnieper, had cooked field porridge on the other side of the river, in the thick, bitter-smelling underbrush; had bathed—men and women by turns—in the rapid, warm water; had drunk home-made spiced brandy, sung sonorous songs of Little Russia, and had returned to town only late in the evening, when the dark, broad, running river so eerily and merrily plashed against the sides of their boats, playing with the reflections of the stars, the silvery shimmering paths of the electric lamps, and the bowing lights of the can-buoys. And when they had stepped out on the shore, the palms of each burned from the oars, the muscles of the arms and legs ached pleasantly, and throughout the whole body was a blissful, healthy fatigue.

Then they had escorted the young women to their homes and at the garden-gates and entrances had taken leave of them long and cordially, with laughter and with such swinging hand-shakes as if they were working the lever of a pump.

The whole day had passed in gaiety and noise, even a trifle clamourously, and just the least wee bit tiresomely, but with youth-like continence; without intoxication, and, which happens especially rarely, without the least shadow of mutual affronts, or jealousy, or unvoiced mortifications. Of course, such a benign mood had been helped by the sun, the fresh river breeze, the sweet exhalations of the grasses and the water, the joyous sensation of the strength and alertness of one's body while bathing and rowing, and the restraining influence of the clever, kind, pure and handsome girls from families they were acquainted with. But, almost without the knowledge of their consciousness, their sensuousness—not imagination, but the simple, healthy, instinctive sensuousness of young playful males—kindled from chance encounters of their hands with feminine hands and from comradely obliging embraces, when the occasion arose to help the young ladies enter a boat or jump out on shore; from the tender odour of maiden apparel, warmed by the sun; from the feminine cries of coquettish fright on the river; from the sight of feminine figures, negligently half-reclining with a naive immodesty on the green grass around the samovar—from all these innocent liberties, which are so usual and unavoidable on picnics, country outings and river excursions, when within man, in the infinite depth of his soul, secretly awakens from the care-free contact with earth, grasses, water and sun, the beast—ancient, splendid, free, but disfigured and intimidated of men.

And for that reason, at two o'clock in the night, when *The Sparrows*, a cozy students' restaurant, had barely closed, and all the eight, excited by alcohol and the plentiful food, had come out of the smoky, fumy underground place into the street, into the sweet, disquieting darkness of the night, with its beckoning fires in the sky and on the earth, with its warm, heady air, from which the nostrils dilate avidly, with its aromas, gliding from unseen gardens and flower-beds,—the head of each one of them was aflame and the heart quietly and languishingly yearning from vague desires. It was joyous and arrogant to sense after the rest the new, fresh strength in all the sinews, the deep breathing of the lungs, the red, resilient blood in the veins, the supple obedience of all the members. And—without words, without thoughts, without consciousness—one was drawn on this night to be running without raiment in the somnolent forest, to be sniffing hurriedly the tracks of some one's feet on the dewy grass, with a loud call to be summoning a female unto one's self.

But to separate was now very difficult. The whole day, passed together, had shaken them into an accustomed, tenacious herd. It seemed that if even one were to go away from the company, a certain attained equilibrium would be disturbed and could not be restored afterwards. And so they dallied and stamped upon the sidewalk, near the exit of the tavern's underground vault, interfering with the progress of the infrequent passers-by. They discussed hypocritically where else they might go to wind up the night. It proved to be too far to the Tivoli Garden, and in addition to that one also had to pay for admission tickets, and the prices in the buffet were outrageous, and the program had ended long ago. Volodya Pavlov proposed going to him—he had a dozen of beer and a little cognac home. But it seemed a bore to all of them to go in the middle of the night to a family apartment, to enter on tiptoes up the stairs and to talk in whispers all the time.

"Tell you what, brethren... Let's better ride to the girlies, that will be nearer the mark," said peremptorily Lichonin, an old student, a tall, stooping, morose and bearded fellow. By convictions he was an anarchist-theoretic, but by avocation a passionate gambler at billiards, races and cards—a gambler with a very broad, fatalistic sweep. Only the day before he had won a thousand roubles at macao in the Merchants' Club, and this money still burned his hands.

"And why not? Right-o!" somebody sustained him. "Let's go, comrades?"

"Is it worth while? Why, this is an all night affair..." spoke another with a false prudence and an insincere fatigue.

And a third said through a feigned yawn:

"Let's better go home, gentlemen... a-a-a... go bye-bye... That's enough for to-day."

"You won't work any wonders when you're asleep," Lichonin remarked sneeringly. "Herr professor, are you coming?"

But the sub-professor Yarchenko was obstinate and

seemed really angered, although, perhaps, he himself did not know what was lurking within him, in some dark cranny of his soul.

"Leave me in peace, Lichonin. As I see it, gentlemen, this is downright and plain swinishness—that which you are about to do. We have passed the time so wonderfully, amiably and simply, it seems—but no, you needs must, like drunken cattle, clamber into a cesspool. I won't go."

"Still, if my memory does not play me false," said Lichonin, with calm causticity, "I recollect that no further back than past autumn we with a certain future Mommsen were pouring in some place or other a jug of ice into a pianoforte, delineating a Bouratian god, dancing the belly-dance, and all that sort of thing?"

Lichonin spoke the truth. In his student days, and later, being retained at the university, Yarchenko had led the most wanton and crack-brained life. In all the taverns, cabarets, and other places of amusement his small, fat, roundish little figure, his rosy cheeks, puffed out like those of a painted cupid, and the shining, humid kindly eyes were well known, his hurried, spluttering speech and shrill laughter remembered.

His comrades could never fathom where he found the time to employ in study, but nevertheless he went through all examinations and prescribed work with distinction and from the first course the professors had him in view. Now Yarchenko was beginning little by little to quit his former comrades and bottle companions. He had just established the indispensable connections with the professorial circle; the reading of lectures in Roman history for the coming year had been offered him, and not infrequently in conversation he would use the expression current among the sub-professors: "We, the learned ones!" The student familiarity, the compulsory companionship, the obligatory participation in all meetings, protests and demonstrations, were becoming disadvantageous to him, embarrassing, and even simply tedious. But he knew the value of popularity among the younger element, and for that reason could not decide to sever relations abruptly with his former circle. Lichonin's words, however, provoked him.

"Oh, my God, what does it matter what we did when we were youngsters? We stole sugar, soiled our panties, tore the wings off beetles," Yarchenko began to speak, growing heated, and spluttering. "But there is a limit and a mean to all this. I, gentlemen, do not presume, of course, to give you counsels and to teach you, but one must be consistent. We are all agreed that prostitution is one of the greatest calamities of humanity, and are also agreed, that in this evil not the women are guilty, but we, men, because the demand gives birth to the offer. And therefore if, having drunk a glass of wine too much, I still, notwithstanding my convictions, go to the prostitutes, I am committing a triple vileness: before the unfortunate foolish woman, whom I subject to the most degrading form of slavery for my filthy rouble; before humanity, because, hiring a public woman for an hour or two for my abominable lust, I through this justify and uphold prostitution; and finally, this is a vileness before one's own conscience and mind. And before logic."

"Phew-ew!" Lichonin let out a long-drawn whistle and chanted in a thin, dismal voice, nodding in time with his head hanging down to one side: "The philosopher is off on our usual stuff: 'A rope—is a common cord.'"

"Of course, there's nothing easier than to play the tom-fool," responded Yarchenko. "But in my opinion there is not in the sorrowful life of Russia a more mournful phenomenon than this lackadaisicalness and vitiation of thought. To-day we will say to ourselves: Eh! It's all the same, whether I go to a brothel or whether I do not go, from this one time things will get neither worse nor better. And after five years we will be saying: Un-doubtedly a bribe is a horribly nasty bit of business, but you know—children... the family... And just the same way after ten years we, having remained fortuitous Rus-sian liberals, will be sighing about personal freedom and

bowing low before worthless scoundrels, whom we despise,
and will be cooling our heels in their ante-rooms. 'Because, don't you know,' we will say, tittering, 'when you
live with wolves, you must howl like a wolf.' By God,
it wasn't in vain that some minister called the Russian
students future head-clerks!"

"Or professors," Lichonin put in.

"But most important of all," continued Yarchenko,
letting this pointed remark pass by, "most important of
all is this, that I have seen all of you to-day on the river
and afterwards there... on the other shore... with these
charming, fine girls. How attentive, well-bred, obliging
you all were—but scarcely have you taken leave of them,
when you are drawn to public women. Let each one of
you imagine for a moment, that we all had been visiting
his sisters and straight from them had driven to Yama...
What? Is such a supposition pleasant?"

"Yes, but there must exist some valves for the passions
of society," pompously remarked Boris Sobashnikov,
a tall, somewhat supercilious and affected young man,
upon whom the short, white summer uniform jacket,
which scarcely covered his fat posteriors, the modish
trousers, of a military cut, the *pince-nez* on a broad,
black ribbon, and a cap after a Prussian model, all bestowed the air of a coxcomb. "Surely, it isn't more
respectable to enjoy the caresses of your chambermaid,
or to carry on an intrigue on the side with another man's
wife? What am I to do if woman is indispensable to me!"

"Eh, very indispensable indeed!" said Yarchenko with
vexation and feebly made a despondent gesture.

But here a student who was called Ramses in the
friendly coterie intervened. This was a yellowish-swarthy,
hump-nosed man of small stature; his clean-shaven face
seemed triangular, thanks to a broad forehead, beginning
to get bald with two wedge-like bald spots at the temples,
fallen-in cheeks and a sharp chin. He led a mode of life
sufficiently queer for a student. While his colleagues

employed themselves by turns with politics, love, the theatre, and a little in study, Ramses had withdrawn entirely into the study of all conceivable suits and claims, into the chicane subtleties of property, hereditary, land and other business law-suits, into the memorizing and logical analysis of quashed decisions. Perfectly of his own will, without in the least needing the money, he served for a year as a clerk at a notary's, for another as a secretary to a justice of the peace, while all of the past year, being in the last term, he had conducted in a local newspaper the reports of the city council and had borne the modest duty of an assistant to a secretary in the management of a syndicate of sugar manufacturers. And when this same syndicate commenced the well-known suit against one of its members, Colonel Baskakov, who had put up the surplus sugar for sale contrary to agreement, Ramses from the very beginning guessed before-hand and very subtly engineered precisely that decision which the senate subsequently handed down in this suit.

Despite his comparative youth, rather well-known jurists gave heed to his opinions—true, a little loftily. None of those who knew Ramses closely doubted that he would make a brilliant career, and even Ramses himself did not conceal his confidence in that toward thirty-five he would knock together a million, exclusively through his practice as a civil lawyer. His comrades not infrequently elected him chairman of meetings and head of the class, but this honour Ramses invariably declined, excusing himself with lack of time. But still he did not avoid participation in his comrades' trials by arbitration, and his arguments—always incontrovertibly logical— were possessed of an amazing virtue in ending the trials with peace, to the mutual satisfaction of the litigating parties. He, as well as Yarchenko, knew well the value of popularity among the studying youths, and even if he did look upon people with a certain contempt, from above, still he never, with a single movement of his thin, clever, energetical lips, showed this.

"Well, Gavrila Petrovich, no one is necessarily dragging you into committing a fall from grace," said Ramses
in a conciliatory manner. "What is all this pathos and
melancholy for, when the matter as it stands is altogether
simple? A company of young Russian gentlemen wishes
to pass the remnant of the night modestly and amicably,
to make merry, to sing a little, and to take internally
several gallons of wine and beer. But everything is
closed now, except these very same houses. *Ergo!..*"

"Consequently, we will go merry-making to women
who are for sale? To prostitutes? Into a brothel?"
Yarchenko interrupted him, mocking and inimically.

"And even so? A certain philosopher, whom it was
desired to humiliate, was given a seat at dinner near the
musicians. But he, sitting down, said: 'Here is a sure
means of making the last place the first.' And finally
I repeat: If your conscience does not allow you, as you
express yourself, to buy a woman, then you can go there
and come away, preserving your innocence in all its
blossoming inviolability."

"You overdo it, Ramses," objected Yarchenko with
displeasure. "You remind me of those bourgeois, who,
while it is still dark, have gathered to gape at an execution and who say: we have nothing to do with this, we
are against capital punishment, this is all the prosecuting
attorney's and the executioner's doing."

"Superbly said and partly true, Gavrila Petrovich.
But to us, precisely, this comparison may not even apply.
One cannot, you see, treat some malignant disease while
absent, without seeing the sufferer in person. And yet
all of us, who are now standing here in the street and
interfering with the passers-by, will be obliged at some
time in our work to run up against the terrible problem
of prostitution, and what a prostitution at that—the
Russian! Lichonin, I, Borya Sobashnikov and Pavlov
as jurists, Petrovsky and Tolpygin as medicos. True,
Veltman has a distinct specialty—mathematics. But
then, he will be a pedagogue, a guide of youth, and,

deuce take it, even a father! And if you are going to scare with a bugaboo, it is best to look upon it one's self first. And finally, you yourself, Gavrila Petrovich— expert of dead languages and future luminary of grave digging—is then, the comparison of the contemporary brothels, say, with some Pompeian lupanaria, or the institution of sacred prostitution in Thebes and Nineveh, not important and instructive to you?..."

"Bravo, Ramses, magnificent!" roared Lichonin. "And what's there to talk so much about, fellows? Take the professor under the gills and put him in a cab!"

The students, laughing and jostling, surrounded Yar- chenko, seized him under the arms, caught him around the waist. All of them were equally drawn to the women, but none, save Lichonin, had enough courage to take the initiative upon himself. But now all this complicated, unpleasant and hypocritical business was happily resolved into a simple, easy joke upon the older comrade. Yar- chenko resisted, and was angry, and laughing, trying to break away. But at this moment a tall, black-moustached policeman, who had long been eyeing them keenly and inimically, walked up to the uproarious students.

"I'd ask you stewdent gents not to congregate. It's not allowed! Keep on going!"

They moved on in a throng. Yarchenko was beginning to soften little by little.

"Gentlemen, I am ready to go with you, if you like... Do not think, however, that the sophistries of the Egyp- tian Pharaoh Ramses have convinced me... No, I simply would be sorry to break up the party... But I make one stipulation: we will drink a little there, gab a little, laugh a little, and so forth... but let there be nothing more, no filth of any kind... It is shameful and painful to think that we, the flower and glory of the Russian intelligentzia, will go all to pieces and let our mouths water at the sight of the first skirt that comes our way."

"I swear it!" said Lichonin, putting up his hand.

"I can vouch for myself," said Ramses.

"And I! And I! By God, gentlemen, let's pledge our words . . Yarchenko is right," others took up.

They seated themselves in twos and threes in the cabs—the drivers of which had been long since following them in a file, grinning and cursing each other—and rode off. Lichonin, for the sake of assurance, sat down beside the sub-professor, having embraced him around the waist and seated him on his knees and those of his neighbour, the little Tolpygin, a rosy, pleasant-faced boy on whose face, despite his twenty-three years, the childish white down—soft and light—still showed.

"The station is at Doroshenko's!" called out Lichonin after the cabbies driving off. "The stop is at Doroshenko's," he repeated, turning around.

They all stopped at Doroshenko's restaurant, entered the general room, and crowded about the bar. All were satiated and no one wanted either to drink or to have a bite. But in the soul of each one still remained a dark trace of the consciousness that right now they were getting ready to commit something needlessly shameful, getting ready to take part in some convulsive, artificial, and not at all a merry merriment. And in each one was the yearning to bring himself through intoxication to that misty and rainbow condition when nothing makes any difference, and when the head does not know what the arms and legs are doing, and what the tongue is babbling. And, probably, not the students alone, but all the casual and constant visitors of Yama experienced in greater or lesser degree the friction of this inner psychic heart-sore, because Doroshenko did business only late in the evening and night, and no one lingered long in his place but only turned in in passing, half-way on the journey.

While the students were drinking cognac, beer and vodka, Ramses was constantly and intently looking into the farthest corner of the restaurant hall, where two men were sitting—a tattered, gray, big old man, and, opposite him, his back to the bar, with his elbows spread out upon the table and his chin resting on the fists folded upon each other, some hunched up, stout, closely-cropped gentleman in a gray suit. The old man was picking upon a dulcimer lying before him and quietly singing, in a hoarse but pleasing voice:

> "Oh my valley, my little valley,
> Bro-o-o-o-o-oad land of plenty."

"Excuse me, but that is a co-worker of ours," said Ramses, and went to greet the gentleman in the gray suit. After a minute he led him up to the bar and introduced him to his comrades.

"Gentlemen, allow me to introduce to you my companion in arms in the newspaper game. Sergei Ivanovich Platonov. The laziest and most talented of newspaper workers."

They all introduced themselves, indistinctly muttering out their names.

"And therefore, let's have a drink," said Lichonin, while Yarchenko asked with the refined amiability which never forsook him:

"Pardon me, pardon me, but I am acquainted with you a little, even though not personally. Weren't you in the university when Professor Priklonsky defended the doctor's dissertation?"

"It was I," answered the reporter.

"Ah, that's very nice," smiled Yarchenko charmingly, and for some reason once more pressed Platonov's hand vigorously. "I read your report afterwards: very exactly, circumstantially and skillfully put together... Won't you favor me?.. To your health!"

"Then allow me, too," said Platonov. "Onuphriy Zakharich, pour out for us again... one... two, three, four... nine glasses of cognac..."

"Oh no, you can't do that... you are our guest, colleague," remonstrated Lichonin.

"Well, now, what sort of colleague am I to you?" good-naturedly laughed the reporter. "I was only in the first class and then only for half a year—as an un-matriculated student. Here you are, Onuphriy Zakharich. Gentlemen, I beg you..."

The upshot of it was that after half an hour Lichonin and Yarchenko did not under any consideration want to part with the reporter and dragged him with them to Yama. However, he did not resist.

"If I am not a burden to you, I would be very glad," he said simply. "All the more since I have easy money to-day. *The Dnieper Word* has paid me an honorarium, and this is just as much of a miracle as winning two hundred thousand on a check from a theatre coat room. Pardon me, I'll be right back..."

He walked up to the old man with whom he had been sitting before, shoved some money into his hand, and gently took leave of him.

"Where I'm going, grandpa, there you mustn't go—to-morrow we will meet in the same place as to-day. Good-bye!"

They all walked out of the restaurant. At the door Borya Sobashnikov, always a little finical and unnecessarily supercilious, stopped Lichonin and called him to one side.

"I'm surprised at you, Lichonin," he said squeamishly. "We have gathered together in our own close company, yet you must needs drag in some vagabond. The devil knows who he is!"

"Quit that, Borya," answered Lichonin amicably. "He's a warm-hearted fellow."

CHAPTER IX.

"Well now, gentlemen, this isn't fit for pigs," Yarchenko was saying, grumblingly, at the entrance of Anna Markovna's establishment. "If we finally have gone, we might at least have chosen a decent place, and not some wretched hole. Really, gentlemen, let's better go to Treppel's alongside; there it's clean and light, at any rate."

"If you please, if you please, signior," insisted Lichonin, opening the door before the sub-professor with courtly urbanity, bowing and spreading his arms before him. "If you please."

"But this is an abomination... At Treppel's the women are better-looking, at least."

Ramses, walking behind, burst into dry laughter.

"So, so, Gavrila Petrovich. Let us continue in the same spirit. Let us condemn the hungry, petty thief who has stolen a five-kopeck loaf out of a tray, but if the director of a bank has squandered somebody else's million on race horses and cigars, let us mitigate his lot."

"Pardon me, but I do not understand this comparison," answered Yarchenko with restraint. "However, it's all the same to me; let's go."

"And all the more so," said Lichonin, letting the sub-professor pass ahead; "all the more so, since this house guards within it so many historical traditions. Comrades! Decades of student generations gaze upon us from the heights of the coat-hooks, and, besides that, through the power of the usual right, children and students pay half here, as in a panopticon. Isn't that so, citizen Simeon?"

Simeon did not like to have people come in large parties—this always smacked of scandal in the not distant future; moreover, he despised students in general for their speech, but little comprehensible to him, for their

83

propensity towards frivolous jokes, for their godlessness,
and chiefly because they were in constant revolt against
officialdom and order. It was not in vain that on the day
when on the Bessarabian Square the cossacks, meat-
sellers, flour dealers and fish mongers were massacring
the students, Simeon having scarce found it out had
jumped into a fine carriage passing by, and, standing
just like a chief of police in the victoria, tore off to the
scene of the fray in order to take part in it. He esteemed
people who were sedate, stout and elderly, who came
singly, in secret, peeped in cautiously from the ante-toom
into the drawing room, fearing to meet with acquaintances,
and very soon and with great haste went away, tipping
him generously. Such he always styled "Your Excellency."

And so, while taking the light grey overcoat off Yarchenko, he sombrely and with much significance snarled
back in answer to Lichonin's banter:

"I am no citizen here, but the bouncer."

"Upon which I have the honour to congratulate you,"
answered Lichonin with a polite bow.

There were many people in the drawing room. The
clerks, having danced their fill, were sitting, red and wet,
near their ladies, rapidly fanning themselves with their
handkerchiefs; they smelt strongly of old goats' wool.
Mishka the Singer and his friend the Book-keeper, both
bald, with soft, downy hairs around the denuded skulls,
both with turbid, mother-of-pearl, intoxicated eyes, were
sitting opposite each other, leaning with their elbows on
a little marble table, and were constantly trying to start
singing in unison with such quavering and galloping voices
as though some one was very, very often striking them
in the cervical vertebræ:

"They fe-e-e-l the tru-u-u-uth!"

while Emma Edwardovna and Zociya with all their
might were exhorting them not to behave indecently.
Roly-Poly was peacefully slumbering on a chair, his head

hanging down, having laid one long leg over the other and grasped the sharp knee with his clasped hands.

The girls at once recognized some of the students and ran to meet them.

"Tamarochka, your husband has come—Volodenka. And my husband too!—Mishka!" cried Niura piercingly, hanging herself on the neck of the lanky, big-nosed, solemn Petrovsky. "Hello, Mishenka. Why haven't you come for so long? I grew weary of waiting for you."

Yarchenko with a feeling of awkwardness was looking about him on all sides.

"We'd like to have in some way... don't you know... a little private room," he said with delicacy to Emma Edwardovna who had approached. "And give us some sort of red wine, please... And then, some coffee as well... You know yourself."

Yarchenko always instilled confidence in the servants and *maîtres d'hôtel*, with his dashing clothes and polite but seigniorial ways. Emma Edwardovna started nodding her head willingly, just like an old, fat circus horse.

"It can be done... it can be done... Pass this way, gentlemen, into the parlor. It can be done, it can be done... What liqueur? We have only Benedictine... Benedictine, then? It can be done, it can be done... And will you allow the young ladies to come in?"

"Well, if that is so indispensable?" Yarchenko spread out his hands with a sigh.

And at once the girls one after the other straggled into the parlor with its gray plush furniture and blue lantern. They entered, extended to every one in turn their unbending palms, unused to hand-clasps, gave their names abruptly in a low voice—Manya, Katie, Liuba... They sat down on somebody's knees, embraced him around the neck, and, as usual, began to importune:

"Little student, you're such a little good-looker. May I ask for oranzes?"

"Volodenka, buy me some candy! All right?"

"And me chocolate!"

"Fatty," Vera, dressed as a jockey, wheedled the sub-professor, clambering up on his knees, "I have a friend, only she's sick and can't come out into the drawing room. I'll carry her some apples and chocolate. Will you let me?"

"Well, now, those are all just stories about a friend! But above all, don't be thrusting your tendernesses at me. Sit as smart children sit, right here alongside, on the arm chair, just so. And fold your little hands."

"Ah, but what if I can't!" writhed Vera in coquetry, rolling her eyes up under her upper lids... "When you are so nice."

But Lichonin, in answer to this professional beggary, only nodded his head gravely and good-naturedly, just like Emma Edwardovna, and repeated over and over again, mimicking her German accent:

"Itt can pe done, itt can pe done, itt can pe done..."

"Then I will tell the waiter, honey, to carry my friend some sweets and apples?" pestered Vera.

Such importunity entered the round of their tacit duties. There even existed among the girls some captious, childish, strange rivalry as to the ability to "ease a guest of his money"—strange enough because they did not derive any profit out of this, unless, indeed, a certain affection from the housekeeper or a word of approbation from the proprietress. But in their petty, monotonous, habitually frivolous life there was, in general, a great deal of semi-puerile, semi-hysterical play.

Simeon brought a coffee pot, cups, a squatty bottle of Benedictine, fruits and bon-bons in glass vases, and gaily and easily began making the corks of the beer and wine pop.

"But why don't you drink?" Yarchenko turned to the reporter Platonov. "Allow me... I do not mistake? Sergei Ivanovich, I believe?"

"Right."

"Allow me to offer you a cup of coffee, Sergei Ivanovich.

It's refreshing. Or perhaps, let's drink this same dubious Lafitte?"

"No, you really must allow me to refuse. I have a drink of my own... Simeon, give me..."

"Cognac!" cried out Niura hurriedly.

"And with a pear!" Little White Manka caught up just as fast.

"I heard you, Sergei Ivanich—right away," unhurriedly but respectfully responded Simeon, and, bending down and letting out a grunt, resoundingly drew the cork out of the neck of the bottle.

"It's the first time I hear of cognac being served in Yama," uttered Lichonin with amazement. "No matter how much I asked, they always refused me."

"Perhaps Sergei Ivanich knows some sort of magic word," jested Ramses.

"Or is held here in an especially honoured state?" Boris Sobashnikov put in pointedly, with emphasis.

The reporter listlessly, without turning his head, looked askance at Sobashnikov, at the lower row of buttons on his short, foppish, white summer uniform jacket, and answered with a drawl:

"There is nothing honourable in that I can drink like a horse and never get drunk; but then, I also do not quarrel with anyone or pick upon anybody. Evidently, these good sides of my character are sufficiently known here, and because of that confidence is shown me."

"Good for you, old fellow!" joyously exclaimed Lichonin, who was delighted by a certain peculiar, indolent negligence—of few words, yet at the same time self-confident—in the reporter. "Will you share the cognac with me also?"

"Very, very gladly," affably answered Platonov and suddenly looked at Lichonin with a radiant, almost child-like smile, which beautified his plain face with the prominent cheek-bones. "You, too, appealed to me from the first. And even when I saw you there, at Doroshenko's, I at once thought that you are not at all as rough as you seem."

"Well, now, we have exchanged pleasantries," laughed Lichonin. "But it's amazing that we haven't met once just here. Evidently, you come to Anna Markovna's quite frequently?"

"Even too much so."

"Sergei Ivanich is our most important guest!" naively shrieked Niura. "Sergei Ivanich is a sort of brother among us!"

"Fool!" Tamara stopped her.

"That seems strange to me," continued Lichonin. "I, too, am a habitue. In any case, one can only envy everybody's cordiality toward you."

"The local chieftain!" said Boris Sobashnikov, curling his lips downward, but said it so low that Platonov, if he chose to, could pretend that he had not heard anything distinctly. This reporter had for long aroused in Boris some blind and prickling irritation. That he was not one of his own herd really meant nothing. But Boris, like many students (and also officers, junkers, and high-school boys) had grown accustomed to the fact that the outside "civilian" people, who accidentally fell into a company of students on a spree, should hold themselves somewhat subordinately and with servility in it, flatter the studying youths, be struck with its daring, laugh at its jokes, admire its self-admiration, recall their own student years with a sigh of suppressed envy. But in Platonov there not only was none of this customary wagging of the tail before youth, but, on the contrary, there was to be felt a certain abstracted, calm and polite indifference.

Besides that, Sobashnikov was angered—and angered with a petty, jealous vexation—by that simple and yet anticipatory attention which was shown to the reporter by everybody in the establishment, beginning with the porter and ending with the fleshy, taciturn Katie. This attention was shown in the way he was listened to, in that triumphal carefulness with which Tamara filled his glass, and in the way Little White Manka pared a pear for him solicitously, and in the delight of Zoe, who had caught the cigar case skillfully thrown to her across the table by the reporter, when she had vainly asked for a cigarette from her two neighbours, who were lost in conversation; and in the way none of the girls begged either chocolate or fruits from him, in the lively gratitude for his little services and his treating. "Pimp!" Sobashnikov had almost decided mentally with malice, but did not believe it even himself—the reporter was altogether too homely and too carelessly dressed, and moreover he bore himself with great dignity.

Platonov again made believe that he had not heard the insolent remark made by the student. He only nervously crumpled a napkin in his fingers and lightly threw it aside from him. And again his eyelids quivered in the direction of Boris Sobashnikov.

"Yes, true, I am one of the family here," he continued calmly, moving his glass in slow circles on the table. "Just think, I dined in this very house, day after day, for exactly four months."

"No? Seriously?" Yarchenko wondered and laughed.

"In all seriousness. The table here isn't at all bad, by the way. The food is filling and savory, although exceedingly greasy."

"But how did you ever. . ."

"Why, just because I was tutoring for high school a daughter of Anna Markovna, the lady of this hospitable house. Well, I stipulated that part of my monthly pay should be deducted for my dinners."

"What a strange fancy! said Yarchenko. "And did you do this of your own will? Or. . . Pardon me, I am afraid of seeming indiscreet to you. . . Perhaps at that time. . . extreme necessity?. . ."

"Not at all. Anna Markovna soaked me three times as much as it would have cost in a student's dining room. I simply wanted to live here a while on a somewhat

nearer, closer footing, to enter intimately into this little
world, so to speak."

"A-ah! It seems I am beginning to understand!"
beamed Yarchenko. "Our new friend—pardon me for
the little familiarity—is, apparently, gathering material
from life? And, perhaps, in a few years we will have the
pleasure of reading..."

"A tr-r-ragedy out of a brothel!" Boris Sobashnikov
put in loudly, like an actor.

While the reporter had been answering Yarchenko,
Tamara quietly got up from her place, walked around
the table, and, bending down over Sobashnikov, spoke
in a whisper in his ear:

"Dearie, sweetie, you'd better not touch this gentleman. Honest to God, it will be better for you, even."

"Wass that?" the student looked at her superciliously,
fixing his *pince-nez* with two spread fingers. "Is he your
lover? Your pimp?"

"I swear by anything you want that not once in his
life has he staid with any one of us. But, I repeat, don't
pick on him."

"Why, yes! Why, of course!" retorted Sobashnikov,
grimacing scornfully. "He has such a splendid defense
as the entire brothel. And it's a sure thing that all the
bouncers on Yamskaya are his near friends and cronies."

"No, not that," retorted Tamara in a kind whisper.
"Only, he'll take you by the collar and throw you out of
the window, like a puppy. I've already seen such an
aerial flight. God forbid its happening to anyone. It's
disgraceful, and bad for the health."

"Get out of here, you filth!" yelled Sobashnikov,
swinging his elbow at her.

"I'm going, dearie," meekly answered Tamara, and
walked away from him with her light step.

Everybody for an instant turned toward the student.

"Behave yourself, barberry!" Lichonin threatened him
with his finger. "Well, well, go on," he begged the reporter; "all that you're saying is so interesting."

"No, I'm not gathering anything," continued the reporter calmly and seriously. "But the material here is in reality tremendous, downright crushing, terrible... And not at all terrible are the loud phrases about the traffic in women's flesh, about the white slaves, about prostitution being a corroding fester of large cities, and so on, and so on... an old hurdy-gurdy of which all have tired! No, horrible are the everyday, accustomed trifles, these business-like, daily, commercial recokonings, this thousand year old science of amatory practice, this prosaic usage, determined by the ages. In these unnoticeable nothings are completely dissolved such feelings as resentment, humiliation, shame. There remains a dry profession, a contract, an agreement, a well-nigh honest petty trade, no better, no worse than, say, the trade in groceries. Do you understand, gentlemen, that all the horror is in just this, that there is no horror! Bourgeois work days—and that is all. And also an after taste of an exclusive educational institution, with its *naïveté*, harshness, sentimentality and imitativeness."

"That's right," confirmed Lichonin, while the reporter continued, gazing pensively into his glass:

"We read in the papers, in leading articles, various wailings of anxious souls. And the women-physicians are also endeavouring in this matter, and endeavouring disgustingly enough. 'Oh, dear, regulation! Oh, dear, abolition! Oh, dear, live merchandise! A condition of slavery! The madames, these greedy hæteræ! These heinous degenerates of humanity, sucking the blood of prostitutes!'... But with clamour you will scare no one and will affect no one. You know, there's a little saying: much cry, little wool. More awful than all awful words—a hundredfold more awful—is some such little prosaic stroke or other as will suddenly knock you all in a heap, like a blow on the forehead. Take even Simeon, the porter here. It would seem, according to you, there is no sinking lower—a bouncer in a brothel, a brute, almost certainly a murderer, he plucks the prostitutes, gives them "black eyes", to use a local expression—that is, just simply beats them. But, do you know on what grounds he and I came together and became friendly? On the magnificent details of the divine service of the prelate, on the canon of the honest Andrew, pastor of Crete, on the works of the most beatific father, John the Damascene. He is religious—unusually so! I used to lead him on, and he would sing to me with tears in his eyes: 'Come ye brethren, and we will give the last kiss to him who has gone to his rest...' From the ritual of the burial of laymen. No, just think: it is only in the Russian soul alone that such contradictions may dwell together!"

"Yes. A fellow like that will pray, and pray, then cut a throat, and then wash his hands and put a candle before an image," said Ramses.

"Just so. I know of nothing more uncanny than this fusion of fully sincere devoutness with an innate leaning toward crime. Shall I confess to you? I, when I talk all alone to Simeon—and we talk with each other long and leisurely, for hours—I experience at moments a genuine terror. A superstitious terror! Just as though, for instance, I am standing in the dusk upon a shaking little board, bending over some dark, malodorous well, and just barely distinguish how there, at the bottom, reptiles are stirring. And yet, he is devout in a real way, and I am sure will some time join the monks and will be a great faster and sayer of prayers, and the devil knows how, in what monstrous fashion, a real religious ecstasy will entwine in his soul with blasphemy, with scoffing at sacred things, with some repulsive passion or other, with sadism or something else of that nature?"

"However, you do not spare the object of your observations," said Yarchenko, and carefully indicated the girls with his eyes.

"Eh, it's all the same. Our relations are cool now."

"How so?" asked Volodya Pavlov, who had caught the end of the conversation.

"Just so... It isn't even worth the telling..." smiled the reporter evasively. "A trifle... Let's have your glass here, Mr. Yarchenko."

But the precipitate Niura, who could never keep her tongue behind her teeth, suddenly shot out in rapid patter:

"It's because Sergei Ivanich gave him one in the snout... On account of Ninka. A certain old man came to Ninka... And stayed for the night... And Ninka had the flowers...* And the old man was torturing her all the time... So Ninka started crying and ran away."

"Drop it, Niura; it's boring," said Platonov with a wry face.

"Can it!" (leave off) ordered Tamara severely, in the jargon of houses of prostitution.

But it was impossible to stop Niura, who had gotten a running start.

"But Ninka says: 'I,' she says, 'won't stay with him for anything, though you cut me all to pieces... He,' she says, 'has made me all wet with his spit.' Well, the old man complained to the porter, to be sure, and the porter starts in to beat up Ninka, to be sure. And Sergei Ivanich at this time was writing for me a letter home, to the province, and when he heard that Ninka was hollering..."

"Zoe, shut her mouth!" said Platonov.

"He just jumped up at once and... app!.." and Niura's torrent instantly broke off, stopped up by Zoe's palm.

Everybody burst out laughing, only Boris Sobashnikov muttered under cover of the noise with a contemptuous look:

"*Oh, chevalier sans peur et sans reproche!*"

He was already pretty far gone in drink, stood leaning against the wall, in a provoking pose, and was nervously chewing a cigarette.

---

*The Russian expression is "the red flag."—*Trans.*

"Which Ninka is this?" asked Yarchenko with curiosity. "Is she here?"

"No, she isn't here. Such a small, pug-nosed little girl. Naive and very angry." The reporter suddenly and sincerely burst into laughter. "Excuse me... It's just so... over my thoughts," explained he through laughter. ."I recalled this old man very vividly just now, as he was running along the corridor in fright, having grabbed his outer clothing and shoes... Such a respectable ancient, with the appearance of an apostle, I even know where he serves. Why, all of you know him. But the funniest of all was when he, at last, felt himself out of danger in the drawing room. You understand— he is sitting on a chair, putting on his pantaloons, can't put his foot where it ought to go, by any means, and bawls all over the house: 'It's an outrage! This is an abominable dive! I'll show you up!... To-morrow I'll give you twenty-four hours to clear out!..' Do you know, this combination of pitiful helplessness with the threatening cries was so killing that even the gloomy Simeon started laughing... Well, now, apropos of Simeon... I say, that life dumfounds, with its wondrous muddle and farrago, makes one stand aghast. You can utter a thousand sonorous words against souteneurs, but just such a Simeon you will never think up. So diverse and motley is life! Or else take Anna Markovna, the proprietress of this place. This blood-sucker, hyena, vixen and so on... is the tenderest mother imaginable. She has one daughter—Bertha, she is now in the fifth grade of high school. If you could only see how much careful attention, how much tender care Anna Markovna expends that her daughter may not somehow, accidentally, find out about her profession. And everything is for Birdie, everything is for the sake of Birdie. And she herself dare not even converse before her, is afraid of her lexicon of a bawd and an erstwhile prostitute, looks into her eyes, holds herself servilely, like an old servant, like a foolish, doting nurse, like an old, faithful, mange-eaten poodle.

It is long since time for her to retire to rest, because she
has money, and because her occupation is both arduous
and troublesome, and because her years are already vener-
able. But no and no; one more extra thousand is needed,
and then more and more—everything for Birdie. And
so Birdie has horses, Birdie has an English governess,
Birdie is every year taken abroad, Birdie has diamonds
worth forty thousand—the devil knows whose they are,
these diamonds? And it isn't that I am merely convinced, but I know well, that for the happiness of this
same Birdie, nay, not even for her happiness, but, let
us suppose that Birdie gets a hangnail on her little finger—
well then, in order that this hangnail might pass away—
imagine for a second the possibility of such a state of
things!—Anna Markovna, without the quiver of an eye-
lash, will sell into corruption our sisters and daughters,
will infect all of us and our sons with syphilis. What?
A monster, you will say? But I will say that she is moved
by the same grand, unreasoning, blind, egoistical love
for which we call all our mothers sainted women."

"Go easy around the curves!" remarked Boris Sobashnikov through his teeth.

"Pardon me: I was not comparing people, but merely
generalizing on the first source of emotion. I might
have brought out as an example the self-denying love of
animal-mothers as well. But I see that I have started on
a tedious matter. Better let's drop it."

"No, you finish," protested Lichonin. "I feel that you
have a massive thought."

"And a very simple one. The other day a professor
asked me if I am not observing the life here with some
literary aims. And all I wanted to say was, that I can
see, but precisely can not observe. Here I have given
you Simeon and the bawd for example. I do not know
myself why, but I feel that in them lurks some terrible,
insuperable actuality of life, but either to tell it, or to
show it, I can not. Here is necessary the great ability
to take some picayune trifle, an insignificant, paltry little

stroke, and then will result a dreadful truth, from which the reader, aghast, will forget that his mouth is agape. People seek the terrible in words, in cries, in gestures. Well, now, for example, I am reading a description of some pogrom or of a slaughter in jail, or of a riot being put down. Of course, the policemen are described, these servants of arbitrariness, these life-guards of contemporaneousness, striding up to their knees in blood, or how else do they write in such cases? Of course, it is revolting and it hurts, and is disgusting, but all this is felt by the mind, and not the heart. But here I am walking along Lebyazhia Street, and see that a crowd has collected, a girl of five years in the centre—she has lagged behind the mother and has strayed, or it may be that the mother had abandoned her. And before the girl, squatting down on his heels, is a roundsman. He is interrogating her, how she is called, and where is she from, and how do they call papa, and how do they call mamma. He has broken out into sweat, the poor fellow, from the effort, the cap is at the back of his neck, the whiskered face is such a kindly and woeful and helpless one, while the voice is gentle, so gentle. At last, what do you think? As the girl has become all excited, and has already grown hoarse from tears, and is shy of everybody—he, this same 'roundsman on the beat', stretches out two of his black, calloused fingers, the index and the little, and begins to imitate a nanny goat for the girl and reciting an appropriate nursery rhyme!.. And so, when I looked upon this charming scene and thought that half an hour later at the station house this same patrolman will be beating with his feet the face and chest of a man whom he had not till that time seen once, and whose crime he is entirely ignorant of—then—you understand!—I began to feel inexpressibly eerie and sad. Not with the mind, but the heart. Such a devilish muddle is this life. Shall we drink some cognac, Lichonin?"

"What do you say to calling each other thou?" suddenly proposed Lichonin.

"All right. Only, really, without any of this business of kissing, now. Here's to your health, old man... Or here is another instance... I read a certain French classic, describing the thoughts and sensations of a man condemned to capital punishment. He describes it all sonorously, powerfully, brilliantly, but I read and... well, there is no impression of any sort; neither emotion nor indignation—just *ennui*. But then, within the last few days I come across a brief newspaper notice of a murderer's execution somewhere in France. The Procureur, who was present at the last toilet of the criminal, sees that he is putting on his shoes on his bare feet, and—the blockhead!—reminds him: 'What about the socks?' But the other gives him a look and says, sort of thoughtfully· 'Is it worth while?' Do you understand, these two remarks, so very short, struck me like a blow on the skull! At once all the horror and all the stupidity of unnatural death were revealed to me... Or here is something else about death... A certain friend of mine died, a captain in the infantry—a drunkard, a vagabond, and the finest soul in the world. For some reason we called him the Electrical Captain. I was in the vicinity, and it fell to me to dress him for the last parade. I took his uniform and began to attach the epaulettes to it. There's a cord, you know, that's drawn through the shank of the epaulette buttons, and after that the two ends of this cord are shoved through two little holes under the collar, and on the inside—the lining—are tied together. Well, I go through all this business, and tie the cord with a slipknot, and, you know, the loop won't come out, nohow—either it's too loosely tied, or else one end's too short. I am fussing over this nonsense, and suddenly into my head comes the most astonishingly simple thought, that it's far simpler and quicker to tie it in a knot—for after all, it's all the same, *no one is going to untie it*. And immediately I felt death with all my being. Until that time I had seen the captain's eyes, grown glassy, had felt his cold forehead, and still somehow had not sensed death to the full, but I thought of the knot—and I was all transpierced, and the simple and sad realization of the irrevocable, inevitable perishing of all our words, deeds, and sensations, of the perishing of all the apparent world, seemed to bow me down to the earth... And I could bring forward a hundred such small but staggering trifles... Even, say, about what people experienced in the war... But I want to lead my thought up to one thing. We all pass by these characteristic trifles indifferently, like the blind, as though not seeing them scattered about under our feet. But an artist will come, and he will look over them carefully, and he will pick them up. And suddenly he will so skillfully turn in the sun a minute bit of life that we shall all cry out: 'Oh, my God! But I myself—myself—have seen this with my own eyes. Only it simply did not enter my head to turn my close attention upon it.' But our Russian artists of the word—the most conscientious and sincere artists in the whole world—for some reason have up to this time passed over prostitution and the brothel. Why? Really, it is difficult for me to answer that. Perhaps because of squeamishness, perhaps because of pusillanimity, out of fear of being signalized as a pornographic writer; finally, from the apprehension that our gossiping criticism will identify the artistic work of the writer with his personal life and will start rummaging in his dirty linen. Or perhaps they can find neither the time, nor the self-denial, nor the self-possession to plunge in head first into this life and to watch it right up close, without prejudice, without sonorous phrases, without a sheepish pity, in all its monstrous simplicity and everyday activity. Oh, what a tremendous, staggering and truthful book would result!''

"But they do write!'' unwillingly remarked Ramses.

"They do write,'' wearily repeated Platonov in the same tone as he. "But it is all either a lie, or theatrical effects for children of tender years, or else a cunning symbolism, comprehensible only to the sages of the future. But the life itself no one as yet has touched. One big writer—a man with a crystal-pure soul and a remarkable talent for delineation—once approached this theme,* and then all that could catch the eye of an outsider was reflected in his soul, as in a wondrous mirror. But he could not decide to lie to and to frighten people. He only looked upon the coarse hair of the porter, like that of a dog, and reflected: 'But, surely, even he had a mother.' He passed with his wise, exact gaze over the faces of the prostitutes and impressed them on his mind. But that which he did not know he did not dare to write. It is remarkable, that this same writer, enchanting with his honesty and truthfulness, has looked at the moujik as well, more than once. But he sensed that both the tongue and the turn of mind, as well as the soul of the people, were for him dark and incomprehensible... And he, with an amazing tact, modestly went around the soul of the people, but refracted all his fund of splendid observation through the eyes of townsfolk. I have brought this up purposely. With us, you see, they write about detectives, about lawyers, about inspectors of the revenue, about pedagogues, about attorneys, about the police, about officers, about sensual ladies, about engineers, about baritones—and really, by God, altogether well—cleverly, with finesse and talent. But, after all, all these people are rubbish, and their life is not life but some sort of conjured up, spectral, unnecessary delirium of world culture. But there are two singular realities—ancient as humanity itself: the prostitute and the moujik. And about them we know nothing save some tinsel, gingerbread, debauched depictions in literature. I ask you: what has Russian literature extracted out of all the nightmare of prostitution? Sonechka Marmeladova alone.† What has it given us about the moujik save odious, false, nationalistic pastorals? One, altogether but one, but then, in truth, the greatest work in all the world—a

---

*The reference here is most probably to Chekhov.—*Trans.*
†The heroine of Dostoievsky's *Crime and Punishment.*—*Trans.*

staggering tragedy, the truthfulness of which takes the breath away and makes the hair stand on end. You know what I am speaking of..."

" 'The little claw is sunk in...' "* quietly prompted Lichonin.

"Yes," answered the reporter, and looked kindly at the student with gratefulness.

"But as regards Sonechka—why, this is an abstract type," remarked Yarchenko with assurance. "A psychological scheme, so to speak..."

Platonov, who up to now had been speaking as though unwillingly, at a slow rate, suddenly grew heated:

"A hundred times have I heard this opinion, a hundred times! And it is entirely an untruth. Underneath the coarse and obscene profession, underneath the foulest oaths—about one's mother—underneath the drunken, hideous exterior—Sonechka Marmeladova still lives! The fate of the Russian prostitute—oh, what a tragic, piteous, bloody, ludicrous and stupid path it is! Here everything has been juxtaposed: the Russian God, Russian breadth and unconcern, Russian despair in a fall, Russian lack of culture, Russian *naïveté*, Russian patience, Russian shamelessness. Why, all of them, whom you take into bedrooms,—look upon them, look upon them well,— why, they are all children; why, each of them is but eleven years old. Fate has thrust them upon prostitution and since then they live in some sort of a strange, fairy-like, toy existence, without developing, without being enriched by experience, naive, trusting, capricious, not knowing what they will say and do half an hour later— altogether like children. This radiant and ludicrous childishness I have seen in the very oldest wenches, fallen as low as low can be, broken-winded and crippled like a cabby's nags. And never does this impotent pity,

---

*"The little claw is sunk in, the whole bird is bound to perish" —a folk proverb used by Tolstoi as a sub-title to his *The Power of Darkness.—Trans.*

this useless commiseration toward human suffering die within them... For example..."

Platonov looked over all the persons sitting with a slow gaze, and suddenly, waving his hand despondently, said in a tired voice:

"However... The devil take it all! To-day I have spoken enough for ten years... And all of it to no purpose."

"But really, Sergei Ivanich, why shouldn't you try to describe all this yourself?" asked Yarchenko. "Your attention is so vitally concentrated on this question."

"I did try!" answered Platonov with a cheerless smile. "But nothing came of it. I started writing and at once became entangled in various 'whats,' 'which's,' 'was's.' The epithets prove flat. The words grow cold on the page. It's all a cud of some sort. Do you know, Terekhov was here once, while passing through... You know... The well-known one... I came to him and started in telling him lots and lots about the life here, which I do not tell you for fear of boring you. I begged him to utilize my material. He heard me out with great attention, and this is what he said, literally: 'Don't get offended, Platonov, if I tell you that there's almost not a single person of those I have met during my life, who wouldn't thrust themes for novels and stories upon me, or teach me as to what ought to be written up. That material which you have just communicated to me is truly unencompassable in its significance and weightiness. But what shall I do with it? In order to write a colossal book such as the one you have in mind, the words of others do not suffice—even though they be the most exact—even observations, made with a little note-book and a bit of pencil, do not suffice. One must grow accustomed to this life, without being cunningly wise, without any ulterior thoughts of writing. Then a terrific book will result.'

"His words discouraged me and at the same time gave me wings. Since that time I believe, that now, not soon—

after fifty years or so—but there will come a writer of
genius, and precisely a Russian one, who will absorb
within himself all the burdens and all the abominations
of this life and will cast them forth to us in the form of
simple, fine, and deathlessly-caustic images. And we
shall all say: 'Why, now, we, ourselves, have seen and
known all this, but we could not even suppose that this
is so horrible!' In this coming artist I believe with all
my heart."

"Amen!" said Lichonin seriously. Let us drink to
him."

"But, honest to God," suddenly declared Little Manka,
"If some one would only write the truth about the way
we live here, miserable w---- that we are..."

There was a knock at the door, and at once Jennie
entered in her resplendent orange dress.

CHAPTER X.

She greeted all the men without embarrassment, with the independent bearing of the first personage in the house, and sat down near Sergei Ivanich, behind his chair. She had just gotten free from that same German in the uniform of the benevolent organization, who early in the evening had made Little White Manka his choice, but had afterwards changed her, at the recommendation of the housekeeper, for Pasha. But the provoking and self-assured beauty of Jennie must have smitten deeply his lecherous heart, for, having prowled some three hours through certain beer emporiums and restaurants, and having there gathered courage, he had again returned into the house of Anna Markovna, had waited until her time-guest—Karl Karlovich, from the optical store—had gone away from Jennie, and had taken her into a room.

To the silent question in Tamara's eyes Jennie made a wry face of disgust, shivered with her back and nodded her head affirmatively.

"He's gone... Brrr!.."

Platonov was looking at Jennie with extraordinary attentiveness. He distinguished her from the rest of the girls and almost respected her for her abrupt, refractory, and impudently mocking character. And now, turning around occasionally, by her flaming, splendid eyes, by the vividly and unevenly glowing unhealthy red of her cheeks, by the much bitten parched lips, he felt that her great, long ripening rancour was heavily surging within the girl and suffocating her. And it was then that he thought (and subsequently often recalled this) that he had never yet seen Jennie so radiantly beautiful as on this night. He also noticed, that all the men present in the private cabinet, with the exception of Lichonin, were looking at her—some frankly, others by stealth and as though in passing—with curiosity and furtive desire. The beauty of this woman, together with the thought of her altogether easy accessibility, at any minute, agitated their imagination.

"There's something working upon you, Jennie," said Platonov quietly.

Caressingly, she just barely drew her fingers over his arm.

"Don't pay any attention. Just so... our womanish affairs... It won't be interesting to you."

But immediately, turning to Tamara, she passionately and rapidly began saying something in an agreed jargon, which presented a wild mixture out of the Hebrew, Tzigani and Roumanian tongues and the cant words of thieves and horse-thieves.

"Don't try to put anything over on the fly guy, the fly guy is next," Tamara cut her short and with a smile indicated the reporter with her eyes.

Platonov had, in fact, understood. Jennie was telling with indignation that during this day and night, thanks to the influx of a cheap public, the unhappy Pashka had been taken into a room more than ten times—and all by different men. Only just now she had had a hysterical fit, ending in a faint. And now, scarcely having brought Pashka back to consciousness and braced her up on valerian drops in a glass of spirits, Emma Edwardovna had again sent her into the drawing room. Jennie had attempted to take the part of her comrade, but the house-keeper had cursed the intercessor out and had threatened her with punishment.

"What is it all about?" asked Yarchenko in perplexity, raising high his eyebrows.

"Don't trouble yourself... nothing out of the way..." answered Jennie in a still agitated voice. "Just so... our little family trifles... Sergei Ivanich, may I have some of your wine?"

She poured out half a glass for herself and drank the cognac off at a draught, distending her thin nostrils wide.

Platonov got up in silence and went toward the door.

"It's not worth while, Sergei Ivanich. Drop it..." Jennie stopped him.

"Oh no, why not?" objected the reporter. "I shall do a very simple and innocent thing, take Pasha here, and if need be—pay for her, even. Let her lie down here for a while on the divan and rest, even though a little... Niura, run for a pillow quick!"

Scarcely had the door shut behind his broad, ungainly figure in its gray clothes, when Boris Sobashnikov at once commenced speaking with a contemptuous bitterness:

"Gentlemen, what the devil for have we dragged into our company this peach off the street? We must needs tie up with all sorts of riff-raff? The devil knows what he is—perhaps he's even a dinny? Who can vouch for him? And you're always like that, Lichonin."

"It isn't Lichonin but I who introduced him to everybody," said Ramses. "I know him for a fully respectable person and a good companion."

"Eh! Nonsense! A good companion to drink at some one else's expense. Why, don't you see for yourselves that this is the most ordinary type of habitue attached to a brothel, and, most probably, he is simply the pimp here, to whom a percentage is paid for the entertainment into which he entices the visitors."

"Leave off, Borya. It's foolish," remarked Yarchenko reproachfully.

But Borya could not leave off. He had an unfortunate peculiarity—intoxication acted neither upon his legs nor his tongue, but put him in a morose, touchy frame of mind and egged him on into quarrels. And Platonov had already for a long time irritated him with his negligently sincere, assured and serious bearing, so little suitable to the private cabinet of a brothel. But that seeming indifference with which the reporter let pass the malicious remarks which he interposed into the conversation angered Sobashnikov still more.

"And then, the tone in which he permits himself to speak in our company!" Sobashnikov continued to seethe. "A certain aplomb, condescension, a professorial tone... The scurvy penny-a-liner! The free-lunch grafter!"

Jennie, who had all the time been looking intently at the student, gaily and maliciously flashing with her sparkling dark eyes, suddenly began to clap her hands.

"That's the way! Bravo, little student! Bravo, bravo, bravo!.. That's the way, give it to him good!.. Really, what sort of a disgrace is this! When he'll come, now, I'll repeat everything to him."

"I—if you please! A—as much as you like!" Sobashnikov drawled out like an actor, making superciliously squeamish creases about his mouth. "I shall repeat the very same things myself."

"There's a fine fellow, now,—I love you for that!" exclaimed Jennie joyously and maliciously, striking her fist on the table. "You can tell an owl at once by its flight, a good man by his snot!"

Little White Manya and Tamara looked at Jennie with wonder, but, noting the evil little lights leaping in her eyes and her nervously quivering nostrils, they both understood and smiled.

Little White Manya, laughing, shook her head reproachfully. Jennie always had such a face when her turbulent soul sensed that a scandal was nearing which she herself had brought on.

"Don't get your back up, Borinka," said Lichonin. "Here all are equal."

Niura came with a pillow and laid it down on the divan.

"And what's that for?" Sobashnikov yelled at her. "Git! take it away at once. This isn't a lodging house."

"Now, leave her be, honey. What's that to you?" retorted Jennie in a sweet voice and hid the pillow behind

Tamara's back. "Wait, sweetie, I'd better sit with you for a while."

She walked around the table, forced Boris to sit on a chair, and herself got up on his knees. Twining his neck with her arm, she pressed her lips to his mouth, so long and so vigorously that the student caught his breath. Right up close to his eyes he saw the eyes of the woman— strangely large, dark, luminous, indistinct and unmoving. For a quarter of a second or so, for an instant, it seemed to him that in these unliving eyes was impressed an expression of keen, mad hate; and the chill of terror, some vague premonition of an ominous, inevitable calamity flashed through the student's brain. With difficulty tearing the supple arms of Jennie away from him, and pushing her away, he said, laughing, having turned red and breathing hard:

"There's a temperament for you! Oh, you Messalina Paphnutievna!... They call you Jennka, I think? You're a good-looking little rascal."

Platonov returned with Pasha. Pasha was pitiful and revolting to look at. Her face was pale, with a bluish cast as though the blood had run off; the glazed, half-closed eyes were smiling with a faint, idiotic smile; the parted lips seemed to resemble two frayed, red, wet rags, and she walked with a sort of timid, uncertain step, just as though with one foot she were making a large step, and with the other a small one. She walked with docility up to the divan and with docility laid her head down on the pillow, without ceasing to smile faintly and insanely. Even at a distance it was apparent that she was cold.

"Pardon me, gentlemen, I am going to undress," said Lichonin, and taking his coat off he threw it over the shoulders of the prostitute. "Tamara, give her chocolate and wine."

Boris Sobashnikov again stood up picturesquely in the corner, in a leaning position, one leg in front of the other and his head held high. Suddenly he spoke amid the general silence, addressing Platonov directly, in a most foppish tone:

"Eh... Listen... what's your name?.. This, then, must be your mistress? Eh?" And with the tip of his boot he pointed in the direction of the recumbent Pasha.

"Wha–at?" asked Platonov in a drawl, knitting his eyebrows.

"Or else you are her lover—it's all one... What do they call this duty here? Well, now, these same people for whom the women embroider shirts and with whom they divide their honest earnings?.. Eh?.."

Platonov looked at him with a heavy, intent gaze through his narrowed lids.

"Listen," he said quietly, in a hoarse voice, slowly and ponderously separating his words. "This isn't the first time that you're trying to pick a quarrel with me. But, in the first place, I see that despite your sober appearance you are exceedingly and badly drunk; and, in the second place, I spare you for the sake of your comrades. However, I warn you, that if you think of talking that way to me again, take your eyeglasses off."

"What's this stuff?" exclaimed Boris, raising his shoulders high and snorting through his nose. "What eyeglasses? Why eyeglasses?" But mechanically, with two extended fingers, he fixed the bow of the *pince-nez* on the bridge of his nose.

"Because I'm going to hit you, and the pieces may get in your eye," said the reporter unconcernedly.

Despite the unexpectedness of such a turn of the quarrel, nobody started laughing. Only Little White Manka oh'd in astonishment and clapped her hands. Jennie, with avid impatience, shifted her eyes from one to the other.

"Well, now! I'll give you change back myself so's you won't like it!" roughly, altogether boyishly, cried out Sobashnikov. "Only it's not worth while mussing one's hands with every..." he wanted to add a new invective, but decided not to, "with every... And besides, comrades, I do not intend to stay here any longer. I am too well brought up to be hail-fellow-well-met with such persons."

He rapidly and haughtily walked to the door.

It was necessary for him to pass almost right up against Platonov, who, out of the corner of his eye, animal-like, was watching his every movement. For a moment in the mind of the student flashed a desire to strike Platonov unexpectedly, from the side, and jump away—the comrades would surely part them and not allow a fight. But immediately, almost without looking at the reporter, with some sort of deep, unconscious instinct, he saw and sensed these broad hands, lying quietly on the table, this obdurately bowed head with its broad forehead, and all the ungainly, alert, powerful body of his foe, so negligently hunched up and spread out on the chair, but ready at any second for a quick and terrific blow. And Sobashnikov walked out into the corridor, loudly banging the door after him.

"Good riddance to bad rubbish," said Jennie after him in a mocking patter. "Tamarochka, pour me out some more cognac."

But the lanky student Petrovsky got up from his place and considered it necessary to defend Sobashnikov.

"Just as you wish, gentlemen; this is a matter of your personal view, but out of principle I go together with Boris. Let him be not right and so on, we can express censure to him in our own intimate company, but when an insult has been rendered our comrade—I can't remain here. I am going away."

"Oh, my God!" And Lichonin nervously and vexedly scratched his temple. "Boris behaved himself all the time in the highest degree vulgarly, rudely and foolishly. What sort of corporate honour do you think this is? A collective walk-out from editorial offices, from political meetings, from brothels. We aren't officers to screen the foolishness of each comrade."

"All the same, just as you wish, but I am going away out of a sense of solidarity!" said Petrovsky importantly and walked out.

"May the earth be as down upon you!" Jennie sent after him.

But how tortuous and dark the ways of the human soul! Both of them—Sobashnikov as well as Petrovsky—acted in their indignation rather sincerely, but the first only half so, while the second only a quarter in all. Sobashnikov, despite his intoxication and wrath, still had knocking at the door of his mind the alluring thought that now it would be more convenient and easier before his comrades to call out Jennka on the quiet and to be alone with her. While Petrovsky, with exactly the same aim, went after Sobashnikov in order to make a loan of three roubles from him. In the general drawing room they made things up between them, and after ten minutes Zociya, the housekeeper, shoved in her little, squinting, pink, cunning face through the half-open door of the private room.

"Jennechka," she called, "go, they have brought your linen, go count it. And you, Niura, the actor begs to come for just a minute, to drink some champagne. He's with Henrietta and Big Manya."

The precipitate and incongruous quarrel of Platonov and Sobashnikov long served as a subject of conversation. The reporter, in cases like this, always felt shame, uneasiness, regret and the torments of conscience. And despite the fact that all those who remained were on his side, he was speaking with weariness in his voice:

"By God, gentlemen! I'll go away, best of all. Why should I disrupt your circle? We were both at fault. I'll go away. Don't bother about the bill. I've already paid Simeon, when I was going after Pasha."

Lichonin suddenly rumpled up his hair and stood up.

"Oh, no, the devil take it! I'll go and drag him here. Upon my word of honour, they're both fine fellows—

Boris as well as Vaska. But they're young yet, and bark at their own tails. I'm going after them, and I warrant that Boris will apologize."

He went away, but came back after five minutes.

"They repose," said he sombrely and made a hopeless gesture with his hand. "Both of them."

CHAPTER XI.

At this moment Simeon walked into the cabinet with a tray upon which stood two goblets of a bubbling golden wine and lay a large visiting card.

"May I ask which of you here might be Gavrila Petrovich, Mister Yarchenko?" he said, looking over all those sitting.

"I," responded Yarchenko.

"If youse please. The actor gent sent this."

Yarchenko took the visiting card and read aloud:

Eumenii Poluectovich

E G M O N T — L A V R E T Z K I

Dramatic Artist of Metropolitan Theatres

"It's remarkable," said Volodya Pavlov, "that all the Russian Garricks bear such queer names, on the style of Chrysantov, Thetisov, Mamontov and Epimakhov."

"And besides that, the best known of them must needs either speak thickly, or lisp, or stammer," added the reporter.

"Yes, but most remarkable of all is the fact that I do not at all have the honour of knowing this artist of the metropolitan theatres. However, there's something else written on the reverse of this card. Judging by the handwriting, it was written by a man greatly drunk and little lettered.

"'I dreenk—not drink, but dreenk," explained Yarchenko. "'I dreenk to the health of the luminary of Russian science, Gavrila Petrovich Yarchenko, whom I saw by chance when I was passing by through the collidor. Would like to clink glasses together personally.

112

If you do not remember, recollect the National Theatre,
Poverty Is No Disgrace, and the humble artist who
played African.'

"Yes, that's right," said Yarchenko. "Once, somehow,
they saddled me with the arrangement of this benefit
performance in the National Theatre. Also, there dimly
glimmers some clean-shaven haughty visage, but...
What shall it be, gentlemen?"

Lichonin answered good-naturedly:

"Why, drag him here. Perhaps he's funny."

"And you?" the sub-professor turned to Platonov.

"It's all the same to me. I know him slightly. At
first he'll shout: '*Kellner*, champagne!' then burst into
tears about his wife, who is an angel, then deliver a
patriotic speech and finally raise a row over the bill,
but none too loudly. All in all he's entertaining."

"Let him come," said Volodya, from behind the
shoulder of Katie, who was sitting on his knees, swinging
her legs.

"And you, Veltman?"

"What?" the student came to with a start. He was
sitting on the divan with his back to his companions,
near the reclining Pasha, bending over her, and already
for a long time, with the friendliest appearance of sym-
pathy, had been stroking her now on the shoulder, now
on the hair at the nape of the neck, while she was smiling
at him with her shyly shameless and senselessly passionate
smile through half-closed and trembling eyelashes.
"What? What's it all about? Oh yes,—is it all right
to let the actor in? I've nothing against it. Please do..."

Yarchenko sent an invitation through Simeon, and
the actor came and immediately commenced the usual
actor's play. In the door he paused, in his long frock
coat, shining with its silk lapels, with a glistening opera
hat, which he held with his arm in the middle of his
chest, like an actor portraying in the theatre an elderly
worldly lion or a bank director. And approximately
these persons he was inwardly picturing to himself.

"May I be permitted, gentlemen, to intrude into your intimate company?" he asked in an unctuous, kindly voice, with a half-bow done somewhat to one side.

They asked him in, and he began to introduce himself. Shaking hands, he stuck out his elbow forward and raised it so high that the hand proved to be far lower. Now it was no longer a bank director, but such a clever, splendid fellow, a sportsman and a rake of the golden youths. But his face—with rumpled, wild eyebrows and with denuded lids without lashes—was the vulgar, harsh and low face of a typical alcoholic, libertine, and pettily cruel man. Together with him came two of his ladies: Henrietta—the eldest girl in years in the establishment of Anna Markovna, experienced, who had seen everything and had grown accustomed to everything, like an old horse on the tether of a threshing machine, the possessor of a thick bass, but still a handsome woman; and Big Manka, or Manka the Crocodile. Henrietta since still the preceding night had not parted from the actor, who had taken her from the house to a hotel.

Having seated himself alongside of Yarchenko, he straight off began to play a new role—he became something on the order of an old good soul of a landed proprietor, who had at one time been at a university himself, and now can not look upon the students without a quiet, fatherly emotion.

"Believe me, gentlemen, that one's soul rests from all these worldly squabbles in the midst of youth," he was saying, imparting to his depraved and harsh face an actor-like, exaggerated and improbable expression of being moved. "This faith in a high ideal, these honest impulses!.. What can be loftier and purer than our Russian students as a body?.. *Kellner!* Chompa–a-agne!" he yelled deafeningly all of a sudden and dealt a heavy blow on the table with his fist.

Lichonin and Yarchenko did not wish to remain in debt to him. A spree began. God knows in what manner Mishka the Singer and Nicky the Book-keeper soon found themselves in the cabinet, and at once began singing in their galloping voices:

"They fe-e-e-el the tru-u-u-uth,
Come thou daw-aw-aw-awning quicker..."

There also appeared Roly-Poly, who had awakened. Letting his head drop touchingly to one side and having made little narrowed, lachrymose, sweet eyes in his wrinkled old face of a Don Quixote, he was speaking in a persuasively begging tone:

"Gentlemen students... you ought to treat a little old man. I love education, by God!.. Allow me!"

Lichonin was glad to see everybody, but Yarchenko in the beginning—until the champagne had mounted to his head—only raised high his small, short eyebrows with a timorous, wondering and naive air. It suddenly became crowded, smoky, noisy and close in the cabinet. Simeon, with rattling, closed the blinds with bolts on the outside. The women, just having gotten done with a visit or in the interim between dances, walked into the room, sat on somebody's knees, smoked, sang disjointedly, drank wine, kissed and again went away, and again came. The clerks of Kereshkovsky, offended because the damsels bestowed more attention upon the cabinet than the drawing room, did start a row and tried to enter into a provoking explanation with the students, but Simeon in a moment quelled them with two or three authoritative words, thrown out as though in passing.

Niura came back from her room and a little later Petrovsky followed her. Petrovsky with an extremely serious air declared that he had been walking on the street all this time, thinking over the incident which had taken place and in the end had come to the conclusion that comrade Boris was in reality not in the right, but that there also was a circumstance in extenuation of his fault—intoxication. Also, Jennie came later, but alone—Sobashnikov had fallen asleep in her room.

The actor proved to have no end of talents. He very faithfully imitated the buzzing of a fly which an intoxicated man is catching on a window pane, and the sounds of a saw; drolly performed, standing with his face in the corner, the conversation of a nervous lady over the telephone; imitated the singing of a phonograph record, and in the end, with exceeding likeness to life, showed a little Persian lad with a little trained monkey. Holding on with his hand to an imaginary small chain and at the same time baring his teeth, squatting like a monkey, winking his eyelids often, and scratching now his posteriors, now the hair on his head, he sang through his nose, in a monotonous and sad voice, distorting the words:

> "The i–young cissack to the war has went,
> The i–young ladee underneath the fence lies
>   spraw–aw–ling.
> *Aina, aina, ai–na–na–na, ai–na na–na–na.*"

In conclusion he took Little White Manka in his arms, wrapped her up in the skirts of his frock and, stretching out his hand and making a tearful face, began to nod his head, bent to one side, as is done by little swarthy, dirty, oriental lads who roam over all Russia in long, old, soldiers' overcoats, with bared chest of a bronze colour, holding a coughing, moth-eaten little monkey in their bosom.

"And who may you be?" severely asked fat Kate, who knew and loved this joke.

"Me Serbian, lady–y–y," piteously moaned the actor through his nose. "Give me somethin', lady–y–y."

"And what do they call your little monkey?"

"Matreshka–a–a... Him 'ungry–y–y, lady... him want eat..."

"And have you got a passport?"

"We Serbia–a–an. Gimme somethin', lady–y–y..."

The actor proved not superfluous on the whole. He created at once a great deal of noise and raised the spirits of the company, which were beginning to be depressing. And every minute he cried out in a stentorian voice:

"*Kellner!* Chompa–a–agne!"—although Simeon, who was accustomed to his manner paid very little attention to these cries.

There began a truly Russian hubbub, noisy and sense-less. The rosy, flaxen-haired, pleasing Tolpygin was playing *La Seguidille* from *Carmen* on the piano, while Roly-Poly was dancing a Kamarinsky peasant dance to its tune. His narrow shoulders hunched up, twisted all to one side, the fingers of his hanging hands widely spread, he intricately hopped on one spot from one long, thin leg to the other, then suddenly letting out a piercing grunt, would throw himself upward and shout out in time to his wild dance:

> "Ugh! Dance on, Matthew,
> Don't spare your boots, you!..."

"Eh, for one stunt like that a quartern of brandy isn't enough!" he would add, shaking his long, graying hair.

"They fee–ee–eel! the tru–u–u–uth!" roared the two friends, raising with difficulty their underlids, grown heavy, beneath dull, bleary eyes.

The actor commenced to tell obscene anecdotes, pour-ing them out as from a bag, and the women squealed from delight, bent in two from laughter and threw them-selves against the backs of their chairs. Veltman, who had long been whispering with Pasha, inconspicuously, in the hubbub, slipped out of the cabinet, while a few minutes after him Pasha also went away, smiling with her quiet, insane and bashful smile.

But all of the remaining students as well, save Lichonin, one after the other, some on the quiet, some under one pretext or another, vanished from the cabinet and did not return for long periods. Volodya Pavlov experi-enced a desire to look at the dancing; Tolpygin's head began to ache badly, and he asked Tamara to lead him somewhere where he might wash up; Petrovski, having "touched" Lichonin for three rubles on the quiet, went out into the corridor and only from there despatched the housekeeper Zociya for Little White Manka. Even the prudent and fastidious Ramses could not cope with that spicy feeling which to-day's strange, vivid and unwholesome beauty of Jennie excited in him. It proved that he had some important, undeferrable business this morning; it was necessary to go home and snatch a bit of sleep if only for a couple of hours. But, having told good-bye to his companions, he, before going out of the cabinet, rapidly and with deep significance pointed the door out to Jennie with his eyes. She understood, slowly, scarcely perceptibly, lowered her eyelashes as a sign of consent, and, when she again raised them, Platonov, who almost without looking had seen this silent dialogue, was struck by that expression of malice and menace in her eyes with which she sped the back of the departing Ramses. Having waited for five minutes she got up, said "Excuse me, I'll be right back," and went out, swinging her short orange skirt.

"Well, now? Is it your turn, Lichonin?" asked the reporter banteringly.

"No, brother, you're mistaken!" said Lichonin and clacked his tongue. "And I'm not doing it out of conviction or on principle, either... No! I, as an anarchist, proclaim the gospel that the worse things are, the better... But, fortunately, I am a gambler and spend all my temperament on gaming; on that account simple squeamishness speaks louder within me than this same unearthly feeling. But it's amazing how our thoughts coincided. I just wanted to ask you about the same thing."

"I—no. Sometimes, if I become very much tired out, I sleep here over night. I take from Isaiah Savvich the key to his little room and sleep on the divan. But all the girls here are already used to the fact that I am a being of the third sex."

"And really... never?..."

"Never."

"Well, what's right is right!" exclaimed Niura. "Sergei Ivanich is like a holy hermit."

"Previously, some five years ago, I experienced this also," continued Platonov. "But, do you know, it's really too tedious and disgusting. Something on the nature of these flies which the actor gentleman just represented. They're stuck together on the window sill, and then in some sort of fool wonder scratch their backs with their little hind legs and fly apart forever. And to play at love here?.. Well, for that I'm not a hero out of their novel. I'm not handsome, am shy with women, uneasy, and polite. While here they thirst for savage passions, bloody jealousy, tears, poisonings, beatings, sacrifices,—in a word, hysterical romanticism. And it's easy to understand why. The heart of woman always wants love, while they are told of love every day with various sour, drooling words. Involuntarily one wants pepper in one's love. One no longer wants words of passion, but tragically-passionate deeds. And for that reason thieves, murderers, souteneurs and other riff-raff will always be their lovers."

"And most important of all," added Platonov, "that would at once spoil for me all the friendly relations which have been so well built up."

"Enough of joking!" incredulously retorted Lichonin. "Then what compels you to pass days and nights here? Were you a writer—it would be a different matter. It's easy to find an explanation; well, you're gathering types or something... observing life... After the manner of that German professor who lived for three years with monkeys, in order to study closely their language and manners. But you yourself said that you don't indulge in writing?"

"It isn't that I don't indulge, but I simply don't know how—I can't."

"We'll write that down. Now let's suppose another thing—that you come here as an apostle of a better, honest life, in the nature of a, now, saviour of perishing souls. You know, as in the dawn of Christianity certain holy fathers instead of standing on a column for thirty years or living in a cave in the woods, went to the market places, into houses of mirth, to the harlots and scaramuchios. But you aren't inclined that way."

"I'm not."

"Then why, the devil take it, do you hang around here? I can see very well that a great deal here is revolting and oppressive and painful to your own self. For example, this fool quarrel with Boris or this flunky who beats a woman, and—and, in general, the constant contemplation of every kind of filth, lust, bestiality, vulgarity, drunkenness. Well, now, since you say so—I believe that you don't give yourself up to lechery. But then, still more incomprehensible to me is your *modus vivendi*, to express myself in the style of leading articles."

The reporter did not answer at once:

"You see," he began speaking slowly, with pauses, as though for the first time lending ear to his thoughts and weighing them. "You see, I'm attracted and interested in this life by its... how shall I express it?... its fearful, stark truth. Do you understand, it's as though all the conventional coverings were stripped off it. There is no falsehood, no hypocrisy, no sanctimoniousness, there are no compromises of any sort, neither with public opinion, nor with the importunate authority of our forefathers, nor with one's own conscience. No illusions of any kind, nor any kind of embellishments! Here she is—'I! A public woman, a common vessel, a cloaca for the drainage of the city's surplus lust. Come to me any one who wills—thou shalt meet no denial, therein is my service. But for a second of this sensuality in haste—thou shalt pay in money, revulsion, disease and ignominy.' And that is all. There is not a single phase of human life where the basic main truth should shine with such a monstrous, hideous, stark clearness, without any shade of human prevarication or self-whitewashing."

"Oh, I don't know! These women lie like the very devil. You just go and talk with her a bit about her first fall. She'll spin you such a yarn!"

"Well, don't you ask then. What business is that of yours? But even if they do lie, they lie altogether like children. But then, you know yourself that children are the foremost, the most charming fibsters, and at the same time the sincerest people on earth. And it's remarkable, that both they and the others—that is, both prostitutes and children—lie only to us—men—and grown-ups. Among themselves they don't lie—they only inspiredly improvise. But they lie to us because we ourselves demand this of them, because we clamber into their souls, altogether foreign to us, with our stupid tactics and questionings, because they regard us in secret as great fools and senseless dissemblers. But if you like, I shall right now count off on my fingers all the occasions when a prostitute is sure to lie, and you yourself will be convinced that man incites her to lying."

"Well, well, we shall see."

"First: she paints herself mercilessly, at times even in detriment to herself. Why? Because every pimply military cadet, who is so distressed by his sexual maturity that he grows stupid in the spring, like a wood-cock on a threshing floor, or some sorry petty government clerk or other from the department of the parish, the husband of a pregnant woman and the father of nine infants—why, they both come here not at all with the prudent and simple purpose of leaving here the surplus of their passion. He, the good for nothing, has come to enjoy himself; he needs beauty, d'you see—æsthete that he is! But all these girls, these daughters of the simple, unpretentious, great Russian people—how do they regard æsthetics? 'What's sweet, that's tasty; what's red, that's handsome.' And so, there you are, receive, if you please, a beauty of antimony, white lead and rouge.

"That's one. Secondly, his desire for beauty isn't enough for this resplendent cavalier—no, he must in addition be served with a similitude of love, so that from his caresses there should kindle in the woman this same 'fa–hire of in–sane pahass–ssion!'" which is sung about in idiotical ballads. Ah! Then *that* is what you want? There y'are! And the woman lies to him with countenance, voice, sighs, moans, movements of the body. And even he himself in the depths of his soul knows about this professional deception, but—go along with you!—still deceives himself: 'Ah, what a handsome man I am! Ah, how the women love me! Ah, into what an ecstasy I bring them...' You know, there are cases when a man with the most desperate brazenness, in the most unlikely manner, is flattered to his face, and he himself sees and knows it very plainly, but—the devil take it!—despite everything a delightful feeling of some sort lubricates his soul. And so here. Query: whose is the initiative in the lie?

"And here's a third point for you, Lichonin. You prompted it yourself. They lie most of all when they are asked: 'How did you come to such a life?' But what right have you to ask her about that, may the devil take you! For she does not push her way into your intimate life? She doesn't interest herself with your first, 'holy' love or the virtue of your sisters and your bride. Aha! You pay money? Splendid! The bawd and the bouncer, and the police, and medicine, and the city government, watch over your interests. Polite and seemly conduct on the part of the prostitute hired by you for love is guaranteed you, and your personality is immune... even though in the most direct sense, in the sense of a slap in the face, which you, of course, deserve through your aimless, and perhaps tormenting interrogations. But you desire truth as well for your money? Well, that you are never to discount and to control. They will tell you just such a conventionalized history as you—yourself a man of conventionality and a vulgarian—will digest easiest of all. Because by itself life is either exceedingly humdrum and tedious to you, or else as exceedingly improbable as only life can be improbable. And so you have the eternal mediocre history about an officer, about a shop clerk, about a baby and a superannuated father, who there, in the provinces, bewails his strayed daughter and implores her to return home. But mark you, Lichonin, all that I'm saying doesn't apply to you; in you, upon my word of honour, I sense a sincere and great soul... Let's drink to your health?"

They drank.

"Shall I speak on?" continued Platonov undecidedly. "Are you bored?"

"No, no, I beg of you, speak on."

"They also lie, and lie especially innocently, to those who preen themselves before them on political hobby horses. Here they agree with anything you want. I shall tell her to-day: Away with the modern bourgeois order! Let us destroy with bombs and daggers the capitalists, landed proprietors, and the bureaucracy! She'll warmly agree with me. But to-morrow the hanger-on Nozdrunov will yell that it's necessary to string up all the socialists, to beat up all the students and massacre all the sheenies, who partake of communion in Christian blood. And she'll gleefully agree with him as well. But if in addition to that you'll also inflame her imagination, make her fall in love with yourself, then she'll go with you everywhere you may wish—on a pogrom, on a barricade, on a theft, on a murder. But then, children also are yielding. And they, by God, are children, my dear Lichonin...

"At fourteen years she was seduced, and at sixteen she became a patent prostitute, with a yellow ticket and a venereal disease. And here is all her life, surrounded and fenced off from the universe with a sort of a bizarre, impenetrable and dead wall. Turn your attention to her everyday vocabulary—thirty or forty words, no more—altogether as with a baby or a savage: to eat, to drink, to sleep, man, bed, the madam, rouble, lover, doctor, hospital, linen, policeman—and that's all. And so her mental development, her experience, her interests, remain on an infantile plane until her very death, exactly as in the case of a gray and naive lady teacher who has not crossed over the threshold of a female institute since she was ten, as in the case of a nun given as a child into a convent. In a word, picture to yourself a tree of a genuinely great species, but raised in a glass bell, in a jar from jam. And precisely to this childish phase of their existence do I attribute their compulsory lying—so innocent, purposeless and habitual... But then, how fearful, stark, unadorned with anything the frank truth in this business-like dickering about the price of a night; in these ten men in an evening; in these printed rules, issued by the city fathers, about the use of a solution of boric acid and about maintaining one's self in cleanliness; in the weekly doctors' inspections; in the nasty diseases, which are looked upon as lightly and facetiously, just as simply and without suffering, as a cold would be; in the deep revulsion of these women to men—so deep, that they all, without exception, compensate for it in the Lesbian manner and do not even in the least conceal it. All their incongruous life is here, on the palm of my hand, with all its cynicism, monstrous and coarse injustice; but there is in it none of that falsehood and that hypocrisy before people and before one's self, which enmesh all humanity from top to bottom. Consider, my dear Lichonin, how much nagging, drawn out, disgusting deception, how much hate, there is in any marital cohabitation in ninety-nine cases out of a hundred. How much blind, merciless cruelty—precisely not animal, but human, reasoned, far-sighted, calculated cruelty—there is in the sacred maternal instinct—and behold, with what tender colours this instinct is adorned! Then what about all these unnecessary, tom-fool professions, invented by cultured man for the safeguarding of my nest, my bit of meat, my woman, my child, these different overseers, controllers, inspectors, judges, attorneys, jailers, advocates, chiefs, bureaucrats, generals, soldiers, and hundreds of thousands of titles more. They all subserve human greed, cowardice, viciousness, servility, legitimised sensuality, laziness—beggarliness!— Yes, that is the real word!—human beggarliness. But what magnificent words we have! The altar of the fatherland, Christian compassion for our neighbour, progress, sacred duty, sacred property, holy love. Ugh! I do not believe in a single fine word now, and I am nauseated to infinity with these petty liars, these cowards and gluttons! Beggar women!.. Man is born for great joy, for ceaseless creation, in which he is God; for a broad, free love, unhindered by anything,—love for everything: for a tree, for the sky, for man, for a dog, for the dear, benign, beautiful earth,—oh, especially for the earth with its beatific motherhood, with its mornings and nights, with its magnificent everyday miracles. But man has lied himself out so, has become such an importunate beggar, and has sunk so low!.. Ah, Lichonin, but I am weary!"

"I, as an anarchist, partly understand you," said Lichonin thoughtfully. It was as though he heard and yet did not hear the reporter. Some thought was with difficulty, for the first time, being born in his mind. "But one thing I can not comprehend. If humanity has become so malodorous to you, then how do you stand — and for so long, too,— all this,—" Lichonin took in the whole table with a circular motion of his hand,—"the basest thing that mankind could invent?"

"Well, I don't even know myself," said Platonov with artlessness. "You see, I am a vagabond, and am passionately in love with life. I have been a turner, a compositor; I have sown and sold tobacco—the cheap Silver Makhorka kind—have sailed as a stoker on the Azov Sea, have been a fisherman on the Black—on the Dubinin fisheries; I have loaded watermelons and bricks on the Dnieper, have ridden with a circus, have been an actor—I can't even recall everything. And never did need drive me. No, only an immeasurable thirst for life and an insupportable curiosity. By God, I would like for a few days to become a horse, a plant, or a fish, or to be a woman and experience childbirth; I would like to live with the inner life, and to look upon the universe with the eyes, of every human being I meet. And so I wander care-free over towns and hamlets, bound by nothing; know and love tens of trades and joyously float wherever it suits fate to set my sail... And so it was that I came upon the brothel, and the more I look at it, the more there grows within me alarm, incomprehension, and very great anger. But even this will soon be at an end. When things get well into autumn— away again! I'll get into a rail rolling mill. I've a certain friend, he'll manage it... Wait, wait, Lichonin... Listen to the actor... That's the third act."

Egmont–Lavretzki, who until this had been very successfully imitating now a choate which is being put into a bag, now the altercation of a cat with a dog, was beginning little by little to wilt and droop. Upon him was already advancing the stage of self-revelation, next in order, in the paroxysm of which he several times attempted to kiss Yarchenko's hand. His lids had become red; around the shaven, prickly lips had deepened the tearful wrinkles that gave him an appearance of weeping; and it could be heard by his voice that his nose and throat were already overflowing with tears.

"I serve in a farce!" he was saying, smiting himself on the breast with his fist. "I disport myself in striped drawers for the sport of the sated mob! I have put out my torch, have hid my talent in the earth, like the slothful servant! But fo—ormerly!" he began to bray tragically, "Fo—ormerly-y-y! Ask in Novocherkassk, ask in Tvier, in Ustejne, in Zvenigorodok, in Krijopole.* What a Zhadov and Belugin I was! How I played Max! What a figure I created of Veltishchev—that was my crowning ro—ole... Nadin-Perekopski was beginning with me at Sumbekov's! With Nikiphorov-Pavlenko did I serve. Who made the name for Legunov-Pochainin? I! But no—ow..."

He sniveled, and sought to kiss the sub-professor.

"Yes! Despise me, brand me, ye honest folk. I play the tom-fool. I drink... I have sold and spilt the sacred ointment! I sit in a dive with vendable merchandise. While my wife... she is a saint, and pure, my little dove!.. Oh, if she knew, if she only knew! She works hard, she has a store of fashions, her fingers—the fingers of an angel—are pricked with the needle, but I! Oh, sainted woman! And I—the scoundrel!—whom do I exchange thee for! Oh, horror!" The actor seized his hair. "Professor, let me, I'll kiss your scholarly hand. You alone understand me. Let us go, I'll introduce you, you'll see what an angel this is!.. She awaits me, she does not sleep nights, she folds the tiny hands of my little ones and together with them whispers: 'Lord, save and preserve papa.'"

"You're lying about it all, actor!" said the drunken Little White Manka suddenly, looking with hatred upon Egmont-Lavretzki. "She isn't whispering anything, but most peacefully sleeping with a man in your bed."

"Be still, you w----!" vociferated the actor beside himself; and seizing a bottle by the neck raised it high over his head. "Hold me, or else I'll brain this carrion. Don't you dare besmirch with your foul tongue..."

"My tongue isn't foul—I take communion," impudently replied the woman. "But you, you fool, wear

*All provincial towns.—*Trans.*

horns. You go traipsing around with prostitutes yourself, and yet want your wife not to play you false. And.
look where the dummy's found a place to slaver, till
he looks like he had reins in his mouth. And what did
you mix the children in for, you miserable papa you!
Don't you roll your eyes and gnash your teeth at me.
You won't frighten me! W---- yourself!"

It required many efforts and much eloquence on the
part of Yarchenko in order to quiet the actor and Little
White Manka, who always after Benedictine ached for
a row. The actor in the end burst into copious and
unbecoming tears and blew his nose, like an old man;
he grew weak, and Henrietta led him away to her room.

Fatigue had already overcome everybody. The students, one after another, returned from the bedrooms;
and separately from them, with an indifferent air, came
their chance mistresses. And truly, both these and
the others resembled flies, males and females, just flown
apart on the window pane. They yawned, stretched,
and for a long time an involuntary expression of wearisomeness and aversion did not leave their faces, pale
from sleeplessness, unwholesomely glossy. And when
they, before going their ways, said good-bye to each
other, in their eyes twinkled some kind of an inimical
feeling, just as with the participants of one and the same
filthy and unnecessary crime.

"Where are you going right now?" Lichonin asked
the reporter in a low voice.

"Well, really, I don't know myself. I did want to
spend the night in the cabinet of Isaiah Savvich, but
it's a pity to lose such a splendid morning. I'm thinking
of taking a bath, and then I'll get on a steamer and ride
to the Lipsky monastery to a certain drunken black
friar I know. But why?"

"I would ask you to remain a little while and sit the
others out. I must have a very important word or two
with you."

"It's a go."

Yarchenko was the last to go. He averred a headache and fatigue. But scarcely had he gone out of the house when the reporter seized Lichonin by the hand and quickly dragged him into the glass vestibule of the entrance.

"Look!" he said, pointing to the street.

And through the orange glass of the little coloured window Lichonin saw the sub-professor, who was ringing at Treppel's. After a minute the door opened and Yarchenko disappeared through it.

"How did you find out?" asked Lichonin with astonishment.

"A mere trifle! I saw his face, and saw his hands smoothing Verka's tights. The others were less restrained. But this fellow is bashful."

"Well, now, let's go," said Lichonin. "I won't detain you long."

CHAPTER XII.

Of the girls only two remained in the cabinet—Jennie, who had come in her night blouse, and Liuba, who had long been sleeping under cover of the conversation, curled up into a ball in the large plush armchair. The fresh, freckled face of Liuba had taken on a meek, almost childlike, expression, while the lips, just as they had smiled in sleep, had preserved the light imprint of a radiant, peaceful and tender smile. It was blue and biting in the cabinet from the dense tobacco smoke; guttered, warty little streams had congealed on the candles in the candelabras; the table, flooded with coffee and wine, scattered all over with orange peels, seemed hideous.

Jennie was sitting on the divan, her knees clasped around with her arms. And again was Platonov struck by the sombre fire in her deep eyes, that seemed fallen in underneath the dark eyebrows, formidably contracted downward, toward the bridge of the nose.

"I'll put out the candles," said Lichonin.

The morning half-light, watery and drowsy, filled the room through the slits of the blinds. The extinguished wicks of the candles smoked with faint streams. The tobacco smoke swirled in blue, layered shrouds, but a ray of sunlight that had cut its way through the heart-shaped hollow in a window shutter, transpierced the cabinet obliquely with a joyous, golden sword of dust, and in liquid, hot gold splashed upon the paper on the wall.

"That's better," said Lichonin, sitting down. "The conversation will be short, but... the devil knows... how to approach it."

He looked at Jennie in abstraction.

"Shall I go away, then?" said she indifferently.

130

"No, you sit a while," the reporter answered for Lichonin. "She won't be in the way," he turned to the student and slightly smiled. "For the conversation will be about prostitution? Isn't that so?"

"Well, yes... sort of..."

"Very well, then. You listen to her carefully. Her opinions happen to be of an unusually cynical nature but at times of exceeding weight."

Lichonin vigorously rubbed and kneaded his face with his palms, then intertwined his fingers and nervously cracked them twice. It was apparent that he was agitated and was himself constrained about that which he was getting ready to say.

"Oh, but isn't it all the same!" he suddenly exclaimed angrily. "You were to-day speaking about these women ... I listened... True, you haven't told me anything new. But—strangely—I, for some reason, as though for the first time in my loose life, have looked upon this question with open eyes... I ask you, what is prostitution, in the end? What is it? The extravagant delirium of large cities, or an eternal historical phenomenon? Will it cease some time? Or will it die only with the death of all mankind? Who will answer me that?"

Platonov was looking at him intently, narrowing his eyes slightly, through habit. He wanted to know what main thought was inflicting such sincere torture on Lichonin.

"When it will cease, none will tell you. Perhaps when the magnificent utopias of the socialists and anarchists will materialize, when the world will become everyone's and no one's, when love will be absolutely free and subject only to its own unlimited desires, while mankind will fuse into one happy family, wherein will perish the distinction between mine and thine, and there will come a paradise upon earth, and man will again become naked, glorified and without sin. Perhaps it may be then..."

"But now? Now?" asks Lichonin with growing

agitation. "Shall I look on, with my little hands folded? 'It's none of my affair?' Tolerate it as an unavoidable evil? Put up with it, and wash my hands of it? Shall I pronounce a benediction upon it?"

"This evil is not unavoidable, but insuperable. But isn't it all the same to you?" asked Platonov with cold wonder. "For you're an anarchist, aren't you?"

"What the devil kind of an anarchist am I! Well, yes, I am an anarchist, because my reason, when I think of life, always leads me logically to the anarchistic beginning. And I myself think in theory: let men beat, deceive, and fleece men, like flocks of sheep—let them!—violence will breed rancour sooner or later. Let them violate the child, let them trample creative thought underfoot, let there be slavery, let there be prostitution, let them thieve, mock, spill blood... Let them! The worse, the better, the nearer the end. There is a great law, I think, the same for inanimate objects as well as for all the tremendous and many-millioned human life: the power of effort is equal to the power of resistance. The worse, the better. Let evil and vindictiveness accumulate in mankind, let them grow and ripen like a monstrous abscess—an abscess the size of the whole terrestrial sphere. For it will burst some time! And let there be terror and insufferable pain. Let the pus deluge all the universe. But mankind will either choke in it and perish, or, having gone through the illness, will be regenerated to a new, beautiful life."

Lichonin avidly drank off a cup of cold black coffee and continued vehemently:

"Yes. Just so do I and many others theorize, sitting in our rooms, over tea with white bread and cooked sausage, when the value of each separate human life is so-so, an infinitesimally small numeral in a mathematical formula. But let me see a child abused, and the red blood will rush to my head from rage. And when I look and look upon the labour of a moujik or a labourer, I am thrown into hysterics for shame at my algebraic calculations. There is—the devil take it!—there is something incongruous, altogether illogical, but which at this time is stronger than human reason. Take to-day, now... Why do I feel at this minute as though I had robbed a sleeping man or deceived a three-year-old child, or hit a bound person? And why does it seem to me to-day that I myself am guilty of the evil of prostitution—guilty in my silence, my indifference, my indirect permission? What am I to do, Platonov!" exclaimed the student with grief in his voice.

Platonov kept silent, squinting at him with his little narrow eyes. But Jennie unexpectedly said in a caustic tone:

"Well, you do as one Englishwoman did... A certain red-haired clodhopper came to us here. She must have been important, because she came with a whole retinue... all some sort of officials... But before her had come the assistant of the commissioner, with the precinct inspector Kerbesh. And the assistant directly forewarned us, just like that: 'If you carcasses and so on and so on, will let out even one little rude word, or something, then I won't leave one stone upon another of your establishment, while I'll flog all the wenches soundly in the station-house and make 'em rot in jail!' Well, at last this galoot came. She gibbered and she gibbered something in a foreign language, all the time pointed to heaven with her hand, and then distributed a five-kopeck Testament to every one of us and rode away. Now you ought to do the same, dearie."

Platonov burst into loud laughter. But seeing the naive and sad face of Lichonin, who did not seem to understand, nor even suspect mockery, he restrained his laughter and said seriously:

"You won't accomplish anything, Lichonin. While there will be property, there will also be poverty. While marriage exists, prostitution also will not die. Do you know who will always sustain and nourish prostitution? It is the so-called decent people, the noble paterfamiliases, the irreproachable husbands, the loving brothers. They will always find a seemly motive to legitimize, normalize and put a wrapper all around paid libertinage, because they know very well that otherwise it would rush in a torrent into their bedrooms and nurseries. Prostitution is for them a deflection of the sensuousness of others from their personal, lawful alcove. And even the respectable paterfamilias himself is not averse to indulge in a love debauch in secret. And really, it is palling to have always the one and the same thing— the wife, the chambermaid, and the lady on the side. Man, as a matter of fact, is a poly—and exceedingly so— a polygamous animal. And to his rooster-like amatory instincts it will always be sweet to unfold in such a magnificent nursery garden, *à la* Treppel's or Anna Markovna's. Oh, of course, a well-balanced spouse or the happy father of six grown-up daughters will always be clamouring about the horror of prostitution. He will even arrange with the help of a lottery and an amateur entertainment a society for the saving of fallen women, or an asylum in the name of St. Magdalene. But the existence of prostitution he will bless and sustain."

"Magdalene asylums!" with quiet laughter, full of an ancient hatred the ache of which had not yet healed, repeated Jennie.

"Yes, I know that all these false measures undertaken are stuff and a total mockery," cut in Lichonin. "But let me be ridiculous and stupid, yet I do not wish to remain a commiserating spectator, who sits on a warm ledge, gazes upon a conflagration, and is saying all the time: 'Oh, my, but it's burning... by God, it is burning! Perhaps there are even people burning!'—but for his part merely laments and slaps his thighs."

"Well, now," said Platonov harshly, "would you take a child's syringe and go to put out the fire with it?"

"No!" heatedly exclaimed Lichonin... "Perhaps— who knows?—perhaps I'll succeed in saving at least one living soul? It was just this that I wanted to ask you about, Platonov, and you must help me... Only, I implore you, without jeers, without cooling off..."

"You want to take a girl out of here? To save her?" asked Platonov, looking at him attentively. He now understood the drift of this entire conversation.

"Yes... I don't know... I'll try..." answered Lichonin uncertainly.

"She'll come back," said Platonov.

"She will," Jennie repeated with conviction.

Lichonin walked up to her, took her by the hands and began to speak in a trembling whisper:

"Jennechka... Perhaps you... eh? For I don't call you as a mistress... but a friend... It's all a trifle, half a year of rest... and then we'll master some trade or other... we'll read..."

Jennie snatched her hands out of his with vexation.

"Oh, into a bog with you!" she almost shouted. "I know you! Want me to darn socks for you? Cook on a kerosene stove? Pass nights without sleeping on account of you when you'll be chitter-chattering with your short-haired friends? But when you get to be a doctor or a lawyer, or a government clerk, then it's me will get a knee in the back: 'Out on the street with you, now, you public hide, you've ruined my young life. I want to marry a decent girl, pure, and innocent!...'"

"I meant it as a brother... I meant it without that..." mumbled Lichonin in confusion.

"I know that kind of brothers. Until the first night... Leave off and don't talk nonsense to me! It makes me tired to listen to it!"

"Wait, Lichonin!" began the reporter seriously. "Why, you will pile a load beyond your strength upon yourself as well. I've known idealists, among the populists, who married peasant girls out of principle. This is just the way they thought—nature, black-loam, untapped forces... But this black-loam after a year turned into the fattest of women, who lies the whole day in bed and chews cookies, or studs her fingers with penny rings, spreads them out and admires them. Or else sits in the kitchen, drinks sweet liquor with the coachman and carries on a natural romance with him. Look out, here it will be worse!"

All three became silent. Lichonin was pale and was wiping his moist forehead with a handkerchief.

"No, the devil take it!" he cried out suddenly with obstinacy. "I don't believe you! I don't want to believe! Liuba!" he called loudly the girl who had fallen asleep. "Liubochka!"

The girl awoke, passed her palm over her lips, first to one side, then the other, yawned, and smiled, in a funny, child-like manner.

"I wasn't sleeping, I heard everything," she said. "I only dozed off for a teeny-weeny bit."

"Liuba, do you want to go away from here with me?" asked Lichonin and took her by the hand. "But entirely, forever, to go away so's never to return either to a brothel or the street?"

Liuba questioningly, with perplexity, looked at Jennie, as though seeking from her an explanation of this jest.

"That's enough for you," she said slyly. "You're still studying yourself. Where do you come in, then, to take a girl and set her up?"

"Not to set you up, Liuba... I simply want to help you... For it isn't very sweet for you in a brothel, is it now!"

"Naturally, it isn't all sugar! If I was as proud as Jennechka, or so enticing like Pasha... but I won't get used to things here for anything...."

"Well, then, let's go, let's go!..." entreated Lichonin. "Surely, you know some manual work—well, now, sewing something, embroidering, cutting?"

"I don't know anything!" answered Liuba bashfully and started laughing and turned red, covering her mouth with the elbow of her free arm. "What's asked of us in the village, that I know, but anything more I don't know. I can cook a little... I lived at the priest's—cooked for him."

"That's splendid! That's excellent!" Lichonin grew joyous. "I will assist you, you'll open a dining room... A cheap dining room, you understand... I'll advertise it for you... The students will come! That's magnificent!..."

"That's enough of making fun of me!" retorted Liuba, a bit offended, and again looked askance and questioningly at Jennie.

"He's not joking," answered Jennie with a voice which quavered strangely. "He's in earnest, seriously."

"Here's my word of honour that I'm serious! Honest to God, now," the student caught her up with warmth and for some reason even made the sign of the cross in the direction of the empty corner.

"And really," said Jennie, "take Liubka. That's not the same thing as taking me. I'm like an old, dragoon's nag, and used to it. You can't make me over, neither with hay nor a stick. But Liubka is a simple girl and a kind one. And she hasn't grown used to our life yet. What are you popping your eyes out at me for, you ninny? Answer when you're asked. Well? Do you want to or don't you want to?"

"And why not? If they ain't laughing, but for real... And you, Jennechka, what would you advise me..."

"Oh, you're such wood!" Jennie grew angry. "What's better according to you—to rot on straw with a nose fallen through? To croak under the fence like a dog? Or to turn honest? Fool! You ought to kiss his hands; but no, you're getting particular."

The naive Liuba did, in fact, extend her lips toward Lichonin's hand, and this movement made everybody laugh, and touched them just the least trifle.

"And that's very good! It's like magic!" bustled the overjoyed Lichonin. "Go and notify the proprietress at once that you're going away from here forever.

And take the most necessary things; it isn't as it used to be; now a girl can go away from a brothel whenever she wants to."

"No, it can't be done that way," Jennie stopped him; "she can go away, that's so, but you'll have no end of unpleasantnesses and hullabaloo. Here's what you do, student. You won't regret ten roubles?"

"Of course, of course... if you please."

"Let Liuba tell the housekeeper that you're taking her to your rooms for to-day. That's the fixed rate— ten roubles. And afterwards, well, even to-morrow— come after her ticket and things. That's nothing; we'll work this thing roundly. And after that you must go to the police with her ticket and declare, that Liubka so-and-so has hired herself to you as chambermaid, and that you desire to exchange her blank for a real passport. Well, Liubka, lively! Take the money and march. And, look out, be as quick as possible with the housekeeper, or else she, the bitch, will read it in your eyes. And also don't forget," she cried, now after Liuba, "wipe the rouge off your puss, now. Or else the drivers will be pointing their fingers at you."

After half an hour Liuba and Lichonin were getting on a cab at the entrance. Jennie and the reporter were standing on the sidewalk.

"You're committing a great folly, Lichonin," Platonov was saying listlessly, "but I honour and respect the fine impulse within you. Here's the thought—and here's the deed. You're a brave and a splendid fellow."

"Here's to your commencement!" laughed Jennie. "Look out, don't forget to send for me to the christening."

"You won't see it, no matter how long you wait for it!" laughed Lichonin, waving his cap about.

They rode off. The reporter looked at Jennie, and with astonishment saw tears in her softened eyes.

"God grant it, God grant it," she was whispering.

"What has been the matter with you to-day, Jennie?"

he asked kindly. "What? Are you oppressed? Can't I do anything?"

She turned her back to him and leaned over the bent balustrade of the stoop.

"How shall I write to you, if need be?" she asked in a stifled voice.

"Why, it's simple. Editorial rooms of *Echoes*. So-and-so. They'll pass it on to me pretty fast.

"I... I... I..." Jennie just began, but suddenly burst into loud, passionate sobs and covered her face with her hands, "I'll write you..."

And without taking her hands away from her face, her shoulders quivering, she ran up the stoop and disappeared in the house, loudly banging the door after her.

PART TWO

CHAPTER I.

Even to this day, after a lapse of ten years, the erstwhile inhabitants of the Yamkas recall that year, abounding in unhappy, foul, bloody events, which began with a series of trifling, small affrays, but terminated in the administration's, one fine day, taking and destroying completely the ancient, long-warmed nest of legalized prostitution, which nest it had itself created—scattering its remains over the hospitals, jails and streets of the big city. Even to this day a few of the former proprietresses who have remained alive and have reached the limit of decrepitude, and quondam housekeepers, fat and hoarse, like pug-dogs grown old, recall this common destruction with sorrow, horror, and stolid perplexity.

Just like potatoes out of a sack, brawls, robberies, diseases, murders and suicides began to pour down, and, it seemed, no one was to blame for this. All these misfortunes just simply began to be more frequent of their own accord, to pile one upon the other, to expand and grow; just as a small lump of snow, pushed by the feet of urchins, becomes constantly bigger and bigger by itself from the thawing snow sticking to it, grows bigger than the stature of a man, and, finally, with one last, small effort is precipitated into a ravine and rolls down as an enormous avalanche. The old proprietresses and housekeepers, of course, had never heard of fatality; but inwardly, with the soul, they sensed its mysterious presence in the inevitable calamities of that terrible year.

And, truly, everywhere in life where people are bound by common interests, blood relationship, or the benefits of a profession into close, individualized groups—there

143

inevitably can be observed this mysterious law of sudden accumulation, of a piling up, of events; their epidemicity, their strange succession and connectedness, their incomprehensible lingering. This occurs, as popular wisdom has long ago noted, in isolated families, where disease or death suddenly falls upon the near ones in an inevitable, enigmatic order. "Misfortune does not come alone." "Misfortune without waits—open wide the gates " This is to be noticed also in monasteries, banks, governmental departments, regiments, places of learning and other public institutions, where for a long time, almost for decades, life flows evenly, like a marshy river; and, suddenly, and after some altogether insignificant incident or other, there begin transfers, changes in positions, expulsions from service, losses, sicknesses. The members of society, just as though they had conspired, die, go insane, are caught thieving, shoot or hang themselves; vacancy after vacancy is freed; promotions follow promotions, new elements flow in, and, behold, after two years there is not a one of the previous people on the spot; everything is new, if only the institution has not fallen into pieces completely, has not crept apart. And is it not the same astounding destiny which overtakes enormous social, universal organizations—cities, empires, nations, countries, and, who knows, perhaps whole planetary worlds?

Something resembling this incomprehensible fatality swept over the Yamaskya Borough as well, bringing it to a rapid and scandalous destruction. Now in place of the boisterous Yamkas is left a peaceful, humdrum outskirt, in which live truck-farmers, cat's-meat men, Tartars, swineherds and butchers from the near-by slaughterhouses. At the petition of these worthy people even the designation of Yamaskya Borough itself, as disgracing the inhabitants with its past, has been named over into Golubovka, in honour of the merchant Golubov, owner of a shop dealing in groceries and delicacies, and warden of the local church.

The first subterranean shocks of this catastrophe began in the heat of summer, at the time of the annual summer fair, which this year was unbelievably brilliant. Many circumstances contributed to its extraordinary success, multitudes, and the stupendousness of the deals concluded during it: the building in the vicinity of three new sugar refineries, and the unusually abundant crop of wheat, and, in particular, of sugar beets; the commencement of work in the laying of an electric trolley and of canalization; the building of a new road to the distance of 750 versts; but mainly, the fever of building which seized the whole town, all the banks and financial institutions, and all the houseowners. Factories for making bricks sprang up on the outskirts of the town like mushrooms. A grandiose agricultural exposition opened. Two new steamer lines came into being, and they, together with the previously established ones, frenziedly competed with each other, transporting freight and pilgrims. In competition they reached such a state, that they lowered their passenger rates for the third class from seventy-five kopecks to five, three, two, and even one kopeck. In the end, ready to fall from exhaustion in the unequal struggle, one of the steamship companies offered a free passage to all the third-class passengers. Then its competitor at once added to the free passage half a loaf of white bread as well. But the biggest and most significant enterprise of this city was the engineering of the extensive river port, which had attracted to it hundreds of thousands of labourers and which cost God knows what money.

It must also be added, that the city was at this time celebrating the millennial anniversary of its famous abbey, the most honoured and the richest among all the monasteries of Russia. From all the ends of Russia, out of Siberia, from the shores of the Frozen Ocean, from the extreme south—the Black and Caspian Seas—countless pilgrims had gathered for the worship of the local sanctities: the abbey's saints, reposing deep underground in calcareous caverns. Suffice it to say, that the monastery gave shelter, and food of a sort, to forty thousand people daily; while those for whom there was not enough room lay, at night, side by side, like logs, in the extensive yards and lanes of the abbey.

This was a summer out of some fairy-tale. The population of the city increased well-nigh fourfold through every sort of newly-come people. Stone-masons, carpenters, painters, engineers, technicians, foreigners, agriculturists, brokers, shady business men, river navigators, unoccupied knaves, tourists, thieves, card sharpers—they all overflowed the city, and not in a single hotel, the most dirty and dubious one, was there a vacant room. Insane prices were paid for quarters. The stock exchange gambled on a grand scale, as never before or since that summer. Money in millions simply flowed from hands to hands, and thence to a third pair. In one hour colossal riches were created, but then many former firms burst, and yesterday's men of wealth turned into beggars. The commonest of labourers bathed and warmed themselves in this golden flood. Stevedores, draymen, street porters, roustabouts, hod carriers and ditch diggers still remember to this day what money they earned by the day during this mad summer. Any tramp received no less than four or five roubles a day at the unloading of barges laden with watermelons. And all this noisy, foreign band, locoed by the easy money, intoxicated with the sensual beauty of the ancient, seductive city, enchanted by the delightful warmth of the southern nights, made drunk by the insidious fragrance of the white acacias—these hundreds of thousands of insatiable, dissolute beasts in the image of men, with all their massed will clamoured: "Give us woman!"

In a single month new amusement enterprises—chic Tivolis, *Chateaux des Fleurs*, Olympias, Alcazars, etc., with a chorus and an operetta; many restaurants and beerhouses, with little summer gardens, and common little taverns—sprang up by the score in the city, in the vicinity of the building port. On every crossing new "violet-wine" houses were opened every day—little booths of boards, in each of which, under the pretext of selling bread-cider, old wenches trafficked in themselves by twos and threes, right alongside behind a partition of deal, and to many mothers and fathers is this summer painful and memorable through the degrading diseases of their sons—schoolboys and military cadets. For the casual arrivals servants were demanded, and thousands of peasant girls started out from the surrounding villages toward the city. It was inevitable that the demand on prostitution should become unusually high. And so, from Warsaw, from Lodz, from Odessa, from Moscow, and even from St. Petersburg, even from abroad, flocked together an innumerable multitude of foreign women; *cocottes* of Russian fabrication, the most ordinary prostitutes of the rank and file, and chic Frenchwomen and Viennese. Imperiously told the corrupting influence of the hundreds of millions of easy money. It was as though this cascade of gold had lashed down upon, had set to whirling and deluged within it, the whole city. The number of thefts and murders increased with astounding rapidity. The police, collected in augmented proportions, lost its head and was swept off its feet. But it must also be said that, having gorged itself with plentiful bribes, it resembled a sated python, willy-nilly drowsy and listless. People were killed for anything and nothing, just so. It happened that men would walk up to a person in broad daylight somewhere on an unfrequented street and ask: "What's your name?" "Fedorov." "Aha, Fedorov? Then take this!" and they would slit his belly with a knife. They nicknamed these blades just that in the city—"rippers"; and there were among them names of which the city news seemed actually proud: the two brothers Polishchuk (Mitka and Dundas), Volodka the Greek, Fedor Miller, Captain Dmitriev, Sivocho, Dobrovolski, Shpachek, and many others.

Both day and night on the main streets of the frenzied city stood, moved, and yelled the mob, as though at a fire. It would be almost impossible to describe what went on in the Yamkas then. Despite the fact that the madams had increased the staff of their patients to more than double and increased their prices trebly, their poor demented girls could not catch up in satisfying the demands of the drunken, crazed public, which threw money around like chips. It happened that in the drawing room, filled to overflowing with people, each girl would be awaited for by some seven, eight, at times even ten, men. It was, truly, some kind of a mad, intoxicated, convulsive time!

And from that very time began all the misfortunes of the Yamkas, which brought them to ruin. And together with the Yamkas perished also the house, familiar to us, of the stout, old, pale-eyed Anna Markovna.

CHAPTER II.

The passenger train sped merrily from the south to the north, traversing golden fields of wheat and beautiful groves of oak, careering with rumbling upon iron bridges over bright rivers, leaving behind it whirling clouds of smoke.

In the *coupé* of the second class, even with open windows, there was fearful stuffiness, and it was hot. The smell of sulphurous smoke irritated the throat. The rocking and the heat had completely tired out the passengers, save one, a merry, energetic, mobile Hebrew, splendidly dressed, accommodating, sociable and talkative. He was travelling with a young woman, and it was at once apparent, especially through her, that they were newly-weds; so often did her face flare up with an unexpected colour at every tenderness of her husband, even the least. And when she raised her eyelashes, to look upon him, her eyes would shine like stars and grow humid. And her face was as beautiful as only the faces of young Hebrew maidens in love can be beautiful—all tenderly rosy, with rosy lips, rounded out in beautiful innocence, and with eyes so black that their pupils could not be distinguished from the irises.

Unabashed by the presence of three strange people, he showered his caresses upon his companion every minute, and, it must be said, sufficiently coarse ones. With the unceremoniousness of an owner, with that especial egoism of one in love, who, it would seem, is saying to the whole universe: "See, how happy we are—this makes you happy also, isn't that so?"—he would now pass his hand over her leg, which resiliently and in relief stood out beneath her dress, now pinch her on the cheek, now tickle her neck with his stiff, black, turned-

up moustache... But, even though he did sparkle with
delight, there was still something rapacious, wary, uneasy
to be glimpsed in his frequently winking eyes, in the
twitching of the upper lips, and in the harsh outline of
his shaved, square chin, jutting out, with a scarcely
noticeable dent in the middle.

Opposite this infatuated couple were placed three
passengers—a retired general, a spare, neat little old
man, with pomade on his hair, with curls combed forward
to the temples; a stout land-owner, who had taken off
his starched collar, but was still gasping from the heat
and mopping his face every minute with a wet handkerchief; and a young infantry officer. The endless talk-
ativeness of Simon Yakovlevich (the young man had
already managed to inform his neighbours that he was
called Simon Yakovlevich Horizon) tired and irritated
the passengers a trifle, just like the buzzing of a fly,
that on a sultry summer day rhythmically beats against
a window pane of a closed, stuffy room. But still, he
knew how to raise their spirits: he showed tricks of
magic; told Hebrew anecdotes, full of a fine humour of
their own. When his wife would go out on the platform
to refresh herself, he would tell such things that the
general would melt into a beatific smile, the land-owner
would neigh, rocking his black-loam stomach, while the
sub-lieutenant, a smooth-faced boy, only a year out of
school, scarcely controlling his laughter and curiosity,
would turn away to one side, that his neighbours might
not see him turning red.

His wife tended Horizon with a touching, naive attention; she wiped his face with a handkerchief, waved
upon him with a fan, adjusted his cravat every minute.
And his face at these times became laughably supercilious and stupidly self-conceited.

"But allow me to ask," asked the spare little general,
coughing politely, "allow me to ask, my dear sir, what
occupation might you pursue?"

"Ah, my God!" with a charming frankness retorted Simon Yakovlevich. "Well, what can a poor Jew do in our time? It's a bit of a travelling salesman and a commission broker by me. At the present time I'm far from business. You—he! he! he!—understand yourselves, gentlemen. A honeymoon—don't turn red, Sarochka—it don't repeat itself three times in a year. But afterwards I'll have to travel and work a great deal. Here we'll come with Sarochka to town, will pay the visits to her relatives, and then again on the road. On my first trip I'm thinking of taking my wife. You know, sort of a wedding journey. I'm a representative from Sidris and two English firms. Wouldn't you like to have a look? Here are the samples with me..."

He very rapidly took out of a small, elegant case of yellow leather a few long cardboard folding books, and with the dexterity of a tailor began to unfold them, holding one end, from which their folds fell downward with a light crackling.

"Look, what splendid samples: they don't give in to foreign ones at all. Please notice. Here, for instance, is Russian and here English tricot, or here, cangan and cheviot. Compare, feel it, and you'll be convinced that the Russian samples almost don't give in to the foreign. Why, that speaks of progress, of the growth of culture. So it's absolutely for nothing that Europe counts us Russians such barbarians.

"And so we'll pay our family visits, will look at the fair, pay a visit to the *Chateau des Fleurs*, enjoy ourselves a little, stroll a bit, and then to the Volga down to Tzaritzin, to the Black Sea, and then again home to our native Odessa."

"That's a fine journey," said the sub-lieutenant modestly.

"I should say it's fine," agreed Simon Yakovlevich; "but there are no roses without thorns. The work of a travelling salesman is exceedingly difficult and requires many kinds of knowledge, and not so much the knowledge of business as the knowledge of—how shall I say it?—the knowledge of the human soul. Another man may not even want to give an order, but you must work like an elephant to convince him, and argue until he feels the clearness and justice of your words. Because I take only absolutely clean lines exclusively, of which there can be no doubts. A fake or a bad line I will not take, although they should offer me millions for it. Ask wherever you like, in any store which deals in cloths or suspenders *Gloire*—I'm also a representative from this firm—or buttons *Helios*—you just ask who Simon Yakovlevich Horizon is, and everyone will answer you: 'Simon Yakovlevich is not a man, but gold; this is a disinterested man, as honest as a diamond.'" And Horizon was already unpacking long boxes with patented suspenders, and was showing the glistening leaves of cardboard, covered with regular rows of vari-coloured buttons.

"There happen great unpleasantnesses, when the place has been worked out, when a lot of travelling salesmen have appeared before you. Here you can't do anything; they absolutely won't listen to you, only wave their arms. But that's only for others. I am Horizon! I can talk him over, the same like a camel from a menagerie. But it happens still more unpleasant, when two competitors in one and the same line come together in the same town. And it happens even worse when it's some chimney sweep and can't do business himself and spoils business for you too. Here you go to all sorts of tricks: let him drink till he's drunk or let him go off somewhere on a false track. Not an easy trade! Besides that, I have one more line—that's false eyes and teeth. But it ain't a profitable line. I want to drop it. And besides I'm thinking of leaving all this business. I understand, it's all right for a young man, in the bloom of his powers, to flutter around like a moth, but once you have a wife, and may be a whole family even...." he playfully patted the woman on the knee, from which she became scarlet and looked uncommonly better. "For the Lord has

blessed us Jews with fecundity for all our misfortunes...
Then you want to have some business of your own, you
want, you understand, to become settled in one place,
so's there should be a shack of your own, and your own
furniture, and your own bedroom, and kitchen...
Isn't that so, your excellency?"

"Yes... Yes... eh—eh... Yes, of course, of course,"
condescendingly responded the general.

"And so I took with Sarochka a little dowry. What do
I mean, a little dowry? Such money that Rothschild
would not even want to look at it are in my hands a
whole capital already. But it must be said that there
are some savings by me, too. The firms I know will
give me credit. If God grant it, we shall still eat a piece
of bread and a little butter—and on the Sabbaths the
tasty *gefilteh fisch*."

"That's fine fish: pike the way the sheenies make it!"
said the gasping land-owner.

"We shall open up for ourselves the firm of 'Horizon
and Son.' Isn't that true, Sarochka—'and Son?' And
you, I hope, will honour me with your esteemed orders?
When you see the sign, 'Horizon and Son,' then straight
off recollect that you once rode in a car together with a
young man, who had grown as foolish as hell from love
and from happiness."

"Ab–solutely!" said the land-owner.

And Simon Yakovlevich at once turned to him:

"But I also work by commission broking. To sell an
estate, to buy an estate, to arrange a second mortgage—
you won't find a better specialist than me, and such a
cheap one at that. I can be of service to you, should
the need arise," and he extended his visiting card to the
land-owner with a bow, and, by the way, handed a card
each to his two neighbours as well.

The land-owner dived into a side pocket and also
dragged out a card.

"Joseph Ivanovich Vengjenovski," Simon Yakov-levich read out loud. "Very, very pleased! And so, should you need me..."

"Why not? It's possible..." said the land-owner meditatively. "Why, yes: perhaps, indeed, a favour-able chance has brought us together! Why, I'm just journeying to K—— about the sale of a certain forest country house. Suppose you do that, then,—drop in to see me. I always stop at the Grand Hotel. Perhaps we may be able to strike up a deal."

"Oh, I'm already almost sure, my dearest Joseph Ivanovich!" exclaimed the rejoicing Horizon, and slightly, with the very tips of his fingers, patted Veng-jenovski's kneecap carefully. "You just rest assured; if Horizon has undertaken anything, then you'll be thanking him like your own father, no more, no less."

Half an hour later Simon Yakovlevich and the smooth-faced sub-lieutenant were standing on the platform of the car and smoking.

"Do you often visit K——, mister sub-lieutenant?" asked Horizon.

"Only for the first time—just imagine! Our regiment is stationed at Chernobob. I was born in Moscow, myself."

"*Ai, ai, ai!* How'd you come to get into such a far-away place?"

"Well, it just fell out so. There was no other vacancy when I was let out."

"But then—Chernobob is a hole! The worst little town in all Podolia."

"That's true, but it just fell out so."

"That means, then, that the young officer gent is going to K—— to divert himself a little?"

"Yes. I'm thinking of stopping there for two or three days. I'm travelling to Moscow, really. I have received a two months' leave, but it would be interesting to look over the city on the way. It's very beautiful, they say."

"Oh, what are you trying to tell me? A remarkable city! Well, absolutely a European city. If you only knew, what streets, electricity, trolleys, theatres! And if you only knew what cabarets! You'll lick your own fingers. Positively, positively, I advise you, young man, to pay a visit to the *Chateau des Fleurs*, to the Tivoli, and also to ride out to the island. That's something special. What women, wha–a–at women!"

The lieutenant turned red, took his eyes away, and asked in a voice that quavered:

"Yes, I've happened to hear that. Is it possible that they're really so handsome?"

"*Oi!* Strike me God! Believe me, there are no handsome women there at all."

"But—how's that?"

"Why, this way: there are only raving beauties there. You understand—what a happy blending of bloods! Polish, Little Russian, and Hebrew. How I envy you, young man, that you're free and alone. In my time I sure would have shown myself! And what's most remarkable of all, they're unusually passionate women! Well, just like fire! And do you know something else?" he asked in a whisper of great significance.

"What?" asked the sub-lieutenant in a fright.

"It's remarkable, that nowheres, neither in Paris, nor in London—believe me, this was told me by people who had seen the whole wide world—never, nowhere, will you meet with such exquisite ways of making love as in this town. That's something especial, as us little Jews say. They think up such things that no imagination can picture to itself. It's enough to drive you crazy!"

"But is that possible?" quietly spoke the sub-lieutenant, whose breath had been cut off.

"Well, strike me God! But permit me, young man, by the way! You understand yourself. I was single, and, of course, every man is liable to sin... It's different now, of course. I've had myself written in with the invalids. But from the former days a remarkable collection has remained to me. Just wait, I'll show it to you right away. Only, please, be as careful as possible in looking at it."

Horizon with trepidation looked around to the right and left and extracted from his pocket a long, narrow little box of morocco, in the style of those in which playing cards are usually kept, and extended it to the sub-lieutenant.

"Here you are, have a look. Only, I beg of you, be very careful."

The sub-lieutenant applied himself to picking out, one after the other, the cards of plain and coloured photography, in which in all possible aspects was depicted in the most beastly ways, in the most impossible positions, that external side of love which at times makes man immeasurably lower and viler than a baboon. Horizon would look over his shoulder, nudge him with his elbow, and whisper:

"Tell me, ain't that swell, now? Why, this is genuine Parisian and Viennese chic!"

The sub-lieutenant looked through the whole collection from the beginning to the end. When he was giving back the little box, his hand was shaking, the temples and forehead were moist, the eyes had dimmed, and over the cheeks had mantled a blush, mottled like marble.

"But do you know what?" Horizon exclaimed gaily, all of a sudden. "It's all the same to me—the Indian sign has been put upon me. I, as they used to say in the olden times, have burned my ships... I have burned all that I used to adore before. For a long time already I've been looking for an opportunity to pass these cards on to some one. I ain't especially chasing after a price. You wish to acquire them, mister officer?"

"Well, now... I,— that is...Why not?...Let's..."

"That's fine! On account of such a pleasant acquaintanceship, I'll take fifty kopecks apiece. What, is that expensive? Well, what's the difference, God be with you! I see you're a travelling man, I don't want to rob

you; let it go at thirty, then. What? That ain't cheap
either? Well, shake hands on it! Twenty-five kopecks
apiece. *Oi!* What an intractable fellow you are! At
twenty! You'll thank me yourself later! And then, do
you know what else? When I come to K——, I always
stop at the Hotel Hermitage. You can very easily find
me there either very early in the morning, or about
eight o'clock in the evening. I know an awful lot of the
finest little ladies. So I'll introduce you. And, you
understand, not for money. Oh, no. It's just simply
nice and gay for them to pass the time with a young,
healthy, handsome man of your sort. There's absolutely
no money of any kind necessary. And for that matter—
they themselves will willingly pay for wine, for a bottle
of champagne! So remember then; The Hermitage,
Horizon. And if it isn't that, then remember it anyway!
Maybe I can be of use to you. And the cards are
such a thing, such a thing, that it will never lay on the
shelf by you. Those who like that sort of thing give
three roubles for each specimen. But these, of course,
are rich people, little old men. And then, you know"—
Horizon bent over to the officer's very ear, winked one
eye, and pronounced in a sly whisper—"you know, many
ladies adore these cards. Why, you're a young man,
and handsome; how many romances you will have yet!"

Having received the money and counted it over painstakingly, Horizon had the brazenness to extend his hand
in addition, and to shake the hand of the sub-lieutenant,
who did not dare to lift up his eyes to him; and, having
left him on the platform, went back into the passageway
of the car, as though nothing had happened.

This was an unusually communicative man. On the
way to his *coupé* he came to a stop before a beautiful
little girl of three years, with whom he had for some time
been flirting at a distance and making all sorts of funny
grimaces at. He squatted down on his heels before her,
began to imitate a nanny goat for her, and questioned her
in a lisping voice:

"May I athk where the young lady ith going? *Oi, oi, oi!* Thuch a big girl! Travelling alone, without mamma? Bought a ticket all by herthelf and travelth alone! *Ai!* What a howwid girl! And where ith the girl'th mamma?"

At this moment a tall, handsome, self-assured woman appeared from the *coupé* and said calmly:

"Get away from the child. What a despicable thing to annoy strange children!"

Horizon jumped up on his feet and began to bustle:

"Madam! I could not restrain myself... Such a wonderful, such a magnificent and swell child! A regular cupid! You must understand, madam, I am a father myself—I have children of my own... I could not restrain myself from delight...!"

But the lady turned her back upon him, took the girl by the hand and went with her into the *coupé*, leaving Horizon shuffling his feet and muttering his compliments and apologies.

*   *   *

Several times during the twenty-four hours Horizon would go into the third class, of two cars, separated from each other by almost the entire train. In one car were sitting three handsome women, in the society of a black-bearded, taciturn, morose man. Horizon and he would exchange strange phrases in some special jargon. The women looked at him uneasily, as though wishing, yet not daring, to ask him about something. Only once, toward noon, did one of them allow herself to utter:

Then that's the truth? That which you said about the place?.. You understand — I'm somewhat uneasy at heart!"

"Ah, what do you mean, Margarita Ivanovna? If I said it, then it's right, just like by the National Bank. Listen, Lazer," he turned to him of the beard. "There will be a station right away. Buy the girls all sorts of sandwiches, whichever they may desire. The train stops here for twenty-five minutes."

"I'd like to have bouillon," hesitatingly uttered a little blonde, with hair like ripened rye, and with eyes like corn-flowers.

"My dear Bella, anything you please! At the station I'll go and see that they bring you bouillon with meat and even stuffed dumplings. Don't you trouble yourself, Lazer, I'll do all that myself."

In another car he had a whole nursery garden of women, twelve or fifteen people, under the leadership of an old, stout woman, with enormous, awesome, black eyebrows. She spoke in a bass, while her fat chins, breasts and stomachs swayed under a broad morning dress in time to the shaking of the car, just like apple jelly. Neither the old woman nor the young women left the least doubt as to their profession.

The women were lolling on the benches, smoking, playing cards—at "sixty-six,"—drinking beer. Frequently the male public of the car provoked them, and they swore back in unceremonious language, in hoarse voices. The young people treated them with wine and cigarettes.

Horizon was here altogether unrecognizable; he was majestically negligent and condescendingly jocose. On the other hand, cringing ingratiation sounded in every word addressed to him by his female clients. But he, having looked over all of them—this strange mixture of Roumanians, Jewesses, Poles and Russians—and having assured himself that all was in order, gave orders about the sandwiches and majestically withdrew. At these moments he very much resembled a drover, who is transporting by railroad cattle for slaughter, and at a station drops in to look it over and to feed it. After that he would return to his *coupé* and again begin to toy with his wife, and Hebrew anecdotes just poured from his mouth.

At the long stops he would go out to the buffet only to see about his lady clients. But he himself said to his neighbours:

"You know, it's all the same to me if it's *treif* or *kosher*. I don't recognize any difference. But what can I do

with my stomach! The devil knows what stuff they'll
feed you sometimes at these stations. You'll pay some
three or four roubles, and then you'll spend a hundred
roubles on the doctors curing yourself. But maybe you,
now, Sarochka"—he would turn to his wife—"maybe
you'll get off at the station to eat something? Or shall I
send it up to you here?"

Sarochka, happy over his attention, would turn red,
beam upon him with grateful eyes, and refuse.

"You're very kind, Senya, only I don't want to. I'm
full."

Then Horizon would reach out of a travelling hamper
a chicken, boiled meat, cucumbers, and a bottle of Pales-
tine wine; have a snack, without hurrying, with appetite;
regale his wife, who ate very genteely, sticking out the
little fingers of her magnificent white hands; then painstakingly wrap up the remnants in paper and, without
hurrying, lay them away accurately in the hamper.

In the distance, far ahead of the locomotive, the cupolas
and belfries were already beginning to sparkle with fires
of gold. Through the *coupé* passed the conductor and
made some imperceptible sign to Horizon. He immediately followed the conductor out to the platform.

"The inspector will pass through right away," said
the conductor, "so you'll please be so kind as to stand
for a while here on the platform of the third class with
your spouse."

"*Nu, nu, nu!*" concurred Horizon.

"And the money as agreed, if you please."

"How much is coming to you, then?"

"Well, just as we agreed; half the extra charge, two
roubles eighty kopecks."

"What?" Horizon suddenly boiled over. "Two
roubles eighty kopecks? You think you got it a crazy
one in me, what? Here's a rouble for you and thank
God for that!"

"Pardon me, sir. This is even absurd—didn't you and
I agree?"

"Agree, agree!.. Here's a half more, and not a thing besides. What impudence! I'll tell the inspector yet that you carry people without tickets. Don't you think it, brother—you ain't found one of that sort here!"

The conductor's eyes suddenly widened, became blood-shot.

"O-oh! You sheeny!" he began to roar. "I ought to take a skunk like you and under the train with you!"

But Horizon at once flew at him like a cock.

"What? Under the train? But do you know what's done for words like that? A threat by action! Here, I'll go right away and will yell 'help!' and will turn the signal handle," and he seized the door-knob with such an air of resolution that the conductor just made a gesture of despair with his hand and spat.

"May you choke with my money, you mangy sheeny!"

Horizon called his wife out of the *coupé*:

"Sarochka! Let's go out on the platform for a look; one can see better there. Well, it's so beautiful—just like on a picture!"

Sarah obediently went after him, holding up with an unskilled hand the new dress, in all probability put on for the first time, bending out and as though afraid of touching the door or the wall.

In the distance, in the rosy gala haze of the evening glow, shone the golden cupolas and crosses. High up on the hill the white, graceful churches seemed to float in this flowery, magic mirage. Curly woods and coppices had run down from above and had pushed on over the very ravine. And the sheer, white precipice, which bathed its foot in the blue river, was all furrowed over with occasional young woods, just like green little veins and warts. Beautiful as in a fairy tale, the ancient town appeared as though it were itself coming to meet the train.

When the train stopped, Horizon ordered three porters to carry the things into the first class, and told his wife to follow him. But he himself lingered at the exit in order to let through both his parties. To the old woman looking after the dozen women he threw briefly in passing:

"So remember, madam Berman! Hotel America, Ivanukovskaya, twenty-two!"

While to the black-bearded man he said:

"Don't forget, Lazer, to feed the girls at dinner and to bring them somewhere to a movie show. About eleven o'clock at night wait for me. I'll come for a talk. But if some one will be calling for me extra, then you know my address—The Hermitage. Ring me up. But if I'm not there for some reason, then run into Reiman's cafe, or opposite, into the Hebrew dining room. I'll be eating *gefilteh fisch* there. Well, a lucky journey!"

CHAPTER III.

All the stories of Horizon about his commercial travelling were simply brazen and glib lying. All the samples of drapers' goods, suspenders *Gloire* and buttons *Helios*, the artificial teeth and insertible eyes, served only as a shield, screening his real activity—to wit, the traffic in the body of woman. True, at one time, some ten years ago, he had travelled over Russia as the representative for the dubious wines of some unknown firm; and this activity had imparted to his tongue that free-and-easy unconstraint for which, in general, travelling salesmen are distinguished. This former activity had, as well, brought him up against his real profession. In some way, while going to Rostov-on-the-Don, he had contrived to make a very young sempstress fall in love with him. This girl had not as yet succeeded in getting on the official lists of the police, but upon love and her body she looked without any lofty prejudices. Horizon, at that time altogether a green youth, amorous and light-minded, dragged the sempstress after him on his wanderings, full of adventures and unexpected things. After half a year she palled upon him dreadfully. She, just like a heavy burden, like a millstone, hung around the neck of this man of energy, motion and aggressiveness. In addition to that, there were the eternal scenes of jealousy, mistrust, the constant control and tears... the inevitable consequences of long living together... Then he began little by little to beat his mate. At the first time she was amazed, but from the second time quieted down, became tractable. It is known, that "women of love" never know a mean in love relations. They are either hysterical liars, deceivers, dissemblers, with a coolly-perverted mind and a sinuous dark soul; or else unboundedly

self-denying, blindly devoted, foolish, naive animals, who
know no bounds either in concessions or loss of self-
esteem. The sempstress belonged to the second category,
and Horizon was soon successful, without great effort,
in persuading her to go out on the street to traffic in
herself. And from that very evening, when his mistress
submitted to him and brought home the first five roubles
earned, Horizon experienced an unbounded loathing
toward her. It is remarkable, that no matter how many
women Horizon met after this—and several hundred of
them had passed through his hands—this feeling of
loathing and masculine contempt toward them would
never forsake him. He derided the poor woman in every
way, and tortured her morally, seeking out the most
painful spots. She would only keep silent, sigh, weep,
and getting down on her knees before him, kiss his hands.
And this wordless submission irritated Horizon still
more. He drove her away from him. She would not go
away. He would push her out into the street; but she,
after an hour or two, would come back shivering from
cold, in a soaked hat, in the turned-up brims of which
the rain-water splashed as in waterspouts. Finally,
some shady friend gave Simon Yakovlevich the harsh
and crafty counsel which laid a mark on all the rest of
his life activity—to sell his mistress into a brothel.

To tell the truth, in going into this enterprise, Horizon
almost disbelieved at soul in its success. But contrary
to his expectation, the business could not have adjusted
itself better. The proprietress of an establishment (this
was in Kharkov) willingly met his proposition half-way.
She had known long and well Simon Yakovlevich, who
played amusingly on the piano, danced splendidly, and
set the whole drawing room laughing with his pranks;
but chiefly, could, with unusually unabashed dexterity,
make any carousing party "shell out the coin." It only
remained to convince the mate of his life, and this proved
the most difficult of all. She did not want to detach
herself from her beloved for anything; threatened suicide,

swore that she would burn his eyes out with sulphuric
acid, promised to go and complain to the chief of police—
and she really did know a few dirty little transactions of
Simon Yakovlevich's that smacked of capital punishment.
Thereupon Horizon changed his tactics. He suddenly
became a tender, attentive friend, an indefatigable lover.
Then suddenly he fell into black melancholy. The
uneasy questionings of the woman he let pass in silence;
at first let drop a word as though by chance; hinted in
passing at some mistake of his life; and then began to
lie desperately and with inspiration. He said that the
police were watching him; that he could not get by the
jail, and, perhaps, even hard labour and the gallows;
that it was necessary for him to disappear abroad for
several months. But mainly, what he persisted in especially strongly, was some tremendous fantastic business,
in which he stood to make several hundred thousands
of roubles. The sempstress believed and became alarmed
with that disinterested, womanly, almost holy alarm,
in which, with every woman, there is so much of something maternal. It was not at all difficult now to convince
her that for Horizon to travel together with her presented
a great danger for him; and that it would be better for
her to remain here and to bide the time until the affairs
of her lover would adjust themselves fortuitously. After
that to talk her into hiding, as in the most trustworthy
retreat, in a brothel, where she would be in full safety
from the police and the detectives, was a mere nothing.
One morning Horizon ordered her to dress a little better,
curl her hair, powder herself, put a little rouge on her
cheeks, and carried her off to a den, to his acquaintance.
The girl made a favourable impression there, and that
same day her passport was changed by the police to a
so-called yellow ticket. Having parted with her, after
long embraces and tears, Horizon went into the room
of the proprietress and received his payment, fifty roubles
(although he had asked for two hundred). But he did
not grieve especially over the low price; the main thing

was, that he had found his calling at last, all by himself, and had laid the cornerstone of his future welfare.

Of course, the woman sold by him just remained forever so in the tenacious hands of the brothel. Horizon forgot her so thoroughly that after only a year he could not even recall her face. But who knows... perhaps he merely pretended?

Now he was one of the chief speculators in the body of woman in all the south of Russia. He had transactions with Constantinople and with Argentine; he transported, in whole parties, girls from the brothels of Odessa into Kiev; those from Kiev he brought over into Kharkov; and those from Kharkov into Odessa. He it was also who stuck away over second rate capital cities, and those districts which were somewhat richer, the goods which had been rejected or had grown too noticeable in the big cities. He had struck up an enormous clientele, and in the number of his consumers Horizon could have counted not a few people with a prominent social position: lieutenant governors, colonels of the gendarmerie, eminent advocates, well-known doctors, rich land-owners, carousing merchants. All the shady world: the proprietresses of brothels, *cocottes solitaires*, go-betweens, madams of houses of assignation, souteneurs, touring actresses and chorus girls—was as familiar to him as the starry sky to an astronomer. His amazing memory, which permitted him prudently to avoid notebooks, held in mind thousands of names, family names, nicknames, addresses, characteristics. He knew to perfection the tastes of all his highly placed consumers: some of them liked unusually odd depravity, others paid mad sums for innocent girls, for others still it was necessary to seek out girls below age. He had to satisfy both the sadistic and the masochistic inclinations of his clients, and at times to cater to altogether unnatural sexual perversions, although it must be said that the last he undertook only in rare instances which promised a large, undoubted profit. Two or three times he had to sit in jail, but these sittings went to his benefit; he not only did not lose his rapacious high-handedness and springy energy in his transactions, but with every year became more daring, inventive, and enterprising. With the years to his brazen impetuousness was joined a tremendous worldly business wisdom.

Fifteen times, during this period, he had managed to marry and every time had contrived to take a decent dowry. Having possessed himself of his wife's money, he, one fine day, would suddenly vanish without a trace, and, if there was a possibility, he would sell his wife profitably into a secret house of depravity or into a *chic* public establishment. It would happen that the parents of the deluded victim would search for him through the police. But while inquiries would be carried on everywhere about him as Shperling, he would already be travelling from town to town under the name of Rosenblum. During the time of his activity, in despite of an enviable memory, he had changed so many names that he had not only forgotten what year he had been Nathanielson, and during what Bakalyar, but even his own name was beginning to seem to him one of his pseudonyms.

It was remarkable, that he did not find in his profession anything criminal or reprehensible. He regarded it just as though he were trading in herrings, lime, flour, beef or lumber. In his own fashion he was pious. If time permitted, he would with assiduity visit the synagogue of Fridays. The Day of Atonement, Passover, and the Feast of the Tabernacles were invariably and reverently observed by him everywhere wherever fate might have cast him. His mother, a little old woman, and a hunchbacked sister, were left to him in Odessa, and he undeviatingly sent them now large, now small sums of money, not regularly but pretty frequently, from all towns from Kursk to Odessa and from Warsaw to Samara. Considerable savings of money had already accumulated to him in the Credit Lyonnaise, and he gradually increased them, never touching the interest. But to greed

or avarice he was almost a stranger. He was attracted
to the business rather by its tang, risk and a professional
self-conceit. To the women he was perfectly indifferent,
although he understood and could value them, and in
this respect resembled a good chef, who together with a
fine understanding of the business, suffers from a chronic
absence of appetite. To induce, to entice a woman, to
compel her to do all that he wanted, did not require any
efforts on his part; they came of themselves to his call
and became in his hands passive, obedient and yielding.
In his treatment of them a certain firm, unshakable,
self-assured aplomb had been worked out, to which they
submitted just as a refractory horse submits instinctively
to the voice, glance, stroking of an experienced horseman.

He drank very moderately, and without company
never drank. Toward eating he was altogether indifferent.
But, of course, as with every man, he had a little weakness of his own: he was inordinately fond of dress and
spent no little money on his toilet. Modish collars of
all possible fashions, cravats, diamond cuff links, watch
charms, the underwear of a dandy, and *chic* footwear
constituted his main distractions.

*   *   *

From the depot he went straight to The Hermitage.
The hotel porters, in blue blouses and uniform caps,
carried his things into the vestibule. Following them,
he too entered, arm in arm with his wife; both smartly
attired, imposing, but he just simply magnificent, in his
wide, bell-shaped English overcoat, in a new broad-
brimmed panama, holding negligently in his hand a
small cane with a silver handle in the form of a naked
woman.

"You ain't supposed to be here without a permit for
your residence," said an enormous, stout doorkeeper,
looking down upon him from above and preserving on his
face a sleepy and immovably-frigid expression.

"Ach, Zachar! Again 'you ain't suposed to!' " merrily exclaimed Horizon, and patted the giant on his

shoulder. "What does it mean, 'you ain't supposed to'? Every time you shove this same 'you ain't supposed to' at me. I must be here for three days in all. Soon as I conclude the rent agreement with Count Ipatiev, right away I go away. God be with you! Live even all by yourself in all your rooms. But you just give a look, Zachar, what a toy I brought you from Odessa! You'll be just tickled with it!"

With a careful, deft, accustomed movement he thrust a gold piece into the doorkeeper's hand, who was already holding it behind his back, ready and folded in the form of a little boat.

The first thing that Horizon did upon installing himself in the large, spacious room with an alcove, was to put out into the corridor at the door of the room six pairs of magnificent shoes, saying to the bell-hop who ran up in answer to the bell:

"Immediately all should be cleaned! So it should shine like a mirror! They call you Timothy, I think? Then you should know me—if you work by me it will never go for nothing. So it should shine like a mirror!"

CHAPTER IV.

Horizon lived at the Hotel Hermitage for not more than three days and nights, and during this time he managed to see some three hundred people. His arrival seemed to enliven the big, gay port city. To him came the keepers of employment offices for servants, the proprietresses of cheap hotels, and old, experienced go-betweens, grown gray in the trade in women. Not so much out of an interest in booty as out of professional pride, Horizon tried, at all costs, to bargain for as much profit as possible, to buy a woman as cheaply as possible. Of course, to receive ten, fifteen roubles more was not the reason for him, but the mere thought that competitor Yampolsky would receive at the sale more than he brought him into a frenzy.

After his arrival, the next day, he set off to Mezer the photographer, taking with him the straw-like girl Bella, and had pictures taken in various poses together with her; at which for every negative he received three roubles, while he gave the woman a rouble. After that he rode off to Barsukova.

This was a woman, or, speaking more correctly, a retired wench, whose like can be found only in the south of Russia; neither a Pole nor a Little Russian; already sufficiently old and rich in order to allow herself the luxury of maintaining a husband (and together with him a cabaret), a handsome and kindly little Pole. Horizon and Barsukova met like old friends. They had, it seemed, no fear, no shame, no conscience when they conversed with each other.

"Madam Barsukova! I can offer you something special! Three women: one a large brunette, very modest; another a little one, a blonde, but who, you

170

understand, is ready for everything; the third is a woman of mystery, who merely smiles and doesn't say anything, but promises much and is a beauty!"

Madam Barsukova was gazing at him with mistrust, shaking her head.

"Mister Horizon! What are you trying to fill my head with? Do you want to do the same with me that you did last time?"

"By God, I should live so, how I want to deceive you! But that's not the main thing. I'm also offering you a perfectly educated woman. Do with her what you like. In all probability you'll find a connoisseur."

Barsukova smiled artfully and asked:

"Again a wife?"

"No. But she's of the nobility."

"Then that means unpleasantnesses with the police again?"

"*Ach!* My God! I don't take big money from you; all the three for a lousy thousand roubles."

"Well, let's talk frankly; five hundred. I don't want to buy a cat in a bag."

"It seems, Madam Barsukova, that it isn't the first time you and I have done business together. I won't deceive you and will bring her here right away. Only I beg you not to forget that you're my aunt, and please work in that direction. I won't be more than three days here in the city."

Madam Barsukova, with all her breasts, bellies and chins, began to sway merrily.

"We won't dicker over trifles. All the more so since you don't deceive me, nor I you. There's a great demand for women now. What would you say, Mister Horizon, if I offered you some red wine?"

"Thank you, Madam Barsukova, with pleasure."

"Let's talk a while like old friends. Tell me, how much do you make a year?"

"*Ach*, madam, what shall I say? Twelve, twenty thousand, approximately. But think what tremendous expenses there are in constantly travelling."

"Do you put away a little?"

"Well, that's trifles; some two or three thousand a year."

"I thought ten, twenty..."

Horizon grew wary. He sensed that he was beginning to be drawn out and asked insidiously:

"But why does this interest you?"

Anna Michailovna pressed the button of an electric bell and ordered the dressy maid to bring coffee with steamed cream and a bottle of Chambertaine. She knew the tastes of Horizon. Then she asked:

"Do you know Mr. Shepsherovich?"

Horizon simply pounced upon her.

"My God! Who don't know Shepsherovich! This is a god, this is a genius!"

And, having become animated, forgetting that he was being dragged into a trap, be hegan speaking exaltedly:

"Just imagine what Shepsherovich did last year! He carried to Argentine thirty women from Kovno, Vilno, Zhitomir. Each one of them he sold at a thousand roubles—a total, madam—count it—of thirty thousand! Do you think Shepsherovich calmed down with this? For this money, in order to repay his expenses on the steamer, he bought several negresses and stuck them about in Moscow, Petersburg, Kiev, Odessa, and Kharkov. But, you know, madam, this isn't a man, but an eagle. There's a man who can do business!"

Barsukova caressingly laid her hand on his knee. She had been waiting for this moment and said to him amicably:

"And so I propose to you, Mr.—— however, I don't know how you are called now..."

"Horizon, let's say..."

"So I propose to you, Mr. Horizon—could you find some innocent girls among yours? There's an enormous demand for them now. I'm playing an open hand with you. We won't stop at money. Now it's in fashion. Notice, Horizon, your lady clients will be returned to you in exactly the same state in which they were. This, you understand, is a little depravity, which I can in no way make out..."

Horizon cast down his eyes, rubbed his head, and said:

"You see, I've a wife... You've almost guessed it."

"So. But why almost?"

"I'm ashamed to confess, that she—how shall I say it... she is my bride..."

Barsukova gaily burst into laughter.

"You know, Horizon, I couldn't at all expect that you're such a nasty villain! Let's have your wife, it's all the same. But is it possible that you've really refrained?"

"A thousand?" asked Horizon seriously.

"Ah! What trifles; a thousand let's say. But tell me, will I be able to manage her?"

"Nonsense!" said Horizon self-assuredly. "Let's again suppose that you're my aunt, and I leave my wife with you. Just imagine, Madam Barsukova, that this woman is in love with me like a cat. And if you'll tell her, that for my good she must do so and so and thus and thus—then there won't be no arguments!"

Apparently, there was nothing more for them to talk over. Madam Barsukova brought out a promissory note, whereon she with difficulty wrote her name, her father's name, and her last name. The promissory note, of course, was fantastic; but there is a tie, a welding, an honour among thieves. In such deals people do not deceive. Death threatens otherwise. It is all the same, whether in prison, or on the street, or in a brothel.

Right after that, just like an apparition out of a trapdoor, appeared the friend of her heart, the master of the cabaret, a young little Pole, with moustaches twirled high. They drank some wine, talked a bit about the fair, about the exposition, complained a little about bad

business.   After that Horizon telephoned to his room in
the hotel, and called out his wife.   He introduced her to
his aunt and his aunt's second cousin, and said that
mysterious political reasons were calling him out of
town.   He tenderly kissed Sarah, shed a tear, and rode
away.

CHAPTER V.

With the arrival of Horizon (however, God knows how he was called: Gogolevich, Gidalevich, Okunev, Rosmitalsky), in a word, with the arrival of this man everything changed on Yamskaya Street. Enormous shufflings commenced. From Treppel girls were transferred to Anna Markovna, from Anna Markovna into a rouble establishment, and from the rouble establishment into a half-rouble one. There were no promotions: only demotions. At each change of place Horizon earned from five to a hundred roubles. Verily, he was possessed of an energy equal, approximately, to the waterfall of Imatra! Sitting in the daytime at Anna Markovna's, he was saying, squinting from the smoke of the cigarette, and swinging one leg crossed over the other:

"The question is... What do you need this same Sonka for? It's no place for her in a decent establishment. If we'll float her down the stream, then you'll make a hundred roubles for yourself, I twenty-five for myself. Tell me frankly, she isn't in demand, is she, now?"

"Ah, Mr. Shatzky! You can always talk a person over! But just imagine, I'm sorry for her. Such a nice girl..."

Horizon pondered for a moment. He was seeking an appropriate citation and suddenly let out:

"Give the falling a shove!* And I'm convinced, Madam Shaibes, that there's no demand of any sort for her."

Isaiah Savvich, a little, sickly, touchy old man, but in moments of need very determined, supported Horizon:

"And that's very simple. There is really no demand of any sort for her. Think it over for yourself, Annechka;

---

*Horizon is quoting a Nietzscheism of Gorky's.—*Trans.*

her outfit costs fifty roubles, Mr. Shatzky will receive twenty-five roubles, fifty roubles will be left for you and me. And, glory be to God, we have done with her! At least, she won't be compromising our establishment."

In such a way Sonka the Rudder, avoiding a rouble establishment, was transferred into a half-rouble one, where all kinds of riff-raff made sport of the girls at their own sweet will, whole nights through. There tremendous health and great nervous force were requisite. Sonka once began shivering from terror, in the night, when Thekla, a mountain of a woman of some two hundred pounds, jumped out into the yard to fulfill a need of nature, and cried out to the housekeeper who was passing by her:

"Housekeeper, dear! Listen—the thirty-sixth man!.. Don't forget!"

Fortunately, Sonka was not disturbed much; even in this establishment she was too homely. No one paid any attention to her splendid eyes, and they took her only in those instances when there was no other at hand. The pharmacist sought her out and came every evening to her. But cowardice, or a special Hebrew fastidiousness, or, perhaps, even physical aversion, would not permit him to take the girl and carry her away with him from the house. He would sit whole nights through near her, and, as of yore, patiently waited until she would return from a chance guest; created scenes of jealousy for her and yet loved her still, and, sticking in the daytime behind the counter in his drug store and rolling some stinking pills or other, ceaselessly thought of her and yearned.

CHAPTER VI.

Immediately at the entrance to a suburban cabaret an artificial flower bed shone with vari-coloured lights, with electric bulbs instead of flowers; and just such another fiery alley of wide, half-round arches, narrowing toward the end, led away from it into the depths of the garden. Further on was a broad, small square, strewn with yellow sand; to the left an open stage, a theatre, and a shooting gallery; straight ahead a stand for the military band (in the form of a seashell) and little booths with flowers and beer; to the right the long terrace of the restaurant. Electric globes from their high masts illuminated the small square with a pale, dead-white brightness. Against their frosted glass, with wire nets stretched over them, beat clouds of night moths, whose shadows—confused and large—hovered below, on the ground. Hungry women, too lightly, dressily, and fancifully attired, preserving on their faces an expression of care-free merriment or haughty, offended unapproachability, strolled back and forth in pairs, in a walk already tired and dragging.

All the tables in the restaurant were taken—and over them floated the continuous noise of knives upon plates and a motley babel, galloping in waves. It smelt of rich and pungent kitchen fumes. In the middle of the restaurant, upon a stand, Roumanians in red frocks were playing; all swarthy, white-toothed, with the faces of whiskered, pomaded apes, with their hair licked down. The director of the orchestra, bending forward and affectedly swaying, was playing upon a violin and making unseemly sweet eyes at the public—the eyes of a man-prostitute. And everything together—this abundance of tiresome electric lights, the exaggeratedly bright

177

toilettes of the ladies, the odours of modish, spicy perfumes, this ringing music, with willful slowings up of the tempo, with voluptuous swoonings in the transitions, with the tempestuous passages screwed up—everything fitted the one to the other, forming a general picture of insane and stupid luxury, a setting for an imitation of a gay, unseemly carouse.

Above, around the entire hall, ran open galleries, upon which, as upon little balconies, opened the doors of the private cabinets. In one of these cabinets four were sitting—two ladies and two men; an artiste known to all Russia, the cantatrice Rovinskaya, a large, handsome woman, with long, green, Egyptian eyes, and a long, red, sensuous mouth, the lips of which were rapaciously drooping at the corners; the baroness Tefting, little, exquisite, pale—she was everywhere seen with the artiste; the famous lawyer Ryazanov; and Volodya Chaplinsky, a rich young man of the world, a composer-dilettante, the author of several darling little ballads and many witticisms upon the topics of the day, which circulated all over town.

The walls of the cabinet were red, with a gold design. On the table, among the lighted candelabra, two white, tarred necks of bottles stuck up out of an electroplated vase, which had sweated from the cold, and the light in a tenuous gold played in the shallow goblets of wine. Outside, near the doors, a waiter was on duty, leaning against the wall; while the stout, tall, important *maître d'hôtel*, on whose right little finger, always sticking out, sparkled a huge diamond, would frequently stop at these doors, and attentively listen with one ear to what was going on in the cabinet.

The baroness, with a bored, pale face, was listlessly gazing through a lorgnette down at the droning, chewing, swarming crowd. Among the red, white, blue and straw-coloured feminine dresses the uniform figures of the men resembled large, squat, black beetles. Rovinskaya negligently, yet at the same time intently as well, was looking down upon the stand and the spectators, and her face expressed fatigue, ennui, and perhaps also that satiation with all spectacles, which are such matters of course to celebrities. The splendid, long, slender fingers of her left hand were lying upon the crimson velvet of the box-seat. Emeralds of a rare beauty hung upon them so negligently that it seemed as though they would fall off at any second, and suddenly she began laughing.

"Look!" she said; "what a funny figure, or, to put it more correctly, what a funny profession! There, there, that one who's playing on a 'syrinx of seven reeds.'"

Everyone looked in the direction of her hand. And really, the picture was funny enough. Behind the Roumanian orchestra was sitting a stout, whiskered man, probably the father, and perhaps even the grandfather, of a numerous family, and with all his might was whistling into seven little pipes glued together. As it was difficult for him, probably, to move this instrument between his lips, he therefore, with an unusual rapidity, turned his head now to the left, now to the right.

"An amazing occupation," said Rovinskaya. "Well now, Chaplinsky, you try to toss your head about like that."

Volodya Chaplinsky, secretly and hopelessly in love with the artiste, immediately began obediently and zealously to do this, but after half a minute desisted.

"It's impossible," he said, "either long training, or, perhaps, hereditary abilities, are necessary for this."

The baroness during this time was tearing away the petals of her rose and throwing them into a goblet; then, with difficulty suppressing a yawn, she said, making just the least bit of a wry face:

"But, my God, how drearily they divert themselves in our K——! Look: no laughter, no singing, no dances. Just like some herd that's been driven here, in order to be gay on purpose!"

Ryazanov listlessly took his goblet, sipped it a little, and answered apathetically in his enchanting voice:

"Well, and is it any gayer in your Paris, or Nice? Why, it must be confessed—mirth, youth and laughter have vanished forever out of human life, and it is scarcely possible that they will ever return. One must regard people with more patience, it seems to me. Who knows, perhaps for all those sitting here, below, the present evening is a rest, a holiday?"

"The speech for the defense," put in Chaplinsky in his calm manner.

But Rovinskaya quickly turned around to the men, and her long emerald eyes narrowed. And this with her served as a sign of wrath, from which even crowned personages committed follies at times. However, she immediately restrained herself and continued languidly:

"I don't understand what you are talking about. I don't understand even what we came here for. For there are no longer any spectacles in the world. Now I, for instance, have seen bull-fights in Seville, Madrid and Marseilles—an exhibition which does not evoke anything save loathing. I have also seen boxing and wrestling— nastiness and brutality. I also happened to participate in a tiger hunt, at which I sat under a baldachin on the back of a big, wise white elephant... in a word, you all know this well yourselves. And out of all my great, chequered, noisy life, from which I have grown old..."

"Oh, what are you saying, Ellena Victorovna!" said Chaplinsky with a tender reproach.

"Abandon compliments, Volodya! I know myself that I'm still young and beautiful of body, but, really, it seems to me at times that I am ninety. So worn out has my soul become. I continue. I say, that during all my life only three strong impressions have sunk into my soul. The first, while still a girl, when I saw a cat stealing upon a cock-sparrow, and I with horror and with interest watched its movements and the vigilant gaze of the bird. Up to this time I don't know myself which I sympathized with more: the skill of the cat or the slipperiness of the sparrow. The cock-sparrow proved the

quicker. In a moment he flew up on a tree and began
from there to pour down upon the cat such sparrow
swearing that I would have turned red for shame if I
had understood even one word. While the cat, as though
it had been wronged, stuck up its tail like a chimney
and tried to pretend to itself that nothing out of the way
had taken place. Another time I had to sing in an opera
a duet with a certain great artist..."

"With whom?" asked the baroness quickly.

"Isn't it all the same? Of what need names? And so,
when he and I were singing, I felt all of me in the sway of
genius. How wonderfully, into what a marvelous har-
mony, did our voices blend! Ah! It is impossible to
describe this impression. Probably, it happens but once
in a lifetime. According to the role, I had to weep, and
I wept with sincere, genuine tears. And when, after the
curtain, he walked up to me and patted my hair with his
big warm hand and with his enchanting radiant smile
said, 'Splendid! for the first time in my life have I sung
so'... and so I—and I am a very proud being—I kissed
his hand. And the tears were still standing in my eyes..."

"And the third?" asked the baroness, and her eyes lit
up with the evil sparks of jealousy.

"Ah, the third," answered the artiste sadly, "the
third is as simple as simple can be. During the last
season I lived at Nice, and so I saw *Carmen* on the open
stage at Fréjus with the participation of Cecile Ketten,
who is now," the artiste earnestly made the sign of the
cross, "dead—I don't really know, fortunately or unfortunately for herself?"

Suddenly, in a moment, her magnificent eyes filled
with tears and began to shine with a magic green light,
such with which the evening star shines, on warm summer
twilights. She turned her face around to the stage,
and for some time her long, nervous fingers convulsively
squeezed the upholstery of the barrier of the box. But
when she again turned around to her friends, her eyes

were already dry, and the enigmatic, vicious and wilful lips were resplendent with an unconstrained smile.

Then Ryazanov asked her politely, in a tender but purposely calm tone:

"But then, Ellena Victorovna, your tremendous fame, admirers, the roar of the mob... finally, that delight which you afford to your spectators. Is it possible that even this does not titillate your nerves?"

"No, Ryazanov," she answered in a tired voice. "You know no less than myself what this is worth. A brazen interviewer, who needs passes for his friends, and, by the way, twenty-five roubles in an envelope. High school boys and girls, students and young ladies attending courses, who beg you for autographed photographs. Some old blockhead with a general's rank, who hums loudly with me during my aria. The eternal whisper behind you, when you pass by: 'there she is, that same famous one!' Anonymous letters, the brazenness of back-stage habitues... why, you can't enumerate everything! But surely, you yourself are often beset by female psy-chopathics of the court-room?"

"Yes," said Ryazanov decisively.

"That's all there is to it. But add to that the most terrible thing, that every time I have come to feel a genuine inspiration, I tormentingly feel on the spot the consciousness that I'm pretending and grimacing before people... And the fear of the success of your rival? And the eternal dread of losing your voice, of straining it or catching a cold? The eternal tormenting bother of throat bandages? No, really, it is heavy to bear renown on one's shoulders."

"But the artistic fame?" retorted the lawyer. "The might of genius! This, verily, is a true moral might, which is above the might of any king on earth!"

"Yes, yes, of course you're right, my dear. But fame, celebrity, are sweet only at a distance, when you only dream about them. But when you have attained them you feel only their thorns. But then, with what anguish you feel every dram of their decrease. And I have forgotten to say something else. Why, we artists undergo a sentence at hard labour. In the morning, exercises; in the daytime, rehearsals; and then there's scarcely time for dinner and you're due for the performance. An hour or so for reading or such diversion as you and I are having now, may be snatched only by a miracle. And even so... the diversion is altogether of the mediocre..."

She negligently and wearily made a slight gesture with the fingers of the hand lying on the barrier.

Volodya Chaplinsky, agitated by this conversation, suddenly asked:

"Yes, but tell me, Ellena Victorovna, what would you want to distract your imagination and ennui?"

She looked at him with her enigmatic eyes and answered quietly, even a trifle shyly, it seemed:

"Formerly, people lived more gaily and did not know prejudices of any sort. Well, it seems to me that then I would have been in my place and would have lived with a full life. O, ancient Rome!"

No one understood her, save Ryazanov, who, without looking at her, slowly pronounced in his velvety voice, like that of an actor, the classical, universally familiar, Latin phrase:

"*Ave, Cæsar, morituri te salutant!*"

"Precisely! I love you very much, Ryazanov, because you are a clever child. You will always catch a thought in its flight; although, I must say, that this isn't an especially high property of the mind. And really, two beings come together, the friends of yesterday, who had conversed with each other and eaten at the same table, and this day one of them must perish. You understand— depart from life forever. But they have neither malice nor fear. There is the most real, magnificent spectacle, which I can only picture to myself!"

"How much cruelty there is in you," said the baroness meditatively.

"Well, nothing can be done about it now! My an-

cestors were cavaliers and robbers. However, shan't
we go away now?"

They all went out of the garden. Volodya Chaplinsky
ordered his automobile called. Ellena Victorovna was
leaning upon his arm. And suddenly she asked:

"Tell me, Volodya, where do you usually go when
you take leave of so-called decent women?"

Volodya hemmed and hawed. However, he knew
positively that he could not lie to Rovinskaya.

"M–m–m... I'm afraid of offending your hearing.
To the Tzigani, for instance... to night cabarets..."

"And somewhere else? Worse?"

"Really, you put me in an awkard position. From
the time that I've become so madly in love with you..."

"Leave out the romancing!"

"Well, how shall I say it?" murmured Volodya,
feeling that he was turning red, not only in the face, but
with his body, his back. "Well, of course, to the women.
Now, of course, this does not occur with me personally..."

Rovinskaya maliciously pressed Chaplinsky's elbow to
her side.

"To a brothel?"

Volodya did not answer anything. Then she said:

"And so, you'll carry us at once over there in the
automobile and acquaint us with this existence, which
is foreign to me. But remember, that I rely upon your
protection."

The remaining two agreed to this, unwillingly, in all
probability; but there was no possibility of opposing
Ellena Victorovna. She always did everything that she
wanted to. And then they had all heard and knew that
in Petersburg carousing worldly ladies, and even girls,
permit themselves, out of a modish snobbism, pranks
far worse than the one which Rovinskaya had proposed.

CHAPTER VII.

On the way to Yamskaya Street Rovinskaya said to Chaplinsky:

"You'll bring me at first into the most luxurious place, then into a medium one, and then into the filthiest."

"My dear Ellena Victorovna," warmly retorted Chaplinsky, "I'm ready to do everything for you. It is without false boasting when I say that I would give my life away at your order, ruin my career and position at a mere sign of yours... But I dare not bring you to these houses. Russian manners are coarse, and often simply inhuman manners. I'm afraid that you will be insulted by some pungent, unseemly word, or that a chance visitor will play some senseless prank before you..."

"Ah, my God," impatiently interrupted Rovinskaya; "when I was singing in London, there were many at that time paying court to me, and I did not hesitate to go and see the filthiest dens of Whitechapel in a choice company. I will say, that I was treated there very carefully and anticipatingly. I will also say, that there were with me at that time two English aristocrats; lords, both sportsmen, both people unusually strong physically and morally, who, of course, would never have allowed a woman to be offended. However, perhaps you, Volodya, are of the race of cowards?"

Chaplinsky flared up:

"Oh, no, no, Ellena Victorovna. I forewarned you only out of love for you. But if you command, then I'm ready to go where you will. Not only on this dubious undertaking, but even very death itself."

By this time they had already driven up to the most
luxurious establishment in the Yamkas—Treppel's. Ryazanov the lawyer said, smiling with his usual ironic smile:

"And so, the inspection of the menagerie begins."

They were led into a cabinet with crimson wall paper,
and on the wall paper was repeated, in the "empire"
style, a golden design in the form of small laurel wreaths.
And at once Rovinskaya recognized, with the keen
memory of an artiste, that exactly the same paper had
also been in that cabinet in which they had just been
sitting.

Four German women from the Baltic provinces came
out. All of them stout, full-breasted, blonde, powdered,
very important and respectful. The conversation did
not catch on at first. The girls sat immovable, like
carvings of stone, in order to pretend with all their might
that they were respectable ladies. Even the champagne,
which Ryazanov called for, did not improve the mood.
Rovinskaya was the first to come to the aid of the party.
Turning to the stoutest, fairest German of all, who resembled a loaf, she asked politely in German:

"Tell me, where were you born? Germany, in all
probability?"

"No, *gnädige Frau*, I am from Riga."

"What compels you to serve here, then? Not poverty,
I hope?"

"Of course not, *gnädige Frau*. But, you understand,
my bridegroom, Hans, works as a *kellner* in a restaurant-
automat, and we are too poor to be married now. I
bring my savings to a bank, and he does the same. When
we have saved the ten thousand roubles we need, we will
open our own beer-hall, and, if God will bless us, then we
shall allow ourselves the luxury of having children. Two
children. A boy and a girl."

"But, listen to me, *mein Fräulein!*" Rovinskaya was
amazed. "You are young, handsome, know two languages..."

"Three, madam," proudly put in the German. "I know Esthonian as well. I finished the municipal school and three classes of high school."

"Well, then, you see, you see..." Rovinskaya became heated. "With such an education you could always find a place with everything found, and about thirty roubles. Well, in the capacity of a housekeeper, *bonne*, senior clerk in a good store, a cashier, let's say... And if your future bridegroom... Fritz..."

"Hans, madam..."

"If Hans proved to be an industrious and thrifty man, then it would not be at all hard for you to get up on your feet altogether, after three or four years. What do you think?"

"Ah, madam, you are a little mistaken. You have overlooked that, in the very best of positions, I, even denying myself in everything, will not be able to put aside more than fifteen, twenty roubles a month; whereas here, with a prudent economy, I gain up to a hundred roubles and at once carry them away with a book into the savings bank. And besides that, just imagine, *gnädige Frau*, what a humiliating position to be the servant in a house! Always to depend on the caprice or the disposition of the spirits of the masters! And the master always pesters you with foolishnesses. *Pfui!*.. And the mistress is jealous, picks, and scolds."

"No... I don't understand..." meditatively drawled Rovinskaya, without looking the German in the eyes, but casting hers on the floor. "I've heard a great deal of your life here, in these... what do you call them?... these houses. They say it is something horrible. That you're forced to love the most repulsive, old and hideous men, that you are plucked and exploited in the most cruel manner..."

"Oh, never, madam... Each one of us has an account book, wherein is written accurately the income and expense. During last month I earned a little more than five hundred roubles. As always, two-thirds went to the proprietress for board, quarters, fuel, light, linen... There remains to me more than a hundred and fifty, is it not so? Fifty I spent on costumes and all sorts of trifles. A hundred I save. What exploitation is it, then, madam, I ask you? And if I do not like a man at all— true, there are some who are exceedingly nasty—I can always say I am sick, and instead of me will go one of the newest girls...''

"But then... pardon me, I do not know your name...''

"Elsa.''

"They say, that you're treated very roughly... beaten at times... compelled to do that which you don't want to and which is repulsive to you?''

"Never, madam!'' dropped Elsa haughtily. "We all live here as a friendly family of our own. We are all natives of the same land or relatives, and God grant, that many should live so in their own families as we live here. True, on Yamskaya Street there happen various scandals and fights and misunderstandings. But that's there... in these... in the rouble establishments. The Russian girls drink a lot and always have one lover. And they do not think at all of their future.''

"You are prudent, Elsa,'' said Rovinskaya in an oppressed tone. "All this is well. But, what of the chance disease? Infection? Why, that is death? And how can you guess?''

"And again—no, madam. I won't let a man into my bed before I make a detailed medical inspection of him... I am guaranteed, at the least, against seventy-five per cent.''

"The devil!'' suddenly exclaimed Rovinskaya with heat and hit the table with her fist. "But, then, what of your Albert...''

"Hans,'' the German corrected her meekly.

"Pardon me... Your Hans surely does not rejoice greatly over the fact that you are living here, and that you betray him every day?"

Elsa looked at her with sincere, lively amazement.

"But, *gnädige Frau*... I have never yet betrayed him! It is other lost wenches, especially Russian, who have lovers for themselves, on whom they spend their hard-earned money. But that I should ever let myself go as far as that? *Pfui!*"

"A greater fall I have not imagined!" said Rovinskaya loudly and with aversion, getting up. "Pay, gentlemen, and let's go on from here."

When they had gone out into the street, Volodya took her arm and said in an imploring voice:

"For God's sake, isn't one experiment enough for you?"

"Oh, what vulgarity! What vulgarity!"

"That's why I'm saying, let's drop this experiment."

"No, in any case I am going through with it to the finish. Show me something simpler, more of the medium."

Volodya Chaplinsky, who was all the time in a torment over Ellena Victorovna, offered the most likely thing— to drop into the establishment of Anna Markovna, which was only ten steps away.

But it was just here that strong impressions awaited them. Simeon did not want to let them in, and only several gold pieces, which Ryazanov gave him, softened him. They took up a cabinet, almost the same as at Treppel's, only somewhat shabbier and more faded. At the command of Emma Edwardovna, the girls were herded into the cabinet. But it was the same as letting a goat into a truck-garden or mixing soda and acid. The main mistake, however, was that they let Jennka in there as well—wrathful, irritated, with impudent fires in her eyes. The modest, quiet Tamara was the last to walk in, with her shy and depraved smile of a Monna Lisa.

In the end, almost the entire personnel of the establishment gathered in the cabinet. Rovinskaya no longer risked asking "How did you come to this life?" But it must be said, that the inmates of the house met her with an outward hospitality. Ellena Victorovna asked them to sing their usual canonical songs, and they willingly sang:

> Monday now is come again,
> They're supposed to get me out;
> Doctor Krassov won't let me out,
> Well, the devil take him then.

And further:

> Poor little, poor little, poor little me,
> The public house is closed,
> My head's aching me...

* * *

> The love of a loafer
> Is spice, is spice;
> But the prostitute
> Is as cold as ice.
> Ha–ha–ha!

* * *

> They came together
> Matched as well as might be,
> She is a prostitute,
> A pickpocket he.
> Ha–ha–ha!

* * *

> Now morning has come,
> He is planning a theft;
> While she lies in her bed
> And laughs like she's daft.
> Ha–ha–ha!

Comes morning, the laddie
Is led to the pen;
But for the prostitute
His pals await then.
Ha–ha–ha!..*

And still further a convict song:

I'm a ruined laddie,
Ruined for alway;
While year after year
The days go away.

And also:

Don't you cry, my Mary,
You'll belong to me;
When I've served the army
I will marry thee.

But here suddenly, to the general amazement, the stout Kitty, usually taciturn, burst into laughter. She was a native of Odessa.

---

*While there can be but little doubt that these four stanzas are an actual transcript from life, Heinrich Heine's *Ein Weib* is such a striking parallel that it may be reproduced here as a matter of interest. The translation is by Mr. Louis Untermeyer.—*Trans*.

A WOMAN

They loved each other beyond belief—
She was a strumpet, he was a thief;
Whenever she thought of his tricks, thereafter
She'd throw herself on the bed with laughter.

The day was spent with a reckless zest;
At night she lay upon his breast.
So when they took him, a while thereafter
She watched at the window—with laughter.

He sent word pleading, "Oh come to me,
I need you, need you bitterly,
Yes, here and in the hereafter."
Her little head shook with laughter.

At six in the morning they swung him high;
At seven the turf on his grave was dry;
At eight, however, she quaffed her
Red wine and sang with laughter!

"Let me sing one song, too. It's sung by thieves and badger queens in the drink shops on our Moldavanka and Peresip."

And in a horrible bass, in a rusty and unyielding voice, she began to sing, making the most incongruous gestures, but, evidently, imitating some cabaret cantatrice of the third calibre that she had sometime seen:

"Ah, I'll go to Dukovka,
Sit down at the table,
Now I throw my hat off,
Toss it under table.
Then I athk my dearie,
'What will you drink, sweet?'
But all the answer that she makes:
'My head aches fit to split.'
'I ain't a–athking you
What your ache may be
But I am a–athking you
What your drink may be:
Will it be beer, or for wine shall I
    call,
Or for violet wine, or nothing else
    at all?' "

And all would have turned out well, if suddenly Little White Manka, in only her chemise and in white lace drawers, had not burst into the cabinet. Some merchant, who the night before had arranged a paradisaical night, was carousing with her, and the ill-fated Benedictine, which always acted upon the girl with the rapidity of dynamite, had brought her into the usual quarrelsome condition. She was no longer "Little Manka" and "Little White Manka," but she was "Manka the *Scandaliste.*" Having run into the cabinet, she suddenly, from unexpectedness, fell down on the floor, and, lying on her back, burst into such sincere laughter that all the rest burst out laughing as well. Yes. But this laughter was not prolonged... Manka suddenly sat up on the floor and began to shout:

"Hurrah! new wenches have joined our place!"

This was altogether an unexpected thing. The baroness did a still greater tactlessness. She said:

"I am a patroness of a convent for fallen girls, and therefore, as a part of my duty, I must gather information about you."

But here Jennka instantly flared up:

"Get out of here right away, you old fool! You rag! You floor mop!.. Your Magdalene asylums—they're worse than a prison. Your secretaries use us, like dogs carrion. Your fathers, husbands, and brothers come to us, and we infect them with all sorts of diseases... Purposely!.. And they in their turn infect you. Your female superintendents live with the drivers, janitors and policemen, while we are put in a cell if we happen to laugh or joke a little among ourselves. And so, if you've come here as to a theatre, then you must hear the truth out, straight to your face."

But Tamara calmly stopped her:

"Stop, Jennie, I will tell them myself... Can it be that you really think, baroness, that we are worse than the so-called respectable women? A man comes to me, pays me two roubles for a visit or five roubles for a night, and I don't in the least conceal this, from any one in the world... But tell me, baroness, do you possibly know even one married lady with a family who isn't in secret giving herself up either for the sake of passion to a young man, or for the sake of money to an old one? I know very well that fifty per cent. of you are kept by lovers, while the remaining fifty, of those who are older, keep young lads. I also know that many—ah, how many!— of you cohabit with your fathers, brothers, and even sons, but these secrets you hide in some sort of a hidden casket. And that's all the difference between us. We are fallen, but we don't lie and don't pretend, but you

all fall, and lie to boot. Think it over for yourself, now—
in whose favour is this difference?"

"Bravo, Tamarochka, that's the way to serve them!"
shouted Manka, without getting up from the floor;
dishevelled, fair, curly, resembling at this moment a
thirteen-year-old girl.

"Now, now!" urged Jennka as well, flashing with her
flaming eyes.

"Why not, Jennechka? I'll go further than that.
Out of us scarcely, scarcely one in a thousand has committed abortion. But all of you several times over.
What? Or isn't that the truth? And those of you who've
done this, did it not out of desperation or cruel provety,
but you simply were afraid of spoiling your figure and
beauty—that's your sole capital! Or else you've been
seeking only beastly carnal pleasure, while pregnancy
and feeding interfered with your giving yourself up to it!"

Rovinskaya became confused and uttered in a quick
whisper:

"*Faites attention, baronne, que dans sa position cette
demoiselle est instruite.*"*

"*Figurez-vous, que moi, j'ai aussi remarqué cet étrange
visage. Comme si je l'ai déjà vu... est-ce en rêve?... en
demi-delire? Ou dans sa petite enfance?*"†

"*Ne vous donnez pas la peine de chercher dans vos souve-
nirs, baronne,*" Tamara suddenly interposed insolently.
"*Je puis de suite vous venir en aide. Rappelez-vous seule-
ment Kharkoff, et la chambre d'hôtel de Koniakine, l'entre-
preneur Solovieitschik, et le ténor di grazzia... A ce
moment vous n'etiez pas encore m-me la baronne de...*"**

---

*"Pay attention, baroness, the girl is rather educated for one of
her position."

†"Just imagine, I, too, have remarked this strange face. But
where have I seen it...was it in a dream?..in semi-delirium? Or
in her early infancy?"

**"Don't trouble to strain your memory, baroness. I will come
to your aid at once. Just recall Kharkov, a room in Koniakine's
hotel, the theatrical manager, Solovieitschik, and a certain lyrical
tenor...At that time you were not yet baroness de..."

However, let's drop the French tongue... You were a common chorus girl and served together with me."

"*Mais, dites-moi, au nom de dieu, comment vous trouvez vous ici, Mademoiselle Marguerite.*"*

"Oh, they ask us about that every day. I just up and came to be here..."

And with an inimitable cynicism she asked:

"I trust you will pay for the time which we have passed with you?"

"No, may the devil take you!" suddenly shouted out Little White Manka, quickly getting up from the rug.

And suddenly, pulling two gold pieces out of her stocking, she flung them upon the table.

"There, you!.. I'm giving you that for a cab. Go away right now, otherwise I'll break up all the mirrors and bottles here..."

Rovinskaya got up and said with sincere, warm tears in her eyes:

"Of course, we'll go away, and the lesson of Mlle. Marguerite will prove of benefit to us. Your time will be paid for—take care of it, Volodya. Still, you sang so much for us, that you must allow me to sing for you as well."

Rovinskaya went up to the piano, took a few chords, and suddenly began to sing the splendid ballad of Dragomyzhsky:

"We parted then with pride—
    Neither with sighs nor words
    Proffered I thee reproach of jealousy...
    We went apart for aye,
    Yet only if with thee
    I might but chance to meet!..
    Ah, that with thee I might but chance to meet!

---

*"But tell me, in God's name, how you have come to be here, Mademoiselle Marguerite."

"I weep not nor complain—
To fate I bend my knee...
I know not, if you loved,
So greatly wronging me?
Yet only if with thee
I might but chance to meet!..
Ah, that with thee I might but chance to meet!"

This tender and passionate ballad, executed by a great artiste, suddenly reminded all these women of their first love; of their first fall; of a late leave-taking at a dawn in the spring, in the chill of the morning, when the grass is gray from the dew, while the red sky paints the tips of the birches a rosy colour; of last embraces, so closely entwined, and of the unerring heart's mournful whispers: "No, this will not be repeated, this will not be repeated!" And the lips were then cold and dry, while the damp mist of the morning lay upon the hair.

Silence seized Tamara; silence seized Manka the *Scandaliste;* and suddenly Jennka, the most untamable of all the girls, ran up to the artiste, fell down on her knees, and began to sob at her feet.

And Rovinskaya, touched herself, put her arms around her head and said:

"My sister, let me kiss you!"

Jennka whispered something into her ear.

"Why, that's a silly trifle," said Rovinskaya. "A few months of treatment and it will all go away."

"No, no, no... I want to make all of them diseased. Let them all rot and croak."

"Ah, my dear," said Rovinskaya, "I would not do that in your place."

And now Jennka, the proud Jennka, began kissing the knees and hands of the artiste and was saying:

"Then why have people wronged me so?... Why have they wronged me so? Why? Why? Why?"

Such is the might of genius!

The only might which takes into its beautiful hands not the abject reason, but the warm soul of man. The self-respecting Jennka was hiding her face in Rovinskaya's dress; Little White Manka was sitting meekly on a chair, her face covered with a handkerchief; Tamara, with elbow propped on her knee and head bowed on the palm of her hand, was intently looking down, while Simeon the porter, who had been looking in against any emergency, only opened his eyes wide in amazement.

Rovinskaya was quietly whispering into Jennka's very ear:

"Never despair. Sometimes things fall out so badly that there's nothing for it but to hang one's self—but, just look, to-morrow life has changed abruptly. My dear, my sister, I am now a world celebrity. But if you only knew what seas of humiliation and vileness I have had to wade through! Be well, then, my dear, and believe in your star."

She bent down to Jennka and kissed her on the forehead. And never afterwards could Volodya Chaplinsky, who had been watching this scene with a painful tension, forget those warm and beautiful rays, which at this moment kindled in the green, long, Egyptian eyes of the artiste.

The party departed gloomily, but Ryazanov lingered behind for a minute.

He walked up to Jennka, respectfully and gently kissed her hand, and said:

"If possible, forgive our prank... This, of course, will not be repeated. But if you ever have need of me, I am always at your service. Here is my visiting card. Don't stick it out on your bureau; but remember, that from this evening I am your friend."

And he, having kissed Jennka's hand once more, was the last to go down the stairs.

CHAPTER VIII.

On Thursday, since very morning, a ceaseless, fine drizzle had begun to fall, and so the leaves of the chestnuts, acacias, and poplars had at once turned green. And, suddenly, it became somehow dreamily quiet and protractedly tedious. Pensive and monotonous.

During this all the girls had gathered, as usual, in Jennka's room. But something strange was going on within her. She did not utter witticisms, did not laugh, did not read, as always, her usual yellow-back novel which was now lying aimlessly either on her breast or stomach; but was vicious, wrapped up in sadness, and in her eyes blazed a yellow fire that spoke of hatred. In vain did Little White Manka, Manka the *Scandaliste*, who adored her, try to turn her attention to herself—Jennka seemed not to notice her, and the conversation did not at all get on. It was depressing. But it may have been that the August drizzle, which had steadily set in for several weeks running, reacted upon all of them. Tamara sat down on Jennka's bed, gently embraced her, and, having put her mouth near her very ear, said in a whisper:

"What's the matter, Jennechka? I've seen for a long time that something strange is going on in you. And Manka feels that too. Just see, how she's wasted without your caressing. Tell me. Perhaps I'll be able to help you in some way?"

Jennka closed her eyes and shook her head in negation. Tamara moved away from her a little, but continued to stroke her shoulder gently.

"It's your affair, Jennechka. I daren't butt into your soul. I only asked because you're the only being who..."

198

Jennka with decision suddenly jumped out of bed, seized Tamara by the hand and said abruptly and commandingly:

"All right! Let's get out of here for a minute. I'll tell you everything. Girls, wait for us a little while."

In the light corridor Jennka laid her hands on the shoulders of her mate and with a distorted, suddenly blanched face, said:

"Well, then, listen here: some one has infected me with syphilis."

"Oh, my poor darling. Long?"

"Long. Do you remember, when the students were here? The same ones who started a row with Platonov? I found out about it for the first time then. I found out in the daytime."

"Do you know," quietly remarked Tamara, "I almost guessed about this, and particularly then, when you went down on your knees before the singer and talked quietly about something with her. But still, my dear Jennechka, you must attend to yourself."

Jennka wrathfully stamped her foot and tore in half the batiste handkerchief which she had been nervously crumpling in her hands.

"No! Not for anything! I won't infect any one of you. You may have noticed yourself, that during the last weeks I don't dine at the common table, and that I wash and wipe the dishes myself. That's why I'm trying to break Manka away from me, whom, you know, I love sincerely, in the real way. But these two-legged skunks I infect purposely, infect every evening, ten, fifteen of them. Let them rot, let them carry the syphilis on to their wives, mistresses, mothers—yes, yes, their mothers also, and their fathers, and their governesses, and even their grand-grandmothers. Let them all perish, the honest skunks!"

Tamara carefully and tenderly stroked Jennka's head.

"Can it be that you'll go the limit, Jennechka?"

"Yes. And without any mercy. All of you, however, don't have to be afraid of me. I choose the man myself. The stupidest, the handsomest, the richest and the most important, but not to one of you will I let them go afterward. Oh! I make believe I'm so passionate before them, that you'd burst out laughing if you saw. I bite them, I scratch, I cry and shiver like an insane woman. They believe it, the pack of fools."

"It's your affair, it's your affair, Jennechka," meditatively uttered Tamara, looking down. "Perhaps you're right, at that. Who knows? But tell me, how did you get away from the doctor?"

Jennka suddenly turned away from her, pressed her face against the angle of the window frame and suddenly burst into bitter, searing tears—the tears of wrath and vengefulness—and at the same time she spoke, gasping and quivering:

"Because... because... Because God has sent me especial luck: I am sick there where, in all probability, no doctor can see. And ours, besides that, is old and stupid..."

And suddenly, with some unusual effort of the will, Jennka stopped her tears just as unexpectedly as she had started crying.

"Come to me, Tamarochka," she said. "Of course, you won't chatter too much?"

"Of course not."

And they returned into Jennka's room, both of them calm and restrained.

*   *   *

Simeon walked into the room. He, contrary to his usual brazenness, always bore himself with a shade of respect toward Jennka. Simeon said:

"Well, now, Jennechka, their Excellency has come to Vanda. Allow her to go away for ten minutes."

Vanda, a blue-eyed, light blonde, with a large red mouth, with the typical face of a Lithuanian, looked

imploringly at Jennka. If Jennka had said "No" she
would have remained in the room, but Jennka did not
say anything and even shut her eyes deliberately. Vanda
obediently went out of the room.

This general came accurately twice a month, every
two weeks (just as to Zoe, another girl, came daily
another honoured guest, nicknamed the Director in the
house).

Jennka suddenly threw the old, tattered book behind
her. Her brown eyes flared up with a real golden fire.

"You're wrong in despising this general," said she.
"I've known worse Ethiopians. I had a certain guest
once—a real blockhead. He couldn't make love to me
otherwise than... otherwise than... well, let's say it
plainly: he pricked me with pins in the breast... While
in Vilno a Polish Catholic priest used to come to me. He
would dress me all in white, compel me to powder myself,
lay me down on the bed. He'd light three candles near
me. And then, when I seemed to him altogether like a
dead woman, he'd throw himself upon me."

Little White Manka suddenly exclaimed:

"It's the truth you're telling, Jennka! I had a certain
old bugger, too. He made me pretend all the time that
I was an innocent girl, so's I'd cry and scream. But,
Jennechka, though you're the smartest one of us, yet
I'll bet you you won't guess who he was..."

"The warden of a prison?"

"A fire chief."

Suddenly Katie burst into laughter in her bass:

"Well, now, I had a certain teacher. He taught some
kind of arithmetic, I disremember which. He always
made me believe, that I was the man, and he the woman,
and that I should do it to him... by force... And
what a fool! Just imagine, girls, he'd yell all the time:
'I'm your woman! I'm all yours! Take me! Take me!'"

"Loony!" said the blue-eyed, spry Verka in a positive
and unexpectedly low contralto: "Loony."

"No, why?" suddenly retorted the kindly and modest Tamara. "Not crazy at all, but simply, like all men, a libertine. At home it's tiresome for him, while here for his money he can receive whatever pleasure he desires. That's plain, it seems?"

Jennka, who had been silent up to now, suddenly, with one quick movement, sat up in bed.

"You're all fools!" she cried. "Why do you forgive them all this? Before I used to be foolish myself, too, but now I compel them to walk before me on all fours, compel them to kiss my soles, and they do this with delight... You all know, girlies, that I don't love money, but I pluck the men in whatever way I can. They, the nasty beasts, present me with the portraits of their wives, brides, mothers, daughters... However, you've seen, I think, the photographs in our water-closet? But now, just think of it, my children... A woman loves only once, but for always, while a man like a he-greyhound... That he's unfaithful is nothing; but he never has even the commonest feeling of gratitude left either for the old, or the new mistress. I've heard it said, that now there are many clean boys among the young people. I believe this, though I haven't seen, haven't met them, myself. But all those I have seen are all vagabonds, nasty brutes and skunks. Not so long ago I read some novel of our miserable life. It's almost the same thing as I'm telling you now."

*   *   *

Vanda came back. She slowly, carefully, sat down on the edge of Jennka's bed; there, where the shadow of the lamp fell. Out of that deep, though deformed psychical delicacy, which is peculiar to people sentenced to death, prisoners at hard labour, and prostitutes, none had the courage to ask her how she had passed this hour and a half. Suddenly she threw upon the table twenty-five roubles and said:

"Bring me white wine and a watermelon."

And, burying her face in her arms, which had sunk on

the table, she began to sob inaudibly. And again no one took the liberty of putting any question to her. Only Jennka grew pale from wrath and bit her lower lip so that a row of white spots was left upon it.

"Yes," she said; "here, now, I understand Tamara. You hear, Tamara, I apologize before you. I've often laughed over your being in love with your thief Senka. But here, now, I'll say that of all the men the most decent is a thief or a murderer. He doesn't hide the fact that he loves a girlie, and, if need be, will commit a crime for her—a theft or a murder. But these—the rest of them! All lying, falsehood, petty cunning, depravity on the sly. The nasty beast has three families, a wife and five children. A governess and two children abroad. The eldest daughter from the first marriage, and a child by her. And this everybody, everybody in town knows, save his little children. And even they, perhaps, guess it and whisper among themselves. And, just imagine, he's a respected person, honoured by the whole world... My children, it seems we've never had occasion to enter into confidences with each other, and yet I'll tell you, that I, when I was ten and a half, was sold by my own mother in the city of Zhitomir to Doctor Tarabukin. I kissed his hands, implored him to spare me, I cried out to him: 'I'm little!' But he'd answer me: 'That's nothing, that's nothing: you'll grow up.' Well, of course, there was pain, aversion, nastiness... And he afterwards spread it around as a current anecdote. The desperate cry of my soul."

"Well, as long as we do speak, let's speak to the end," suddenly and calmly said Zoe, and smiled negligently and sadly. "I was deprived of innocence by a teacher in the ministerial school, Ivan Petrovich Sus. He simply called me over to his rooms, and his wife at that time had gone to market for a suckling pig—it was Christmas. Treated me with candies, and then said it was going to be one of two things: either I must obey him in everything, or he'd at once expel me out of school for bad conduct.

But then you know yourselves, girls, how we feared the teachers. Here they aren't terrible to us, because we do with them whatever we want—but at that time! For then he seemed to us greater than Czar and God."

"And me a stewdent. He was teaching the master's boys in our place. There, where I was a servant. . ."

"No, but I. . ." exclaimed Niura, but, turning around unexpectedly, remained as she was with her mouth open. Looking in the direction of her gaze, Jennka had to wring her hands. In the doorway stood Liubka, grown thin, with dark rings under her eyes, and, just like a somnambulist, was searching with her hand for the door-knob, as a point of support.

"Liubka, you fool, what's the matter with you?" yelled Jennka loudly. "What is it?"

"Well, of course, what: he took and chased me out."

No one said a word. Jennka hid her eyes with her hands and started breathing hard, and it could be seen how under the skin of her cheeks the taut muscles of the jaws were working.

"Jennechka, all my hope is only in you," said Liubka with a deep expression of weary helplessness. "Everybody respects you so. Talk it over, dearie, with Anna Markovna or with Simeon. . . Let them take me back."

Jennka straightened up on the bed, fixed Liubka with her dry, burning, yet seemingly weeping eyes, and asked brokenly:

"Have you eaten anything to-day?"

"No. Neither yesterday, nor to-day. Nothing."

"Listen, Jennechka," asked Vanda quietly, "suppose I give her some white wine? And Verka meanwhile will run to the kitchen for meat? What?"

"Do as you know best. Of course, that's all right. And give a look, girlies, why, she's all wet. Oh, what a booby! Well! Lively! Undress yourself! Little White Manka, or you, Tamarochka, give her dry drawers, warm stockings and slippers. Well, now," she turned to Liubka, "tell us, you idiot, all that happened to you!"

CHAPTER IX.

On that early morning when Lichonin so suddenly, and, perhaps, unexpectedly even to himself, had carried off Liubka from the gay establishment of Anna Markovna, it was the height of summer. The trees still remained green, but in the scent of the air, the leaves, and the grass there was already to be felt, as though from afar, the tender, melancholy, and at the same time bewitching scent of the nearing autumn. With wonder the student gazed at the trees, so clean, innocent and quiet, as though God, imperceptibly to men, had planted them about here at night; and the trees themselves were looking around with wonder upon the calm blue water, that still seemed slumbering in the pools and ditches and under the wooden bridge thrown across the shallow river; upon the lofty, as though newly washed sky, which had just awakened and, in the glow of dawn, half asleep, was smiling with a rosy, lazy, happy smile in greeting to the kindling sun.

The heart of the student expanded and quivered; both from the beauty of the beatific morning, and from the joy of existence, and from the sweet air, refreshing his lungs after the night, passed without sleep, in a crowded and smoke-filled compartment. But the beauty and loftiness of his own action moved him still more.

Yes, he had acted like a man, like a real man, in the highest sense of that word! Even now he is not repenting of what he had done. It's all right for them (to whom this "them" applied, Lichonin did not properly understand even himself), it's all right for them to talk about the horrors of prostitution; to talk, sitting at tea, with rolls and sausage, in the presence of pure and cultured girls. But had any one of his colleagues taken some

205

actual step toward liberating a woman from perdition?
Eh, now? And then there is also the sort that will come
to this same Sonechka Marmeladova, will tell her all
sorts of taradiddles, describe all kinds of horrors to her,
butt into her soul, until he brings her to tears; and right
off will start in crying himself and begin to console her,
embrace her, pat her on the head, kiss her at first on the
cheek, then on the lips; well, and everybody knows
what happens next! Faugh! But with him, with Lichonin, the word and the deed were never at odds.

He clasped Liubka around the waist, and looked at her
with kindly, almost loving, eyes; although, the very same
minute, he himself thought that he was regarding her
as a father or a brother.

Sleep was fearfully besetting Liubka; her eyes would
close, and she with an effort would open them wide, so as
not to fall asleep again; while on her lips lay the same
naive, childish, tired smile, which Lichonin had noticed
still there, in the cabinet. And out of one corner of her
mouth ran a thin trickle of saliva.

"Liuba, my dear! My darling, much-suffering woman!
Behold how fine it is all around! Lord! Here it's five
years that I haven't seen the sunrise. Now play at
cards, now drinking, now I had to hurry to the university.
Behold, my dearest, over there the dawn has burst into
bloom. The sun is near! This is your dawn, Liubochka!
This is your new life beginning. You will fearlessly lean
upon my strong arm. I shall lead you out upon the
road of honest toil, on the way to a brave combat with
life, face to face with it!"

Liubka eyed him askance. "There, the fumes are still
playing in his head," she thought kindly. "But that's
nothing—he's kind and a good sort. Only a trifle homely."
And, having smiled with a half-sleepy smile, she said in
a tone of capricious reproach:

"Ye-es! You'll fool me, never fear. All of you men
are like that. You just gain yours at first, to get your
pleasure, and then—no attention whatsoever!"

"I? Oh! That I should do this!" Lichonin exclaimed warmly and even smote himself on the chest with his free hand. "Then you know me very badly! I'm too honest a man to be deceiving a defenseless girl. No! I'll exert all my powers and all my soul to educate your mind, to widen your outlook, to compel your poor heart, which has suffered so, to forget all the wounds and wrongs which life has inflicted upon it. I will be a father and a brother to you! I shall safeguard your every step! And if you will come to love somebody with a truly pure, holy love, then I shall bless that day and hour when I had snatched you out of this Dantean hell!"

During the continuation of this flaming tirade the old cabby with great significance, although silently, began laughing, and from this inaudible laughter his back shook. Old cabbies hear very many things, because to the cabby, sitting in front, everything is readily audible, which is not at all suspected by the conversing fares; and many things do the old cabbies know of that which takes place among people. Who knows, perhaps he had heard more than once even more disordered, more lofty speeches?

It seemed to Liubka for some reason that Lichonin had grown angry at her, or that he was growing jealous beforehand of some imaginary rival. He was declaiming with entirely too much noise and agitation, She became perfectly awake, turned her face to Lichonin with wide open, uncomprehending, and at the same time submissive eyes, and slightly touched his right hand, lying on her waist, with her fingers.

"Don't get angry, my sweetie. I'll never exchange you for another. Here's my word of honour, honest to God! My word of honour, that I never will! Don't you think I feel you're wanting to take care of me? Do you think I don't understand? Why, you're such an attractive, nice little young fellow. There, now, if you were an old man and homely..."

"Ah! You haven't got the right idea!" shouted Lichonin, and again in high-flown style began to tell her about the equal rights of women, about the sacredness of toil, about human justice, about freedom, about the struggle against reigning evil.

Of all his words Liubka understood exactly not a one. She still felt herself guilty of something and somehow shrank all up, grew sad, bowed her head and became quiet. A little more and she, in all probability, would have burst out crying in the middle of the street; but, fortunately, they by this time had driven up to the house where Lichonin was staying.

"Well, here we are at home," said the student. "Stop, driver!"

And when he had paid him, he could not refrain from declaiming with pathos, his hand extended theatrically straight before him:

> "And into my house, calm and fearless,
>   As its full mistress walk thou in!"

And again the unfathomable, prophetic smile wrinkled the aged brown face of the cabby.

CHAPTER X.

The room in which Lichonin lived was situated on the fifth story and a half. And a half, because there are such five, six, and seven-story profitable houses, packed to overflowing and cheap, on top of which are erected still other sorry bug-breeders of roof iron, something in the nature of mansards; or, more exactly, bird-houses, in which it is fearfully cold in winter, while in the summer time it is just as torrid as in the tropics. Liubka with difficulty clambered upward. It seemed to her that now, now, two steps more, and she would drop straight down on the steps and fall into a sleep from which nothing would be able to wake her. But Lichonin was saying all the time:

"My dear! I can see you are tired. But that's nothing. Lean upon me. We are going upwards all the time! Always higher and higher! Is this not a symbol of all human aspirations? My comrade, my sister, lean upon my arm!"

Here it became still worse for poor Liubka. As it was, she could barely go up alone, but here she also had to drag in tow Lichonin, who had grown extremely heavy. And his weight would not really have mattered; his wordiness, however, was beginning to irritate her little by little. So irritates at times the ceaseless, wearisome crying, like a toothache, of an infant at breast; the piercing whimpering of a canary; or someone whistling without pause and out of tune in an adjoining room.

Finally, they reached Lichonin's room. There was no key in the door. And, as a rule, it was never even locked with a key. Lichonin pushed the door and they entered. It was dark in the room, because the window curtains were lowered. It smelt of mice, kerosene, yesterday's vegetable soup, long-used bed linen, stale tobacco smoke.

209

In the half-dusk some one who could not be seen was snoring deafeningly and with variations.

Lichonin raised the shade. There were the usual furnishings of a poor student: a sagging, unmade bed with a crumpled blanket; a lame table, and on it a candlestick without a candle; several books on the floor and on the table; cigarette stubs everywhere; and opposite the bed, along the other wall, an old, old divan, upon which at the present moment was sleeping and snoring, with mouth wide open, some young man with black hair and moustache. The collar of his shirt was unbuttoned and through its opening could be seen the chest and black hair, the like of which for thickness and curliness could be found only on Persian lambs.

"Nijeradze! Hey, Nijeradze, get up!" cried Lichonin and prodded the sleeper in the ribs. "Prince!"

"M-m-m . . ."

"May your race be even accursed in the person of your ancestors and descendants! May they even be exiled from the heights of the beauteous Caucasus! May they even never behold the blessed Georgia! Get up, you skunk! Get up, you Aravian dromedary! Kintoshka! . ."

But suddenly, altogether unexpectedly for Lichonin, Liubka intervened. She took him by the arm and said timidly:

"Darling, why torture him? Maybe he wants to sleep, maybe he's tired? Let him sleep a bit. I'd better go home. Will you give me a half for a cabby? To-morrow you'll come to me again. Isn't that so, sweetie?"

Lichonin was abashed. So strange did the intervention of this silent, apparently sleepy girl, appear to him. Of course, he did not grasp that she was actuated by an instinctive, unconscious pity for a man who had not had enough sleep; or, perhaps, a professional regard for the sleep of other people. But the astonishment was only momentary. For some reason he became offended. He raised the hand of the recumbent man, which hung down to the floor, with the extinguished cigarette still remaining between its fingers, and, shaking it hard, he said in a serious, almost severe voice:

"Listen, now, Nijeradze, I'm asking you seriously. Understand, now, may the devil take you, that I'm not alone, but with a woman. Swine!"

It was as though a miracle had happened: the lying man suddenly jumped up, as though some spring of unusual force had instantaneously unwound under him. He sat down on the divan, rapidly rubbed with his palms his eyes, forehead, temples; saw the woman, became confused at once, and muttered, hastily buttoning his blouse:

"Is that you, Lichonin? And here I was waiting and waiting for you and fell asleep. Request the unknown comrade to turn away for just a minute."

He hastily pulled on his gray, everyday student's coat, and rumpled up with all the fingers of both his hands his luxuriant black curls. Liubka, with the coquetry natural to all women, no matter in what years or situation they find themselves, walked up to the sliver of a mirror hanging on the wall, to fix her hair-dress. Nijeradze askance, questioningly, only with the movement of his eyes, indicated her to Lichonin.

"Never mind. Don't pay any attention," answered the other aloud. "But let's get out of here, however. I'll tell you everything right away. Excuse me, Liubochka, it's only for a minute. I'll come back at once, fix you up, and then evaporate, like smoke."

"But don't trouble yourself," replied Liubka: "it'll be be all right for me here, right on this divan. And you fix yourself up on the bed."

"No, that's no longer like a model, my angel! I have a colleague here. And so I'll go to him to sleep. I'll return in just a minute."

Both students went out into the corridor.

"What meaneth this dream?" asked Nijeradze, opening wide his oriental, somewhat sheepish eyes. "Whence this beauteous child, this comrade in a petticoat?"

Lichonin shook his head with great significance and made a wry face. Now, when the ride, the fresh air, the morning, and the business-like, everyday, accustomed setting had entirely sobered him, he was beginning to experience within his soul an indistinct feeling of a certain awkwardness, needlessness of this sudden action; and at the same time something in the nature of an unconscious irritation both against himself and the woman he had carried off. He already had a presentiment of the onerousness of living together, of a multiplicity of cares, unpleasantnesses and expenses; of the equivocal smiles or even simply the unceremonious questionings of comrades; finally, of the serious hindrance during the time of government examinations. But, having scarcely begun speaking with Nijeradze, he at once became ashamed of his pusillanimity, and having started off listlessly, towards the end he again began to prance on his heroic steed.

"Do you see, prince," he said, in his confusion twisting a button of his comrade's coat and without looking in his eyes, "you've made a mistake. This isn't a comrade in a petticoat at all, but this is...simply, I was just now with my colleagues...that is, I wasn't, but just dropped in for just a minute with my friends into the Yamkas, to Anna Markovna..."

"With whom?" asked Nijeradze, becoming animated.

"Well, isn't it all the same to you, prince? There was Tolpygin, Ramses, a certain sub-professor—Yarchenko—Borya Sobashnikov, and others...I don't recall. We had been boat-riding the whole evening, then dived into a publican's, and only after that, like swine, started for the Yamkas. I, you know, am a very abstemious man. I only sat and soaked up cognac, like a sponge, with a certain reporter I know. Well, all the others fell from grace, however. And so, toward morning, for some reason or other, I went all to pieces. I got so sad and full of pity from looking at these unhappy women. I also thought, now, of how our sisters enjoy our regard, love, protection; how our mothers are surrounded with reverent adoration. Just let

some one say one rude word to them, shove them, offend
them; we are ready to chew his throat off! Isn't that
the truth?"

"M-m?.." drawled out the Georgian, half questioningly, half expectantly, and squinted his eyes to one side.

"Well, then I thought: why, now, any blackguard, any
whippersnapper, any shattered ancient can take any one
of these women to himself for a minute or for a night, as a
momentary whim; and indifferently, one superfluous time
more—the thousand and first—profane and defile in her
that which is the most precious in a human being—love...
Do you understand—revile, trample it underfoot, pay for
the visit and walk away in peace, his hands in his pockets,
whistling. But the most horrible of all is that all this has
come to be a habit with them; it's all one to her, and it's
all one to him. The feelings have dulled, the soul has
dimmed. That's so, isn't it? And yet, in every one of
them perishes both a splendid sister and a sainted mother.
Eh? Isn't that the truth?"

"N-na?.." mumbled Nijeradze and again shifted his
eyes to one side.

"And so I thought: wherefore words and superfluous
exclamations! To the devil with hypocritical speeches during conventions. To the devil with abolition, regulation
(suddenly, involuntarily, the recent words of the reporter
came to his mind), Magdalene asylums and all these dis-
tributions of holy books in the establishments! Here, I'll
up and act as a really honest man, snatch a girl out of this
slough, implant her in real firm soil, calm her, encourage
her, treat her kindly."

"H-hm!" grunted Nijeradze with a grin.

"Eh, prince! You always have salacious things on your
mind. For you understand that I'm not talking about a
woman, but about a human being; not about flesh, but
about a soul."

"All right, all right, me soul, go on!"

"Furthermore, as I thought, so did I act. I took her
to-day from Anna Markovna's and brought her for the

present to me. And later—whatever God may grant.
I'll teach her in the beginning to read, to write; then open
up for her a little cook-shop, or a grocery store, let's say.
I think that the comrades won't refuse to help me. The
human heart, prince, my brother—every heart—is in
need of cordiality, of warmth. And lo and behold! in a
year, in two, I will return to society a good, industrious,
worthy member, with a virgin soul, open to all sorts of
great possibilities... For she has given only her body,
while her soul is pure and innocent."

"*Tse, tse, tse,*" the prince smacked his tongue.

"What does this mean, you Tifflissian he-mule?"

"And will you buy her a sewing machine?"

"Why a sewing machine, in particular? I don't understand."

"It's always that way in the novels, me soul. Just as
soon as the hero has saved the poor, but lost, creature, he
at once sets up a sewing machine for her."

"Stop talking nonsense," Lichonin waved him away
angrily with his hand. "Clown!"

The Georgian suddenly grew heated, his black eyes
began to sparkle, and immediately Caucasian intonations
could be heard in his voice.

"No, not nonsense, me soul. It's one of two things here,
and it'll all end in one and the same result. Either you'll
get together with her and after five months chuck her out
on the street; and she'll return to the brothel or take to
walking the street. That's a fact! Or else you won't get
together with her, but will begin to load her up with manual or mental labours and will try to develop her ignorant,
dark mind; and she from tedium will run away from you,
and will again find herself either walking the street, or in
a brothel. That's a fact, too! However, there is still a
third combination. You'll be vexing yourself about her
like a brother, like the knight Lancelot, but she, secretly
from you, will fall in love with another. Me soul, believe
me, that wooman, when she is a wooman, is always—a
wooman. And the other will play a bit with her body, and

after three months chuck her out into the street or into a brothel."

Lichonin sighed deeply. Somewhere deep—not in his mind, but in the hidden, almost unseizable secret recesses of his consciousness—something resembling the thought that Nijeradze was right flashed through him. But he quickly gained control of himself, shook his head, and, stretching out his hand to the prince, uttered triumphantly:

"I promise you, that after half a year you'll take your words back and as a mark of apology, you Erivanian billy goat, you Armavirian egg-plant, you'll stand me to a dozen of Cakhetine wine."

"*Va!* That's a go!" the prince struck Lichonin's hand with his palm with all his might. "With pleasure. But if it comes out as I say—then you do it."

"Then I do it. However, *au revoir*, prince. Whom are you lodging with?"

"Right here, in this corridor, at Soloviev's. But you, of course, like a mediaeval knight, will lay a two-edged sword between yourself and the beauteous Rosamond? Yes?"

"Nonsense! I did want to pass the night at Soloviev's myself. But now I'll go and wander about the streets a bit and turn in into somebody's; to Zaitzevich or Strump. Farewell, prince!"

"Wait, wait!" Nijeradze called him, when he had gone a few steps. "I have forgotten to tell you the main thing: Partzan has tripped up!"

"So that's how?" wondered Lichonin and at once yawned long, deeply and with enjoyment.

"Yes. But there's nothing dreadful; only the possession of some illegal brochures and stuff. He won't have to sit for more than a year."

"That's nothing; he's a husky lad, he can stand it."

"He's husky, all right," confirmed the prince.

"Farewell!"

"*Au revoir*, knight Grunwaldus!"

"*Au revoir*, you Cabardinian stallion."

CHAPTER XI.

Lichonin was left alone. In the half-dark corridor it smelt of kerosene fumes from the guttering little tin lamp and of the odour of stagnant bad tobacco. The daylight dully penetrated only near the top, from two small glass frames, made in the roof at both ends of the corridor.

Lichonin found himself in that simultaneously weakened and elevated mood which is so familiar to every man who has happened to be thoroughly sleepless for a long time. It was as though he had gone out of the limitations of everyday human life, and this life had become to him distant and of indifference; but at the same time his thoughts and emotions obtained a certain peaceful clarity and apathetic distinctness, and there was a tedious and languishing allurement in this crystal Nirvanah.

He stood near his room, leaning against the wall, and seemed to see, feel, and hear how near him and below him were sleeping several score of people; sleeping with the last, fast morning sleep, with open mouths, with measured deep breathing, with a wilted pallor on their faces, glistening from sleep; and through his head flashed the thought, remote yet familiar since childhood, of how horrible sleeping people are—far more horrible than dead people. Then he remembered about Liubka. His subterranean, submerged, mysterious "I" rapidly, rapidly whispered that he ought to drop into the room, and see if the girl were all right, as well as make certain dispositions about tea in the morning; but he made believe to himself that he was not at all even thinking of this, and walked out into the street.

He walked, looking closely at everything that met his eyes, with an idle and exact curiosity new to him; and every feature was drawn for him in relief to such a degree that it seemed to him as though he were feeling it with his fingers... There a peasant woman passed by. Over her shoulder is a yoke staff, while at each end of the yoke is a large pail of milk; her face is not young, with a net of fine wrinkles on the temples and with two deep furrows from the nostrils to the corners of the mouth; but her cheeks are rosy, and, probably, hard to the touch, while her hazel eyes radiate a sprightly peasant smile. From the movement of the heavy yoke and from the smooth walk her hips sway rhythmically now to the left, now to the right, and in their wave-like movements there is a coarse, sensual beauty.

"A mischievous dame, and she's lived through a checkered life," reflected Lichonin. And suddenly, unexpectedly to himself, he had a feeling for, and irresistibly desired, this woman, altogether unknown to him, homely and not young; in all probability dirty and vulgar, but still resembling, as it seemed to him, a large Antonovka* apple which had fallen to the ground—somewhat bored by a worm, and which had lain just a wee bit too long, but which has still preserved its bright colour and its fragrant, winey aroma.

Getting ahead of her, an empty, black, funereal catafalque whirled by; with two horses in harness, and two tied behind to the little rear columns. The torch-bearers and grave-diggers, already drunk since morning, with red, brutish faces, with rusty opera hats on their heads, were sitting in a disorderly heap on their uniform liveries, on the reticular horse-blankets, on the mourning lanterns; and with rusty, hoarse voices were roaring out some incoherent song. "They must be hurrying to a funeral procession; or, perhaps, have even finished it already," reflected Lichonin; "merry fellows!" On the boulevard he came to a stop and sat down on a small wooden bench, painted green. Two rows of mighty centenarian chestnuts went away into the distance, merging together somewhere afar into one straight green arrow. The prickly large nuts

---

*Somewhat like a Spitzbergen, but a trifle rounder.—*Trans.*

were already hanging on the trees. Lichonin suddenly recalled that at the very beginning of the spring he had been sitting on this very boulevard, and at this very same spot. Then it had been a calm, gentle evening of smoky purple, soundlessly falling into slumber, just like a smiling, tired maiden. Then the stalwart chestnuts, with their foliage—broad at the bottom and narrow toward the top —had been strewn all over with clusters of blossoms, growing with bright, rosy, thin cones straight to the sky; just as though some one by mistake had taken and fastened upon all the chestnuts, as upon lustres, pink Christmas-tree candles. And suddenly, with extraordinary poignancy —every man sooner or later passes through this zone of inner emotion—Lichonin felt, that here are the nuts ripening already, while then there had been little pink blossoming candles, and that there would be many more springs and many blossoms, but the one which had passed no one and nothing had the power to bring back. Sadly gazing into the depths of the retreating dense alley, he suddenly noticed that sentimental tears were making his eyes smart.

He got up and went on farther, looking closely at everything that he met with an incessant, sharpened, and at the same time calm attention, just as though he were looking at the God-created world for the first time. A gang of stone masons went past him on the pavement, and all of them were reflected in his inner vision with an exaggerated vividness and brilliance of colour, just as though on the frosted glass of a camera obscura. The foreman, with a red beard, matted to one side, and with blue austere eyes; and a tremendous young fellow, whose left eye was swollen, and who had a spot of a dark-blue colour spreading from the forehead to the cheek-bone and from the nose to the temple; and a young boy with a naive, country face, with a gaping mouth like a fledgling's, weak, moist; and an old man who, having come late, was running after the gang at a funny, goat-like trot; and their clothes, soiled with lime, their aprons and their chisels—all this flickered before him in an inanimate file—a colourful, motley, but dead cinematographic film.

He had to cut across the New Kishenevsky Market. Suddenly the savoury, greasy odour of something roasted compelled him to distend his nostrils. Lichonin recalled that he had not eaten anything since noon yesterday, and at once felt hunger. He turned to the right, into the centre of the market.

In the days of his starvings—and he had had to experience them more than once—he would come here to the market, and for the pitiful coppers, gotten with difficulty, would buy himself bread and fried sausage. This was in winter, oftenest of all. The huckstress, wrapped up in a multiplicity of clothes, usually sat upon a pot of coals for warmth; while before her, on the iron dripping-pan, hissed and crackled the thick, home-made sausage, cut into pieces a quarter of a yard in length, plentifully seasoned with garlic. A piece of sausage usually cost ten kopecks, the bread two kopecks.

There were very many folk at market to-day. Even at a distance, edging his way to the familiar, loved stall, Lichonin heard the sounds of music. Having made his way through the crowd, which in a solid ring surrounded one of the stalls, he saw a naive and endearing sight, which may be seen only in the blessed south of Russia. Ten or fifteen huckstresses, during ordinary times gossips of evil tongue and addicted to unrestrainable swearing, inexhaustible in its verbal diversity, but now, evidently, flattering and tender cronies, had started celebrating even since last evening; had caroused the whole night through and now had carried their noisy merrymaking out to the market. The hired musicians—two fiddles, a first and a second, and a tambourine—were strumming a monotonous but a lively, bold, daring and cunning tune. Some of the wives were clinking glasses and kissing each other, pouring vodka over one another; others poured it out into glasses and over the tables; others still, clapping their palms in time with the music, oh'd, squealed, and danced, squatting in one place. And in the middle of the ring, upon the cobbles of the pavement, a stout woman of about forty-five, but still handsome, with red, fleshy lips, with humid, intoxicated, seemingly unctuous eyes, merrily sparkling from under the high bows of black, regular, Little Russian eyebrows, was whirling around and stamping out a tattoo on one spot. All the beauty and all the art of her dance consisted in that she would now bow her little head and look out provokingly from under her eyebrows, then suddenly toss it back and let her eyelashes down and spread her hands out at her sides; and also in that in measure with the dance her enormous breasts swayed and quivered under her red calico waist. During the dance she was singing, now shuffling her heels, now the toes, of her goat-skin shoes:

> "The fiddle's playing on the street,
>   You can hear its bass so sweet;
>   My mother has me locked up neat,
>   My waitin' dearie I can't meet."

That was the very country-wife whom Lichonin knew; the self-same who not only had had him for a client during hard times, but had even extended him credit. She suddenly recognized Lichonin, darted to him, embraced him, squeezed him to her bosom and kissed him straight on his lips with her moist, warm, thick lips. Then she spread her arms out wide, smote one palm against the other, intertwined her fingers, and sweetly, as only Podolian wives can do it, began to coo:

"My little master, my little silver gold trove, my lovie! You forgive a drunken wife like me, now. Well, what of it? I've gone on a spree!" She then darted at him in an attempt to kiss his hand. "But then, I know you ain't proud, like other gentry. Well, give me your hand, dearie-dear; why, I want to kiss your little hand! No, no, no! I athk, I athk you!.."

"Well, now, that's nonsense, Aunt Glycera!" Lichonin interrupted her, unexpectedly becoming animated. "Let's best kiss just so, now. Your lips are just too sweet!"

"Ah, my little sweetheart! My little bright sun, my little apple of paradise, you," Glycera waxed tender, "give me your lips, then! Give me your little lips to buss, then!..."

She pressed him warmly to her gigantean bosom and again slavered over him with her moist, warm, Hottentot lips. After that, she seized him by his sleeve, brought him out into the middle of the ring, and began to walk around him with a stately, mincing step, having bent her waist coquettishly and vociferating:

"Oh, each to his taste, I want Paraska more,
   For I've a divel in my pants
   Her skirt holds somethin' for!"

And then suddenly she passed on, sustained by the musicians, to a most rollicking, Little Russian, thumping *hopak* dance:

"Oh, Chook, that is too much,
   You have soiled your apron too much.
   Well, Prisko, don't you fret,
   Wipe it off, then, if you're wet!
      Tralala, tralala...

Sleeps, Khima, and won't stir
That a Kossack sleeps with her,
You feel all, Khima—why deceive?
Just to yourself you make believe.
      Tai, tai, tralalai..."

Lichonin, completely grown merry, suddenly began jumping like a goat about her, just like a satellite around a whirling planet—long-legged, long-armed, stooping and altogether incongruous. His entrance was greeted by a general but pretty friendly neighing. He was made to sit down at the table, was helped to vodka and sausage. He, for his part, sent a tramp he knew after beer, and, glass in hand, delivered three absurd speeches: one about the self-determination of Ukraine; another about the goodness of Little Russian sausage, in connection with the beauty and domesticity of the women of Little Russia; and the third, for some reason, about trade and industry in the south of Russia. Sitting alongside of Lukeriya, he was all the time trying to embrace her around the waist, and she did not oppose this. But even his long arms could not encompass her amazing waist. However, she clasped his hand power-fully under the table, until it hurt, with her enormous, soft hand, as hot as fire.

At this moment among the huckstresses, who up to now had been tenderly kissing, certain old, unsettled quarrels and grievances flickered up. Two of the wives, bending toward each other just like roosters ready to enter battle, their arms akimbo, were pouring upon each other the most choice, out-of-the-way oaths:

"Fool, stiff, daughter of a dog!" one was yelling. "Youse ain't fit to kiss me right here." And, turning her back around to her foe, she loudly slapped herself below the spine. "Right here! Here!"

While the other, infuriated, squealed in answer:

"You lie, you slut, for I am fit, I am fit!"

Lichonin utilized the minute. As though he had just recalled something, he hurriedly jumped up from the bench and called out:

"Wait for me, Aunty Luckeriya, I'll come in three minutes!" and dived through the living ring of spectators.

"Master! Master!" his neighbor cried after him: "Come back the quickest you can, now! I've one little word to say to you."

Having turned the corner, he for some time racked his head trying to recall what it was that he absolutely had to do, now, this very minute. And again, in the very depths of his soul, he knew just what he had to do, but he pro-crastinated confessing this to his own self. It was already a clear, bright day, about nine or ten o'clock. Janitors were watering the streets with rubber hose. Flower girls were sitting on the squares and near the gates of the boulevards, with roses, stock-gillyflowers and narcissi. The radiant, gay, rich southern town was beginning to get animated. Over the pavement jolted an iron cage filled with dogs of every possible colour, breed, and age. On the coach box were sitting two dog-catchers, or, as they deferentially style themselves, "the king's dog-catchers"—i. e., hunters of stray dogs—returning home with this morning's catch.

"She must be awake by now," Lichonin's secret thought finally took form; "but if she isn't yet awake, then I'll quietly lie down on the divan and sleep a little."

In the corridor the dying kerosene lamp emitted a dim light and smoked as before, and the watery, murky half light penetrated into the narrow, long box. The door of the room had remained unlocked, after all. Lichonin opened it without a sound and entered.

The faint, blue half light poured in through the interstices between the blinds and the windows. Lichonin stopped in the middle of the room and with an intensified avidity heard the quiet, sleeping breathing of Liubka. His lips became so hot and dry that he had to lick them incessantly. His knees began to tremble.

"Ask if she needs anything," suddenly darted through his head.

Like a drunkard, breathing hard, with mouth open, staggering on his shaking legs, he walked up to the bed.

Liubka was sleeping on her back, with one bare arm stretched out along the body, and the other on her breast. Lichonin bent nearer, to her very face. She was breathing evenly and deeply. This breathing of her young, healthy body was, despite sleep, pure and almost aromatic. He cautiously ran his fingers over her bare arm and stroked her breast a little below the clavicle. "What am I doing?" his reason suddenly cried out within him in terror; but some one else answered for Lichonin: "But I'm not doing anything. I only want to ask if she's sleeping comfortably, and whether she doesn't want some tea."

But Liubka suddenly awoke, opened her eyes, blinked them for a moment and opened them again. She gave a long, long stretch, and with a kindly, not yet fully reasoning smile, encircled Lichonin's neck with her warm, strong arm.

"Sweetie! Darling!" caressingly uttered the woman in a crooning voice, somewhat hoarse from sleep. "Why, I was waiting for you and waiting, and even became angry. And after that I fell asleep and all night long saw you in my sleep. Come to me, my baby, my lil' precious!" She drew him to her, breast against breast.

Lichonin almost did not resist; he was all atremble, as from a chill, and meaninglessly repeating in a galloping whisper with chattering teeth:

"No, now, Liuba, don't... Really, don't do that, Liuba ...Ah, let's drop this, Liuba... Don't torture me. I won't vouch for myself... Let me alone, now, Liuba, for God's sake!.."

"My-y little silly!" she exclaimed in a laughing, joyous voice. "Come to me, my joy!"—and, overcoming the last, altogether insignificant opposition, she pressed his mouth to hers and kissed him hard and warmly—kissed him sincerely, perhaps for the first and last time in her life.

"Oh, you scoundrel! What am I doing?" declaimed some honest, prudent, and false body in Lichonin.

"Well, now? Are you eased up a bit?" asked Liubka kindly, kissing Lichonin's lips for the last time. "Oh, you, my little student!.."

CHAPTER XII.

With pain at soul, with malice and repulsion toward himself and Liubka, and, it would seem, toward all the world, Lichonin without undressing flung himself upon the wooden, lopsided, sagging divan and even gnashed his teeth from the smarting shame. Sleep would not come to him, while his thoughts revolved around this fool action—as he himself called the carrying off of Liubka, —in which an atrocious vaudeville had been so disgustingly intertwined with a deep drama. "It's all one," he stubbornly repeated to himself. "Once I have given my promise, I'll see the business through to the end. And, of course, that which has occurred just now will never, never be repeated! My God, who hasn't fallen, giving in to a momentary laxity of the nerves? Some philosopher or other has expressed a deep, remarkable truth, when he affirmed that the value of the human soul may be known by the depth of its fall and the height of its flight. But still, the devil take the whole of this idiotical day and that equivocal reasoner—the reporter Platonov, and his own— Lichonin's—absurd outburst of chivalry! Just as though, in reality, this had not taken place in real life, but in Chernishevski's novel, *What's to be done?* And how, devil take it, with what eyes will I look upon her tomorrow?"

His head was on fire; the eyelids were smarting, the lips dry. He was nervously smoking a cigarette and frequently got up from the divan to take the decanter of water off the table, and avidly, straight from its mouth, drink several big draughts. Then, by some accidental effort of the will, he succeeded in tearing his thoughts away from the past night, and at once a heavy sleep, without any visions and images, enveloped him as though in black cotton.

He awoke long past noon, at two or three o'clock; at first could not come to himself for a long while; smacked his lips and looked around the room with glazed, heavy eyes. All that had happened during the night seemed to have flown out of his memory. But when he saw Liubka, who was quietly and motionlessly sitting on the bed, with head lowered and hands crossed on her knees, he began to groan and grunt from vexation and confusion. Now he recalled everything. And at that minute he experienced in his own person how heavy it is to see in the morning, with one's own eyes, the results of folly committed the night before.

"Are you awake, sweetie?" asked Liubka kindly.

She got up from the bed, walked up to the divan, sat down at Lichonin's feet, and cautiously patted his blanket-covered leg.

"Why, I woke up long ago and was sitting all the while; I was afraid to wake you up. You were sleeping so very soundly!"

She stretched toward him and kissed him on the cheek. Lichonin made a wry face and gently pushed her away from him.

"Wait, Liubochka! Wait; that's not necessary. Do you understand—absolutely, never necessary. That which took place yesterday—well, that's an accident. My weakness, let's say. Even more, a momentary baseness, perhaps. But, by God, believe me, I didn't at all want to make a mistress out of you. I want to see you my friend, my sister, my comrade... Well, that's nothing, then; everything will adjust itself, grow customary. Only one mustn't fall in spirit. And in the meanwhile, my dear, go to the window and look out of it a bit; I just want to put myself in order."

Liubka slightly pouted her lips and walked off to the window, turning her back on Lichonin. All these words about friendship, brotherhood and comradeship she could not understand with her brain of a hen and her simple peasant soul. That a student—after all, not just anybody, but an educated man, who could learn to be a doctor, or a lawyer, or a judge—had taken her on maintenance flattered her imagination far more... And here, now, it turned out that he had just fulfilled his caprice, had gotten what he wanted, and was now trying to back out. They are all like that, the men!

Lichonin hastily got up, splashed a few handfuls of water in his face, and dried himself with an old napkin. Then he raised the blinds and threw open both window shutters. The golden sunlight, the azure sky, the rumble of the city, the foliage of the thick linden trees and the chestnuts, the bells of the horse trams, the dry smell of the hot, dusty street—all this at once burst into the tiny garret room. Lichonin walked up to Liubka and amicably patted her on the shoulder.

"Never mind, my joy... What's done can't be undone, but it's a lesson for the future. You haven't yet asked tea for yourself, Liubochka?"

"No, I was waiting for you all the while. Besides, I didn't know who to ask. And you're all right, too. Why, I heard you, after you went off with your friend, come back and stand a while near the door. But you never even said good-bye to me. Is that right?"

"The first family quarrel," thought Lichonin, but thought it without malice, in jest.

The wash-up, the beauty of the gold and blue southern sky, and the naive, partly submissive, partly displeased face of Liubka, as well as the consciousness that after all he was a man, and that he and not she had to answer for the porridge he had cooked—all this together braced up his nerves and compelled him to take himself in hand. He opened the door and roared into the darkness of the stinking corridor:

"Al-lexa-andra! A samova-ar! Two lo-oaves, bu-utter, and sausage! And a small bottle of vo-odka!"

The patter of slippers was heard in the corridor, and an aged voice, even from afar, began to speak thickly:

"What are you bawling for? What are you bawling for, eh? Ho, ho, ho! Like a stallion in a stall. You ain't little, to look at you; you're grown up already, yet you carry on like a street boy! Well, what do you want?"

Into the room walked a little old woman, with red-lidded eyes, like little narrow cracks, and with a face amazingly like parchment, upon which a long, sharp nose stuck downward, morosely and ominously. This was Alexandra, the servant of old of the student bird-houses; the friend and creditor of all the students; a woman of sixty-five, argumentative, and a grumbler.

Lichonin repeated his order to her and gave her a rouble note. But the old woman would not go away; shuffled in one place, snorted, chewed with her lips and looked inimically at the girl sitting with her back to the light.

"What's the matter with you now, Alexandra, that you seem ossified?" asked Lichonin, laughing. "Or are you lost in admiration? Well, then, know: this is my cousin, my first cousin, that is—Liubov..."* he was confused for only a second, but immediately fired away: "Liubov Vasilievna, but for me—simply Liubochka. I've known her when she was only that high," he showed a quarter of a yard off the table. "And I pulled her ears and slapped her for her caprices over the place where the legs grow from. And then... I caught all sorts of bugs for her... But, however... However, you go on, go on, you Egyptian mummy, you fragment of former ages! Let one leg be here and the other there!"

But the old woman lingered. Stamping all around herself, she barely, barely turned to the door and kept a keen, spiteful, sidelong glance on Liubka. And at the same time she muttered with her sunken mouth:

"First cousin! We know these first cousins! There's lots of them walking around Kashtanovaya Street. There, these he-dogs can never get enough!"

---

*Love.—*Trans.*

"Well, you old barque! Lively and don't growl!" Lichonin shouted after her. "Or else, like your friend, the student Triassov, I'll take and lock you up in the dressing room for twenty-four hours!"

Alexandra went away, and for a long time her aged, flapping steps and indistinct muttering could be heard in the corridor. She was inclined, in her austere, grumbling kindliness, to forgive a great deal to the studying youths, whom she had served for nigh unto forty years. She forgave drunkenness, card playing, scandals, loud singing, debts; but, alas! she was a virgin, and there was only one thing her continent soul could not abide—libertinage.

CHAPTER XIII.

"And that's splendid... And fine and charming," Lichonin was saying, bustling about the lame table and without need shifting the tea things from one place to another. "For a long time, like an old crocodile, I haven't drunk tea as it should be drunk, in a Christian manner, in a domestic setting. Sit down, Liuba, sit down my dear, right here on the divan, and keep house. Vodka, in all probability, you don't drink of a morning, but I, with your permission, will drink some... This braces up the nerves right off. Make mine a little stronger, please, with a piece of lemon. Ah, what can taste better than a glass of hot tea, poured out by charming feminine hands?"

Liubka listened to his chatter, a trifle too noisy to seem fully natural; and her smile, in the beginning mistrusting, wary, was softening and brightening. But she did not get on with the tea especially well. At home, in the back-woods village, where this beverage was still held a rarity, the dainty luxury of well-to-do families, to be brewed only for honoured guests and on great holidays—there over the pouring of the tea officiated the eldest man of the family. Later, when Liubka served with "all found" in the little provincial capital city, in the beginning at a priest's, and later with an insurance agent (who had been the first to put her on the road of prostitution)—she was usually left some strained, tepid tea, which had already been drunk off, with a bit of gnawn sugar, by the mistress herself— the thin, jaundiced, malicious wife of the priest; or the wife of the agent, a fat, old, wrinkled, malignant, greasy, jealous and stingy common woman. Therefore, the simple business of preparing the tea was now as difficult for her as it is difficult for all of us in childhood to distinguish the left hand from the right, or to tie a rope into a small noose. The bustling Lichonin only hindered her and threw her into confusion.

"My dear, the art of brewing tea is a great art. It ought to be studied at Moscow. At first a dry tea-pot is slightly warmed up. Then the tea is put into it and is quickly scalded with boiling water. The first liquid must at once be poured off into the slop-bowl—the tea thus becomes purer and more aromatic; and by the way, it's also known that Chinamen are pagans and prepare their herb very filthily. After that the tea-pot must be filled anew, up to a quarter of its volume; left on the tray, covered over with a towel and kept so for three and a half minutes. Afterwards pour in more boiling water almost up to the top, cover it again, let it stay just a bit, and you have ready, my dear, a divine beverage; fragrant, refreshing, and strengthening."

The homely, but pleasant-looking face of Liubka, all spotted from freckles, like a cuckoo's egg, lengthened and paled a little.

"Well, for God's sake, don't you be angry at me... You're called Vassil Vassilich, isn't that so? Don't get angry, darling Vassil Vassilich. Really, now, I'll learn fast, I'm quick. And why do you say you and you* to me all the time? It seems that we aren't strangers now?"

She looked at him kindly. And truly, she had this morning, for the first time in all her brief but distorted life, given her body to a man—even though without enjoyment but more out of gratitude and pity, yet voluntarily—not for money, not under compulsion, not under threat of dismissal and scandal. And her feminine heart, always unwithering, always drawn to love, like a sunflower to the sun, was at this moment pure and inclined to tenderness.

But Lichonin suddenly felt a prickling, shameful awkwardness and something inimical toward this woman, yesterday unknown to him, now—his chance mistress.

---

*In contradistinction to "thou", as used to familiars and inferiors in Russia.—*Trans*.

"The charms of the family hearth have begun," he thought involuntarily; still, he got up from his chair, walked up to Liubka, and having taken her by the hand, drew her to him and patted her on the head.

"My dear, my darling sister," he said touchingly and falsely; "that which has happened to-day must never more be repeated. In everything only I alone am guilty, and, if you desire, I am ready to beg forgiveness of you on my knees. Understand—oh, understand, that all this came about against my will, somehow elementally, suddenly, unexpectedly. And I myself didn't think that it would be like that! You understand, for a very long time... I have not known woman intimately... A repulsive, unbridled beast awoke within me... and... But, Lord, is my fault so great, then? Holy people, anchorites, recluses, ascetics, stylites, hermits in deserts, are no match for me in fortitude of spirit—yet even they fell in the struggle with the temptation of the diabolical flesh. But then, I swear by whatever you wish, that this won't be repeated any more... Isn't that so?"

Liubka was stubbornly trying to pull his hand away from hers. Her lips had become a little stuck out and the lowered lids began to wink frequently.

"Ye-es," she drawled, like a child that stubbornly refuses to "make up." "Well, I can see that I don't please you. Well, then, you'd best tell me so straight and give me a little for a cab, and some more, now; as much as you want... The money for the night is paid anyway, and I only have to ride up to...there."

Lichonin seized his hair, flung himself about the room and began to declaim:

"Ah, not that, not that, not that! Just understand me, Liuba! To go on with that which happened in the morning—that's...that's swinishness, bestiality, and unworthy of a man who respects himself. Love! Love—this is a full blending of minds, thoughts, souls, interests, and not of the bodies alone. Love is a tremendous, great emotion, mighty as the universe, and not the sprawling in bed.

There's no such love between us, Liubochka. If it'll come, it will be wonderful happiness both for you and for me. But in the meantime—I'm your friend, your faithful comrade, on the path of life. And that's enough, and that will do... And though I'm no stranger to human frailties, still, I count myself an honest man."

Liubka seemed to wilt. "He thinks I want him to marry me. And I absolutely don't need that," she thought sadly. "It's possible to live just so. There are others, now, living on maintenance. And, they say, far better than if they had twirled around an altar. What's so bad about that? Peaceful, quiet, genteel...I'd darn socks for him, wash floors, cook...the plainer dishes. Of course, he'll be in line to get married to a rich girl some time. Well, now, to be sure, he wouldn't throw me out in the street just so, mother-naked. Although he's a little simpleton, and chatters a lot, still, it's easy to tell he's a decent man. He'll provide for me with something, somehow. And, perhaps, he'll get to like me, will get used to me? I'm a simple girl, modest, and would never consent to be false to him. For, they say, things do fall out that way...Only I mustn't let him see anything. But that he'll come again into my bed, and will come this very night—that's as sure as God is holy."

And Lichonin also fell into thought, grew quiet and sad; he was already feeling the weight of a great deed which he had undertaken beyond his powers. That was why he was even glad when some one knocked on the door, and to his answer, "Come in!" two students entered; Soloviev, and Nijeradze, who had slept that night at his place.

Soloviev, well-grown and already obese, with a broad, ruddy Volga face and a light, scandent little beard, belonged to those kindly, merry and simple fellows, of which there are sufficiently many in any university. He divided his leisure—and of leisure he had twenty-four hours in the day—between the beer-shop and rambling over the boulevards; among billiards, whist, the theatre, reading of newspapers and novels, and the spectacles of circus wrestling; while the short intervals in between he used for eating, sleeping, the home repair of his wardrobe, with the aid of thread, cardboard, pins and ink; and for succinct, most realistic love with the chance woman from the kitchen, the anteroom or the street. Like all the youths of his circle, he deemed himself a revolutionary, although he was oppressed by political disputes, dissensions, and mutual reproaches; and not being able to stand the reading of revolutionary brochures and journals, was almost a complete ignoramus in the work. For that reason he had not attained even the very least party initiation; although at times there were given him instructions of a sort, not at all of a safe nature, the meaning of which was not made clear to him. And not in vain was his steadfast faithfulness relied upon; he carried out everything rapidly, exactly, with a courageous faith in the universal importance of the work; with a care-free smile and with a broad contempt of possible destruction. He concealed outlawed comrades, guarded forbidden literature and printing types, transmitted passports and money. He had a great deal of physical strength, black-loam amiability and elemental simple-heartedness. Not infrequently he would receive from home, somewheres in the depth of the Simbirskaya or Ufimskaya province, sums of money sufficiently large for a student; but in two days he scattered and dispersed it everywhere, with the carelessness of a French grandee of the seventeenth century, while he himself remained during winter in only his everyday coat, with boots restored by his own devices.

Beside all these naive, touching, laughable, lofty and shiftless qualities of the old Russian student, passing—and God knows if for the better?—into the realm of historical memories, he possessed still another amazing ability—to invent money and arrange for credit in little restaurants and cook-shops. All the employees of pawnshops and loan offices, secret and manifest usurers, and old-clo'-men were on terms of the closest friendship with him.

But if for certain reasons he could not resort to them, then even here Soloviev remained at the height of his resourcefulness. At the head of a knot of impoverished friends, and weighed down with his usual business responsibility, he would at times be illumined by an inner inspiration; make at a distance, across the street, a mysterious sign to a Tartar passing with his bundle behind his shoulders, and for a few seconds would disappear with him into the nearest gates. He would quickly return without his everyday coat, only in his blouse with the skirts outside, belted with a thin cord; or, in winter, without his overcoat, in the thinnest of small suits; or instead of the new, just purchased uniform cap—in a tiny jockey cap, holding by a miracle on the crown of his head.

Everybody loved him: comrades, servants, women, children. And all were familiar with him. He enjoyed especial good-will from his bosom cronies, the Tartars, who, apparently, deemed him a little innocent. They would sometimes, in the summer, bring as a present the strong, intoxicating *koumyss* in big quartern bottles, while at Bairam they would invite him to eat a suckling colt with them. No matter how improbable it may seem, still, Soloviev at critical moments gave away for safe-keeping certain books and brochures to the Tartars. He would say at this with the most simple and significant air: "That which I am giving you is a Great Book. It telleth, that Allah Akbar, and that Mahomet is his prophet, that there is much evil and poverty on earth, and that men must be merciful and just to each other."

He also had two other abilities: he read aloud very well; and played at chess amazingly, like a master, like a downright genius, defeating first-class players in jest. His attack was always impetuous and rigorous; his defense wise and cautious, preferably in an oblique direction; his concessions to his opponent full of refined, far-sighted calculation and murderous craftiness. With this, he made moves as though under the influence of some inner instinct, or inspiration; not pondering for more than four or five seconds and resolutely despising the respected traditions.

He was not willingly played with; his manner of play was held barbarous, but still they played, sometimes for large sums of money; which, invariably winning, Soloviev readily laid down upon the altar of his comrades' needs. But he steadfastly declined from participation in competitions, which could have created for him the position of a star in the world of chess: "There is in my nature neither love for this nonsense, nor respect," he would say. "I simply possess some sort of a mechanical ability of the mind, some sort of a psychic deformity. Well, now, just as there are lefties. And for that reason I've no professional self-respect, nor pride at victory, nor spleen at losing."

Such was the generously built student Soloviev. And Nijeradze filled the post of his closest comrade; which did not hinder them both, however, from jeering at each other, disputing, and swearing, from morning till night. God knows, wherewithal and how the Georgian prince existed. He said of himself, that he possessed the ability of a camel, of nourishing himself for the future, for several weeks ahead; and then eating nothing for a month. From home, from his blessed Georgia, he received very little; and then, for the most part, in victuals. At Christmas, at Easter, or on his birthday (in August) he was sent—and inevitably through arriving fellow-countrymen—whole cargoes of hampers with mutton, grapes, goat-flesh, sausages, dried hawthorn berries, *rakhat loukoum*, egg-plants, and very tasty cookies; as well as leathern bottles of excellent home-made wine, strong and aromatic, but giving off just the least bit of sheep-skin. Then the prince would summon together to one of his comrades (he never had quarters of his own) all his near friends and fellow-countrymen; and arranged such a magnificent festival—*toi* in Caucasian— that at it were extirpated to the last shred the gifts of fertile Georgia. Georgian songs were sung, the first place, of course, being given to *Mravol-djamiem* and *Every guest is sent down to us from Heaven by God, no matter of what country he be;* the *Lezginka* was danced without tiring, with table knives brandished wildly in the air; and the *tulum-bash* (or, perhaps, he is called *tomada*?) spoke his improvisations; for the greater part Nijeradze himself spoke.

He was a great hand at talking and could, when he warmed up, pronounce about three hundred words a minute. His style was distinguished for mettle, pomp, and imagery; and his Caucasian accent with characteristic lisping and throaty sounds, resembling now the hawking of a woodcock, now the clucking of an eagle, not only did not hinder his discourse, but somehow even strangely adorned it. And no matter of what he spoke, he always led up the monologue to the most beautiful, most fertile, the very foremost, most chivalrous, and at the same time the most injured country—Georgia. And invariably he cited lines from *The Panther's Skin* of the Georgian poet Rustavelli; with assurances, that this poem was a thousand times above all of Shakespeare, multiplied by Homer.

Even though he was hot-headed, he was not spiteful; and in his demeanour femininely soft, gentle, engaging, without losing his native pride... One thing only did his comrades dislike in him—some exaggerated, exotic love of women. He was unshakably, unto sacredness or folly, convinced that he was irresistibly splendid of person; that all men envied him, all women were in love with him, while husbands were jealous... This self-conceited, obtrusive dangling after women did not forsake him for a minute, probably not even in his sleep. Walking along the street he would every minute nudge Lichonin, Soloviev or some other companion with his elbow, and would say, smacking his lips and jerking his head backward at a woman who had passed by: "*Tse, tse, tse...vai-vai!* A ree-markable wooman! What a look she gave me. If I wish it, she'll be mine!.."

This funny shortcoming about him was known; this trait of his was ridiculed good-naturedly and unceremoniously, but willingly forgiven for the sake of that indepen-

dent comradely obligingness and faithfulness to his word,
given to a man (oaths to women did not count), of which
he was so naturally possessed. However, it must be said
that he did in reality enjoy great success with women.
Sempstresses, modistes, chorus girls, girls in candy stores,
and telephone girls melted from the intense gaze of his
heavy, soft, and languishing dark-blue eyes.

"Un-to this house and all those righteously, peacefully
and without sin inhabiting it..." Soloviev started in to
vociferate like an arch-deacon and suddenly missed fire.
"Father-prelates," he began to murmur in astonishment,
trying to continue the unsuccessful jest. "Why, but this
is... This is...ah, the devil...this is Sonya, no, my
mistake, Nadya... Well, yes! Liubka from Anna Markovna's..."

Liubka blushed hotly, to the verge of tears, and covered
her face with her palms. Lichonin noticed this, understood, sensed the thoroughly agitated soul of the girl, and
came to her aid. He sternly, almost rudely, stopped
Soloviev.

"Perfectly correct, Soloviev. As in a directory. Liubka
from the Yamkas. Formerly a prostitute. Even more,
still yesterday a prostitute. But from to-day—my friend,
my sister. And so let everyone, who respects me to any
extent, regard her. Otherwise..."

The ponderous Soloviev hurriedly, sincerely, and powerfully embraced and rumpled Lichonin.

"Well, dear fellow, well, that's enough... I committed
a stupidity in the flurry. It won't be repeated any more.
Hail, my pale-faced sister." He extended his hand with a
broad sweep across the table to Liubka, and squeezed her
listless, small and short fingers with gnawed, tiny nails.
It's fine—your coming into our modest wigwam. This
will refresh us and implant in our midst quiet and decent
customs. Alexandra! Be-er!" he began to call loudly.
"We've grown wild, coarse; have become mired in foul
speech, drunkenness, laziness and other vices. And all
because we were deprived of the salutary, pacifying influ-

ence of feminine society. Once again I press your hand. Your charming, little hand. Beer!"

"Coming," the displeased voice of Alexandra could be heard on the other side of the door. "I'm coming. What you yelling for? How much you want?"

Soloviev went out into the corridor to explain. Lichonin smiled after him gratefully; while the Georgian on his way slapped him benignly on the back, between his shoulder blades. Both understood and appreciated the belated, somewhat coarse delicacy of Soloviev.

"Now," said Soloviev, coming back into the room and sitting down cautiously upon an ancient chair, "now let's come to the order of the day. Can I be of service to you in any way? If you'll give me half an hour's time, I'll run down to the coffee house for a minute and lick the guts out of the very best chess player there. In a word—I'm at your disposal!"

"What a funny fellow you are!" said Liubka, ill at ease and laughing. She did not understand the jocose and unusual style of speech of the student, but something drew her simple heart to him.

"Well, that's not at all necessary," Lichonin put in. "I am as yet beastly rich. I think we'll all go together to some little tavern somewhere. I must have your advice about some things. After all, you're the people closest to me; and of course not as stupid and inexperienced as you seem at first glance. After that, I'll go and try to arrange about her...about Liuba's passport. You wait for me. That won't take long... In a word, you understand what this whole business consists of, and won't be lavish of any superfluous jokes. I,"—his voice quivered sentimentally and falsely—"I desire that you take upon yourselves a part of my care. Is that a go?"

"*Va!* It's a go!" exclaimed the prince (it sounded like "idiot," when he said it*), and for some reason looked significantly at Liubka and twirled his moustache. Li-

---

*The Russian phrase is "Eedët!"—*Trans.*

chonin gave him a sidelong look.   As for Soloviev, he said simple-heartedly:

"That's the way.   You've begun something big and splendid, Lichonin.   The prince told me about it during the night.   Well, what of it, that's what youth is for—to commit sacred follies.   Give me the bottle, Alexandra, I'll open it myself, or else you'll rupture yourself and burst a vein.   To a new life, Liubochka, pardon me...Liubov... Liubov..."

"Nikonovna.   But call me just as it comes...Liuba."

"Well, yes, Liuba.   Prince, *Allahverdi!*"

"*Yakshi-ol,*" answered Nijeradze and clinked his glass of beer with him.

"And I'll also say, that I rejoice over you, friend Lichonin," continued Soloviev, setting down his glass and licking his moustache.   "Rejoice, and bow before you. It's precisely you, only, who are capable of such a genuinely Russian heroism, expressed simply, modestly, without superfluous words."

"Drop it...   Well, where's the heroism?" Lichonin made a wry face.

"That's true, too," confirmed Nijeradze.   "You're reproaching me all the time that I chatter a lot, but see what nonsense you're spouting yourself."

"That makes no difference!" retorted Soloviev.   "It may be even grandiloquent, but still that makes no difference!   As an elder of our garret commune, I declare Liuba an honourable member with full rights!"   He got up, made a sweeping gesture with his hand, and uttered with pathos:

"And into our house, free and fearless,
    Its charming mistress walk thou in!"

Lichonin recalled vividly, that to-day at dawn he had spoken the very same phrase, like an actor; and even blinked his eyes from shame.

That's enough of tom-foolery.   Let's go, gentlemen. Dress yourself, Liuba."

CHAPTER XIV.

It was not far to *The Sparrows* restaurant; some two hundred steps. On the way Liuba, unnoticed, took Lichonin by the sleeve and pulled him toward her. In this wise they lagged a few steps behind Soloviev and Nijeradze, who were walking ahead.

"Then you mean it seriously, my darling Vassil Vassilich?" she asked, looking up at him with her kindly, dark eyes. "You're not playing a joke on me?"

"What jokes can there be here, Liubochka! I'd be the lowest of men if I permitted myself such jokes. I repeat, that to you I am more than a friend, brother, comrade. And let's not talk about it any more. And that which happened to-day toward morning, that, you may be sure, won't be repeated. And I'll rent a separate room for you this very day."

Liubka sighed. Not that she was offended by the chaste resolution of Lichonin, in which, to tell the turth, she believed but badly; but somehow her dark, narrow mind could not even theoretically picture any other attitude of a man toward a woman than the sensual. Besides that, she experienced the ancient discontent of a preferred or rejected female; a feeling strongly intrenched in the house of Anna Markovna, in the form of boastful rivalry, but now dulled; yet still angry and sincere. And for some reason she believed Lichonin but illy, unconsciously seizing much of the assumed, not altogether sincere, in his words. Soloviev, now—although he did speak incomprehensibly, like the rest of the majority of the students known to her, when they joked among themselves or with the young ladies in the general room (by themselves, in the room, all the men without an exception—all as one—said and did one and the same thing)—she would rather believe Soloviev, far more readily and willingly. A certain simplicity shone in his merry, sparkling gray eyes, placed widely apart.

At *The Sparrows* Lichonin was esteemed for his sedateness, kind disposition, and accuracy in money matters. Because of that he was at once assigned a little private room—an honour of which but very few students could boast. The gas burned all day in this room, because light penetrated only through the narrow bottom of a window, cut short by the ceiling. Only the boots, shoes, umbrellas and canes of the people walking by on the sidewalk could be seen through this window.

They had to let still another student, Simanovsky (whom they ran against near the coat room), join the party. "What does he mean, by leading me around as though for a show?" thought Liubka: "it looks like he's showing off before them." And, snatching a free moment, she whispered to Lichonin who had bent over her:

"But why are there so many people, dearie? For I'm so bashful. I can't hold my own in company."

"That's nothing, that's nothing, my dear Liubochka," Lichonin whispered rapidly, tarrying at the door of the cabinet. "That's nothing, my sister; these are all fine people, good comrades. They'll help you, help us both. Don't mind their having fun at times and their silly lying. But their hearts are of gold."

"But it's so very awkward for me; I'm ashamed. All of them already know where you took me from."

"Well, that's nothing, that's nothing! Why, let 'em know!" warmly contradicted Lichonin. "Why be embarrassed with your past, why try to pass it by in silence? In a year you'll look bravely and directly in the eyes of every man and you'll say: 'He who has not fallen, has not gotten up.' Come on, come on, Liubochka!"

While the inelaborate appetizers were being served, and each one was ordering the meal, everybody, save Simanovsky, felt ill at ease and somehow constrained. And Simanovsky himself was partly the reason for this; he was a clean-shaven man, with *pince-nez* and long hair, with head proudly thrown back and with a contemptuous expression on the tight lips, drooping at the corners. He had no intimate. hearty friends among his comrades; but his opinions and judgments had a considerable authoritativeness among them. It is doubtful whether any one of them could explain to himself whence this influence came; whether from his self-assured appearance, his ability to seize and express in general words the dismembered and indistinct things which are dimly sought and desired by the majority, or because he always saved his conclusions for the most appropriate moment. Among any society there are many of this sort of people: some of them act upon the circle through sophistries; others through adamant, unalterable steadfastness of convictions; the third group with a loud mouth; the fourth through a malicious sneer; the fifth simply by silence, which compels the supposition of profound thought behind it; the sixth through a chattering, outward erudition; others still through a slashing sneer at everything that is said...many with the terrible Russian word *yerunda*: "Fiddlesticks!"—"Fiddlesticks!" they say contemptuously in reply to the warm, sincere, probably truthful but clumsily put word. "But why fiddlesticks?" "Because it's twaddle, nonsense," answer they, shrugging their shoulders; and it is as though they did for a man by hitting him with a stone over the head. There are many more sorts of such people, bearing the bell at the head of the meek, the shy, the nobly modest; and often even the big minds; and to their number did Simanovsky belong.

However, toward the middle of the dinner everybody's tongue became loosened—except Liubka's, who kept silent, answered "yes" and "no," and left her food practically untouched. Lichonin, Soloviev, and Nijeradze talked most of all. The first, in a decisive and businesslike manner, trying to hide under the solicitous words something real, inward, prickling and inconvenient. Soloviev, with a puerile delight, with the most sweeping of gestures, hitting the table with his fist. Nijeradze, with a slight doubtfulness and with unfinished phrases, as though he knew that which must be said, but concealed it. The queer fate of the girl, however, had seemingly engrossed, interested them all; and each one, in expressing his opinion, for some reason inevitably turned to Simanovsky. But he kept his counsel for the most part, and looked at each one from under the glasses of the *pince-nez*, raising his head high to do so.

"So, so, so," he said at last, drumming with his fingers upon the table. "What Lichonin has done is splendid and brave. And that the prince and Soloviev are going to meet him half-way is also very good. I, for my part, am ready to co-operate with your beginnings with whatever lies in my power. But will it not be better, if we lead our friend along the path of her natural inclinations and abilities, so to speak? Tell me, my dear," he turned to Liubka, "what do you know, what can you do? Well, now, some kind of work, or something. Sewing, knitting, embroidering or something."

"I don't know anything," said Liubka in a whisper, letting her eyes drop low, all red, squeezing her fingers under the table. "I don't understand anything of this."

"And really, now," interposed Lichonin; "why, we haven't begun the business from the right end. By talking about her in her presence we merely place her in an awkward position. Just see—even her tongue doesn't move from confusion. Let's go, Liubka, I'll escort you home for just a little while, and return in ten minutes. And in the meanwhile we'll think over ways and means here, without you. All right?"

"As for me, I don't mind," almost inaudibly answered Liubka. "I'll do just as you like, Vassil Vassilich. Only I wouldn't like to go home."

"Why so?"

"It's awkward for me there alone. I'd best wait for you on the boulevard, at the very entrance, on a bench."

"Ah, yes!" Lichonin recollected: "It's Alexandra who has inspired her with such a terror. My, but I'll make it hot for this old lizard! Well, let's go, Liubochka."

She timidly, in some sidelong way, put out her hand to each one, folding it like a little spade; and walked out under the escort of Lichonin.

After several minutes he returned and sat down at his place. He felt that something had been said about him during his absence, and he ran his eyes uneasily over his comrades. Then, putting his hands on the table, he began:

"Gentlemen, I know that you're all good, close friends," he gave a quick and sidelong look at Simanovsky, "and responsive people. I heartily beg of you to come to my aid. The deed was done by me in a hurry—this I must confess— but done through a sincere, pure inclination of the heart."

"And that's the main thing," put in Soloviev.

"It's absolutely all one to me what acquaintances and strangers will begin saying about me; but from my intention to save—pardon the fool word, which slipped out— to encourage, to sustain this girl, I will not decline. Of course, I'm able to rent an inexpensive, small room for her; to give her something for board at first; but what's to be done further—that's what presents difficulties to me. The matter, of course; isn't one of money, which I'd always find for her; but, then, to compel her to eat, drink, and with all that to do nothing—that would mean to condemn her to idleness, indifference, apathy; and you know what the end will be then. Therefore, we must think of some occupation for her. And that's the very matter which we must exert our brains about. Make an effort, gentlemen; advise something."

"We must know what she's fitted for," said Simanovsky. "For she must have been doing something before getting into the house."

Lichonin, with an air of hopelessness, spread out his hands.

"Almost nothing. She can sew just the least bit, just like any country lass. Why, she wasn't fifteen when some

246 YAMA

government clerk led her astray. She can sweep up a room, wash a little, and, if you will, cook cabbage soup and porridge. Nothing more, it seems."

"Rather little," said Simanovsky, and clacked his tongue.

"And in addition to that, she's illiterate as well."

"But that's not at all important!" warmly defended Soloviev. "If we had to do with a well-educated girl, or, worse still, with a half-educated one, then only nonsense would result out of all that we're preparing to do, a mere soap-bubble; while here before us is maiden ground, untouched virgin soil."

"He-ee!" Nijeradze started neighing equivocally.

Soloviev, now no longer joking, but with real wrath, pounced upon him:

"Listen, prince! Every holy thought, every good deed, can be made disgusting, obscene. There's nothing clever or worthy in that. If you regard that which we're preparing to do so like a stallion, then there's the door and God be with you. Go away from us!"

"Yes, but you yourself just now in the room..." retorted the prince in confusion.

"Yes, I too," Soloviev at once softened and cooled down. "I popped out with a stupidity and I regret it. But now I willingly admit that Lichonin is a fine fellow and a splendid man; and I'm ready to do everything, for my part. And I repeat, that knowledge of reading and writing is a secondary matter. It is easy to attain it in play. For such an untouched mind to learn reading, writing, counting, and especially without school, of one's free will, is like biting a nut in two. And as far as a manual trade is concerned, through which it would be possible to live and earn one's keep, then there are hundreds of trades, which can be easily mastered in two weeks."

"For instance?" asked the prince.

"Well, for instance... for instance... well, now, for instance, making artificial flowers. Yes, and still better, to get a place as a flower clerk. A charming business, clean and nice."

"Taste is necessary," Simanovsky dropped carelessly.

"There are no inborn tastes, as well as abilities. Otherwise talents would be born only in refined, highly educated society; while artists would be born only to artists, and singers to singers; but we don't see this. However, I won't argue. Well, if not a flower girl, then something else. I, for instance, saw not long ago in a store show window a miss sitting, and some sort of a little machine with foot-power before her."

"*V-va!* Again a little machine!" said the prince, smiling and looking at Lichonin.

"Stop it, Nijeradze," answered Lichonin, quietly but sternly. "You ought to be ashamed."

"Blockhead!" Soloviev threw at him, and continued.

"So, then, the machine moves back and forth, while upon it, on a square frame, is stretched a thin canvas, and really, I don't know how it's contrived, I didn't grasp it; only the miss guides some metallic thingamajig over the screen, and there comes out a fine drawing in vari-coloured silks. Just imagine, a lake, all grown over with pond-lilies with their white corollas and yellow stamens, and great green leaves all around. And on the water two white swans are floating toward each other, and in the background is a dark park with an alley; and all this shows finely, distinctly, as on a picture from life. And I became so interested that I went in on purpose to find out how much it costs. It proved to be just the least bit dearer than an ordinary sewing machine, and it's sold on terms. And any one who can sew a little on a common machine can learn this art in an hour. And there's a great number of charming original designs. And the main thing is that such work is very readily taken for fire-screens, albums, lamp-shades, curtains and other rubbish, and the pay is decent."

"After all, that's a sort of a trade, too," agreed Lichonin, and stroked his beard in meditation. "But, to confess, here's what I wanted to do. I wanted to open up for her...to open up a little cook-shop or dining room, the very tiniest to start with, of course, but one in which all the food is cheap, clean and tasty. For it's absolutely all the same to many students where they dine and what they eat. There are almost never enough places to go round in the students' dining room. And so we may succeed, perhaps, in pulling in all our acquaintances and friends, somehow."

"That's true," said the prince, "but impractical as well; we'll begin to board on credit. And you know what accurate payers we are. A practical man, a knave, is needed for such an undertaking; and if a woman, then one with a pike's teeth; and even then a man must absolutely stick right at her back. Really, it's not for Lichonin to stand at the counter and to watch that somebody shouldn't suddenly wine and dine and slip away."

Lichonin looked straight at him, insolently, but only set his jaws and let it pass in silence.

Simanovsky began in his measured, incontrovertible tone, toying with the glasses of his *pince-nez*:

"Your intention is splendid, gentlemen, beyond dispute. But have you turned your attention to a certain shady aspect, so to speak? For to open a dining room, to start some business—all this in the beginning demands money, assistance—somebody else's back, so to speak. The money is not grudged—that is true, I agree with Lichonin; but then, does not such a beginning of an industrious life, when every step is provided for—does it not lead to inevitable laxity and negligence, and, in the very end, to an indifferent disdain for business? Even a child does not learn to walk until it has flopped down some fifty times. No; if you really want to help this poor girl, you must give her a chance of getting on her feet at once, like a toiling being, and not like a drone. True, there is a great temptation here—the burden of labour, temporary need; but then, if she will surmount this, she will surmount the rest as well."

"What, then, according to you, is she to become—a dish-washer?" asked Soloviev with unbelief.

"Well, yes," calmly retorted Simanovsky. "A dish-washer, a laundress, a cook. All toil elevates a human being."

Lichonin shook his head.

"Words of gold. Wisdom itself speaks with your lips, Simanovsky. Dish-washer, cook, maid, housekeeper... but, in the first place, it's doubtful if she's capable for that; in the second place, she has already been a maid and has tasted all the sweets of masters' bawlings out, and masters' pinches behind doors, in the corridor. Tell me, is it possible you don't know that ninety per cent. of prostitution is recruited from the number of female servants? And, therefore, poor Liuba, at the very first injustice, at the first rebuff, will the more easily and readily go just there where I have gotten her out of; if not even worse, because for her that's customary and not so frightful; and, perhaps, it will even seem desirable after the masters' treatment. And besides that, is it worth while for me— that is, I want to say—is it worth while for all of us, to go to so much trouble, to try so hard and put ourselves out so, if, after having saved a being from one slavery, we only plunge her into another?"

"Right," confirmed Soloviev.

"Just as you wish," drawled Simanovsky with a disdainful air.

"But as far as I'm concerned," said the prince, "I'm ready, as a friend and a curious man, to be present at this experiment and to participate in it. But even this morning I warned you, that there have been such experiments before and that they have always ended in ignominious failure, at least those of which we know personally; while those of which we know only by hearsay are dubious as regards authenticity. But you have begun the business— and go on with it. We are your helpers."

Lichonin struck the table with his palm.

"No!" he exclaimed stubbornly. "Simanovsky is partly right concerning the great danger of a person's being led in leading strings. But I don't see any other way out. In the beginning I'll help her with room and board... find some easy work, buy the necessary accessories for her. Let be what may! And let us do everything in order to educate her mind a little; and that her heart and soul are beautiful, of that I'm sure. I've no grounds for the faith, but I am sure, I almost know. Nijeradze! Don't clown!" he cried abruptly, growing pale. "I've restrained myself several times already at your fool pranks. I have until now held you as a man of conscience and feeling. One more inappropriate witticism, and I'll change my opinion of you; and know, that it's forever."

"Well, now, I didn't mean anything...Really, I... Why go all up in the air, me soul? You don't like that I'm a gay fellow, well, I'll be quiet. Give me your hand, Lichonin, let's drink!"

"Well, all right, get away from me. Here's to your health! Only don't behave like a little boy, you Ossetean ram. Well, then, I continue, gentlemen. If we find anything which might satisfy the just opinion of Simanovsky about the dignity of independent toil, unsustained by anything, then I shall stick to my system: to teach Liuba whatever is possible, to take her to the theatre, to expositions, to popular lectures, to museums; to real aloud to her, give her the possibility of hearing music—comprehensible music, of course. It's understood, I alone won't be able to manage all this. I expect help from you; and after that, whatever God may will."

"Oh, well," said Simanovsky, "the work is new, not threadbare; and how can we know the unknowable—perhaps you, Lichonin, will become the spiritual father of a good being. I, too, offer my services."

"And I! And I!" the other two seconded; and right there, without getting up from the table, the four students worked out a very broad and very wondrous program of education and enlightenment for Liubka.

Soloviev took upon himself to teach the girl grammar
and writing. In order not to tire her with tedious lessons,
and as a reward for successes, he would read aloud for her
artistic fiction, Russian and foreign, easy of comprehen-
sion. Lichonin left for himself the teaching of arithmetic,
geography and history.

While the prince said simple-heartedly, without his
usual facetiousness this time:

"I, my children, don't know anything; while that which
I do know, I know very badly. But I'll read to her the
remarkable production of the great Georgian poet Rustavelli, and translate it line by line. I confess to you, that
I'm not much of a pedagogue: I tried to be a tutor, but
they politely chased me out after only the second lesson.
Still, no one can teach better playing on a guitar, mandolin, and the bagpipes!"

Nijeradze was speaking with perfect seriousness, and for
that reason Lichonin with Soloviev good-naturedly started
laughing; but with entire unexpectedness, to the general
amazement of all, Simanovsky sustained him.

"The prince speaks common sense. To have the mastery of an instrument elevates the æsthetic sense, in any
case; and is even a help in life. And I, for my part, gentlemen...I propose to read with the young person the *Capital* of Marx, and the history of human culture. And to
take up chemistry and physics with her, besides."

If it were not for the customary authority of Simanovsky
and the importance with which he spoke, the remaining
three would have burst into laughter in his face. They
only stared a him, with eyes popping out.

"Well, yes," continued Simanovsky imperturbably,
"I'll show her a whole series of chemical and physical
experiments, which it is possible to carry on at home;
which are always amusing and beneficial to the mind;
and which eradicate prejudices. Incidentally, I'll explain
something of the structure of the world, of the properties
of matter. And as far as Karl Marx is concerned, just

remember, that great books are equally accessible to the understanding both of a scholar and an unlettered peasant, if only comprehensibly presented. And every great thought is simple."

*   *   *

Lichonin found Liubka at the place agreed upon, on a bench of the boulevard. She went home with him very unwillingly. Just as Lichonin had supposed, meeting the grumbling Alexandra was a fearful thing to her, who had long since grown unused to every-day actuality; harsh, and plentiful with all sorts of unpleasantnesses. And besides that, the fact that Lichonin did not want to conceal her past acted oppressively upon her. But she, who had long ago lost her will in the establishment of Anna Markovna, deprived of her personality, ready to follow after the call of every stranger, did not tell him a word and walked after him.

The crafty Alexandra had already managed during this time to run to the superintendent of the houses and to complain to him, that, now, Lichonin had come with some miss, had passed the night with her in the room; but who she is, that Alexandra don't know; that Lichonin says she is his first cousin, like; but did not present a passport. It was necessary to explain things at great length, diffusedly and tiresomely, to the superintendent, a coarse and insolent man, who bore himself to all the tenants in the house as toward a conquered city; and feared only the students slightly, because they gave him a severe rebuff at times. Lichonin propitiated him only when he rented on the spot another room, several rooms away from his, for Liubka; under the very slope of the roof, so that it represented on the inside a sharply cut-off, low, four-sided pyramid, with one little window.

"But still, Mr. Lichonin, just you present the passport to-morrow without fail," said the superintendent insistently at parting. "Since you're a respectable man, hardworking, and you and I are long acquainted, also you pay punctually, I am willing to do it only for you. You know yourself what hard times these are. If some one tells on me, they'll not only fine me, but they can put me out of town as well. They're strict now."

In the evening Lichonin strolled with Liubka through Prince Park, listened to the music playing in the aristocratic club, and returned home early. He escorted Liubka to the door of her room and at once took leave of her; kissing her, however, tenderly on the brow, like a father. But after ten minutes, when he was already lying in bed undressed and reading the statutes of state, Liubka, having scratched on his door like a cat, suddenly entered his room.

"Darling, sweetie! Excuse me for troubling you. Haven't you a needle and thread? But don't get angry at me; I'll go away at once."

"Liuba! I beg of you to go away not at once, but this second. Finally, I demand it!"

"My dearie, my pretty," Liubka began to intone laughably and piteously, "well, what are you yelling at me for all the time?" and, in a moment, having blown upon the candle, she nestled up to him in the darkness, laughing and crying.

"No, Liuba, this must not be. It's impossible to go on like this," Lichonin was saying ten minutes later, standing at the door, wrapped up in his blanket, like a Spanish hidalgo in a cape. "To-morrow at the latest I'll rent a room for you in another house. And, in general, don't let this occur! God be with you, and good night! Still, you must give me your word of honour that our relations will be merely friendly."

"I give it, dearie, I give it, I give it, I give it!" she began to prattle, smiling; and quickly smacked him first on the lips and then on his hand.

The last action was altogether instinctive; and, perhaps, unexpected even to Liubka herself. Never yet in her life had she kissed a man's hand, save a priest's. Perhaps she wanted to express through this her gratitude to Lichonin, and a prostration before him as before a higher being.

CHAPTER XV.

Among Russian intelligents, as has already been noted by many, there is a decent quantity of wonderful people; true children of the Russian land and culture, who would be able heroically, without the quivering of a single muscle, to look straight in the face of death; who are capable for the sake of an idea of bearing unconceivable privations and sufferings, equal to torture; but then, these people are lost before the haughtiness of a doorman; shrink from the yelling of a laundress; while into a police station they enter in an insufferable and timid distress. And precisely such a one was Lichonin. On the following day (yesterday it had been impossible on account of a holiday and the lateness), having gotten up very early and recollecting that to-day he had to take care of Liubka's passport, he felt just as bad as when in former times, as a high-school boy, he went to an examination, knowing that he would surely fall through. His head ached, while his arms and legs somehow seemed another's; in addition, a drizzling and seemingly dirty rain had been falling on the street since morning. "Always, now, when there's some unpleasantness in store, there is inevitably a rain falling," reflected Lichonin, dressing slowly.

It was not especially far from his street to the Yamskaya, not more than two-thirds of a mile. In general, he was not infrequently in those parts, but he had never had occasion to go there in the daytime; and on the way it seemed to him all the time that every one he met, every cabby and policeman, was looking at him with curiosity, with reproach, or with disdain, as though surmising the destination of his journey. As always on a nasty and muggy morning, all the faces that met his eyes seemed pale, ugly, with monstrously underlined defects. Scores of times he imagined all that he would say in the beginning at the house; and later at the station house; and every time the outcome was different. Angry at himself for this premature rehearsal, he would at times stop himself:

"Ah! You mustn't think, you mustn't presuppose what you're going to say. It always turns out far better when it's done right off..."

And then again imaginary dialogues would run through his head:

"You have no right to hold this girl against her wish."

"Yes, but let her herself give notice about going away."

"I act at her instruction."

"All right; but how can you prove this?" and again he would mentally cut himself short.

The city common began, on which cows were browsing; a board sidewalk along a fence; shaky little bridges over little brooklets and ditches. Then he turned into the Yamskaya. In the house of Anna Markovna all the windows were closed with shutters, with openings, in the form of hearts, cut out in the middle. And all of the remaining houses on the deserted street, desolated as though after a pestilence, were closed as well. With a contracting heart Lichonin pulled the bell-handle.

A maid, barefooted, with skirt caught up, with a wet rag in her hand, with face striped from dirt, answered the bell—she had just been washing the floor.

"I'd like to see Jennka," timidly requested Lichonin.

"Well, now, the young lady is busy with a guest. They haven't waked up yet."

"Well, Tamara then."

The maid looked at him mistrustfully.

"Miss Tamara—I don't know... I think she's busy too. But what you want—to pay a visit, or what?"

"Ah, isn't it all the same! A visit, let's say."

"I don't know. I'll go and look. Wait a while."

She went away, leaving Lichonin in the half-dark drawing room. The blue pillars of dust, coming from the openings in the shutters, pierced the heavy obscurity in all directions. Like hideous spots stood out of the gray murkiness the bepainted furniture and the sweetish oleographs on the walls. It smelt of yesterday's tobacco, of dampness, sourness; and of something else peculiar, indeterminate, uninhabited, of which places that are lived in only temporarily always smell in the morning—such as empty theatres, dance-halls, auditoriums. Far off in the city a droshky rumbled intermittently. The wall-clock monotonously ticked behind the wall. In a strange agitation Lichonin walked back and forth through the drawing room and rubbed and kneaded his trembling hands, and for some reason was stooping and felt cold.

"I shouldn't have started all this false comedy," he thought with irritation. "It goes without saying that I've now become the by-word of the entire university. The devil nudged me! And even during the day yesterday it wasn't too late, when she was saying that she was ready to go back. All I had to do was to give her for a cabby and a little pin money, and she'd have gone, and all would have been fine; and I would be independent now, free, and wouldn't be undergoing this tormenting and ignominious state of spirits. But it's too late to retreat now. To-morrow it'll be still later, and the day after to-morrow— still more. Having pulled off one fool stunt, it must be immediately put a stop to; but on the other hand, if you don't do that in time, it draws two others after it, and they—twenty new ones. Or, perhaps, it's not too late now? Why, she's silly, undeveloped, and, probably, a hysteric, like the rest of them. She's an animal, fit only for stuffing herself and for the bed. Oh! The devil!" Lichonin forcefully squeezed his cheeks and his forehead between his hands and shut his eyes. "And if I had but held out against the common, coarse, physical temptation! There, you see for yourself, this has happened twice already; and then it'll go on and on..."

But side by side with these ran other thoughts, opposed to them:

"But then, I'm a man. I am master of my word. For that which urged me on to this deed was splendid, noble, lofty. I remember very well that rapture which seized me when my thought transpired into action! That was a pure, tremendous feeling. Or was it simple an extravagance of the mind, whipped up by alcohol; the consequence of a sleepless night, smoking, and long, abstract conversations?"

And immediately Liubka would appear before him, appear at a distance, as though out of the misty depths of time; awkward, timid, with her homely and endearing face, which had at once come to seem of infinitely close kinship; long, long familiar, and at the same time unpleasant—unjustly, without cause.

"Can it be that I'm a coward and a rag?" cried Lichonin inwardly and wrung his hands. "What am I afraid of, before whom am I embarrassed? Have I not always prided myself upon being sole master of my life? Let's suppose, even, that the phantasy, the extravagance, of making a psychological experiment upon a human soul— a rare experiment, unsuccessful in ninety-nine per cent.— has entered my head. Is it possible that I must render anybody an account in this, or fear anybody's opinion? Lichonin! Look down upon mankind from above!"

Jennie walked into the room, dishevelled, sleepy, in a night jacket on top of a white underskirt.

"A-a!" she yawned, extending her hand to Lichonin. "How d'you do, my dear student! How does your Liubochka feel herself in the new place? Call me in as a guest some time. Or are you spending your honeymoon on the quiet? Without any outside witnesses?"

"Drop the silly stuff, Jennechka. I came about the passport."

"So-o. About the passport," Jennka went into thought. "That is, there's no passport here, but you must take a blank from the housekeeper. You understand, our usual prostitute's blank; and then they'll exchange it for you for a real book at the station house. Only you see, my dear, I will be but ill help to you in this business. They are as like as not to beat me up if I come near a housekeeper or a porter. But here's what you do. You'd best send the maid for the housekeeper; tell her to say that a certain guest, now, a steady one, has come on business; that it's very urgent to see her personally. But you must excuse me—I'm going to back out, and don't you be angry, please. You know yourself—charity begins at home. But why should you hang around by yourself in this here darkness? You'd better go into the cabinet. If you want to, I'll send you beer there. Or, perhaps you want coffee? Or else," and her eyes sparkled slyly, "or else a girlie, perhaps? Tamara is busy, but may be Niura or Verka will do?"

"Stop it, Jennie! I came about a serious and important matter, but you..."

"Well, well, I won't, I won't! I said it just so. I see that you observe faithfulness. That's very noble on your part. Let's go, then."

She led him into the cabinet, and, opening the inner bolt of the shutter, threw it wide open. The daylight softly and sadly splashed against the red and gold walls, over the candelabra, over the soft red velveteen furniture.

"Right here it began," reflected Lichonin with sad regret.

"I am going," said Jennka. "Don't you knuckle down too much before her, and Simeon too. Abuse them for all you're worth. It's daytime now, and they won't dare do anything to you. If anything happens, tell them straight that, now, you're going to the governor immediately and are going to tell on them. Tell 'em, that they'll be closed up and put out of town in twenty-four hours. Bawl 'em out and they get like silk. Well, now, I wish you success."

She went away. After ten minutes had passed, into the cabinet floated Emma Edwardovna, the housekeeper, in a blue satin *pegnoir;* corpulent, with an important face, broadening from the forehead down to the cheeks, just like a monstrous squash; with all her massive chins and breasts; with small, keen eyes, without eyelashes; with thin, malicious, compressed lips. Lichonin, arising, pressed the puffy hand extended to him, studded with rings, and suddenly thought with aversion:

"The devil take it! If this vermin had a soul, if it were possible to read this soul—then how many direct and indirect murders are lurking hidden within it!"

It must be said, that in starting out for the Yamkas, Lichonin, besides money, had fetched a revolver along with him; and on the road, while walking, he had frequently shoved his hand into his pocket and had there felt the chill contact of the metal. He expected affront, violence, and was prepared to meet them in a suitable manner. But, to his amazement, all that he had presupposed and had feared proved a timorous, fantastic fiction. The business was far more simple, more wearisome and more prosaic, and at the same time more unpleasant.

"*Ja, mein Herr*," said the housekeeper indifferently and somewhat loftily, settling into a low chair and lighting a cigarette. "You pay for one night and instead of that took already the girl for one more night and one more day. *Also*, you owe twenty-five more roubles yet. When we let off a girlie for a night we take ten roubles, and for the twenty-four hours twenty-five roubles. That's a tax, like. Don't you want a smoke, young man?" she stretched out her case, and Lichonin, without himself knowing why, took a cigarette.

"I wanted to talk with you about something else entirely."

"O! Don't trouble yourself to speak: I understand everything very well. Probably the young man wants to take these girl, those Liubka, altogether to himself to set her up, or in order to—how do you Russians call it?—in order to safe her? Yes, yes, yes, that happens. Twenty-two years I live in a brothel, and I know, that this happens with very foolish young peoples. But only I assure you, that from this will come nothing out."

"Whether it will come out or whether it won't come out—that is already my affair," answered Lichonin dully, looking down at his fingers, trembling on his knees.

"O, of course, it's your affair, my young student," and the flabby cheeks and majestic chins of Emma Edward- ovna began to jump from inaudible laughter. "From my soul I wish for you love and friendship; but only trouble yourself to tell this nasty creature, this Liubka, that she shouldn't dare to show even her nose here, when you throw her out into the street like a little doggie. Let her croak from hunger under a fence, or go into a half-rouble estab- lishment for the soldiers!"

"Believe me, she won't return. I ask you merely to give me her certificate, without delay."

"The certificate? *Ach*, if you please! Even this very minute. Only I will first trouble you to pay for everything that she took here on credit. Have a look, here is her account book. I took it along with me on purpose. I knew already with what our conversation would end." She took out of the slit of her *pegnoir*—showing Lichonin for just a minute her fat, full-fleshed, yellow, enormous breast—a little book in a black cover, with the heading: *Account of Miss Irene Voschhenkova in the house of ill-fame, maintained by Anna Markovna Shaibes, on Yamskaya Street, No. So-and-so*, and extended it to him across the table. Lichonin turned over the first page and read through four or five paragraphs of the printed rules. There dryly and briefly it was stated that the account book consists of two copies, of which one is kept by the proprie- tress while the other remains with the prostitute; that all income and expense were entered into both books; that by agreement the prostitute receives board, quarters, heat, light, bed linen, baths and so forth, and for this pays out to the proprietress in no case more than two-thirds of her earnings; while out of the remaining money she is bound to dress neatly and decently, having no less than two dresses for going out. Further, mention was made of the fact that payment was made with the help of stamps, which the proprietress gives out to the prostitute upon receipt of money from her; while the account is drawn up at the end of every month. And, finally, that the prostitute can at any time leave the house of prostitution, even if there does remain a debt of hers, which, however, she binds herself to cancel on the basis of general civil laws.

Lichonin prodded the last point with his finger, and, having turned the face of the book to the housekeeper, said triumphantly:

"Aha! There, you see: she has the right to leave the house at any time. Consequently, she can at any time quit your abominable dive of violence, baseness, and depravity, in which you..." Lichonin began rattling off, but the housekeeper calmly cut him short:

"O! I have no doubt of this. Let her go away. Let her only pay the money."

"What about promissory notes? She can give promissory notes."

"Pst! Promissory notes! In the first place, she's illiterate; while in the second, what are her promissory notes worth? A spit and no more. Let her find a surety who would be worthy of trust, and then I have nothing against it."

"But, then, there's nothing said in the rules about sureties."

"There's many a thing not said! In the rules it also does not say that it's permitted to carry a girlie out of the house, without giving warning to the owners."

"But in any case you'll have to give me her blank."

"I will never do such a foolishness! Come here with some respectable person and with the police; and let the police certify that this friend of yours is a man of means; and let this man stand surety for you; and let, besides that, the police certify that you are not taking the girl in order to trade in her, or to sell her over to another establishment—then as you please! Hand and foot!"

"The devil!" exclaimed Lichonin. "But if that surety will be I, I myself! If I'll sign your promissory notes right away..."

"Young man! I don't know what you are taught in your different universities, but is it possible that you reckon me such a positive fool? God grant, that you have, besides those which are on you, still some other pants! God grant, that you should even the day after have for dinner the remnants of sausages from the sausage shop, and yet you say—a promissory note! What are you bothering my head for?"

Lichonin grew completely angry. He drew his wallet out of his pocket and slapped it down on the table.

"In that case I pay in cash and immediately!"

"*Ach*, that's a business of another kind," sweetly, but still with mistrust, the housekeeper intoned. "I will trouble you to turn the page, and see what the bill of your beloved is."

"Keep still, you carrion!"

"I'm still, you fool," calmly responded the housekeeper. On the small ruled pages on the left side was designated the income, on the right were the expenses.

"Received in stamps, 15th of April," read Lichonin, "10 roubles; 16th—4r.; 17th—12r.; 18th—sick; 19th—sick; 20th—6r.; 21st—24r."

"My God!" with loathing, with horror, reflected Lichonin. "Twelve men in one night!"

At the end of the month stood:

"Total 330 roubles."

"Lord! Why, this is some sort of delirium! One hundred and sixty-five visits," thought Lichonin, having mechanically calculated it, and still continued turning the pages. Then he went over to the columns on the right.

"Made, a red dress of silk with lace 84r. Dressmaker Eldokimova. Dressing sack of lace 35r. Dressmaker Eldokimova. Silk stockings 6 pair 36 roubles," &c., &c.

"Given for cab-fare, given for candy, perfumes bought," &c., &c. "Total 205 roubles." After that from the 330r. were deducted 220r.—the share of the proprietress for board and lodging. The figure of 110r. resulted. The end of the monthly account declared:

"Total after the payment to the dressmaker and for other articles, of 110r., a debt of ninety ninety-five (95) roubles remains for Irene Voshshenkova and with the four hundred and eighteen roubles remaining from last year—five hundred and thirteen (513) roubles."

Lichonin's spirits fell. He did try, at first, to be indignant at the expensiveness of the materials supplied; but the housekeeper retorted with *sang froid* that that did not concern her at all; that the establishment demanded only that the girl dress decently, as becomes a girl from a decent, genteel house; while it did not concern itself with the rest. The establishment merely extended her credit in paying her expenses.

"But this is a vixen, a spider in human shape—this dressmaker of yours!" yelled Lichonin beside himself. "Why, she's in a conspiracy with you, cupping glass that you are, you abominable tortoise! Scuttlefish! Where's your conscience?"

The more agitated he grew, the more calm and jeering Emma Edwardovna became.

"Again I repeat: that is not my business. And you, young man, don't express yourself like that, because I will call the porter, and he will throw you out of the door."

Lichonin was compelled to bargain with the cruel woman long, brutally, till he grew hoarse, before she agreed, in the end, to take two hundred and fifty roubles in cash, and two hundred roubles in promissory notes. And even that only when Lichonin with his half-yearly certificate proved to her that he was finishing this year and would become a lawyer.

The housekeeper went after the ticket, while Lichonin took to pacing the cabinet back and forth. He had already looked over all the pictures on the walls: Leda with the swan, and the bathing on the shore of the sea, and the odalisque in a harem, and the satyr, bearing a naked nymph in his arms; but suddenly a small printed placard, framed and behind glass, half covered by a portiere, attracted his attention. It was the first time that it had come across Lichonin's eyes, and the student with amazement and aversion read these lines, expressed in the dead, official language of police stations. There with shameful, business-like coldness, were mentioned all possible measures and precautions against infections; the intimacies of feminine toilet; the weekly medical inspections and all the adaptations for them. Lichonin also read that no establishment was to be situated nearer than a hundred steps from churches, places of learning, and court buildings; that only persons of the female sex may maintain houses of prostitution; that only her relatives, and even then of the female sex exclusively, and none older than seven years, may live with the proprietress; and that the proprietors and the owners of the house, as well as the girls, must in their relations among themselves and the guests as well, observe politeness, quiet, civility and decency, by no means allowing themselves drunkenness, swearing and brawls. And also that the prostitute must not allow herself the caresses of love when in an intoxicated condition or with an intoxicated man; and in addition to that, during the time of certain functions. Here also the prostitutes were most strictly forbidden to commit abortions. "What a serious and moral view of things!" reflected Lichonin with a malicious sneer.

Finally the business with Emma Edwardovna was concluded. Having taken the money and written out a receipt, she stretched it out to Lichonin together with the blank, while he stretched out the money to her; at which, during the time of the operation, they both looked at each other's eyes and hands intently and warily. It was apparent that they both felt no especially great mutual trust. Lichonin put the documents away in his wallet and was preparing to depart. The housekeeper escorted him to the very stoop, and when the student was already standing in the street, she, remaining on the steps, leaned out and called after him:

"Student! Hey! Student!"

He stopped and turned around.

"What now?"

"And here's another thing. Now I must tell you, that your Liubka is trash, a thief, and sick with syphilis! None of our good guests wanted to take her; and anyway, if you had not taken her, then we would have thrown her out to-morrow! I will also tell you, that she had to do with the porter, with policemen, with janitors, and with petty thieves. Congratulations on your lawful marriage!"

"Oo-ooh! Vermin!" Lichonin roared back at her.

"You green blockhead!" called out the housekeeper and banged the door.

Lichonin went to the station house in a cab. On the way he recalled that he had not had time to look at the blank properly, at this renowned "yellow ticket", of which he had heard so much. This was an ordinary small white sheet, no larger than a postal envelope. On one side, in the proper column, were written out the name, father's name, and family name of Liubka, and her profession—"Prostitute"; and on the other side, concise extracts from the paragraphs of that placard which he had just read through—infamous, hypocritical rules about behaviour and external and internal cleanliness. "Every visitor," he read, "has the right to demand from the prostitute the written certificate of the doctor who has inspected her the last time." And again sentimental pity overcame the heart of Lichonin.

"Poor women!" he reflected with grief. "What only don't they do with you, how don't they abuse you, until you grow accustomed to everything, just like blind horses on a treadmill!"

In the station house he was received by the district inspector, Kerbesh. He had spent the night on duty, had not slept his fill, and was angry. His luxurious, fan-shaped red beard was crumpled. The right half of the ruddy face was still crimsonly glowing from lying long on the uncomfortable oilcloth pillow. But the amazing, vividly blue eyes, cold and luminous, looked clear and hard, like blue porcelain. Having ended interrogating, recording, and cursing out with obscenities the throng of ragamuffins, taken in during the night for sobering up and now being sent out over their own districts, he threw himself against the back of the divan, put his hands behind his neck, and stretched with all his enormous, heroic body so hard that all his ligaments and joints cracked. He looked at Lichonin just as at a thing, and asked:

"And what will you have, Mr. Student?"

Lichonin stated his business briefly.

"And so I want," he concluded, "to take her to me... how is this supposed to be done with you?.. in the capacity of a servant, or, if you want, a relative, in a word...how is it done?.."

"Well, in the capacity of a kept mistress or a wife, let's say," indifferently retorted Kerbesh and twirled in his hands a silver cigar case with monograms and little figures. "I can do absolutely nothing for you...at least right now. If you desire to marry her, present a suitable permit from your university authorities. But if you're taking her on maintenance—then just think, where's the logic in that? You're taking a girl out of a house of depravity, in order to live with her in depraved cohabitation."

"A servant, finally," Lichonin put in.

"And even a servant. I'd trouble you to present an affidavit from your landlord—for, I hope, you're not a houseowner? Very well, then, an affidavit from your landlord, as to your being in a position to keep a servant; and besides that, all the documents, testifying that you're that very person you give yourself out to be; an affidavit, for instance, from your district and from the university, and all that sort of thing. For you, I hope, are registered? Or, perhaps, you are now, eh?.. Of the illegal ones?

"No, I am registered!" retorted Lichonin, beginning to lose patience.

"And that's splendid. But the young lady, about whom you're troubling yourself?"

"No, she's not registered as yet. But I have her blank in my possession, which, I hope, you'll exchange for a real passport for me, and then I'll register her at once."

Kerbesh spread his arms out wide, then again began toying with the cigar case.

"Can't do anything for you, Mr. Student, just nothing at all, until you present all the papers required. As far as the girl's concerned, why, she, as one not having the right of residence, will be sent to the police without delay, and there detained; unless she personally desires to go there, where you've taken her from. I've the honour of wishing you good day."

Lichonin abruptly pulled his hat over his eyes and went toward the door. But suddenly an ingenious thought flashed through his head, from which, however, he himself became disgusted. And feeling nausea in the pit of his stomach, with clammy, cold hands, experiencing a sickening pinching in his toes, he again walked up to the table and said as though carelessly, but with a catch in his voice:

"Pardon me, inspector. I've forgotten the most important thing; a certain mutual acquaintance of ours has instructed me to transmit to you a small debt of his."

"Hm! An acquaintance?" asked Kerbesh, opening wide his magnificent azure eyes. "And who may he be?"

"Bar...Barbarisov."

"Ah, Barbarisov? So, so, so, I recollect, I recollect!"

"So then, won't you please accept these ten roubles?"

Kerbesh shook his head, but did not take the bit of paper.

"Well, but this Barbarisov of yours—that is, ours—is a swine. It isn't ten roubles he owes me at all, but a quarter of a century. What a scoundrel! Twenty-five roubles and some small change besides. Well, the small change, of course, I won't count up to him. God be with him! This, you see, is a billiard debt. I must say that he's a blackguard, plays crookedly... And so, young man, dig up fifteen more."

"Well, but you are a knave, Mr. Inspector!" said Lichonin, getting out the money.

"Oh, mercy!" by now altogether good-naturedly retorted Kerbesh. "A wife, children... You know yourself what our salary is... Receive the little passport, young man. Sign your receipt. Best wishes."

*   *   *

A queer thing! The consciousness that the passport was, finally, in his pocket, for some reason suddenly calmed and again braced up and elevated Lichonin's nerves.

"Oh, well!" he thought, walking quickly along the street, "the very beginning has been laid down, the most difficult part has been done. Hold fast, now, Lichonin, and don't fall in spirit! What you've done is splendid and lofty. Let me be even a victim of this deed—it's all one! It's a shame, having done a good deed, to expect rewards for it right away. I'm not a little circus dog, and not a trained camel, and not the first pupil of a young ladies' genteel institute. Only it was useless for me to let loose yesterday before these bearers of enlightenment. It all turned out to be silly, tactless, and, in any case, premature. But everything in life is reparable. A person will sustain the heaviest, most disgraceful things; but, time passes, and they are recalled as trifles..."

To his amazement, Liubka was not especially struck, and did not at all become overjoyed when he triumphantly showed her the passport. She was only glad to see Lichonin again. Perhaps, this primitive, naive soul had already contrived to cleave to its protector? She did throw herself upon his neck, but he stopped her, and quietly, almost in her ear, asked her:

"Liubka, tell me...don't be afraid to tell the truth, no matter what it may be... They told me just now, there

in the house, that you're sick with a certain disease...
you know, that which is called the evil sickness. If you
believe in me even to some extent, tell me, my darling,
tell me, is that so or not?"

She turned red, covered her face with her hands, fell
down on the divan and burst into tears.

"My dearie! Vassil Vassilich! Vasinka! Honest to
God! Honest to God, now, there never was anything of
the kind! I always was so careful! I was awfully afraid
of this. I love you so! I would have told you without
fail." She caught his hands, pressed them to her wet face
and continued to assure him with the absurd and touching
sincerity of an unjustly accused child.

And he at once believed her in his soul.

"I believe you, my child," he said quietly, stroking her
hair. "Don't excite yourself, don't cry. Only let us not
again give in to our weaknesses. Well, it has happened—
let it have happened; but let us not repeat it any more."

"As you wish," prattled the girl, kissing now his hands,
now the cloth of his coat. "If I displease you so, then,
of course, let it be as you wish."

However, this evening also the temptation was again
repeated, and kept on repeating until the falls from grace
ceased to arouse a burning shame in Lichonin, and turned
into a habit, swallowing and extinguishing remorse.

CHAPTER XVI.

Justice must be rendered to Lichonin; he did everything to create for Liubka a quiet and secure existence. Since he knew that they would have to leave their mansard anyway—this bird house, rearing above the whole city—leave it not so much on account of its inconvenience and lack of space as on account of the old woman Alexandra, who with every day became more ferocious, captious and scolding—he resolved to rent a little bit of a flat, consisting of two rooms and a kitchen, on the Borschhagovka, at the edge of the town. He came upon an inexpensive one, for nine roubles a month, without fuel. True, Lichonin had to run very far from there to his pupils, but he relied firmly upon his endurance and health, and would often say:

"My legs are my own. I don't have to be sparing of them."

And, truly, he was a great master at walking. Once, for the sake of a joke, having put a pedometer in his vest pocket, he towards evening counted up twenty versts; which, taking into consideration the unusual length of his legs, equalled some twenty-five versts.* And he did have to run about quite a bit, because the fuss about Liubka's passport and the acquisition of household furnishings of a sort had eaten up all his accidental winnings at cards. He did try to take up playing again, on a small scale at first, but was soon convinced that his star at cards had now entered upon a run of fatal ill luck.

By now, of course, the real character of his relations with Liubka was a mystery to none of his comrades; but he still continued in their presence to act out the comedy of friendly and brotherly relations with the girl. For some reason he could not, or did not want to, realize that it

*A verst is equal to two-thirds of a mile.—*Trans.*

would have been far wiser and more advantageous for him not to lie, not to be false, and not to pretend. Or, perhaps, although he did know this, he still could not change the established tone. As for the intimate relations, he inevitably played a secondary, passive role. The initiative, in the form of tenderness, caressing, always had to come from Liubka (she had remained Liubka, after all, and Lichonin had somehow entirely forgotten that he himself had read her real name—Irene—in the passport).

She, who had so recently given her body up impassively—or, on the contrary, with an imitation of burning passion—to tens of people in a day, to hundreds in a month, had become attached to Lichonin with all her feminine being, loving and jealous; had grown attached to him with body, feeling, thoughts. The prince was funny and entertaining to her, and the expansive Soloviev interestingly amusing; toward the crushing authoritativeness of Simanovsky she felt a supernatural terror; but Lichonin was for her at the same time a sovereign, and a divinity; and, which is the most horrible of all, her property and bodily joy.

It has long ago been observed, that a man who has lived his fill, has been worn out, gnawed and chewed by the jaws of amatory passions, will never again love with a strong and only love, simultaneously self-denying, pure, and passionate. But for a woman there are neither laws nor limitations in this respect. This observation was especially confirmed in Liubka. She was ready to crawl before Lichonin with delight, to serve him as a slave; but, at the same time, desired that he belong to her more than a table, than a little dog, than a night blouse. And he always proved wanting, always failing before the onslaught of this sudden love, which from a modest little stream had so rapidly turned into a river and had overflowed its banks. And not infrequently he thought to himself, with bitterness and a sneer:

"Every evening I play the role of the beauteous Joseph; still, he at least managed to tear himself away, leaving his underwear in the hands of the ardent lady; but when will I at last get free of my yoke?"

And a secret enmity for Liubka was already gnawing him. All the more and more frequently various crafty plans of liberation came into his head. And some of them were to such an extent dishonest, that, after a few hours, or the next day, Lichonin squirmed inwardly from shame, recalling them.

"I am falling, morally and mentally!" he would at times think with horror. "It's not in vain that I read somewhere, or heard from some one, that the connection of a cultured man with a woman of little intellect will never elevate her to the level of the man, but, on the contrary, will bow him down and sink him to the mental and moral outlook of the woman."

And after two weeks she ceased to excite his imagination entirely. He gave in, as to violence, to the long-continued caresses, entreaties, and often even to pity.

Yet at the same time Liubka, who had rested and felt living, real soil under her, began to improve in looks with unusual rapidity, just as a flower bud, that but yesterday was almost dying, suddenly unfolds after a plentiful and warm rain. The freckles ran off her soft face, and the uncomprehending, troubled expression, like that of a young jackdaw, had disappeared from the dark eyes, and they had grown brighter and had begun to sparkle. The body grew stronger and filled out; the lips grew red. But Lichonin, seeing Liubka every day, did not notice this and did not believe those compliments which were showered upon her by his friends. "Fool jokes," he reflected, frowning. "The boys are spoofing."

As the lady of the house, Liubka proved to be less than mediocre. True, she could cook fat stews, so thick that the spoon stood upright in them; prepare enormous, unwieldy, formless cutlets; and under the guidance of Lichonin familiarized herself pretty rapidly with the great art of brewing tea (at seventy-five kopecks a pound); but further than that she did not go, probably because for each art and for each being there are extreme limitations of their own, which cannot in any way be surmounted. But then, she loved to wash floors very much; and carried out this occupation so often and with such zeal, that dampness soon set in in the flat and multipedes appeared.

Tempted once by a newspaper advertisement, Lichonin procured a stocking knitting machine for her, on terms. The art, the mastery of this instrument—promising, to judge by the advertisement, three roubles of clear profit a day—proved to be so uncomplicated that Lichonin, Soloviev, and Nijeradze easily mastered it in a few hours; while Lichonin even contrived to knit a whole stocking of uncommon durability, and of such dimensions that it would have proven big even for the feet of Minin and Pozharsky, whose statues are in Moscow, on Krasnaya Square. Only Liubka alone could not master this trade. At every mistake or tangle she was forced to turn to the co-operation of the men. But then, she learned pretty rapidly to make artificial flowers and, despite the opinion of Simanovsky, made them very exquisitely, and with great taste; so that after a month the hat and specialty stores began to buy her work. And, what is most amazing, she had taken only two lessons in all from a specialist; while the rest she learned through a self-instructor, guiding herself only by the drawings supplemental to it. She did not contrive to make more than a rouble's worth of flowers in a week; but this money was her pride, and for the very first half-rouble that she made she bought Lichonin a mouthpiece for smoking.

Several years later Lichonin confessed to himself at soul, with regret and with a quiet melancholy, that this period of time was the most quiet, peaceful and comfortable one of all his life in the university and as a lawyer. This unwieldy, clumsy, perhaps even stupid Liubka, possessed some instinctive domesticity, some imperceptible ability of creating a bright and easy quietude around her. It was precisely she who attained the fact that Lichonin's quarters very soon became a charming, quiet centre; where

all the comrades of Lichonin, who, as well as the majority
of the students of that time, were forced to sustain a bitter
struggle with the harsh conditions of life, felt somehow at
ease, as though in a family; and rested at soul after heavy
tribulations, need, and starvation. Lichonin recalled with
grateful sadness her friendly complaisance, her modest
and attentive silence, on those evenings around the samovar, when so much had been spoken, argued and dreamt.

In learning, things went with great difficulty. All these
self-styled cultivators, collectively and separately, spoke
of the fact that the education of the human mind, and the
upbringing of the human soul must flow out of individual
motives; but in reality they stuffed Liubka with just that
which seemed to them the most necessary and indispensable, and tried to overcome together with her those
scientific obstacles, which, without any loss, might have
been left aside.

Thus, for example, Lichonin did not want, under any
conditions, to become reconciled, in teaching her arithmetic, to her queer, barbarous, savage, or, more correctly,
childish, primitive method of counting. She counted
exclusively in ones, twos, threes and fives. Thus, for
example, twelve to her was two times two threes; nineteen
—three fives and two twos; and, it must be said, that
through her system she with the rapidity of a counting
board operated almost up to a hundred. To go further
she dared not; and besides she had no practical need of this.
In vain did Lichonin try to transfer her to a digital system.
Nothing came of this, save that he flew into a rage, yelled
at Liubka; while she would look at him in silence, with
astonished, widely open and guilty eyes, the lashes of
which stuck into long black arrows from tears. Also,
through a capricious turn of her mind, she began to master
addition and multiplication with comparative ease, but
subtraction and division were for her an impenetrable wall.
But then, she could, with amazing speed and wit, solve all
possible jocose oral head-breaking riddles, and even remembered very many of them herself from the thousand

year old usage of the village. Toward geography she was perfectly dull. True, she could orientate herself as to the four cardinal points on the street, in the garden, and in the room; hundreds of times better than Lichonin—the ancient peasant instinct in her asserted itself—but she stubbornly denied the sphericity of the earth and did not recognize the horizon; and when she was told that the terrestrial globe moves in space, she only snorted from laughter. Geographical maps to her were always an incomprehensible daubing in several colours; but separate figures she memorized exactly and quickly. "Where's Italy?" Lichonin would ask her. "Here it is, a boot," Liubka would say and triumphantly jabbed the Apennine Peninsula. "Sweden and Norway?" "This dog, which is jumping off a roof." "The Baltic sea?" "A widow standing on her knees." "The Black Sea?" "A shoe." "Spain?" "A fatty in a cap"...&c. With history matters went no better; Lichonin did not take into consideration the fact that she, with her childlike soul thirsting for fiction, would have easily become familiarized with historic events through various funny and heroically touching anecdotes; but he, accustomed to pulling through examinations and tutoring high-school boys of the fourth or fifth grade, starved her on names and dates. Besides that, he was very impatient, unrestrained, irascible; grew fatigued soon, and a secret—usually concealed but constantly growing—hatred for the girl who had so suddenly and incongruously warped all his life, more and more frequently and unjustly broke forth during the time of these lessons.

A far greater success as a pedagogue enjoyed Nijeradze. His guitar and mandolin always hung in the dining room, secured to the nails with ribbons. The guitar, with its soft, warm sounds, drew Liubka more than the irritating, metallic bleating of the mandolin. When Nijeradze would come to them as a guest (three or four times a week, in the evening), she herself would take the guitar down from the wall, painstakingly wipe it off with a handkerchief, and hand it over to him. He, having fussed for some time with

the tuning, would clear his throat, put one leg over the
other, negligently throw himself against the back of the
chair, and begin in a throaty little tenor, a trifle hoarse,
but pleasant and true:

> "The trea-cha-rous sa-ound av akissing
> Resahounds through the quiet night air;
> Tuh all fla-ming hearts it is pleasing,
> And given tuh each lovin' pair.
>
> . . . .
>
> For a single mohoment of mee-ting. . ."

And at this he would pretend to swoon away from his
own singing, shut his eyes, toss his head in the passionate
passages or during the pauses, tearing his right hand away
from the strings; would suddenly turn to stone, and for a
second would pierce Liubka's eyes with his languorous,
humid, sheepish eyes. He knew an endless multitude of
ballads, catches, and old-fashioned, jocose little pieces.
Most of all pleased Liubka the universally familiar
Armenian couplets about Karapet:

> "Karapet has a buffet,
> On the buffet's a confet,
> On the confet's a portret—
> That's the self-same Karapet."*

Of these couplets (in the Caucasus they are called
kinto-uri—the song of the peddlers) the prince knew an
infinite many, but the absurd refrain was always one and
the same:

> "Bravo, bravo, Katenka,
> Katerin Petrovna,
> Don't you kiss me on the cheek-a,
> Kiss the backs of my head."

These couplets Nijeradze always sang in a diminished
voice, preserving on his face an expression of serious
astonishment about Karapet; while Liubka laughed until
it hurt, until tears came, until she had nervous spasms.

---

*Anglice, "confet" is a bon-bon; "portret," a portrait.—*Trans.*

Once, carried away, she could not restrain herself and began to chime in with him, and their singing proved to be very harmonious. Little by little, when she had by degrees completely ceased to be embarrassed before the prince, they sang together more and more frequently. Liubka proved to have a very soft and low contralto, even though thin, on which her past life with its colds, drinking, and professional excesses had left absolutely no traces. And mainly—which was already a curious gift of God—she possessed an instinctive, inherent ability very exactly, beautifully, and always originally, to carry on the second voice. There came a time toward the end of their acquaintance, when Liubka did not beg the prince, but the prince Liubka, to sing some one of the beloved songs of the people, of which she knew a multitude. And so, putting her elbow on the table, and propping up her head with her palm, like a peasant woman, she would start off to the cautious, painstaking, quiet accompaniment:

"Oh, the nights have grown tiresome to me, and
    wearisome;
  To be parted from my dearie, from my mate!
  Oh, haven't I myself, woman-like, done a foolish
    thing—
  Have stirred up the wrath of my own darling:
  When I did call him a bitter drunkard!.."

"Bitter drunkard!" the prince would repeat the last words together with her, and would forlornly toss his curly head, inclined to one side; and they both tried to end the song so that the scarcely seizable quivering of the guitar strings and the voice might by degrees grow quiet, and that it might not be possible to note when the sound ended and the silence came.

But then, in the matter of *The Panther's Skin*, the work of the famous Georgian poet Rustavelli, prince Nijeradze fell down completely. The beauty of the poem, of course, consisted in the way it sounded in the native tongue; but scarcely would he begin to read in sing-song his throaty, sibilant, hawking phrases, when Liubka would at first shake for a long time from irresistible laughter; then, finally, burst into laughter, filling the whole room with explosive, prolonged peals. Then Nijeradze in wrath would slam shut the little tome of the adored writer, and swear at Liubka, calling her a mule and a camel. However, they soon made up.

There were times when fits of goatish, mischievous merriment would come upon Nijeradze. He would pretend that he wanted to embrace Liubka, would roll exaggeratedly passionate eyes at her, and would utter with a theatrically languishing whisper:

"Me soul! The best rosa in the garden of Allah! Honey and milk are upon thy lips, and thy breath is better than the aroma of *cabob*. Give me to drink the bliss of Nirvanah from the goblet of thy lips, O thou, my best Tifflissian she-goat!"

But she would laugh, get angry, strike his hands, and threaten to complain to Lichonin.

"*V-va!*" the prince would spread out his hands. "What is Lichonin? Lichonin is my friend, my brother, and bosom crony. But then, does he know what loffe is? Is it possible that you northern people understand loffe? It's we, Georgians, who are created for loffe. Look, Liubka! I'll show you right away what loffe is!" He would clench his fists, bend his body forward, and would start rolling his eyes so ferociously, gnash his teeth and roar with a lion's voice so, that a childish terror would encompass Liubka, despite the fact that she knew this to be a joke, and she would dash off running into another room.

It must be said, however, that for this lad, in general unrestrained in the matter of light, chance romances, existed special firm moral prohibitions, sucked in with the milk of his mother Georgian; the sacred *adates* concerning the wife of a friend. And then, probably he understood—and it must be said that these oriental men, despite their seeming naiveness—and, perhaps, even owing to it—possess, when they wish to, a fine psychic intuition—he understood, that having made Liubka his mistress for even one minute, he would be forever deprived of this charming, quiet, domestic evening comfort, to which he had grown so used. For he, who was on terms of thou-ing with almost the whole university, nevertheless felt himself so lonely in a strange city and in a country still strange to him!

These studies afforded the most pleasure of all to Soloviev. This big, strong, and negligent man somehow involuntarily, imperceptibly even to himself, began to submit to that hidden, unseizable, exquisite witchery of femininity; which not infrequently lurks under the coarsest covering, in the harshest, most gnarled environment. The pupil dominated, the teacher obeyed. Through the qualities of a primitive, but on the other hand a fresh, deep, and original soul, Liubka was inclined not to obey the method of another, but to seek out her own peculiar, strange processes. Thus, for example, she—like many children, however,—learned writing before reading. Not she herself, meek and yielding by nature, but some peculiar quality of her mind, obstinately refused in reading to harness a vowel alongside of a consonant, or vice versa; in writing, however, she would manage this. For penmanship along slanted rulings she, despite the general wont of beginners, felt a great inclination; she wrote bending low over the paper; blew on the paper from exertion, as though blowing off imaginary dust; licked her lips and stuck out with the tongue, from the inside, now one cheek, now the other. Soloviev did not thwart her, and followed after along those ways which her instinct laid down. And it must be said, that during this month and a half he had managed to become attached with all his huge, broad, mighty soul to this chance, weak, transitory being. This was the circumspect, droll, magnanimous, somewhat wondering love, and the careful concern, of a kind elephant for a frail, helpless, yellow-downed chick.

The reading was a delectation for both of them, and here again the choice of works was directed by the taste of Liubka, while Soloviev only followed its current and its sinuosities. Thus, for example, Liubka did not overcome Don Quixote, tired, and, finally, turning away from him, with pleasure heard Robinson Crusoe through, and wept with especial copiousness over the scene of his meeting with his relatives. She liked Dickens, and very easily grasped his radiant humour; but the features of English manners were foreign to her and incomprehensible. They also read Chekhov more than once, and Liubka very freely, without difficulty, penetrated the beauty of his design, his smile and his sadness. Stories for children moved her, touched her to such a degree that it was laughable and joyous to look at her. Once Soloviev read to her Chekhov's story, *The Fit*, in which, as it is known, a student for the first time finds himself in a brothel; and afterwards, on the next day, writhes about, as in a fit, in the spasms of a keen psychic suffering and the consciousness of common guilt. Soloviev himself did not expect that tremendous impression which this narrative would make upou her. She cried, swore, wrung her hands, and exclaimed all the while:

"Lord! Where does he take all that stuff from, and so skillfully! Why, it's every bit just the way it is with us!"

Once he brought with him a book entitled *The History of Manon Lescaut and the Chevalier de Grieux*, the work of Abbé Prevost. It must be said that Soloviev himself was reading this remarkable book for the first time. But still, Liubka appraised it far more deeply and finely. The absence of a plot, the naiveness of the telling, the surplus of sentimentality, the olden fashion of the style—all this taken together cooled Soloviev; whereas Liubka received the joyous, sad, touching and flippant details of this quaint immortal novel not only through her ears, but as though with her eyes and with all her naively open heart.

" 'Our intention of espousal was forgotten at St. Denis,' " Soloviev was reading, bending his tousled, golden-haired head, illuminated by the shade of the lamp, low over the book; "'we transgressed against the laws of the church and, without thinking of it, became espoused.'"

"What are they at? Of their own will, that is? Without a priest? Just so?" asked Liubka in uneasiness, tearing herself away from her artificial flowers.

"Of course. And what of it? Free love, and that's all there is to it. Like you and Lichonin, now."

"Oh, me! That's an entirely different matter. You know yourself where he took me from. But she's an innocent and genteel young lady. That's a low-down thing for him to do. And, believe me, Soloviev, he's sure to leave her later. Ah, the poor girl. Well, well, well, read on."

But already after several pages all the sympathies and commiserations of Liubka went over to the side of the deceived chevalier.

"'However, the visits and departures by thefts of M. de B. threw me into confusion. I also recollected the little purchases of Manon, which exceeded our means. All this smacked of the generosity of a new lover. "But no, no," I repeated, "it is impossible that Manon should deceive me! She is aware, that I live only for her, she is exceedingly well aware that I adore her."'"

"Ah, the little fool, the little fool!" exclaimed Liubka. "Why, can't you see right off that she's being kept by this rich man. Ah, trash that she is!"

And the further the novel unfolded, the more passionate and lively an interest did Liubka take in it. She had nothing against Manon's fleecing her subsequent patrons with the help of her lover and brother, while de Grieux occupied himself with sharping at the club; but her every new betrayal brought Liubka into a rage, while the sufferings of the gallant chevalier evoked her tears. Once she asked:

"Soloviev, dearie, who was he—this author?"

"He was a certain French priest."

"He wasn't a Russian?"

"No, a Frenchman, I'm telling you. See, he's got every-thing so—the towns are French and the people have French names."

"Then he was a priest, you say? Where did he know all this from, then?"

"Well, he knew it, that's all. Because he was an ordi-nary man of the world, a nobleman, and only became a monk afterwards. He had seen a lot in his life. Then he again left the monks. But, however, here's everything about him written in detail in front of this book."

He read the biography of Abbé Prevost to her. Liubka heard it through attentively, shaking her head with great significance; asked over again about that which she did not understand in certain places, and when he had finished she thoughtfully drawled out:

"Then that's what he is! He's written it up awfully good. Only why is she so low down? For he loves her so, with all his life; but she's playing him false all the time."

"Well, Liubochka, what can you do? For she loved him too. Only she's a vain hussy, and frivolous. All she wants is only rags, and her own horses, and diamonds."

Liubka flared up and hit one fist hard against the other.

"I'd rub her into powder, the low-down creature! So that's called her having loved, too! If you love a man, then all that comes from him must be dear to you. He goes to prison, and you go with him to prison. He's be-come a thief, well, you help him. He's a beggar, but still you go with him. What is there out of the way, that there's only a crust of black bread, so long as there's love? She's low down, and she's low down, that's what! But I, in his place, would leave her; or, instead of crying, give her such a drubbing that she'd walk around in bruises for a whole month, the varmint!"

The end of the novel she could not manage to hear to the finish for a long time, and always broke out into sincere warm tears, so that it was necessary to interrupt the reading; and the last chapter they overcame only in four doses.

The calamities and misadventures of the lovers in prison, the compulsory despatch of Manon to America and the self-denial of de Grieux in voluntarily following her, so possessed the imagination of Liubka and shook her soul, that she even forgot to make her remarks. Listening to the story of the quiet, beautiful death of Manon in the midst of the desert plain, she, without stirring, with hands clasped on her breast, looked at the light; and the tears ran and ran out of her staring eyes and fell, like a shower, on the table. But when the Chevalier de Grieux, who had lain two days near the corpse of his dear Manon, finally began to dig a grave with the stump of his sword—Liubka burst into sobbing so that Soloviev became scared and dashed after water. But even having calmed down a little, she still sobbed for a long time with her trembling, swollen lips and babbled:

"Ah! Their life was so miserable! What a bitter lot that was! And I don't know whom to pity more—him or her. And is it possible that it's always like that, darling Soloviev; that just as soon as a man and a woman fall in love with each other, in just the way they did, then God is sure to punish them? Dearie, but why is that? Why?"

CHAPTER XVII.

But if the Georgian and the kind-souled Soloviev served as a palliating beginning against the sharp thorns of great worldly wisdom, in the curious education of the mind and soul of Liubka; and if Liubka forgave the pedantism of Lichonin for the sake of a first sincere and limitless love for him, and forgave just as willingly as she would have forgiven curses, beatings, or a heavy crime—the lessons of Simanovsky, on the other hand, were a downright torture and a constant, prolonged burden for her. For it must be said that he, as though in spite, was far more accurate and exact in his lessons than any pedagogue working out his weekly stipulated tutorings.

With the incontrovertibility of his opinions, the assurance of his tone and the didacticism of his presentation he took away the will of poor Liubka and paralyzed her soul; in the same way that he sometimes, during university gatherings or at mass meetings, influenced the timid and bashful minds of newcomers. He was an orator at meetings; he was a prominent member in the organization of students' mess halls; he took part in the recording, lithographing and publication of lectures; he was chosen the head of the course; and, finally, took a very great interest in the students' treasury. He was of that number of people who, after they leave the student auditoriums, become the leaders of parties, the unrestrained arbiters of pure and self-denying conscience; serve out their political stage somewhere in Chukhlon, directing the keen attention of all Russia to their heroically woeful situation; and after that, beautifully leaning on their past, make a career for themselves, thanks to a solid advocacy, a deputation, or else a marriage joined with a goodly piece of black loam land and provincial activity. Unnoticeably to themselves and altogether unnoticeably, of course, to the casual glance, they cautiously right themselves; or, more correctly, fade until they grow a belly unto themselves, and acquire podagra and diseases of the liver. Then they grumble at the whole world; say that they were not understood, that their time was the time of sacred ideals. While in the family they are despots and not infrequently give money out at usury.

The path of the education of Liubka's mind and soul was plain to him, as was plain and incontrovertible everything that he conceived; he wanted at the start to interest Liubka in chemistry and physics.

"The virginally feminine mind," he pondered, "will be astounded, then I shall gain possession of her attention, and from trifles, from hocus-pocus, I shall pass on to that which will lead her to the centre of universal knowledge, where there is no superstition, no prejudices; where there is only a broad field for the testing of nature."

It must be said that he was inconsistent in his lessons. He dragged in all that came to his hand for the astonishment of Liubka. Once he brought along for her a large self-made serpent—a long cardboard hose, filled with gunpowder, bent in the form of a harmonica, and tied tightly across with a cord. He lit it, and the serpent for a long time with crackling jumped over the dining room and the bedroom, filling the place with smoke and stench. Liubka was scarcely amazed and said that this was simply fireworks, that she had already seen this, and that you couldn't astonish her with that. She asked, however, permission to open the window. Then he brought a large phial, tinfoil, rosin and a cat's tail, and in this manner contrived a Leyden jar. The discharge, although weak, was produced, however.

"Oh, the unclean one take you, Satan!" Liubka began to cry out, having felt the dry fillip in her little finger.

Then, out of heated peroxide of manganese, mixed with sand, with the help of a druggist's vial, the gutta-percha end of a syringe, a basin filled with water, and a jam jar—

oxygen was derived. The red-hot cork, coal and phosphorus burnt in the jar so blindingly that it pained the eyes. Liubka clapped her palms and squealed out in delight:

"Mister Professor, more! Please, more, more!.."

But when, having united the oxygen with the hydrogen brought in an empty champagne bottle, and having wrapped up the bottle for precaution in a towel, Simanovsky ordered Liubka to direct its neck toward a burning candle, and when the explosion broke out, as though four cannons had been fired off at once—an explosion through which the plastering fell down from the ceiling—then Liubka grew timorous, and, only getting to rights with difficulty, pronounced with trembling lips, but with dignity:

"You must excuse me now, but since I have a flat of my own, and I'm not at all a wench any longer, but a decent woman, I'd ask you therefore not to misbehave in my place. I thought you, like a smart and educated man, would do everything nice and genteel, but you busy yourself with silly things. They can even put one in jail for that."

Subsequently, much, much later, she told how she had a student friend, who made dynamite before her.

It must have been, after all, that Simanovsky, this enigmatic man, so influential in his youthful society, where he had to deal with theory for the most part, and so incoherent when a practical experiment with a living soul had come into his hands—was just simply stupid, but could skillfully conceal this sole sincere quality of his.

Having suffered failure in applied sciences, he at once passed on to metaphysics. Once he very self-assuredly, and in a tone such that after it no refutation was possible, announced to Liubka that there is no God, and that he would undertake to prove this during five minutes. Whereupon Liubka jumped up from her place, and told him firmly that she, even though a quondam prostitute, still believed in God and would not allow Him to be offended in her presence; and if he would continue such nonsense, then she would complain to Vassil Vassilich.

"I will also tell him," she added in a weeping voice, "that you, instead of teaching me, only rattle off all kinds of stuff and all that sort of nastiness, while you yourself hold your hand on my knees. And that's even not at all genteel." And for the first time during all their acquaint-anceship she, who had formerly been so timorous and constrained, sharply moved away from her teacher.

However, having suffered a few failures, Simanovsky still obstinately continued to act upon the mind and imagina-tion of Liubka. He tried to explain to her the theory of the origin of species, beginning with an amœba and ending with Napoleon. Liubka listened to him attentively, and during this there was an imploring expression in her eyes: "When will you stop at last?" She yawned into a hand-kerchief and then guiltily explained: "Excuse me, that's from my nerves." Marx also had no success—goods, supplementary value, the manufacturer and the worker, which had become algebraic formulas, were for Liubka merely empty sounds, vibrating the air; and she, very sincere at soul, always jumped up with joy from her place, when hearing that, apparently, the vegetable soup had boiled up, or the samovar was getting ready to boil over.

It cannot be said that Simanovsky did not have success with women. His aplomb and his weighty, decisive tone always acted upon simple souls, especially upon fresh, naive, trusting souls. Out of protracted ties he always got out very easily; either he was dedicated to a tremen-dously responsible call, before which domestic love relations were nothing; or he pretended to be a superman, to whom all is permitted (O, thou, Nietszche, so long ago and so disgracefully misconstrued for high-school boys!). The passive, almost imperceptible, but firmly evasive resist-ance of Liubka irritated and excited him. What particu-larly incensed him was the fact that she, who had formerly been so accessible to all, ready to yield her love in one day to several people in succession, to each one for two roubles, was now all of a sudden playing at some pure and disinterested inamoration!

"Nonsense," he thought. "This can't be. She's making believe, and, probably, I don't strike the right tone with her."

And with every day he became more exacting, captious, and stern. Hardly consciously, more probably through habit, he relied on his usual influence, intimidating the thought and subduing the will, which rarely betrayed him.

Once Liubka complained about him to Lichonin:

"He's too strict with me, now, Vassil Vassilievich; and I don't understand anything he says, and I don't want to take lessons with him any more."

Somehow or other, Lichonin lamely quieted her down; but still he had an explanation with Simanovsky. The other answered him with *sang froid*:

"Just as you wish, my dear fellow; if my method displeases you or Liubka, then I'm even ready to resign. My problem consists only of bringing in a genuine element of discipline into her education. If she does not understand anything, then I compel her to learn it by heart, aloud. With time this will cease. That is unavoidable. Recall, Lichonin, how difficult the transition from arithmetic to algebra was for us, when we were compelled to replace common numerals with letters, and did not know why this was done. Or why did they teach us grammar, instead of simply advising us to write tales and verses?"

And on the very next day, bending down low under the hanging shade of the lamp over Liubka's body, and sniffing all over her breast and under her arm pits, he was saying to her:

"Draw a triangle... Well, yes, this way and this way. On top I write 'Love.' Write simply the letter L, and below M and W. That will be: the Love of Man and Woman."

With the air of an oracle, unshakable and austere, he spoke all sorts of erotic balderdash and almost unexpectedly concluded:

"And so look, Liuba. The desire to love—it's the same as the desire to eat, to drink, and to breathe the air." He would squeeze her thigh hard, considerably above the knee; and she again, becoming confused and not wishing to offend him, would try almost imperceptibly to move her leg away gradually.

"Tell me, would it be offensive, now, for your sister, mother, or for your husband, that you by chance had not dined at home, but had gone into a restaurant or a cookshop, and had there satisfied your hunger? And so with love. No more, no less. A physiological enjoyment. Perhaps more powerful, more keen, than all others, but that's all. Thus, for example, now: I want you as a woman. While you..."

"Oh, drop it, Mister," Liubka cut him short with vexation. "Well, what are you harping on one and the same thing for all the time? Change your act. You've been told: no and no. Don't you think I see what you're trying to get at? But only I'll never agree to unfaithfulness, seeing as how Vasilli Vasillievich is my benefactor, and I adore him with all my soul... And you're even pretty disgusting to me with your nonsense."

Once he caused Liubka a great and scandalous hurt, and all because of his theoretical first principles. As at the university they were already for a long time talking about Lichonin's having saved a girl from such and such a house; and that now he is taken up with her moral regeneration; that rumour, naturally, also reached the studying girls, who frequented the student circles. And so, none other than Simanovsky once brought to Liubka two female medicos, one historian, and one beginning poetess, who, by the way, was already writing critical essays as well. He introduced them in the most serious and fool-like manner.

"Here," he said, stretching out his hand, now in the direction of the guests, now of Liubka, "here, comrades, get acquainted. You, Liuba, will find in them real friends, who will help you on your radiant path; while you— comrades Liza, Nadya, Sasha and Rachel— you will regard as elder sisters a being who has just struggled out of that horrible darkness into which the social structure places the modern woman."

He spoke not exactly so, perhaps; but in any case, approximately in that manner. Liubka turned red, ex- tended her hand, with all the fingers clumsily folded together, to the young ladies in coloured blouses and in leather belts; regaled them with tea and jam; promptly helped them with lights for cigarettes; but, despite all invitations, did not want to sit down for anything. She would say: "Yes-ss, n-no, as you wish." And when one of the young ladies dropped a handkerchief on the floor, she hurriedly made a dash to pick it up.

One of the maidens, red, stout, and with a bass voice, whose face, all in all, consisted of only a pair of red cheeks, out of which mirth-provokingly peeped out a hint at an upturned nose, and with a pair of little black eyes, like tiny raisins, sparkling out of their depths, was inspecting Liubka from head to feet, as though through an imaginary lorgnette; directing over her a glance which said nothing, but was contemptuous. "Why, I haven't been getting anybody away from her," thought Liubka guiltily. But another was so tactless, that she—perhaps for the first time for her, but the hundredth for Liubka—began a conversation about: how had she happened upon the path of prostitution? This was a bustling young lady, pale, very pretty, ethereal; all in little light curls, with the air of a spoiled kitten and even with a little pink cat's bow on her neck.

"But tell me, who was this scoundrel, now...who was the first to...well, you understand?..."

In the mind of Liubka quickly flashed the images of her former mates, Jennka and Tamara, so proud, so brave and resourceful—oh, far brainier than these maidens—and she, almost unexpectedly for herself, suddenly said sharply:

"There was a lot of them. I've already forgotten. Kolka, Mitka, Volodka, Serejka, Jorjik, Troshka, Petka, and also Kuzka and Guska with a party. But why are you interested?"

"Why...no...that is, I ask as a person who fully sympathizes with you."

"But have you a lover?"

"Pardon me, I don't understand what you're saying. People, it's time we were going."

"That is, what don't you understand? Have you ever slept with a man?"

"Comrade Simanovsky, I had not presupposed that you would bring us to such a person. Thank you. It was exceedingly charming of you!"

It was difficult for Liubka to surmount the first step. She was of those natures which endure long, but tear loose rapidly; and she, usually so timorous, was unrecognizable at this moment.

"But I know!" she was screaming in wrath. "I know, that you're the very same as I! But you have a papa, a mamma; you're provided for, and if you have to, then you'll even commit abortion—many do so. But if you were in my place, when there's nothing to stuff your mouth with, and a girlie doesn't understand anything yet, because she can't read or write; while all around the men are shoving like he-dogs—then you'd be in a sporting house too. It's a shame to put on airs before a poor girl—that's what!"

Simanovsky, who had gotten into trouble, said a few general consolatory words in a judicious bass, such as the noble fathers used in olden comedies, and led his ladies off.

But he was fated to play one more very shameful, distressing, and final role in the free life of Liubka. She had already complained to Lichonin for a long time that the presence of Simanovsky was oppressive to her; but Lichonin paid no attention to womanish trifles: the vacuous, fictitious, wordy hypnosis of this man of commands was strong within him. There are influences, to get rid of which is difficult, almost impossible. On the other hand, he was already for a long time feeling the burden of co-habitation with Liubka. Frequently he thought to himself: "She is spoiling my life; I am growing common, foolish; I have become dissolved in fool benevolence; it will end up in my marrying her, entering the excise or the assay office, or getting in among pedagogues; I'll be taking bribes, will gossip, and become an abominable provincial morel. And where are my dreams of the power of thought, the beauty of life, of love and deeds for all humanity?" he would say, at times even aloud, and pull his hair. And for that reason, instead of attentively going into Liubka's complaints, he would lose his temper, yell, stamp his feet, and the patient, meek Liubka would grow quiet and retire into the kitchen, to have a good cry there.

Now more and more frequently, after family quarrels, in the minutes of reconciliation he would say to Liubka:

"My dear Liuba, you and I do not suit each other, comprehend that. Look: here are a hundred roubles for you, ride home. Your relatives will receive you as their own. Live there a while, look around you. I will come for you after half a year; you'll have become rested, and, of course, all that's filthy, nasty, that has been grafted upon you by the city, will go away, will die off. And you'll begin a new life independently, without any assistance, alone and proud!"

But then, can anything be done with a woman who has come to love for the first, and, of course, as it seems to her, for the last time? Can she be convinced of the necessity for parting? Does logic exist for her?

Always reverent before the firmness of the words and decisions of Simanovsky, Lichonin, however, surmised and by instinct understood his real relation to Liubka; and in his desire to free himself, to shake off a chance load beyond his strength, he would catch himself in a nasty little thought: "She pleases Simanovsky; and as for her, isn't it all the same if it's he or I or a third? Guess I'll make a clean breast of it, explain things to him and yield Liubka up to him like a comrade. But then, the fool won't go. Will raise a rumpus."

"Or just to come upon the two of them together, some-how," he would ponder further, "in some decisive pose... to raise a noise, make a row... A noble gesture...a little money and...a getaway."

He now frequently, for several days, would not return home; and afterwards, having come, would undergo tor-turesome hours of feminine interrogations, scenes, tears, even hysterical fits. Liubka would at times watch him in secret, when he went out of the house; would stop oppo-site the entrance that he went into, and for hours would await his return in order to reproach him and to cry in the street. Not being able to read, she intercepted his letters and, not daring to turn to the aid of the prince or Soloviev, would save them up in her little cupboard together with sugar, tea, lemon and all sorts of other trash. She had even reached the stage when, in minutes of anger, she threatened him with sulphuric acid.

"May the devil take her," Lichonin would ponder during the minutes of his crafty plans. "It's all one, let there even be nothing between them. But I'll take and make a fearful scene for him and her."

And he would declaim to himself:

"Ah, so!.. I have warmed you in my bosom, and what do I see now? You are paying me with black ingratitude. ...And you, my best comrade, you have attempted my sole happiness!.. O, no, no, remain together; I go hence with tears in my eyes. I see, that I am one too many! I do not wish to oppose your love, etc., etc."

And precisely these dreams, these hidden plans, such momentary, chance, and, at bottom, vile ones—of those to which people later do not confess to themselves—were suddenly fulfilled. It was the turn of Soloviev's lesson. To his great happiness, Liubka had at last read through almost without faltering: "A good plough has Mikhey, and a good one has Sisoi as well...a swallow...a swing...the children love God..." And as a reward for this Soloviev read aloud to her *Of the Merchant Kalashnikov and of Kiribeievich, Life-guardsman of Czar Ivan the Fourth.* Liubka from delight bounced in her armchair, clapped her hands. The beauty of this monumental, heroic work had her in its grasp. But she did not have a chance to express her impressions in full. Soloviev was hurrying to a business appointment. And immediately, coming to meet Soloviev, having barely exchanged greetings with him in the doorway, came Simanovsky. Liubka's face sadly lengthened and her lips pouted. For this pedantic teacher and coarse male had become very repugnant to her of late.

This time he began a lecture on the theme that for man there exist no laws, no rights, no duties, no honour, no vileness; and that man is a quantity self-sufficient, independent of anyone and anything.

"It's possible to be a God, possible to be an intestinal worm, a tape worm—it's all the same."

He already wanted to pass on to the theory of amatory emotions; but, it is to be regretted, he hurried a trifle from impatience: he embraced Liubka, drew her to him and began to squeeze her roughly. "She'll become intoxicated from caressing. She'll give in!" thought the calculating Simanovsky. He sought to touch her mouth with his lips for a kiss, but she screamed and snorted spit at him. All the assumed delicacy had left her.

"Get out, you mangy devil, fool, swine, dirt. I'll smash your snout for you!..."

All the lexicon of the establishment had come back to her; but Simanovsky, having lost his *pince-nez*, his face distorted, was looking at her with blurred eyes and jabbering whatever came into his head:

"My dear... It's all the same...a second of enjoyment!.. You and I will blend in enjoyment!.. No one will find out!.. Be mine!..."

It was just at this very minute that Lichonin walked into the room.

Of course, at soul he did not admit to himself that this minute he would commit a vileness; but only somehow from the side, at a distance, reflected that his face was pale, and that his immediate words would be tragic and of great significance.

"Yes!" he said dully, like an actor in the fourth act of a drama; and, letting his hands drop impotently, began to shake his chin, which had fallen upon his breast. "I expected everything, only not this. You I excuse, Liuba— you are a cave being; but you, Simanovsky... I esteemed you...however, I still esteem you a decent man. But I know, that passion is at times stronger than the arguments of reason. Right here are fifty roubles—I am leaving them for Liuba; you, of course, will return them to me later, I have no doubt of that. Arrange her destiny... You are a wise, kind, honest man, while I am... ("A skunk!" somebody's distinct voice flashed through his head.) I am going away, because I will not be able to bear this torture any more. Be happy."

He snatched out of his pocket and with effect threw his wallet on the table; then seized his hair and ran out of the room.

Still, this was the best way out for him. And the scene had been played out precisely as he had dreamt of it.

PART THREE

CHAPTER I.

All this Liubka told at length and disjointedly, sobbing on Jennka's shoulder. Of course, in her personal elucidation this tragi-comical history proved altogether unlike what it had been in reality.

Lichonin, according to her words, had taken her to him only to entice, to tempt her; to have as much use as possible out of her foolishness, and then to abandon her. But she, the fool, had in truth fallen in love with him, and since she was very jealous about him and all these tousled girls in leather belts, he had done a low-down thing: had sent up his comrade on purpose, had framed it up with him, and the other had begun to hug Liubka, and Vasska came in, saw it and kicked up a great row, and chased Liubka out into the street.

Of course, in her version there were two almost equal parts of truth and untruth; but so, at least, all this had appeared to her.

She also told with great details how, having found herself without masculine support or without anybody's powerful extraneous influence, she had hired a room in a rather bad little hotel, on a retired street; how even from the first day the boots, a tough bird, a hard-boiled egg, had attempted to trade in her, without even having asked her permission thereto; how she had moved from the hotel to a private room, but even there had been overtaken by an experienced old woman go-between, with whose like the houses inhabited by poverty swarm.

Therefore, even with quiet living, there was in the face, in the conversation, and in the entire manner of Liubka something peculiar, specific to the casual eye; perhaps even entirely imperceptible, but for the business scent as plain and as irrefutable as the day.

But the chance, brief, sincere love had given her the strength to oppose the inevitability of a second fall. In her heroic courage she even went so far as putting in a few notices in the newspapers, that she was seeking a place with "all found." However, she had no recommendation of any sort. In addition, she had to do exclusively with women when it came to the hiring; and they also, with some sort of an inner, infallible instinct, surmised in her their ancient foe—the seductress of their husbands, brothers, fathers, and sons.

There was neither sense nor use in going home. Her native Vassilkovsky district is distant only fifteen versts from the state capital; and the rumour that she had entered that sort of an establishment had long since penetrated, by means of her fellow-villagers, into the village. This was written of in letters, and transmitted verbally, by those village neighbours who had seen her both on the street and at Anna Markovna's place itself—porters and bell-hops of hotels, waiters at small restaurants, cabbies, small contractors. She knew what odour this fame would give off if she were to return to her native spots. It were better to hang one's self than to endure this.

She was as uneconomical and impractical in money matters as a five-year-old child, and in a short while was left without a kopeck; while to go back to the brothel was fearful and shameful. But the temptations of street prostitution turned up of themselves, and at every step begged to be seized. In the evenings, on the main street, old hardened street prostitutes at once unerringly guessed her former profession. Ever and anon one of them, having come alongside of her, would begin in a sweet, ingratiating voice:

"How is it, young lady, that you're walking alone? Let's be mates. Let's walk together. That's always more convenient. Whenever men want to pass the time pleasantly with girls, they always love to start a party of four."

And right here the experienced, tried recruiting agent, at first casually, but after that warmly, with all her heart, would begin to praise up all the conveniences of living at your own landlady's—the tasty food, full freedom of going out, the possibility of always concealing from the landlady of your rooms the surplus over the agreed pay. Here also much of the malicious and the offensive was said, by the way, against the women of the private houses, who were called "government hides", "government stuff", "genteel maidens" and "institutes." Liubka knew the value of these sneers, because the dwellers in brothels also bear themselves with the greatest contempt toward street prostitutes, calling them "bimmies" and "venereals."

To be sure, in the very end that happened which had to happen. Seeing in perspective a whole series of hungry days, and in the very depth of them the dark horror of an unknown future, Liubka consented to a very civil invitation of some respectable little old man; important, grayish, well-dressed and correct. For this ignominy Liubka received a rouble, but did not dare to protest: the previous life in the house had entirely eaten away her personal initiative, mobility and energy. Later, several times running, he even did not pay her anything at all.

One young man, easy of manner and handsome, in a cap with a flattened brim, put on at a brave slant over one ear, in a silk blouse, girdled by a cord with tassels, also led her with him into a hotel, asked for wine and a snack; for a long time lied to Liubka about his being an earl's son on the wrong side of the blanket, and that he was the first billiardist in the whole city; that all the wenches like him and that he would make a swell Jane out of Liubka as well. Then he went out of the room for just one minute, as though on business of his own, and vanished forever. The stern, cross-eyed porter beat her with contentment, long, in silence, with a business-like air; breathing hard and covering up Liubka's mouth with his hand. But in the end, having become convinced, probably, that the fault was not hers, but the guest's, he took her purse, in which was a rouble with some small change, away from her; and took as security her rather cheap little hat and small outer jacket.

Another man of forty-five years, not at all badly dressed, having tortured the girl for some two hours, paid for the room and gave her 80 kopecks; but when she started to complain, he with a ferocious face put an enormous red-haired fist up to her very nose, the first thing, and said decisively:

"You just snivel a bit more to me... I'll snivel you... I'll yell for the police, now, and say that you robbed me when I was sleeping. Want me to? Is it long since you've been in a station house?"

And went away.

And of such cases there were many.

On that day, when her landlords—a boatman and his wife—had refused to let her have a room and just simply threw her things out into the yard; and when she had wandered the night through on the streets, without sleep, under the rain, hiding from the policemen—only then, with aversion and shame, did she resolve to turn to Lichonin's aid. But Lichonin was no longer in town—pusillanimously, he had gone away the very same day when the unjustly wronged and disgraced Liubka had run away from the flat. And it was in the morning that there came into her head the desperate thought of returning into the brothel and begging forgiveness there.

*   *   *

"Jennechka, you're so clever, so brave, so kind; beg Emma Edwardovna for me—the little housekeeper will listen to you," she implored Jennka and kissed her bare shoulders and wetted them with tears.

"She won't listen to anybody," gloomily answered Jennka. "And you did have to tie up with a fool and a low-down fellow like that."

"Jennechka, but you yourself advised me to," timidly retorted Liubka.

"I advised you?.. I didn't advise you anything. What are you lying on me for, just as though I was dead... Well, all right then—let's go."

Emma Edwardovna had already known for a long while about the return of Liubka; and had even seen her at that moment when she had passed through the yard of the house, looking all around her. At soul she was not at all against taking Liubka back. It must be said, that she had even let her go only because she had been tempted by the money, one-half of which she had appropriated for herself. And in addition to that, she had reckoned that with the present seasonal influx of new prostitutes she would have a large choice; in which, however, she had made a mistake, because the season had terminated abruptly. But in any case, she had firmly resolved to take Liubka. Only it was necessary, for the preservation and rounding out of prestige, to give her a scare befittingly.

"Wha-at?" she began to yell at Liubka, scarcely having heard her out, babbling in confusion. "You want to be taken on again?.. You wallowed the devil knows with whom in the streets, under the fences; and now, you scum, you're again shoving your way into a respectable, decent establishment!.. *Pfui*, you Russian swine! Out!.."

Liubka was catching her hands, aiming to kiss them, but the housekeeper roughly snatched them away. Then, suddenly paling, with a distorted face, biting her trembling, twisted lower lip, Emma calculatingly and with good aim struck Liubka on her cheek, with all her might; from which the other went down on her knees, but got up right away, gasping for breath and stammering from the sobs.

"Darlingest, don't beat me... Oh my dear, don't beat me..."

And again fell down, this time flat upon the floor.

And this systematic, malignant slaughter, in cold blood, continued for some two minutes. Jennka, who had at first been looking on with her customary malicious, disdainful air, suddenly could not stand it; she began to squeal savagely, threw herself upon the housekeeper, clutched her by the hair, tore off her *chignon* and began to vociferate in a real hysterical fit:

"Fool!.. Murderer!.. Low-down go-between!.. Thief!.."

All the three women vociferated together, and at once enraged wails resounded through all the corridors and rooms of the establishment. This was that general fit of grand hysterics, which takes possession of those confined in prisons, or that elemental insanity (*raptus*), which envelops unexpectedly and epidemically an entire lunatic asylum, from which even experienced psychiatrists grow pale.

Only after the lapse of an hour was order restored by Simeon and two comrades by profession who had come to his aid. All the thirteen girls got it hot; but Jennka, who had gone into a real frenzy, more than the others. The beaten-up Liubka kept on crawling before the housekeeper until she was taken back. She knew that Jennka's outbreak would sooner or later be reflected upon her in a cruel repayment. Jennka sat on her bed until the very night, her legs crossed Turkish fashion; refused dinner, and chased out all her mates who went in to her. Her eye was bruised, and she assiduously applied a five-kopeck copper to it. From underneath the torn shirt a long, transversal scratch reddened on the neck, just like a mark from a rope. That was where Simeon had torn off her skin in the struggle. She sat thus, alone, with eyes that glowed in the dark like a wild beast's, with distended nostrils, with spasmodically moving cheek-bones, and whispered wrathfully:

"Just you wait... Watch out, you damned things— I'll show you... You'll see yet... Ooh-ooh, you man-eaters..."

But when the lights had been lit, and the junior housekeeper, Zociya, knocked on her door with the words: "Miss, get dressed!.. Into the drawing room!" she rapidly washed herself, dressed, put some powder on the bruise, smeared the scratch over with *Crême de Simon* and pink powder, and went out into the drawing room, pitiful but proud; beaten-up but with eyes flaming with an unbearable wrathfulness and a beauty not human.

Many people, who have happened to see suicides a few hours before their horrible death, say that in their visages in those fateful hours before death they have noticed some enigmatic, mysterious, incomprehensible allurement. And all who saw Jennka on this night, and on the next day for a few hours, for long, intently and in wonder, kept their gaze upon her.

And strangest of all (this was one of the sombre wiles of fate) was the fact that the indirect culprit of her death, the last grain of sand which draws down the pan of the scales, appeared none other than the dear, most kind, military cadet Kolya Gladishev.

CHAPTER II.

Kolya Gladishev was a fine, merry, bashful young lad, with a large head; pink-cheeked, with a funny little white, bent line, as though from milk, upon his upper lip, under the light down of the moustache, sprouting through for the first time; with gray, naive eyes, placed far apart; and so closely cropped, that from underneath his flaxen little bristles the skin glistened through, just as with a thorough-bred Yorkshire suckling pig. It was precisely he with whom Jennka during the past winter had played either at maternal relations, or at dolls; and thrust upon him a little apple or a couple of bon-bons on his way, when he would be going away from the house of ill repute, squirming from shame.

This time, when he came, there could at once be felt in him, after long living in camps, that rapid change in age, which so often imperceptibly and rapidly transforms a boy into a youth. He had already finished the cadet academy and with pride counted himself a junker; although he still walked around in a cadet's uniform, with aversion. He had grown taller, had become better formed and more adroit; the camp life had done him good. He spoke in a bass, and during these months to his most great pride the nipples of his breasts had hardened; the most important—he already knew about this—and undeniable sign of virile maturity. Now, in the meanwhile, until the eyes-front severities of a military school, he had a period of alluring freedom. Already he was permitted to smoke at home, in the presence of grown-ups; and even his father had himself presented him with a leather cigar case with his monogram, and also, in the elevation of family joy, had assigned him fifteen roubles monthly salary.

And it was just here—at Anna Markovna's—that he had come to know woman for the first time—the very same Jennka.

The fall of innocent souls in houses of ill-fame, or with street solitaries, is fulfilled far more frequently than it is usually thought. When not green youths only, but even honourable men of fifty, almost grandfathers, are interrogated about this ticklish matter, they will tell you, sure enough, the ancient stencilled lie of how they had been seduced by a chambermaid or a governess. But this is one of those lingering, queer lies, going back into the depth of past decades, which are almost never noticed by a single one of the professional observers, and in any case are not described by any one.

If each one of us will try, to put it pompously, to put his hand on his heart, then every one will catch himself in the fact, that having once in childhood said some sort of boastful or touching fiction, which had success, and having repeated it for that reason two and five and ten times more—he afterwards cannot get rid of it all his life, and repeats with entire firmness by now a history which had never been; a firmness such that in the very end he believes the story. With time Kolya also narrated to his comrades how his aunt once removed, a young woman of the world, had seduced him. It must be said, however, that the intimate proximity to this lady—a large, dark-eyed, white faced, sweetly fragrant southern woman—did really exist; but existed only in Kolya's imagination, in those sad, tragic and timid minutes of solitary sexual enjoyments, through which pass if not a hundred percent. of all men, then ninety-nine, in any case.

Having experienced mechanical sexual excitements very early, approximately since nine or nine years and a half, Kolya did not at all have the least understanding of the significance of that end of being in love or of courtship, which is so horrible on the face of it, if it be looked at impartially, or if it be explained scientifically. Unfortunately, there was at that time near him not a one of the present progressive and learned ladies who, having turned away the neck of the classic stork, and torn up by the roots the cabbage underneath which children are found, recommend that the great mystery of love and generation be explained to children in lectures, through comparisons and assimilations, mercilessly and in a well-nigh graphic manner.

It must be said, that at that remote time of which we are speaking, the private institutions—male *pensions* and institutes, as well as academies for cadets—represented some sort of hot-house nurseries. The care of the mind and morality they tried to entrust as much as possible to educators who were bureaucrats-formalists; and in addition impatient, captious, capricious in their sympathies and hysterical, just like old maid lady teachers. Now it is otherwise. But at that time the boys were left to themselves. Barely snatched away, speaking figuratively, from the maternal breast; from the care of devoted nurses; from morning and evening caresses, quiet and sweet; even though they were ashamed of every manifestation of tenderness as "womanishness," they were still irresistibly and sweetly drawn to kisses, contacts, conversations whispered in the ear.

Of course, attentive, solicitous treatment, bathing, exercises in the open air—precisely not gymnastics, but voluntary exercises, each to his own taste—could have always put off the coming of this climacteric period or soften and make it understandable.

I repeat—*then* there was nothing of this.

The longing for family endearment, the endearment of mother, sister, nurse, so roughly and unexpectedly cut short, turned into deformed forms of courting (every whit like the "crushes" in a female institute) of good-looking boys, of "fairies"; they loved to whisper in corners and, walking arm in arm, or embracing in dark corridors, to tell in each other's ears improbable histories of adventures with women. This was partly both childhood's need of the fairy-tale element and partly awakening sensuality as well. Not infrequently some fifteen-year-old chubby, for whom it was just the proper time to be playing at popular tennis or to be greedily putting away buckwheat porridge with milk, would be telling, having read up, of course, on certain cheap novels, of how every Saturday, now, when it is leave, he goes to a certain handsome widow millionairess; and of how she is passionately enamored of him; and how near their couch always stand fruits and precious wine; and how furiously and passionately she makes love to him.

Here, by the bye, came along the inevitable run of prolonged reading, like hard drinking, which, of course, every boy and girl had undergone. No matter how strict in this respect the class surveillance may be, the striplings did read, are reading, and will read just that which is not permitted them. Here is a special passion, *chic*, the allurement of the forbidden. Already in the third class went from hand to hand the manuscript transcrips of Barkov; of a spurious Pushkin; the youthful sins of Lermontov and others: *The First Night, The Cherry, Lucas, The Festival at Peterhof, The She Uhlan, Grief through Wisdom, The Priest*, &c.

But no matter how strange, fictitious or paradoxical this may seem, still, even these compositions, and drawings, and obscene photographic cards, did not arouse a delightful curiosity. They were looked upon as a prank, a lark, and the allurement of contraband risk. In the cadets' library were chaste excerpts from Pushkin and Lermontov; all of Ostrovsky, who only made you laugh; and almost all of Turgenev, who was the very one that played a chief and cruel role in Kolya's life. As it is known, love with the late great Turgenev is always surrounded with a tantalizing veil; some sort of crepe, unseizable, forbidden, but tempting: his maidens have forebodings of love and are agitated at its approach, and are ashamed beyond all measure, and tremble, and turn red. Married women or widows travel this tortuous path somewhat differently: they struggle for a long time with their duty, or with respectability, or with the opinion of the world;

and, in the end—oh!—fall with tears; or—oh!—begin to brave it; or, which is still more frequent, the implacable fate cuts short her or his life at the most—oh!—necessary moment, when it only lacks a light puff of wind for the ripened fruit to fall. And yet all of his personages still thirst after this shameful love; weep radiantly and laugh joyously from it; and it shuts out all the world for them. But since boys think entirely differently than we grown-ups, and since everything that is forbidden, everything not said fully, or said in secret, has in their eyes an enormous, not only twofold but threefold interest—it is therefore natural that out of reading they drew the hazy thought that the grown-ups were concealing something from them.

And it must be mentioned—had not Kolya (like the majority of those of his age) seen the chambermaid Phrociya—so rosy-cheeked, always merry, with legs of the hardness of steel (at times he, in the heat of playing, had slapped her on the back), had he not seen her once, when Kolya had by accident walked quickly into papa's cabinet, scurry out of there with all her might, covering her face with her apron; and had he not seen that during this time papa's face was red, with a dark blue, seemingly lengthened nose? And Kolya had reflected: "Papa looks like a turkey." Had not Kolya—partly through the fondness for pranks and the mischievousness natural to all boys, partly through tedium—accidentally discovered in an unlocked drawer of papa's writing table an enormous collection of cards, whereon was represented just that which shop clerks call the crowning of love, and worldly nincompoops —the unearthly passion?

And had he not seen, that every time before the visit of the sweet-scented and bestarched Paul Edwardovich, some ninny with some embassy, with whom mamma, in imitation of the fashionable St. Petersburg promenades to the Strelka, used to ride to the Dnieper to contemplate the sun setting on the other side of the river, in the Cherni-govskaya district—had he not seen how mamma's bosom went, and how her cheeks glowed under the powder; had he not detected at these moments many new and strange things; had he not heard her voice, an altogether unknown voice, like an actor's; nervously breaking off, mercilessly malicious to those of the family and the servants, and suddenly soft, like velvet, like a green meadow under the sun, when Paul Edwardovich would arrive? Ah, if we people who have been made wise by experience would know how much, and even too much, the urchins and little girls surrounding us know, of whom we usually say:

"Well, why mind Volodya (or Petie, or Katie)?.. Why, they are little. They don't understand anything!.."

So also not in vain passed for Gladishev the history of his elder brother, who had just come out of a military school into one of the conspicuous grenadier regiments; and, being on leave until such time when it would be possible for him to spread his wings, lived in two separate rooms with his family. At that time Niusha, a chambermaid, was in their service; at times they jestingly called her signorita Anita—a seductive black-haired girl, who, if she were to change costumes, could in appearance be taken for a dramatic actress, or a princess of the royal blood, or a political worker. Kolya's mother manifestly countenanced the fact that Kolya's brother, half in jest, half in earnest, was allured by this girl. Of course, she had only the sole, holy, maternal calculation: If it were destined, after all, for her Borenka to fall, then let him give his purity, his innocence, his first physical inclination, not to a prostitute, not to a street-walker, not to a seeker of adventures, but to a pure girl. Of course, only a disinterested, unreasoning, truly-maternal feeling guided her. Kolya at that time was living through the epoch of llanos, pampases, Apaches, track-finders, and a chief by the name of "Black Panther"; and, of course, attentively kept track of the romance of his brother, and made his own syllogisms; at times only too correct, at times fantastic. After six months, from behind a door, he was the witness— or more correctly the auditor—of an outrageous scene. The wife of the general, always so respectable and restrained, was yelling in her boudoir at signorita Anita, and cursing in the words of a cab-driver: the signorita was in the fifth month of pregnancy. If she had not cried, then, probably, they would simply have given her smart-money, and she would have gone away in peace; but she was in love with the young master, did not demand anything, and for that reason they drove her away with the aid of the police.

In the fifth or sixth class many of Kolya's comrades had already tasted of the tree of knowledge of evil. At that time it was considered in their corpus an especial, boastful masculine *chic* to call all secret things by their own names. Arkasha Shkar contracted a disease, not dangerous, but still venereal; and he became for three whole months the object of worship of all the seniors—at that time there were no squads yet. And many of them visited brothels; and, really, about their sprees they spoke far more handsomely and broadly than the hussars of the time of Denis Davidov.* These debauches were esteemed by them the last word in valour and maturity.

And so it happened once, that they did not exactly persuade Gladishev to go to Anna Markovna, but rather he himself had begged to go, so weakly had he resisted temptation. This evening he always recalled with horror, with aversion; and dimly, just like some heavy dream. With difficulty he recalled, how in the cab, to get up courage, he had drunk rum, revoltingly smelling of real bedbugs; how qualmish this beastly drink made him feel; how he had walked into the big hall, where the lights of the lustres and the candelabra on the walls were turning round in fiery wheels; where the women moved as fantastic pink, blue, violet splotches, and the whiteness of their necks, bosoms and arms flashed with a blinding, spicy, victorious splendour. Some one of the comrades whispered something

---

* A Russian *bon vivant*, wit and poet (1781 - 1839), the overwhelming majority of whose lyrics deals with military exploits and debauches.—*Trans.*

in the ear of one of these fantastic figures. She ran up to Kolya and said:

"Listen, you good-looking little cadet, your comrades are saying, now, that you're still innocent... Let's go... I'll teach you everything."

The phrase was said in a kindly manner; but this phrase the walls of Anna Markovna's establishment had already heard several thousand times. Further, that took place which it was so difficult and painful to recall, that in the middle of his recollections Kolya grew tired, and with an effort of the will turned back the imagination to something else. He only remembered dimly the revolving and spreading circles from the light of the lamp; persistent kisses; disconcerting contacts—then a sudden sharp pain, from which one wanted both to die in enjoyment and to cry out in terror; and then with wonder he saw his pale shaking hands, which could not, somehow, button his clothes.

Of course, all men have experienced this primordial *tristia post coitus*; but this great moral pain, very serious in its significance and depth, passes very rapidly, remaining, however, with the majority for a long time—sometimes for all life—in the form of wearisomeness and awkwardness after certain moments. In a short while Kolya became accustomed to it; grew bolder, became familiarized with woman, and rejoiced very much over the fact that when he came into the establishment, all the girls, and Verka before all, would call out:

"Jennechka, your lover has come!"

It was pleasant, in relating this to his comrades, to be plucking at an imaginary moustache.

CHAPTER III.

It was still early—about nine—of a rainy August evening. The illuminated drawing room in the house of Anna Makovna was almost empty. Only near the very doors a young telegraph clerk was sitting, his legs shyly and awkwardly squeezed under his chair, and was trying to start with the thick-fleshed Katie that worldly, unconstrained conversation which is laid down as the proper thing in polite society at quadrille, during the intermissions between the figures of the dance. And, also, the long-legged, aged Roly-Poly wandered over the room, sitting down now next one girl, now another, and entertaining them all with his fluent chatter.

When Kolya Gladishev walked into the front hall, the first to recognize him was the round-eyed Verka, dressed in her usual jockey costume. She began to twirl round and round, to clap her palms, and called out:

"Jennka, Jennka, come quicker, your little lover has come to you... The little cadet... And what a handsome little fellow!"

But Jennka was not in the drawing room at this time; a stout head-conductor had already managed to get hold of her.

This elderly, sedate, and majestic man was a very convenient guest, because he never lingered in the house for more than twenty minutes, fearing to let his train go by; and even so, glanced at his watch all the while. During this time he regularly drank down four bottles of beer, and, going away, infallibly gave the girl half a rouble for candy and Simeon twenty kopecks for drink-money.

Kolya Gladishev was not alone, but with a comrade of the same school, Petrov, who was stepping over the threshold of a brothel for the first time, having given in to the

tempting persuasions of Gladishev. Probably, during
these minutes, he found himself in the same wild, absurd,
feverish state which Kolya himself had gone through a
year and a half ago, when his legs had shook, his mouth
had grown dry, and the lights of the lamps had danced
before him in revolving wheels.

Simeon took their great-coats from them and hid them
separately, on the side, that the shoulder straps and the
buttons might not be seen.

It must be said, that this stern man, who did not approve of students because of their free-and-easy facetiousness and incomprehensible style in conversation, also did
not like when just such boys in uniform appeared in the
establishment.

"Well, what's the good of it?" he would at times say
sombrely to his colleagues by profession. "What if a
whippersnapper like that comes, and runs right up nose to
nose against his superiors? Smash, and they've closed up
the establishment! There, like Lupendikha's three years
back. Of course, it's nothing that they closed it up—she
transferred it in another name right off; and when they sentenced her to sit in jail for a year and a half, why, it came
to a pre-etty penny for her. She had to shell out four hundred for Kerbesh alone... And then it also happens: a
little pig of that kind will cook up some sort of disease for
himself and start in whining: 'Oh, papa! Oh, mamma!
I am dying!' 'Tell me, you skunk, where you got it?'
'There and there...' Well, and so they haul you over the
coals again; judge me, thou unrighteous judge!"

"Pass on, pass on," said he to the cadets sternly.

The cadets entered, blinking from the bright light.
Petrov, who had been drinking to get up courage, swayed
and was pale. They sat down beneath the picture of the
Feast of the Russian Noblemen, and immediately two of the
young ladies—Verka and Tamara—joined them on both
sides.

"Treat me to a smoke, you beautiful little brunet!"
Verka turned to Petrov; and as though by accident put

against his leg her strong, warm thigh, closely drawn over with white tights. "What an agreeable little fellow you are!"

"But where's Jennie?" Gladishev asked of Tamara. "Is she busy with anybody?"

Tamara looked him in the eyes intently—looked so fixedly, that the boy even began to feel uncomfortable, and turned away.

"No. Why should she be busy? Only the whole day to-day her head ached; she was walking through the corridor, and at that time the housekeeper opened the door quickly and accidentally struck her in the forehead—and so her head started in to ache. The poor thing, she's lying the whole day with a cold pack. But why? Or can't you hold out? Wait a while, she'll come out in five minutes. You'll remain very much satisfied with her."

Verka pestered Petrov:

"Sweetie, dearie, what a tootsie-wootsicums you are! I adore such pale brunets; they are jealous and very fiery in love."

And suddenly she started singing in a low voice:

"He's kind of brown,
    My light, my own,
    Won't sell me out, and won't deceive.
    He suffers madly,
    Pants and coat gladly
    All for a woman he will give."

"How do they call you, ducky dear?"

"George," answered Petrov in a hoarse, cadet's bass.

"Jorjik! Jorochka! Ah, how very nice!"

She suddenly drew near to his ear and whispered with a cunning face:

"Jorochka, come to me."

Petrov was abashed and forlornly let out in a bass:

"I don't know... It all depends on what the comrade says, now..."

Verka burst into loud laughter:

"There's a case for you! Say, what an infant it is! Such as you, Jorochka, in a little village would long since have been married; but he says: 'It all depends on the comrade!' You ought to ask a nurse or a wet nurse yet! Tamara, my angel, just imagine: I'm calling him to go sleeping, but he says: 'It all depends on the comrade.' What about you, mister friend, are you his bringer up?"

"Don't be pestering, you devil!" clumsily, altogether like a cadet before a quarrel, grumbled out Petrov in a bass.

The lanky, rickety Roly-Poly, grown still grayer, walked up to the cadets, and, inclining his long, narrow head to one side, and having made a touching grimace, began to patter:

"Messieurs cadets, highly educated young people; the flowers, so to speak, of the intelligentzia; future masters of ordnance, will you not lend to a little old man, an aborigine of these herbiferous regions, one good old cigarette? I be poor. *Omnia mea mecum porto.* But I do adore the weed."

And, having received a cigarette, suddenly, without delay, he got into a free-and-easy, unconstrained pose; put forward the bent right leg, put his hand to his side, and began to sing in a wizened falsetto:

"It used to be that I gave dinners,
    In rivers flowed the champagne wine;
But now I have not even bread crusts,
    Nor for a split, oh brother mine.

It used to be—in the *Saratov*
    The doorman rushed, and was so fine;
But now all drive me in the neck,
    Give for a split, oh brother mine."

"Gentlemen!" suddenly exclaimed Roly-Poly with pathos, cutting short his singing and smiting himself on the chest. "Here I behold you, and know that you are the future generals Skobelev and Gurko; but I, too, in a certain respect, am a military hound. In my time, when I was studying for a forest ranger, all our department of woods and forests was military; and for that reason, knocking at the diamond-studded, golden doors of your hearts, I beg of you—donate toward the raising for an ensign of taxation of a wee measure of *spiritus vini*, which same is taken of the monks also."

"Roly!" cried the stout Kitty from the other end, "show the young officers the lightning; or else, look you, you're taking the money only for nothing, you good-for-nothing camel."

"Right away!" merrily responded Roly-Poly. "Most illustrious benefactors, turn your attention this way. Living pictures. Thunder Storm on a Summer Day in June. The work of the unrecognized dramaturgist who concealed himself under the pseudonym of Roly-Poly. The first picture.

" 'It was a splendid day in June. The scorching rays of the sun illumined the blossoming meadows and environs...' "

Roly-Poly's Don Quixotic phiz spread into a wrinkled, sweetish smile; and the eyes narrowed into half-circles.

" '...But now in the distance the first clouds have appeared upon the horizon. They grew, piled upon each other like crags, covering little by little the blue vault of the sky...' "

By degrees the smile was coming off Roly-Poly's face, and it grew more and more serious and austere.

" 'At last the clouds have overcast the sun... An ominous darkness has fallen...' "

Roly-Poly made his physiognomy altogether ferocious.
" 'The first drops of the rain fell...' "

Roly-Poly began to drum his fingers on the back of a chair.

" '...In the distance flashed the first lightning...' "

Roly-Poly's eye winked quickly, and the left corner of his mouth gave a twitch.

" ' . . . Whereupon the rain began to pour down in torrents, and there came a sudden, blinding flash of lightning. . . ' "

And with unusual artistry and rapidity Roly-Poly, with a successive movement of his eyebrows, eyes, nose, the upper and the lower lip, portrayed a lightning zig-zag.

" ' . . . A jarring thunder clap burst out—trrroo-oo. An oak that had stood through the ages fell down to earth, as though it were a frail reed. . . ' "

And Roly-Poly with an ease and daring not to be expected from one of his years, bending neither the knees nor the back, only drawing down his head, instantaneously fell down; straight, like a statue, with his back to the floor, but at once deftly sprang up on his feet.

" ' . . . But now the thunder storm is gradually abating. The lightning flashes less and less often. The thunder sounds duller, just like a satiated beast—oooooo-oooo-oo. . . The clouds scurry away. The first rays of the blessed sun have peeped out. . . ' "

Roly-Poly made a wry smile.

" ' . . . And now, the luminary of day has at last begun to shine anew over the bathed earth. . . ' "

And the silliest of beatific smiles spread anew over the senile face of Roly-Poly.

The cadets gave him a twenty-kopeck piece each. He laid them on his palm, made a pass in the air with the other hand, said: *ein, zwei, drei,* snapped two of his fingers, and the coins vanished.

"Tamarochka, this isn't honest," he said reproachfully. "Aren't you ashamed to take the last money from a poor retired almost-head-officer? Why have you hidden them here?"

And, having snapped his fingers again, he drew the coins out of Tamara's ear.

"I shall return at once, don't be bored without me," he reassured the young people; "but if you can't wait for me, then I won't have any special pretensions about it. I have the honour!.."

"Roly-Poly!" Little White Manka cried after him, "Won't you buy me candy for fifteen kopecks... Turkish Delight, fifteen kopecks' worth. There, grab!"

Roly-Poly neatly caught in its flight the thrown fifteen-kopeck piece; made a comical curtsey and, pulling down the uniform cap with the green edging at a slant over his eyes, vanished.

The tall, old Henrietta walked up to the cadets, also asked for a smoke and, having yawned, said:

"If only you young people would dance a bit—for as it is the young ladies sit and sit, just croaking from weariness."

"If you please, if you please!" agreed Kolya. "Play a waltz and something else of the sort."

The musicians began to play. The girls started to whirl around with one another, ceremoniously as usual, with stiffened backs and with eyes modestly cast down.

Kolya Gladishev, who was very fond of dancing, could not hold out and invited Tamara; he knew even from the previous winter that she danced more lightly and skillfully than the rest. While he was twirling in the waltz, the stout head-conductor, skillfully making his way between the couples, slipped away unperceived through the drawing room. Kolya did not have a chance to notice him.

No matter how Verka pressed Petrov, she could not, in any way, drag him off his place. The recent light intoxication had by now gone entirely out of his head; and more and more horrible, and unrealizable, and monstrous did that for which he had come here seem to him. He might have gone away, saying that not a one here pleased him; have put the blame on a headache, or something; but he knew that Gladishev would not let him go; and mainly—it seemed unbearably hard to get up from his place and to walk a few steps by himself. And, besides that, he felt that he had not the strength to start talking of this with Kolya.

They finished dancing. Tamara and Gladishev again sat down side by side.

"Well, really, how is it that Jennechka isn't coming by now?" asked Kolya impatiently.

Tamara quickly gave Verka a look with a question, incomprehensible to the uninitiated, in her eyes. Verka quickly lowered her eyelashes. This signified: yes, he is gone.

"I'll go right away and call her," said Tamara.

"But what are you so stuck on your Jennka for," said Henrietta. "You might take me."

"All right, another time," answered Kolya and nervously began to smoke.

* * *

Jennka was not even beginning to dress yet. She was sitting before the mirror and powdering her face.

"What is it, Tamarochka?" she asked.

"Your little cadet has come to you. He's waiting."

"Ah, that's the little baby of last year... Well, the devil with him!"

"And that's right, too. But how healthy and handsome the lad has grown, and how tall... It's a delight, that's all! So if you don't want to, I'll go myself."

Tamara saw in the mirror how Jennka contracted her eyebrows.

"No, you wait a while, Tamara, don't. I'll see. Send him here to me. Say that I'm not well, that my head aches."

"I have already told him, anyway, that Zociya had opened the door unsuccessfully and hit you on the head; and that you're lying down with a cold pack. But the only thing is, is it worth while, Jennechka?"

"Whether it's worth while or not, that's not your business, Tamara," answered Jennka rudely.

Tamara asked cautiously:

"Is it possible, then, that you aren't at all, at all sorry?"

"But for me you aren't sorry?" and she passed her hand over the red stripe that slashed her throat. "And for yourself you aren't sorry? And not sorry for this Liubka, miserable as she is? And not sorry for Pashka? You're huckleberry jelly, and not a human being!"

Tamara smiled craftily and haughtily:

"No, when it comes to a real matter, I'm not jelly. Perhaps you'll see this soon, Jennechka. Only let's better not quarrel—as it is it isn't any too sweet to live. All right, I'll go at once and send him to you."

When she had gone away, Jennka lowered the light in the little hanging blue lantern, put on her night blouse, and lay down. A minute later Gladishev walked in; and after him Tamara, dragging Petrov by the hand, who resisted and kept his head down. And in the rear was thrust in the pink, sharp, foxy little phiz of the cross-eyed housekeeper Zociya.

"And that's fine, now," the housekeeper commenced to bustle. "It's just sweet to look at; two handsome gents and two swell dames. A regular bouquet. What shall I treat you with, young people? Will you order beer or wine?"

Gladishev had a great deal of money in his pocket, as much as he never had before during all his brief life—all of twenty-five roubles; and he wanted to go on a splurge. Beer he drank only out of bravado, but could not bear its bitter taste, and wondered himself how others could ever drink it. And for that reason, squeamishly, like an old rake, sticking out his lower lip, he said mistrustfully:

"But then, you surely must have some awful stuff?"

"What do you mean, what do you mean, good-looking! The very best gentlemen approve of it... Of the sweet, there are Cagore, church wine, Teneriffe; while of the French there's Lafitte... You can get port wine also. The girls just simply adore Lafitte with lemonade."

"And what are the prices?"

"No dearer than money. As is the rule in all good establishments—a bottle of Lafitte five roubles, four bottles of lemonade at a half each, that's two roubles, and only seven in all..."

"That'll do you, Zociya," Jennka stopped her indifferently, "it's a shame to take advantage of boys. Even five is enough. You can see these are decent people, and not just anybody..."

But Gladishev turned red, and with a negligent air threw a ten rouble note on the table.

"Oh, what's the use of talking about it. All right, bring it."

"Whilst I'm at it, I'll take the money for the visit as well. What about you, young people—are you on time or for the night? You know the rates yourself: on time, at two roubles; for the night, at five."

"All right, all right. On time," interrupted Jennka, flaring up. "Trust us in that, at least."

The wine was brought. Tamara through importunity got pastry, besides. Jennka asked for permission to call in Little White Manka. Jennka herself did not drink, did not get up from the bed, and all the time muffled herself up in a gray shawl of Orenburg * manufacture, although it was hot in the room. She looked fixedly, without tearing her eyes away, at the handsome, sunburned face of Gladishev, which had become so manly.

"What's the matter with you, dearie?" asked Gladishev, sitting down on her bed and stroking her hand.

"Nothing special... Head aches a little... I hit myself."

"Well, don't you pay any attention."

"Well, here I've seen you, and already I feel better. How is it you haven't been here for so long?"

"I couldn't snatch away the time, nohow—camping. You know yourself... We had to put away twenty-five versts a day. The whole day drilling and drilling: field, formation, garrison. With a full pack. Used to get so fagged out from morning to night that towards

---

*Orenburg has as high a reputation for woolens as Sheffield has for steel.—*Trans.*

evening you couldn't feel your legs under you... We were at the manœuvres also... It isn't sweet..."

"Oh, you poor little things!" Little White Manka suddenly clasped her hands. "And what do they torture you for, angels that you are? If I was to have a brother like you, or a son—my heart would just simply bleed. Here's to your health, little cadet!"

They clinked glasses. Jennka was just as attentively scrutinizing Gladishev.

"And you, Jennechka?" he asked, extending a glass.

"I don't want to," she answered listlessly, "but, however, ladies, you've drunk some wine, chatted a bit—don't wear the welcome off the mat."

"Perhaps you'll stay with me the whole night?" she asked Gladishev, when the others had gone away. "Don't you be afraid, dearie; if you won't have enough money, I'll pay the difference for you. You see, how good-looking you are, that a wench does not grudge even money for you?" she began laughing.

Gladishev turned around to her; even his unobserving ear was struck by Jennka's strange tone—neither sad, nor kindly, nor yet mocking.

"No, sweetie, I'd be very glad to; I'd like to remain myself, but I can't, possibly; I promised to be home toward ten o'clock."

"That's nothing, dear, they'll wait; you're altogether a grown-up man now. Is it possible that you have to listen to anybody?.. But, however, as you wish. Shall I put out the light entirely, perhaps; or is all right the way it is? Which do you want—the outside or near the wall?"

"It's immaterial to me," he answered in a quavering voice; and, having embraced with his arm the hot, dry body of Jennka, he stretched with his lips toward her face. She slightly repulsed him.

"Wait, bear a while, sweetheart—we have time enough to kiss our fill yet. Just lie still for one little minute... So, now... quiet, peaceful... don't stir..."

These words, passionate and imperious, acted like hypnosis upon Gladishev. He submitted to her and lay down on his back, putting his hands underneath his head. She raised herself a little, leant upon her elbow, and placing her head upon the bent hand, silently, in the faint half-light, was looking his body over—so white, strong, muscular; with a high and broad pectoral cavity; with well-made ribs; with a narrow pelvis; and with mighty, bulging thighs. The dark tan of the face and the upper half of the neck was divided by a sharp line from the whiteness of the shoulders and breast.

Gladishev blinked for a second. It seemed to him that he was feeling upon himself, upon his face, upon the entire body, this intensely fixed gaze, which seemed to touch his face and tickle it, like the cobwebby contact of a comb, which you first rub against a cloth—the sensation of a thin, imponderous, living matter.

He opened his eyes and saw altogether near him the large, dark, uncanny eyes of the woman, who seemed to him now an entire stranger.

"What are you looking at, Jennie?" he asked quietly. "What are you thinking of?"

"My dear little boy!.. They call you Kolya: isn't that so?"

"Yes."

"Don't be angry at me, carry out a certain caprice of mine, please: shut your eyes again... no, even tighter, tighter... I want to turn up the light and have a good look at you. There now, so... If you only knew how beautiful you are now... right now... this second. Later you will become coarse, and you will begin giving off a goatish smell; but now you give off an odour of fur and milk... and a little of some wild flower. But shut them—shut your eyes!"

She added light, returned to her place, and sat down in her favourite pose—Turkish fashion. Both kept silent. In the distance, several rooms away, a broken-down grand piano was tinkling; somebody's vibrating laughter floated in; while from the other side—a little song, and rapid, merry talking. The words could not be heard. A cabby was rumbling by somewhere through the distant street...

"And now I will infect him right away, just like all the others," pondered Jennka, gliding with a deep gaze over his well-made legs, his handsome torso of a future athlete, and over his arms, thrown back, upon which, above the bend of the elbow, the muscles tautened—bulging, firm. "Why, then, am I so sorry for him? Or is it because he is such a good-looking little fellow? No. I am long since a stranger to such feelings. Or is it because he is a boy? Why, only a little over a year ago I shoved apples in his pocket, when he was going away from me at night. Why have I not told him then that which I can, and dare, tell him now? Or would he not have believed me, anyway? Would have grown angry? Would have gone to another? For sooner or later this turn awaits every man... And that he bought me for money—can that be forgiven? Or did he act just as all of them do—blindly?.."

"Kolya!" she said quietly, "Open your eyes."

He obeyed, opened his eyes, turned to her; entwined her neck with his arm, drew her a little to him, and wanted to kiss her in the opening of her chemise—on the breast. She again tenderly but commandingly repulsed him.

"No, wait a while, wait a while—hear me out... one little minute more. Tell me, boy, why do you come here to us—to the women?"

Kolya quietly and hoarsely began laughing.

"How silly you are! Well, what do they all come for? Am I not also a man? For, it seems, I'm at that age when in every man ripens... well, a certain need... for woman. For I'm not going to occupy myself with all sorts of nastiness!"

"Need? Only need? That means, just as for that chamber which stands under my bed?"

"No, why so?" retorted Kolya, with a kindly laugh. "I liked you very much... From the very first time... If you will, I'm even... a little in love with you... at least, I never stayed with any of the others."

"Well, all right! But then, the first time, could it possibly have been need?"

"No, perhaps, it wasn't need even; but somehow, vaguely, I wanted woman... My friends talked me into it... Many had already gone here before me... So then, I too..."

"But, now, weren't you ashamed the first time?"

Kolya became confused; all this interrogation was to him unpleasant, oppressive. He felt, that this was not the empty, idle bed talk, so well known to him out of his small experience; but something else, of more import.

"Let's say... not that I was ashamed... well, but still I felt kind of awkward. I drank that time to get up courage."

Jennie again lay down on her side; leaned upon her elbow, and again looked at him from time to time, near at hand and intently.

"But tell me, sweetie," she asked, in a barely audible voice, so that the cadet with difficulty made out her words, "tell me one thing more; but the fact of your paying money, these filthy two roubles—do you understand?—paying them for love, so that I might caress, kiss you, give all my body to you—didn't you feel ashamed to pay for that? Never?"

"Oh, my God! What strange questions you put to me to-day! But then they all pay money! Not I, then some one else would have paid—isn't it all the same to you?"

"And have you been in love with any one, Kolya? Confess! Well, now, if not in real earnest, then just so... at soul... Have you done any courting? Brought little flowers of some sort... Strolled arm-in-arm with her under the moon? Wasn't that so?"

"Well, yes," said Kolya in a sedate bass. "What follies don't happen in one's youth! It's a matter anyone can understand..."

"Some sort of a little first cousin? An educated young lady? A boarding school miss? A high school girl?.. There has been, hasn't there?"

"Well, yes, of course—everybody has them."

"Why, you wouldn't have touched her, would you?.. You'd have spared her? Well, if she had only said to you: take me, but only give me two roubles—what would you have said to her?"

"I don't understand you, Jennka!" Gladishev suddenly grew angry. "What are you putting on airs for! What sort of comedy are you trying to put over! Honest to God, I'll dress myself at once and go away."

"Wait a while, wait a while, Kolya! One more, one more, the last, the very, very last question."

"Oh, you!" growled Kolya displeased.

"And could you never imagine... well, imagine it right now, even for a second... that your family has suddenly grown poor, become ruined. You'd have to earn your bread by copying papers; or, now, let's say, through carpenter or blacksmith work; and your sister was to go wrong, like all of us... yes, yes, yours, your own sister... if some blockhead seduced her and she was to go travelling... from hand to hand... what would you say then?"

"Bosh!.. That can't be..." Kolya cut her short curtly. "But, however, that's enough—I'm going away!"

"Go away, do me that favour! I've ten roubles lying there, near the mirror, in a little box from chocolates— take them for yourself. I don't need them, anyway. Buy with them a tortoise powder box with a gold setting for your mamma; and if you have a little sister, buy her a good doll. Say: in memory from a certain wench that died. Go on, little boy!"

Kolya, with a frown, angry, with one shove of a well-knit body jumped off the bed, almost without touching it. Now he was standing on the little mat near the bed, naked, well-formed, splendid in all the magnificence of his blooming, youthful body.

"Kolya!" Jennka called him quietly, insistently and caressingly. "Kolechka!"

He turned around to her call, and drew in the air in a short, jerky gust, as though he had gasped: he had never yet in his life met anywhere, even in pictures, such a beautiful expression of tenderness, sorrow, and womanly silent reproach, as the one he was just now beholding in the eyes of Jennka, filled with tears. He sat down on the edge of the bed, and impulsively embraced her around the bared, swarthy arms.

"Let's not quarrel, then, Jennechka," he said tenderly.

And she twined herself around him, placed her arms on his neck, while her head she pressed against his breast. They kept silent so for several seconds.

"Kolya," Jennie suddenly asked dully, "but were you never afraid of becoming infected?"

Kolya shivered. Some chill, loathsome horror stirred and glided through within his soul. He did not answer at once.

"Of course, that would be horrible... horrible... God save me! But then I go only to you alone, only to you! You'd surely have told me?..."

"Yes, I'd have told you," she uttered meditatively. And at once rapidly, consciously, as though having weighed the significance of her words: "Yes, of course, of course, I would have told you! But haven't you ever heard what sort of a thing is that disease called syphilis?"

"Of course, I've heard... The nose falls through..."

"No, Kolya, not only the nose! The person becomes all diseased: his bones, sinews, brains grow diseased... Some doctors say such nonsense as that it's possible to be cured of this disease. Bosh! You'll never cure yourself! A person rots ten, twenty, thirty years. Every second paralysis can strike him down, so that the right side of the face, the right arm, the right leg die—it isn't a human being that's living, but some sort of a little half. Half-man—half-corpse. The majority of them go out of their minds. And each understands... every person... each one so infected understands, that if he eats, drinks, kisses, simply even breathes—he can't be sure that he won't immediately infect some one of those around him, the very nearest—sister, wife, son... To all syphilitics the children are born monsters, abortions, goitrous, consumptives, idiots. There, Kolya, is what this disease means. And now," Jennka suddenly straightened up quickly, seized Kolya fast by his bare shoulders, turned his face to her, so that he was almost blinded by the flashing of her sorrowful, sombre, extraordinary eyes, "and now, Kolya, I will tell you that for more than a month I am sick with this filth. And that's just why I haven't allowed you to kiss me..."

"You're joking!.. You're teasing me on purpose, Jennie!" muttered Gladishev, wrathful, frightened, and out of his wits.

"Joking?.. Come here!"

She abruptly compelled him to get up on his feet, lit a match and said:

"Now look closely at what I'm going to show you..."

She opened her mouth wide and placed the light so that it would illumine her larynx. Kolya looked and staggered back.

"Do you see these white spots? This—is syphilis, Kolya! Do you understand?—syphilis in the most fearful, the most serious stage. Now dress yourself and thank God."

He, silently and without looking around at Jennka, began to dress hurriedly, missing his clothes when he tried to put his legs through. His hands were shaking, and his under jaw jumped so that the lower teeth knocked against the upper; while Jennka was speaking with bowed head:

"Listen, Kolya, it's your good fortune that you've run across an honest woman; another wouldn't have spared you. Do you hear that? We, whom you deprive of innocence and then drive out of your home, while later you pay us two roubles a visit, we always—do you understand?"—she suddenly raised her head—"we always hate you and never have any pity for you!"

The half-clad Kolya suddenly dropped his dressing, sat down on the bed near Jennka and, covering his face with his palms, burst into tears; sincerely, altogether like a child...

"Lord, Lord," he whispered, "why, this is the truth!.. What a vile thing this really is!.. We, also, we had this happen: we had a chambermaid, Niusha...a chambermaid...they also called her signorita Anita...a pretty little girl...and my brother lived with her...my elder brother...an officer...and when he went away, she proved pregnant and mother drove her out...well, yes—drove her out...threw her out of the house, like a floor mop... Where is she now? And father...father...he also with a cham...chambermaid."

And the half-naked Jennka, this Jennka, the atheist, swearer, and brawler, suddenly got up from the bed, stood before the cadet, and slowly, almost solemnly, made the sign of the cross over him.

"And may God preserve you, my boy!" she said with an expression of deep tenderness and gratitude.

And at once she ran to the door, opened it and called out: "Housekeeper!"

Zociya came to her call.

"Tell you what, housekeeper dear," Jennka directed, "go and find out, please, which one of them is free—Tamara or Little White Manka. And the one that's free send here."

Kolya growled out something in the back, but Jennka purposely did not listen to him.

"And please make it as quick as possible, housekeeper dear, won't you be so kind?"

"Right away, right away, miss."

"Why, why do you do this, Jennie?" asked Gladishev with anguish. "Well, what's that for?.. Is it possible that you want to tell about it?.."

"Wait a while, that's not your business... Wait a while, I won't do anything unpleasant for you."

After a minute Little White Manka came in her brown, smooth, deliberately modest dress of a high school girl.

"What did you call me for, Jennie? Or have you quarreled?"

"No, we haven't quarreled, Mannechka, but my head aches very much," answered Jennka calmly, "and for that reason my little friend finds me very cold. Be a friend, Mannechka, stay with him, take my place!"

"That's enough, Jennie, stop it, darling!" in a tone of sincere suffering retorted Kolya. "I understand everything, everything, it's not necessary now... Don't be finishing me off, then!.."

"I don't understand anything of what's happened," the frivolous Manka spread out her hands. "Maybe you'll treat a poor little girl to something?"

"Well, go on, go on!" Jennka sent her away gently. "I'll come right away. We just played a joke."

Already dressed, they stood for long in the open door between the bedroom and the corridor; and without words sadly looked at each other. And Kolya did not understand, but sensed, that at this moment in his soul was taking place one of those tremendous crises which tell imperiously upon the entire life.

Then he pressed Jennie's hand hard and said:

"Forgive!.. Will you forgive me, Jennie? Will you forgive?.."

"Yes, my boy!.. Yes, my fine one!.. Yes...yes...."

She tenderly, softly, like a mother, stroked his closely cropped, harsh head and gave him a slight shove into the corridor.

"Where are you bound now?" she sent after him, half opening her door.

"I'll take my comrade right away, and then home."

"As you know best!.. God bless you, dearie!"

"Forgive me!.. Forgive me!.." once more repeated Kolya, stretching out his hands to her.

"I've already told you, my splendid boy... And you forgive me too... For we won't see each other any more!"

And she, having closed the door, was left alone.

In the corridor Gladishev hesitated, because he did not know how to find the room to which Petrov had retired with Tamara. But the housekeeper Zociya helped him, running past him very quickly, and with a very anxious, alarmed air.

"Oh, I haven't time to bother with you now!" she snarled back at Gladishev's question. "Third door to the left."

Kolya walked up to the door indicated and knocked. Some sort of bustle and whispering sounded in the room. He knocked once more.

"Kerkovius, open! This is me—Soliterov."

Among the cadets, setting out on expeditions of this sort, it was always agreed upon to call each other by fictitious names. It was not so much a conspiracy or a shift against the vigilance of those in authority, or fear of compromising one's self before a chance acquaintance of the family, but rather a play, of its own kind, at mysteriousness and disguise—a play tracing its beginning from those times when the young people were borne away by Gustave Aimard, Mayne Reid, and the detective Lecocq.

"You can't come in!" the voice of Tamara came from behind the door. "You can't come in. We are busy."

But the bass voice of Petrov immediately cut her short:

"Nonsense! She's lying. Come in. It's all right."

Kolya opened the door.

Petrov was sitting on a chair dressed, but all red, morose, with lips pouting like a child's, with downcast eyes.

"Well, what a friend you've brought—I must say!" Tamara began speaking sneeringly and wrathfully. "I thought he was a man in earnest, but this is only some sort of a little girl! He's sorry to lose his innocence, if you please. What a treasure you've found, to be sure! But take back, take back your two roubles!" she suddenly began yelling at Petrov and tossed two coins on the table. "You'll give them away to some poor chambermaid or other! Or else save them for gloves for yourself, you marmot!"

"But what are you cursing for?" grumbled Petrov, without raising his eyes. "I'm not cursing you, am I? Then why do you curse first? I have a full right to act as I want to. But I have passed some time with you, and so take them. But to be forced, I don't want to. And on your part, Gladishev—that is, Soliterov—this isn't at all nice. I thought she was a nice girl, but she's trying to kiss all the time, and does God knows what...."

Tamara, despite her wrath, burst into laughter.

"Oh, you little stupid, little stupid! Well, don't be angry—I'll take your money. Only watch: this very evening you'll be sorry, you'll be crying. Well, don't be angry, don't be angry, angel, let's make up. Put your hand out to me, as I'm doing to you."

"Let's go, Kerkovius," said Gladishev. "*Au revoir*, Tamara!"

Tamara let the money down into her stocking, through the habit of all prostitutes, and went to show the boys the way.

Even at the time that they were passing through the corridor Gladishev was struck by the strange, silent, tense bustle in the drawing room; the trampling of feet and some muffled, low-voiced, rapid conversations.

Near that place where they had just been sitting below the picture, all the inmates of Anna Markovna's house and several outsiders had gathered. They were standing in a close knot, bending down. Kolya walked up with curiosity, and, wedging his way through a little, looked in between the heads: on the floor, sideways, somehow unnaturally drawn up, was lying Roly-Poly. His face was blue, almost black. He did not move, and was lying strangely small, shrunken, with legs bent. One arm was squeezed in under his breast, while the other was flung back.

"What's the matter with him?" asked Gladishev in a fright.

Niurka answered him, starting to speak in a rapid, jerky whisper:

"Roly-Poly just came here... Gave Manka the candy, and then started in to put Armenian riddles to us... 'Of a blue colour, hangs in the parlor and whistles'... We couldn't guess nohow, but he says: 'A herring'... Suddenly he started laughing, had a coughing spell, and began falling sideways; and then—bang on the ground and don't move... They sent for the police... Lord, there's doings for you!.. I'm horribly afraid of corpseses!"

"Wait!" Gladishev stopped her. "It's necessary to feel his forehead; he may be alive yet..."

He did try to thrust himself forward, but Simeon's fingers, just like iron pincers, seized him above the elbows and dragged him back.

"There's nothing, there's nothing to be inspecting," sternly ordered Simeon, "go on, now, young gents, out of here! This is no place for you: the police will come, will summon you as witnesses—then it's scat! to the devil's dam! for you out of the military high school! Better go while you're good and healthy!"

He escorted them to the entrance hall, shoved the greatcoats into their hands and added still more sternly:

"Well, now—go at a run!... Lively! So's there won't be even a whiff of you left. And if you come another time, then I won't let youse in at all. You are wise guys, you are! You gave the old hound money for whisky—so now he's gone and croaked."

"Well, don't you get too smart, now!" Gladishev flew at him, all ruffled up.

"What d'you mean, don't get smart?.." Simeon suddenly began to yell infuriatedly, and his black eyes without lashes and brows became so terrible that the cadets shrank back. "I'll soak you one on the snout so hard you'll forget how to say papa and mamma! Git, this second! Or else I'll bust you in the neck!"

The boys went down the steps.

At this time two men were going up, in cloth caps on the sides of their heads; one in a blue, the other in a red, blouse, with the skirts outside, under the unbuttoned, wide open jackets—evidently, Simeon's comrades in the profession.

"What?" one of them called out gaily from below, addressing Simeon, "Is it bye-bye for Roly-Poly?"

"Yes, it must be the finish," answered Simeon. "We've got to throw him out into the street in the meantime, fellows, or else the spirits will start haunting. The devil with him, let 'em think that he drank himself full and croaked on the road."

"But you didn't...well, now?.. You didn't do for him?"

"Well, now, there's foolish talk! If there'd only been some reason. He was a harmless fellow. Altogether like a little lamb. It must be just that his turn came."

"And didn't he find a place where to die! Couldn't he have thought up something worse?" said the one who was in the red shirt.

"Right you are, there!" seconded the other. "Lived to grin and died in sin. Well, let's go, mate, what?"

The cadets ran with all their might. Now, in the darkness, the figure of Roly-Poly drawn up on the floor, with his blue face, appeared before them in all the horror that the dead possess for early youth; and especially if recalled at night, in the dark.

CHAPTER IV.

A fine rain, like dust, obstinate and tedious, had been drizzling since morning. Platonov was working in the port at the unloading of watermelons. At the mill, where he had since the very summer proposed to establish himself, luck had turned against him; after a week he had already quarreled, and almost had a fight, with the foreman, who was extremely brutal with the workers. About a month Sergei Ivanovich had struggled along somehow from hand to mouth, somewheres in the back-yards of Temnikovskaya Street, dragging into the editorial rooms of *The Echoes*, from time to time, notes of street accidents or little humorous scenes from the court rooms of the justices of the peace. But the hard newspaper game had long ago grown distasteful to him. He was always drawn to adventures, to physical labour in the fresh air, to life completely devoid of even the least hint at comfort; to care-free vagabondage, in which a man, having cast from him all possible external conditions, does not know himself what is going to be with him on the morrow. And for that reason, when from the lower stretches of the Dnieper the first barges with watermelons started coming in, he willingly entered a gang of labourers, in which he was known even from last year, and loved for his merry nature, for his comradely spirit, and for his masterly ability of keeping count.

This labour was carried on with good team work and with skill. Four parties, each of five men, worked on each barge. Number one would reach for a watermelon and pass it on to the second, who was standing on the side of the barge. The second cast it to the third, standing already on the wharf; the third threw it over to the fourth; while the fourth handed it up to the fifth, who stood on a horse cart and laid the watermelons away—now dark-green, now white, now striped—into even glistening rows. This work is clean, lively, and progresses rapidly. When a good party is gotten up, it is a pleasure to see how the watermelons fly from hand to hand, are caught with a circus-like quickness and success, and anew, and anew, without a break, fly, in order to fill up the dray. It is only difficult for the novices, that have not as yet gained the skill, have not caught on to that especial sense of the tempo. And it is not as difficult to catch a watermelon as to be able to throw it.

Platonov remembered well his first experiences of last year. What swearing—virulent, mocking, coarse—poured down upon him when for the third or fourth time he had been gaping and had slowed up the passing: two water-melons, not thrown in time, had smashed against the pavement with a succulent crunch, while the completely lost Platonov dropped the one which he was holding in his hands as well. The first time they treated him gently; on the second day, however, for every mistake they began to deduct from him five kopecks per watermelon out of the common share. The following time when this happened, they threatened to throw him out of the party at once, without any reckoning. Platonov even now still remembered how a sudden fury seized him: "Ah, so? The devil take you!" he had thought. "And yet you want me to be chary of your watermelons? So then, here you are, here you are!.." This flare-up helped him as though instantaneously. He carelessly caught the watermelons, just as carelessly threw them over, and to his amazement suddenly felt that precisely just now he had gotten into the real swing of the work with all his muscles, sight, and breathing; and understood, that the most important thing was not to think at all of the watermelons representing some value, and that then everything went well. When he, finally, had fully mastered this art, it served him for a long time as a pleasant and entertaining athletic game of its own kind. But that, too, passed away. He reached, in the end, the stage where he felt himself a will-less, mechanical wheel in a general machine, consisting of five men and an endless chain of flying watermelons.

Now he was number two. Bending downward rhythmically, he, without looking, received with both hands the cold, springy, heavy watermelon; swung it to the right; and, also almost without looking, or looking only out of the corner of his eye, tossed it downward, and immediately once again bent down for the next watermelon. And his ear seized at this time how smack-smack...smack-smack ...the caught watermelons slapped in the hands; and immediately bent downwards and again threw, letting the air out of himself noisily—ghe...ghe...

The present work was very profitable; their gang, consisting of forty men, had taken on the work, thanks to the great rush, not by the day but by the amount of work done, by the waggon load. Zavorotny, the head—an enormous, mighty Poltavian—had succeeded with extreme deftness in getting around the owner; a young man, and, to boot, in all probability not very experienced as yet. The owner, it is true, came to his senses later and wanted to change the stipulations; but experienced melon growers dissuaded him from it in time: "Drop it. They'll kill you," they told him simply and firmly. And so, through this very stroke of good luck every member of the gang was now earning up to four roubles a day. They all worked with unusual ardour, even with some sort of vehemence; and if it had been possible to measure with some apparatus the labour of each one of them, then, in all probability, the number of units of energy created would have equalled the work day of a large Voronezhian train horse.

However, Zavorotny was not satisfied even with this— he hurried and hurried his lads on all the time. Professional ambition was speaking within him; he wanted to bring the daily earnings of every member of the gang up to five roubles per snout. And gaily, with unusual ease, twinkled from the harbour to the waggon, twirling and flashing, the wet green and white watermelons; and their succulent plashing resounded against accustomed palms.

But now a long blast sounded on the dredging machine in the port. A second, a third, responded to it on the river; a few more on shore; and for a long time they roared together in a mighty chorus of different voices.

"*Ba-a-a-st-a-a!*" hoarsely and thickly, exactly like a locomotive blast, Zavorotny started roaring.

And now the last smack-smack—and the work stopped instantaneously.

Platonov with enjoyment straightened out his back and bent it backward, and spread out his swollen arms. With pleasure he thought of having already gotten over that first pain in all the muscles, which tells so during the first days, when one is just getting back into the work after disuse. While up to this day, awaking in the mornings in his lair on Temnikovskaya—also to the sound of a factory blast agreed upon—he would during the first minutes experience such fearful pains in his neck, back, in his arms and legs, that it seemed to him as if only a miracle would be able to compel him to get up and make a few steps.

"Go-o-o and e-at," Zavorotny began to clamour again.

The stevedores went down to the water; got down on their knees or laid down flat on the gangplank or on the rafts; and, scooping up the water in handfuls, washed their wet, heated faces and arms. Right here, too, on the shore, to one side, where a little grass had been left yet, they disposed themselves for dinner: placed in a circle ten of the most ripe watermelons, black bread, and twenty dried porgies. Gavriushka the Bullet was already running with a half-gallon bottle to the pot-house and was singing as he went the soldiers' signal for dinner:

> "Drag spoon and mess-kit out,
>   If there's no bread, eat without."

A bare-footed urchin, dirty and so ragged that there was more of his bare body than clothes upon him, ran up to the gang.

"Which one of you here is Platonov?" he asked, quickly running over them with his thievish eyes.

"I'm Platonov, and by what name do they tease you?"

"Around the corner here, behind the church, some sort of a young lady is waiting for you... Here's a note for you."

The whole gang neighed deeply.

"What d'you open up your mouths for, you pack of fools!" said Platonov calmly. "Give me the note here."

This was a letter from Jennka, written in a round, naive, rolling, childish handwriting, and not very well spelt.

"Sergei Ivanich. Forgive me that I dis-turbe you. I must talk over a very, very important matter with you. I would not be troubling you if it was Trifles. For only 10 minutes in all. Jennka, whom you know, from Anna Markovna's."

Platonov got up.

"I'm going away for a little while," he said to Zavorotny. "When you begin, I'll be in my place."

"Now you've found somethin' to do," lazily and contemptuously said the head of the gang. "There's the night for that business... Go ahead, go ahead, who's holding you. But only if you won't be here when we begin work, then this day don't count. I'll take any tramp. And as many watermelons as he busts—that's out of your share, too... I didn't think it of you, Platonov—that you're such a he-dog..."

Jennka was waiting for him in the tiny little square, sheltered between a church and the wharf, and consisting of ten sorry poplars. She had on a gray, one-piece street dress; a simple, round, straw hat with a small black ribbon. "And yet, even though she has dressed herself simply," reflected Platonov, looking at her from a distance with his habitually puckered eyes, "and yet, every man will walk past, give a look, and inevitably look back three or four times; he'll feel the especial tone at once."

"Howdy do, Jennka! Very glad to see you," he said cordially, squeezing the girl's hand. "There, now, I didn't expect it!"

Jennka was reserved, sad, and apparently troubled over something. Platonov at once understood and sensed this.

"You excuse me, Jennechka, I must have dinner right away," said he, "so, perhaps, you'll go together with me and tell me what's the matter, while I'll manage to eat at the same time. There's a modest little inn not far from here. At this time there are no people there at all, and there's even a tiny little stall, a sort of a private room; that will be just the thing for you and me. Let's go! Perhaps you'll also have a bite of something."

"No. I won't eat," answered Jennka hoarsely, "and I won't detain you for long...a few minutes. I have to talk things over, have some advice—but I haven't anybody."

"Very well... Let's go then! In whatever way I can, I'm always at your service, in everything. I love you very much, Jennka!"

She looked at him sadly and gratefully.

"I know this, Serge Ivanovich; that's why I've come."

"You need money, perhaps? Just say so. I haven't got much with me, myself; but the gang will trust me with an advance."

"No, thanks...it isn't that at all. I'll tell everything at once, there, where we're going now."

In the dim, low-ceiled little inn, the customary haunt of petty thieves, where business was carried on only in the evening, until very far into the night, Platonov took the little half-dark cubby hole.

"Give me boiled meat, cucumbers, a large glass of vodka, and bread," he ordered the waiter.

The waiter—a young fellow with a dirty face; pug-nosed; as dirty and greasy in all his person as though he had just been pulled out of a cesspool, wiped his lips and asked hoarsely:

"How many kopecks' bread?"

"As much as it comes to."

Then he started laughing:

"Bring as much as possible—we'll reckon it up later... and some bread cider!"

"Well, Jennie, say what your trouble is... I can already see by your face that there's trouble, or something distasteful in general... Go ahead and tell it!"

Jennka for a long time plucked her handkerchief and looked at the tips of her slippers, as though gathering her strength. Timorousness had taken possession of her—the necessary and important words would not come into her mind, for anything. Platonov came to her aid:

"Don't be embarrassed, my dear Jennie, tell all there is! For you know that I'm like one of the family, and will never give you away. And perhaps I may really give you some worth while advice. Well, dive off with a splash into the water—begin!"

"That's just it, I don't know how to begin," said Jennka irresolutely. "Here's what, Sergei Ivanovich, I'm a sick woman... Understand?—sick in a bad way... With the most nasty disease... Do you know—which?"

"Go on!" said Platonov, nodding his head.

"And I've been that way for a long time... more than a month... a month and a half, maybe... Yes, more than a month, because I found out about this on the Trinity..."

Platonov quickly rubbed his forehead with his hand.

"Wait a while, I've recalled it... This was that day I was there together with the students... isn't that so?"

"That's right, Sergei Ivanovich, that's so..."

"Ah, Jennka" said Platonov reproachfully and with regret. "For do you know, that after this two of the students got sick... Wasn't it from you?"

Jennka wrathfully and disdainfully flashed her eyes.

"Perhaps even from me... How should I know? There were a lot of them... I remember there was this one, now, who was even trying to pick a fight with you all the time... A tall sort of fellow, fair-haired, in *pince-nez*..."

"Yes, yes... That's Sobashnikov. They passed the news to me... That's he... this one was nothing—a little coxcomb! But then the other—him I'm sorry for. Although I've known him long, somehow I never made the right inquiries about his name... I only remember that he comes from some city or other—Poliyansk... Zvenigorodsk... His comrades called him Ramses... When the physicians—he turned to several physicians—when they told him irrevocably that he had the lues, he went home and shot himself... And in the note that he wrote there were amazing things, something like this: 'I supposed all the meaning of life to be in the triumph of mind, beauty and good; with this disease I am not a man, but junk, rottenness, carrion; a candidate for a progressive paralytic. My human dignity cannot reconcile itself to this. But guilty in all that has happened, and therefore in my death as well, am I alone; for that I, obeying a momentary bestial inclination, took a woman without love, for money. For that reason have I earned the punishment which I myself lay upon me...'

"I am sorry for him..." added Platonov quietly.

Jennka dilated her nostrils.

"But I, now, not the very least bit."

"That's wrong... You go away now, young fellow. When I'll need you I'll call out," said Platonov to the serving-man. "Absolutely wrong, Jennechka! This was an unusually big and forceful man. Such come only one to the hundreds of thousands. I don't respect suicides. Most frequent of all, these are little boys, who shoot and hang themselves over trifles, like a child that has not been given a piece of candy, and hits himself against the wall to spite those around him. But before his death I reverently and with sorrow bow my head. He was a wise, generous, kindly man, attentive to all; and, as you see, too strict to himself."

"But to me this is absolutely all one," obstinately contradicted Jennka, "wise or foolish, honest or dishonest, old or young—I have come to hate them all. Because—look upon me—what am I? Some sort of universal spittoon, cesspool, privy. Think of it, Platonov; why, thousands, thousands of people have taken me, clutched me; grunted, snorted over me; and all those who were, and all those who might yet have been on my bed—oh, how I hate them all! If I only could, I would sentence them to torture by fire and iron!.. I would order..."

"You are malicious and proud, Jennie," said Platonov quietly.

"I was neither malicious nor proud... It's only now. I wasn't ten yet when my own mother sold me; and since that time I've been travelling from hand to hand... If only some one had seen a human being in me! No!.. I am vermin, refuse, worse than a beggar, worse than a thief, worse than a murderer!.. Even a hangman... we have even such coming to the establishment—and even he would have treated me loftily, with loathing: I—am nothing; I—am a public wench! Do you understand, Sergei Ivanovich, what a horrible word this is? Pub-lic!.. This means nobody's: not papa's, not mamma's, not Russian, not Riyazan, but simply—public! And not once did it enter anybody's head to walk up to me and think: why, now, this is a human being too; she has a heart and a brain; she thinks of something, feels something; for she's not made out of wood, and isn't stuffed with straw, small hay, or excelsior! And yet, only I feel this. I, perhaps, am the only one out of all of them who feels the horror of her position; this black, stinking, filthy pit. But then, all the girls with whom I have met, and with whom I am living right now—understand, Platonov, understand me! —why, they don't realize anything!.. Talking, walking pieces of meat! And this is even worse than my malice!.."

"You are right!" said Platonov quietly. "And this is one of those questions where you'll always run up against a wall. No one will help you..."

"No one, no one!..." passionately exclaimed Jennka.
"Do you remember—this was while you were there: a
student carried away our Liubka..."

"Why, certainly, I remember well!.. Well, and what
then?"

"And this is what, that yesterday she came back tattered, wet... Crying... Left her, the skunk!.. Played
a while at kindliness, and then away with her! 'You,' he
says, 'are a sister.' 'I,' he says, 'will save you, make a
human being of you...'"

"Is that possible?"

"Just so!.. One man I did see, kindly, indulgent,
without the designs of a he-dog—that's you. But then,
you're altogether different. You're somehow queer. You're
always wandering somewhere, seeking something... You
forgive me, Sergei Ivanovich, you're some sort of a little
innocent!.. And that's just why I've come to you, to you
alone!.."

"Speak on, Jennechka..."

"And so, when I found out that I was sick, I almost
went out of my mind from wrath; I choked from wrath...
I thought: and here's the end; therefore, there's no more
use in pitying, there's nothing to grieve about, nothing to
expect... The lid!.. But for all that I have borne—can
it be that there's no paying back for it? Can it be that
there's no justice in the world? Can it be that I can't even
feast myself with revenge?—for that I have never known
love; that of the family I know only by hearsay; that, like
a disgustin', nasty little dog, they call me near, pat me
and then with a boot over the head—get out!—that they
made me over, from a human being, equal to all of them,
no more foolish than all those I've met; made me over
into a floor mop, some sort of a sewer pipe for their filthy
pleasures?.. Ugh!.. Is it possible that for all of this
I must take even such a disease with gratitude as well?..
Or am I a slave?.. A dumb object?.. A pack horse?..
And so, Platonov, it was just then that I resolved to infect

them all; young, old, poor, rich, handsome, hideous—all, all, all!.."

Platonov, who had already long since put his plate away from him, was looking at her with astonishment, and even more—almost with horror. He, who had seen in life much of the painful, the filthy, at times even of the bloody—he grew frightened with an animal fright before this intensity of enormous, unvented hatred. Coming to himself, he said:

"One great writer tells of such a case. The Prussians conquered the French and lorded it over them in every possible way: shot the men, violated the women, pillaged the houses, burned down the fields... And so one handsome woman—a Frenchwoman, very handsome,—having become infected, began out of spite to infect all the Germans who happened to fall into her embraces. She made ill whole hundreds, perhaps even thousands... And when she was dying in a hospital, she recalled this with joy and with pride...* But then, those were enemies, trampling upon her fatherland and slaughtering her brothers... But you, you, Jennechka!.."

"But I—all, just all! Tell me, Sergei Ivanovich, only tell me on your conscience: if you were to find in the street a child, whom some one had dishonoured, had abused... well, let's say, had stuck its eyes out, cut its ears off—and then you were to find out that this man is at this minute walking past you, and that only God alone, if only He exists, is looking at you at this minute from heaven—what would you do?"

"Don't know," answered Platonov, dully and downcast; but he paled, and his fingers underneath the table convulsively clenched into fists. "Perhaps I would kill him..."

"Not 'perhaps', but certainly! I know you, I sense you. Well, and now think: every one of us has been abused so, when we were children!.. Children!.." passionately moaned out Jennka and covered her eyes for a moment

---

*This story is *Lit No. 29*, by Guy de Maupassant.—*Trans.*

with her palm. "Why, it comes to me, you also spoke of
this at one time, in our place—wasn't it on that same
evening before the Trinity?.. Yes, children—foolish,
trusting, blind, greedy, frivolous... And we cannot tear
ourselves out of our harness...where are we to go? what
are we to do?.. And please, don't you think it, Sergei
Ivanovich—that the spite within me is strong only against
those who wronged just me, me personally... No,
against all our guests in general; all these cavaliers, from
little to big... Well, and so I have resolved to avenge
myself and my sisters. Is that good or no?.."

"Jennechka, really I don't know... I can't... I dare
not say anything... I don't understand."

"But even that's not the main thing... For the main
thing is this: I infected them, and did not feel anything
—no pity, no remorse, no guilt before God or my fatherland. Within me was only joy, as in a hungry wolf that
has managed to get at blood... But yesterday something
happened which even I can't understand. A cadet came
to me, altogether a little bit of a lad, silly, with yellow
around his mouth... He used to come to me from still
last winter... And then suddenly I had pity on him...
Not because he was very handsome and very young; and
not because he had always been very polite—even tender,
if you will... No, both the one and the other had come
to me, but I did not spare them: with enjoyment I marked
them off, just like cattle, with a red-hot brand... But
this one I suddenly pitied... I myself don't understand—
why? I can't make it out. It seemed to me, that it would
be all the same as stealing money from a little simpleton,
a little idiot; or hitting a blind man, or cutting a sleeper's
throat...if he only were some dried-up marasmus or a
nasty little brute, or a lecherous old fellow, I would not
have stopped. But he was healthy, robust, with chest
and arms like a statue's...and I could not... I gave him
his money back, showed him my disease; in a word, I acted
like a fool among fools. He went away from me...burst
into tears... And now since last evening I haven't slept.

I walk around as in a fog... Therefore—I'm thinking right now—therefore, that which I meditated; my dream to infect them all; to infect their fathers, mothers, sisters, brides—even all the world—therefore, all this was folly, an empty fantasy, since I have stopped?.. Once again, I don't understand anything... Sergei Ivanovich, you are so wise, you have seen so much of life—help me, then, to find myself now!.."

"I don't know, Jennechka!" quietly pronounced Platonov. "Not that I fear telling you, or advising you, but I know absolutely nothing. This is above my reason... above conscience..."

Jennie crossed her fingers and nervously cracked them.

"And I, too, don't know... Therefore, that which I thought—is not the truth. Therefore, there is but one thing left me... This thought came into my head this morning..."

"Don't, don't do it, Jennechka!.. Jennie!.." Platonov quickly interrupted her.

"There's one thing: to hang myself..."

"No, no, Jennie, only not that!.. If there were other circumstances, unsurmountable, I would, believe me, tell you boldly: well, it's no use, Jennie; it's time to close up shop... But what you need isn't that at all... If you wish, I can suggest one way out to you, no less malicious and merciless; but which, perhaps, will satiate your wrath a hundredfold..."

"What's that?" asked Jennie, wearily, as though suddenly wilted after her flare-up.

"Well, this is it... You're still young, and I'll tell you the truth, you are very handsome; that is, you can be, if you only want to, unusually stunning... That's even more than beauty. But you've never yet known the bounds and the power of your appearance; and, mainly, you don't know to what a degree such natures as yours are bewitching, and how mightily they enchain men to them, and make out of them more than slaves and brutes... You are proud, you are brave, you are independent, you are a clever woman. I know—you have read a great deal, let's presuppose even trashy books, but still you have read, you have an entirely different speech than the others. With a successful turn of life, you can cure yourself, you can get out of these 'Yamkas', these 'Little Ditches', into freedom. You have only to stir a finger, in order to see at your feet hundreds of men; submissive, ready for your sake for vileness, for theft, for embezzlement... Lord it over them with tight reins, with a cruel whip in your hands! ... Ruin them, make them go out of their minds, as long as your desire and energy hold out!.. Look, my dear Jennie, who manages life now if not women! Yesterday's chambermaid, laundress, chorus girl goes through estates worth millions, the way a country-woman of Tver cracks sunflower seeds. A woman scarcely able to sign her name, at times affects the destiny of an entire kingdom through a man. Hereditary princes marry the street-walkers, the kept mistresses of yesterday... Jennechka, there is the scope for your unbridled vengeance; while I will admire you from a distance... For you—you are made of this stuff—you are a bird of prey, a spoliator... Perhaps not with such a broad sweep—but you will cast them down under your feet."

"No," faintly smiled Jennka. "I thought of this before ...But something of the utmost importance has burned out within me. There are no forces within me, there is no will within me, no desires... I am somehow all empty inside, rotted... Well, now, you know, there's a mushroom like that—white, round,—you squeeze it, and snuff pours out of it. And the same way with me. This life has eaten out everything within me save malice. And I am flabby, and my malice is flabby... I'll see some little boy again, will have pity on him, will be punishing myself again... No, it's better...better so!.."

She became silent. And Platonov did not know what to say. It became oppressive and awkward for both. Finally, Jennka got up, and, without looking at Platonov, extended her cold, feeble hand to him.

"Good-bye, Sergei Ivanovich! Excuse me, that I took up your time... Oh, well, I can see myself that you'd help me, if you only could... But, evidently, there's nothing to be done here... Good-bye!"

"Only don't do anything foolish, Jennechka! I implore you!.."

"Oh, that's all right!" said she and made a tired gesture with her hand.

Having come out of the square, they parted; but, having gone a few steps, Jennka suddenly called after him:

"Sergei Ivanovich, oh Sergei Ivanovich!.."

He stopped, turned around, walked back to her.

"Roly-Poly croaked last evening in our drawing room. He jumped and he jumped, and then suddenly plumped down... Oh, well, it's an easy death at least! And also I forgot to ask you, Sergei Ivanovich... This is the last, now... Is there a God or no?"

Platonov knit his eyebrows.

"What answer can I make? I don't know. I think that there is, but not such as we imagine Him. He is more wise, more just..."

"And future life? There, after death? Is there, now, as they tell us, a paradise or hell? Is that the truth? Or is there just nothing at all? A barren void? A sleep without a dream? A dark basement?"

Platonov kept silent, trying not to look at Jennka. He felt oppressed and frightened.

"I don't know," said he, finally, with an effort. "I don't want to lie to you."

Jennka sighed, and smiled with a pitiful, twisted smile.

"Well, thanks, my dear. And thanks for even that much... I wish you happiness. With all my soul. Well, good-bye..."

She turned away from him and began slowly, with a wavering walk, to climb up the hill.

*　*　*

Platonov returned to work just in the nick of time. The gathering of tramps, scratching, yawning, working out their accustomed dislocations, were getting into their places. Zavorotny, at a distance, with his keen eyes caught sight of Platonov and began to yell over the whole port:

"You did manage to get here in time, you round-shouldered devil... But I was already wanting to take you by the tail and chase you out of the gang... Well, get in your place!.."

"Well, but I did get a he-dog in you, Serejka!.." he added, in a kindly manner. "If only it was night; but no, —look you, he starts in playing ring-around-a-rosie in broad daylight..."

CHAPTER V

Saturday was the customary day of the doctor's inspection, for which they prepared very carefully and with quaking in all the houses; as, however, even society ladies prepare themselves, when getting ready for a visit to a physician-specialist; they diligently made their intimate toilet and inevitably put on clean underthings, even as dressy as possible. The windows toward the street were closed with shutters, while at one of those windows, which gave out upon the yard, was put a table with a hard bolster to put under the back.

All the girls were agitated... "And what if there's a disease, which I haven't noticed myself?... And then the despatch to a hospital; disgrace; the tedium of hospital life; bad food; the hard course of treatment..."

Only Big Manka—or otherwise Manka the Crocodile—Zoe, and Henrietta—all thirty years old, and, therefore, in the reckoning of Yama, already old prostitutes, who had seen everything, had grown inured to everything, grown indifferent to their trade, like white, fat circus horses—remained imperturbably calm. Manka the Crocodile even often said of herself:

"I have gone through fire and water and pipes of brass ...Nothing will stick to me any more."

Jennka, since morning, was meek and pensive. She presented to Little White Manka a golden bracelet; a medallion upon a thin little chain with her photograph; and a silver neck crucifix. Tamara she moved through entreaty into taking two rings for remembrance: one of silver, in three hoops, that could be moved apart, with a heart in the middle, and under it two hands that clasped

one another when all the three parts of the ring were
joined; while the other was of thin gold wire with an alman-
dine.

"As for my underwear, Tamarochka—you give it to
Annushka, the chambermaid. Let her wash it out well
and wear it in good health, in memory of me."

The two of them were sitting in Tamara's room. Jennka
had in the very morning sent after cognac; and now slowly,
as though lazily, was imbibing wine-glass after wine-glass,
eating lemon and a piece of sugar after drinking. Tamara
was observing this for the first time and wondered, because
Jennka had always disliked wine, and drank very rarely;
and then only at the constraint of guests.

"What are you giving stuff away so to-day?" asked
Tamara. "Just as though you'd gotten ready to die, or to
go into a convent?..."

"Yes, and I will go away," answered Jennka listlessly.
"I am weary, Tamarochka!..."

"Well, which one of us has a good time?"

"Well, no!.. It isn't so much that I'm weary; but
somehow everything—everything is all the same... I
look at you, at the table, at the bottle; at my hands and
feet; and I'm thinking, that all this is alike and everything
is to no purpose... There's no sense in anything... Just
like on some old, old picture. Look there—there's a soldier
walking on the street, but it's all one to me, as though they
had wound up a doll, and it's moving... And that he's
wet under the rain, is also all one to me... And that he'll
die, and I'll die, and you, Tamara, will die—in this also
I see nothing frightful, nothing amazing... So simple and
wearisome is everything to me..."

Jennka was silent for a while; drank one more wine-
glass; sucked the sugar and, still looking out at the street,
suddenly asked:

"Tell me, please, Tamara, I've never asked you about
it—from where did you get in here, into the house? You
don't at all resemble all of us; you know everything; for
everything that turns up you have a good, clever remark..."

Even French, now—how well you spoke it that time! But none of us knows anything at all about you... Who are you?"

"Darling Jennechka, really, it's not worth while... A life like any life... I went to boarding school; was a governess; sang in a choir; then kept a shooting gallery in a summer garden; and then got mixed up with a certain charlatan and taught myself to shoot with a Winchester... I traveled with circuses—I represented an American Amazon. I used to shoot splendidly... Then I found myself in a monastery. There I passed two years... I've been through a lot... Can't recall everything... I used to steal..."

"You've lived through a great deal...Checkered-like."

"But then, my years are not a few. Well, what do you think—how many?"

"Twenty-two, twenty-four?.."

"No, my angel! It just struck thirty-two a week ago. I, if you like, am older than all of you here in Anna Markovna's. Only I didn't wonder at anything, didn't take anything near to heart. As you see, I never drink... I occupy myself very carefully with the care of my body; and the main thing, the very main thing—I don't allow myself ever to be carried away with men..."

"Well, but what about your Senka?.."

"Senka—that's a horse of another colour; the heart of woman is foolish, inconsistent... Can it possibly live without love? And even so, I don't love him, but just so... a self-deception... But, however, I shall be in very great need of Senka soon."

Jennka suddenly grew animated and looked at her friend with curiosity.

"But how did you come to get stuck right here, in this hole? So clever, handsome, sociable..."

"I'd have to take a long time in telling it... And then I'm too lazy... I got in here out of love; I got mixed up with a certain young man and went into a revolution with him. For we always act so, we women: where the dearie is looking, there we also look; what the dearie sees, that we also see... I didn't believe at soul in his work, but I went. A flattering man he was; smart, a good talker, a good looker... Only he proved to be a skunk and a traitor afterwards. He played at revolution; while he himself gave his comrades away to the gendarmes. A stool-pigeon, he was. When they had killed and shown him up, then all the foolishness left me. However, it was necessary to conceal myself... I changed my passport. Then they advised me, that the easiest thing of all was to screen myself with a yellow ticket... And then the fun began!.. And even here I'm on a sort of pasture ground; when the time comes, the successful moment arrives—I'll go away!"

"Where?" asked Jennie with impatience.

"The world is large... And I love life!.. There, now, I was the same way in the convent: I lived on and I lived on; sang antiphonies and dulias, until I had rested up, and had finally grown weary of it; and then all at once—hop! and into a cabaret... Wasn't that some jump? The same way out of here... I'll get into a theatre, into a circus, into a *corps de ballet*...but do you know, Jennechka, I'm drawn to the thieving trade the most, after all... Daring, dangerous, hard, and somehow intoxicating... It's drawing me!.. Don't you mind that I'm so respectable and modest, and can appear an educated young lady. I'm entirely, entirely different."

Her eyes suddenly blazed up, vividly and gaily.

"There's a devil living within me!"

"It's all very well for you," pensively and with weariness pronounced Jennie. "You at least desire something, but my soul is some sort of carrion... I'm twenty-five years old, now; but my soul is like that of an old woman, shrivelled up, smelling of the earth... And if I had only lived sensibly!.. Ugh!.. There was only some sort of slush."

"Drop it, Jennka; you're talking foolishly. You're smart, you're original; you have that especial power before which men crawl and creep so willingly. You go away from here, too. Not with me, of course—I'm always single—but go away all by your own self."

Jennka shook her head and quietly, without tears, hid her face in her palms.

"No, she responded dully, after a long silence, "no, this won't work out with me: fate has chewed me all up!.. I'm not a human being any more, but some sort of dirty cud... Eh!" she suddenly made a gesture of despair. 'Let's better drink some cognac, Jennechka,'" she addressed herself, " 'and let's suck the lemon a little!..' Brr...what nasty stuff!.. And where does Annushka always get such abominable stuff? If you smear a dog's wool with it, it will fall off... And always, the low-down thing, she'll take an extra half. Once I somehow ask her—'What are you hoarding money for?' 'Well, I,' she says, 'am saving it up for a wedding. What sort,' she says, 'of joy will it be for my husband, that I'll offer him up my innocence alone! I must earn a few hundreds in addition.' She's happy!.. I have here, Tamara, a little money in the little box under the mirror; you pass it on to her, please..."

"And what are you about, you fool; do you want to die, or what?" sharply, with reproach, said Tamara.

"No, I'm saying it just so, if anything happens... Take it, now, take the money! Maybe they'll take me off to the hospital... And how do you know what's going to take place there? I left myself some small change, if anything happens... And supposing that I wanted to do something to myself in downright earnest, Tamarochka—is it possible that you'd interfere with me?"

Tamara looked at her fixedly, deeply, and calmly. Jennie's eyes were sad, and as though vacant. The living fire had become extinguished in them, and they seemed turbid, just as though faded, with whites like moonstone.

"No," Tamara said at last, quietly but firmly. "If it was on account of love, I'd interfere; if it was on account of money, I'd talk you out of it; but there are cases where one must not interfere. I wouldn't help, of course; but I also wouldn't seize you and interfere with you."

At this moment the quick-limbed housekeeper Zociya whirled through the corridor with an outcry:

"Ladies, get dressed!—the doctor has arrived... Ladies, get dressed!.. Lively, ladies!.."

"Well, go on, Tamara, go on!" said Jennka tenderly, getting up. "I'll run into my room for just a minute—I haven't changed my dress yet, although, to tell the truth, this also is all one. When they'll be calling out for me, and I don't come in time, call out, run in after me."

And, going out of Tamara's room, she embraced her by the shoulder, as though by chance, and stroked it tenderly.

*   *   *

Doctor Klimenko—the official city doctor—was preparing in the parlor everything indispensable for an inspection—vaseline, a solution of sublimate, and other things—and was placing them on a separate little table. Here also were arranged for him the white blanks of the girls, replacing their passports, as well as a general alphabetical list. The girls, dressed only in their chemises, stockings, and slippers, were standing and sitting at a distance. Nearer the table was standing the proprietress herself—Anna Markovna—while a little behind her were Emma Edwardovna and Zociya.

The doctor—aged, disheartened, slovenly; a man indifferent to everything—put the *pince-nez* crookedly upon his nose, looked at the list, and called out:

"Alexandra Budzinskaya!.."

The frowning, little, pug-nosed Nina stepped out. Preserving on her face an angry expression, and breathing heavily from shame, from the consciousness of her own awkwardness, and from the exertions, she clumsily climbed up on the table. The doctor, squinting through his *pince-nez* and dropping it every minute, carried out the inspection.

"Go ahead!.. You're sound."

And on the reverse side of the blank he marked off: "Twenty-eighth of August. Sound" and put down a curly-cue. And, when he had not even finished writing, called out: "Voshchenkova, Irene!.."

Now it was the turn of Liubka. She, during the past month and a half of her comparative freedom, had had time to grow unaccustomed to the inspections of every week; and when the doctor turned up the chemise over her breast, she suddenly turned as red as only very bashful women can—even with her back and breast.

After her was the turn of Zoe; then of Little White Manka; after that of Tamara and Niurka—the last, the doctor found, had gonorrhœa, and ordered her to be sent off to a hospital.

The doctor carried out the inspection with amazing rapidity. It was now nearly twenty years that every week, on Saturdays, he had to inspect in such a manner several hundred girls; and he had worked out that habitual technical dexterity and rapidity, a calm carelessness of movements, which is frequently to be found in circus artists, in card sharpers, in furniture movers and packers, and in other professionals. And he carried out his manipulations with the same calmness with which a drover or a veterinary inspects several hundred head of cattle in a day.

Did he ever think that before him were living people; or that he appeared as the last and most important link of that fearful chain which is called legalized prostitution?

No! And even if he did experience this, then it must have been in the very beginning of his career. Now before him were only naked abdomens, naked backs, and opened mouths. Not one exemplar of all this faceless herd of every Saturday would he have recognized subsequently on the street. The main thing was the necessity of finishing as soon as possible the inspection in one establishment, in order to pass on to another, to a third, a ninth, a twentieth...

"Susannah Raitzina!" the doctor finally called out.

No one walked up to the table.

All the inmates of the house began to exchange glances and to whisper.

"Jennka... Where's Jennka?.."

But she was not among the girls.

Then Tamara, just released by the doctor, moved a little forward and said:

"She isn't here. She hasn't had a chance to get herself ready yet. Excuse me, Mr. Doctor, I'll go right away and call her."

She ran into the corridor and did not return for a long time. After her went, at first Emma Edwardovna, then Zociya, several girls, and even Anna Markovna herself.

"*Pfui!* What indecency is this!.." the majestic Emma Edwardovna was saying in the corridor, making an indignant face. "And eternally this Jennka!.. Always this Jennka!.. It seems my patience has already burst..."

But Jennka was nowhere—neither in her room, nor in Tamara's. They looked into other chambers, in all the out-of-the-way corners... But she did not prove to be even there.

"We must look in the water-closet... Perhaps she's there?" surmised Zoe.

But this institution was locked from the inside with a bolt. Emma Edwardovna knocked on the door with her fist.

"Jennie, do come out at last! What foolishness is this?!"

And, raising her voice, she cried out impatiently and threateningly:

"Do you hear, you swine?.. Come out this minute—the doctor's waiting!"

But there was no answer of any sort.

All exchanged glances with fear in their eyes, with one and the same thought in mind.

Emma Edwardovna shook the door by the brass knob, but the door did not yield.

"Go after Simeon!" Anna Markovna directed.

Simeon was called... He came, sleepy and morose, as was his wont. By the distracted faces of the girls and the housekeepers, he already saw that some misunderstanding or other had occurred, in which his professional cruelty and strength were required. When they explained to him what the matter was, he silently took the door-knob with both his hands, braced himself against the wall, and gave a yank.

The knob remained in his hands; and he himself, staggering backward, almost fell on the floor on his back.

"A-a, hell!" he began to growl in a stifled voice. "Give me a table knife."

Through the crack of the door he felt for the inner bolt with the table knife; whittled away with the blade the edges of the crack, and widened it so that he could at last push the end of the knife through it, and began gradually to scrape back the bolt. Only the grating of metal against metal could be heard.

Finally Simeon threw the door wide open.

Jennka was hanging in the middle of the water-closet on a tape from her corset, fastened to the lamp-hook. Her body, already motionless after an unprolonged agony, was slowly swinging in the air, and describing scarcely perceptible turns to the right and left around its vertical axis. Her face was bluishly-purple, and the tip of the tongue was thrust out between the clenched and bared teeth. The lamp which had been taken off was also here, sprawling on the floor.

Some one began to squeal hysterically, and all the girls, like a stampeded herd, crowding and jostling each other in the narrow corridor, vociferating and choking with hysterical sobbings, started in to run.

The doctor came upon hearing the outcries... Came, precisely, and not ran. Seeing what the matter was, he did not become amazed or excited; during his practice as an official city doctor, he had had his fill of seeing such things; so that he had already grown benumbed and hardened to human sufferings, wounds and death. He ordered Simeon to lift the corpse of Jennka a bit upward, and himself, getting up on the seat, cut through the tape. *Proforma*, he ordered Jennka's body to be borne away into the room

that had been hers, and tried with the help of the same
Simeon to produce artificial respiration; but after five
minutes gave it up as a bad job, fixed the *pince-nez*, which
had become crooked, on his nose, and said:

"Call the police in to make a protocol."

Again Kerbesh came, again whispered for a long time
with the proprietress in her little bit of a cabinet, and again
crunched in his pocket a new hundred-rouble bill.

The protocol was made in five minutes; and Jennka,
just as half-naked as she had hung herself, was carted
away in a hired waggon into an anatomical theatre, wrapped up in and covered with two straw mats.

Emma Edwardovna was the first to find the note that
Jennka had left on her night table. On a sheet, torn out
of the income-expense book, compulsory for every prostitute, in pencil, in a naive, rounded, childish handwriting—
by which, however, it could be judged that the hands of the
suicide had not trembled during the last minutes—was
written:

"I beg that no one be blamed for my death. I am dying
because I have become infected, and also because all
people are scoundrels and it is very disgusting to live.
How to divide my things—Tamara knows about that. I
told her in detail."

Emma Edwardovna turned around upon Tamara, who
was right on the spot among a number of other girls, and
with eyes filled with a cold, green hatred, hissed out:

"Then you knew, you low-down thing, what she was
preparing to do?.. You knew, you vermin?.. You knew
and didn't tell?.."

She already had swung back, in order, as was her wont,
to hit Tamara cruelly and calculatingly; but suddenly
stopped just as she was, with gaping mouth and with eyes
wide open. It was just as though she was seeing, for the
first time, Tamara, who was looking at her with a firm,
wrathful, unbearable gaze; and slowly, slowly was raising
from below, and at last brought up to the level of the housekeeper's face, a small object, glistening with white metal.

CHAPTER VI.

That very same day, at evening, a very important event took place in the house of Anna Markovna: the whole institution—with land and house, with live and inanimate stock—passed into the hands of Emma Edwardovna.

They had been speaking of this, on and off, for a long time in the establishment; but when the rumours so unexpectedly, immediately right after the death of Jennka, turned into realities, the misses could not for a long time come to themselves for amazement and fear. They knew well, having experienced the sway of the German upon themselves, her cruel, implacable pedantism; her greed, arrogance, and, finally, her perverted, exacting, repulsive love, now for one, now for another favorite. Besides that, it was no mystery to any one, that out of the fifteen thousand which Emma Edwardovna had to pay the former proprietress for the firm and for the property, one third belonged to Kerbesh, who had, for a long time already, been carrying on half-friendly, half-business relations with the fat housekeeper. From the union of two such people, shameless, pitiless, and covetous, the girls could expect all sorts of disasters for themselves.

Anna Markovna had to let the house go so cheaply not simply because Kerbesh, even if he had not known about certain shady little transactions to her credit, could still at any time he liked trip her up and eat her up without leaving anything. Of pretexts and cavils for this even a hundred could be found every day; and certain ones of them not merely threatened the shutting down of the house alone, but, if you like, even with the court.

But, dissembling, oh-ing and sighing, bewailing her poverty, her maladies and orphanhood, Anna Markovna at soul was glad of even such a settlement. And then it

must be said: she was already for a long time feeling the approach of senile infirmity, together with all sorts of ailments and the thirst for complete, benevolent rest, undisturbed by anything. All, of which she had not even dared dream in her early youth, when she herself had yet been a prostitute of the rank and file—all had now come to her of itself, one in addition to the other: peaceful old age, a house—a brimming cup on one of the quiet, cozy streets, almost in the centre of the city,—the adored daughter Birdie, who—if not to-day then to-morrow— must marry a respected man, an engineer, a house-owner, and member of the city-council; provided for as she was with a respectable dowry and magnificent valuables...
Now it was possible peacefully, without hurrying, with gusto, to dine and sup on sweet things, for which Anna Markovna had always nourished a great weakness; to drink after dinner good, home-made, strong cherry-brandy; and of evenings to play a bit| at "preference", for kopeck stakes, with esteemed elderly ladies of her acquaintance, who, even although they never as much as let it appear that they knew the real trade of the little old woman, did in reality know it very well; and not only did not condemn her business but even bore themselves with respect toward those enormous percentages which she earned upon her capital. And these charming friends, the joy and consola- tion of an untroubled old age, were: one—the keeper of a loan office; another—the proprietress of a lively hotel near the railroad; the third—the owner of a jewelry shop, not large, but all the go and well known among the big thieves, &c. And about them, in her turn, Anna Markovna knew and could tell several shady and not especially flattering anecdotes; but in their society it was not customary to talk of the sources of the family well-being—only clever- ness, daring, success, and decent manners were esteemed.

But, even besides that, Anna Markovna, sufficiently limited in mind and not especially developed, had some sort of an amazing inner intuition, which during all her life permitted her instinctively but irreproachably to avoid unpleasantnesses, and to find prudent paths in time. And so now, after the sudden death of Roly-Poly, and the suicide of Jennka which followed the next day, she, with her unconsciously-penetrating soul foreguessed that fate—which had been favouring her house of ill-fame, sending her good fortunes, turning away all under-water shoals—was now getting ready to turn its back upon her. And she was the first to retreat.

They say, that not long before a fire in a house, or before the wreck of a ship, the wise, nervous rats in droves make their way into another place. And Anna Markovna was directed by the same rat-like, animal, prophetic intuition. And she was right: immediately right after the death of Jennka some fateful curse seemed to hang over the house, formerly Anna Markovna Shaibes', but now Emma Edwardovna Titzner's: deaths, misfortunes, scandals just simply descended upon it ceaselessly, becoming constantly more frequent, on the manner of bloody events in Shakespeare's tragedies; as, however, was the case in all the remaining houses of the Yamas as well.

And one of the first to die, a week after the liquidation of the business, was Anna Markovna herself. However, this frequently happens with people put out of their accustomed rut of thirty years: so die war heroes, who have gone into retirement—people of insuperable health and iron will; so quickly go off the stage former stock brokers, who have happily gone away to rest, but have been deprived of the burning allurement of risk and hazard; so, too, age rapidly, droop, and grow decrepit, the great artists who leave the stage... Her death was the death of the just. Once at a game of cards she felt herself unwell; begged them to wait a while for her; said that she would lie down for just a minute; lay down in the bedroom on a bed; sighed deeply, and passed on into another world—with a calm face, with a peaceful, senile smile upon her lips. Isaiah Savvich—her faithful comrade on the path of life, a trifle downtrodden, who had always played a secondary, subordinate role—survived her only a month.

Birdie was left sole heiress. She very successfully turned the cozy house into money, as well as the land somewhere at the edge of the town; married, as it had been presupposed, very happily; and up to this time is convinced that her father carried on a great commercial business in the export of wheat through Odessa and Novorossiysk into Asia Minor.

*   *   *

On the evening of that day when Jennie's corpse had been carried away to an anatomical theatre; at an hour when not even a chance guest appears on Yamskaya Street, all the girls, at the insistence of Emma Edwardovna, assembled in the drawing room. Not one of them dared murmur against the fact that on this distressing day, when they had not yet recovered from the impression of Jennka's horrible death, they would be compelled to dress up, as usual, in wildly festive finery; and to go into the brightly illuminated drawing room; in order to dance, sing, and to entice lecherous men with their denuded body.

And at last into the drawing room walked Emma Edwardovna herself. She was more majestic than she had ever been—clad in a black silk gown, from which, just like battlements, her enormous breasts jutted out, upon which descended two fat chins; in black silk mittens; with an enormous gold chain wound thrice around her neck, and terminating in a ponderous medallion hanging upon the very abdomen.

"Ladies!.." she began impressively, "I must...Stand up!" she suddenly called out commandingly. "When I speak, you must hear me out standing."

They all exchanged glances with perplexity: such an order was a novelty in the establishment. However, the girls got up one after another, irresolutely, with eyes and mouths gaping.

"*Sie sollen*...you must from this day show me that respect which you are bound to show to your mistress," importantly and weightily began Emma Edwardovna.

"Beginning from to-day, the establishment in a legal manner has passed from our good and respected Anna Markovna to me, Emma Edwardovna Titzner. I hope that we will not quarrel, and that you will behave yourselves like sensible, obedient, and well-brought-up girls. I will be to you like in place of your own mother, but only remember, that I will not stand for laziness, or drunkenness, or notions of any sort; or any kind of disorder. The kind Madam Shaibes, it must be said, held you in too loose reins. O-o, I will be var more strict. Discipline *über alles*...before everything. It's a great pity, that the Russian people are lazy, dirty and stoopid, do not understand this rule; but don't you trouble yourself, I will teach you this for your own good. I say 'for your own good,' because my main thought is to kill the competition of Treppel. I want that my client should be a man of substance, and not some charlatan and ragamuffin, some kind of student, now, or ham actor. I want that my ladies should be the most beautiful, best brought-up, the healthiest and gayest in the whole city. I won't spare any money in order to set up swell furnishings; and you will have rooms with silk furniture and with genuine, beautiful rugs. Your guests will no longer be demanding beer, but only genteel Bordeaux and Burgundy wines and champagne. Remember, that a rich, substantial, elderly man never likes your common, ordinary, coarse love. He requires Cayenne pepper; he requires not a trade, but an art, and you will soon acquire this. At Treppel's they take three roubles for a visit and ten roubles for a night... I will establish it so, that you will receive five roubles for a visit and twenty-five for a night. They will present you with gold and diamonds. I will contrive it so, that you won't have to pass on into establishments of a lower sort, *und so weiter*...right down to the soldier's filthy den. No! Deposits will be put away and saved with me for each one of you every month; and will be put away in your name in a banker's office, where there will increase interest upon them, and interest upon interest. And then, if a girl feels herself tired, or wants to marry a respectable man, there will always be at her disposal not a large, but a sure capital. So is it done in the best establishments in Riga, and everywhere abroad. Let no one say about me, that Emma Edwardovna is a spider, a vixen, a cupping glass. But for disobedience, for laziness, for notions, for lovers on the side, I will punish cruelly and, like nasty weeds, will throw out—on the street, or still worse. Now I have said all that I had to. Nina, come near me. And all the rest of you come up in turn."

Ninka irresolutely walked right up to Emma Edwardovna—and even staggered back in amazement: Emma Edwardovna was extending her right hand to her, with the fingers lowered downward, and slowly nearing it to Ninka's lips.

"Kiss it!..." impressively and firmly pronounced Emma Edwardovna, narrowing her eyes and with head thrown back, in the magnificent pose of a princess ascending her throne.

Ninka was so bewildered that her right arm gave a jerk in order to make the sign of the cross; but she corrected herself, loudly smacked the extended hand, and stepped aside. Following her Zoe, Henrietta, Vanda and others stepped up also. Tamara alone continued to stand near the wall with her back to the mirror; that mirror into which Jennka so loved to gaze, in gone-by times, admiring herself as she walked back and forth through the drawing room.

Emma Edwardovna let the imperious, obstinate gaze of a boa-constrictor rest upon her; but the hypnosis did not work. Tamara bore this gaze without turning away, without flinching; but without any expression on her face. Then the new proprietress put down her hand, produced on her face something resembling a smile, and said hoarsely:

"And with you, Tamara, I must have a little talk separately, eye to eye. Let's go!"

"I hear you, Emma Edwardovna!" calmly answered Tamara.

Emma Edwardovna came to the little bit of a cabinet, where formerly Anna Markovna loved to drink coffee with clotted cream; sat down on the divan and pointed out a place opposite her to Tamara. For some time the women kept silent; searchingly, mistrustfully eyeing each other.

"You acted rightly, Tamara," said Emma Edwardovna finally. "You did wisely in not stepping up, on the manner of those sheep, to kiss my hand. But just the same, I would not have let you come to that. I wanted right there in the presence of all, when you walked up to me, to press your hand and to offer you the place of first house-keeper—you understand?—my chief assistant—and on terms very advantageous to you..."

"I thank you..."

"No, wait a while, don't interrupt me. I will have my say to the end, and then you will express your pros and cons. But will you explain to me, please, when yesterday you were aiming at me out of a revolver, what did you want? Can it possibly be, to kill me?"

"On the contrary, Emma Edwardovna," retorted Tamara respectfully, "on the contrary; it seemed to me that you wanted to strike me."

"*Pfui!* What do you mean, Tamarochka!.. Have you paid no attention to the fact that during all the time of our acquaintance I never permitted myself, not only to hit you, but even to address you with a rude word?.. What do you mean, what do you mean?.. I don't confuse you with this poor Russian trash... Glory be to God, I am an experienced person and one who knows people well. I can very well see that you are a genuinely cultured young lady; far more educated, for example, than I myself. You are refined, elegant, smart. I am convinced of the fact that you even know music not at all badly. Finally, if I were to confess, I was a little...how shall I put it to you?... I always was a little in love with you.

And now you wanted to shoot me! Me, a person who could be a very good friend to you! Well, what will you say to that?"

"Well...nothing at all, Emma Edwardovna," retorted Tamara in the meekest and most plausible tone. "Everything was very simple. Even before that I found the revolver under Jennka's pillow and brought it, in order to give it over to you. I did not want to interfere, when you were reading the letter; but then you turned around to me—I stretched the revolver out to you and wanted to say: 'See, Emma Edwardovna, what I found'—for, don't you see, it surprised me awfully how the late Jennie, having a revolver at her disposal, preferred such a horrible death as hanging? And that's all!"

The bushy, frightful eyebrows of Emma Edwardovna rose upward; the eyes widened joyously; and a real, uncounterfeited smile spread over her cheeks of a behemoth. She quickly extended both hands to Tamara.

"And is this all? *O, mein Kind?* And I thought... God knows what I imagined! Give me your hands, Tamara, your little charming white hands, and allow me to press them *auf mein Herz*, upon my heart, and to kiss you."

The kiss was so long, that Tamara with great difficulty and with aversion barely freed herself from the embraces of Emma Edwardovna.

"Well, and now to business. And so, here are my terms: you will be housekeeper, I give you fifteen percent. out of the clear gain. Mind you, Tamara, fifteen percent. And, besides that, a small salary—thirty, forty, well, if you like, fifty roubles a month. Splendid terms—isn't that the truth? I am deeply convinced, that none other than just you will help me to raise the house to a real height, and make it the swellest not only in our city, but in all the south of Russia as well. You have taste, and an understanding of things!.. Besides that, you will always be able to entertain, and to stir up the most exacting, the most unyielding guests. In rare instances, when a very rich and distinguished gentleman—in Russian they call it one "sun-fish", while with us, *ein Freier,** —when he becomes infatuated with you—for you are so handsome, Tamarochka," (the proprietress looked at her with misty, humid eyes), "then I do not at all forbid you to pass the time with him gaily; only to bear down always upon the fact that you have no right, owing to your duty, your position, *und so weiter, und so weiter...   Aber sagen Sie bitte*, do you easily make yourself understood in German?"

"*Die Deutsche Sprache beherrsche ich in geringerem Grade als die französische; indes kann ich stets in einer Salon-Plauderei mitmachen.*" †

"*O, wunderbar!   Sie haben eine entzückende Rigaer Aussprache, die beste aller deutschen Aussprachen.   Und also—fahren wir in unserer Sprache fort.   Sie klingt viel süsser meinem Ohr, die Muttersprache.   Schön?*"**

"*Schön.*"††

"*Zuletzt werden Sie nachgeben, dem Anschein nach ungern, unwillkürlich, von der Laune des Augenblicks hingerissen— und, was die Hauptsache ist, lautlos, heimlich vor mir.   Sie verstehen?   Dafür zahlen Narren ein schweres Geld.   Übrigens brauche ich Sie wohl nicht zu lernen.*"***

"*Ja, gnädige Frau.   Sie sprechen gar kluge Dinge.   Doch das ist schon keine Plauderei mehr, sondern eine ernste Unterhaltung.*"†††   And for that reason it is more convenient for me, if you will revert to the Russian language... I am ready to obey you."

---

*In English, a "toff"; in American, a "swell."—*Trans.*

†"My mastery of the German language is a trifle worse than that of the French, but I can always keep up my end in parlor small talk."

**"O, splendid!.. You have a bewitching Riga enunciation, the most correct of all the German ones. And so, let us continue in my tongue. That is far sweeter to my ear—my mother tongue. All right?"

††"All right."

***"In the very end you will give in, as though unwillingly, as though against your will, as though from infatuation, a momentary caprice, and—which is the main thing—as though on the sly from me. You understand? For this the fools pay enormous money. However, it seems I will not have to teach you."

†††"Yes, my dear madam. You say very wise things. But this is no longer small talk; it is, rather, serious conversation..."

"Furthermore!.. I was just now talking about a lover.
I dare not forbid you this pleasure, but let us be prudent:
let him not appear here, or appear as rarely as possible.
I will give you days for going out, when you will be perfectly free. But it's best if you would get along without
him entirely. It will serve your benefit too. This is only
a drag and a yoke. I am telling you this from my own
personal experience. Wait a while; after three or four
years we will expand this business so, that you will have
substantial money already, and then I will take you into
the business as a partner with full rights. After ten years
you will still be young and handsome, and then take and
buy men as much as you want to. By that time romantic
follies will go out of your head entirely, and it will not be
you who will be chosen already, but you who will be
choosing with sense and with feeling, as a connoisseur
picks out precious stones. Do you agree with me?"

Tamara cast down her eyes, and smiled just the least
trifle.

"You speak golden truths, Emma Edwardovna. I will
drop mine, but not at once. For that I will need some two
weeks. I will try not to have him appear here. I accept
your proposition."

"And that's splendid!" said Emma Edwardovna, getting up. "Now let us conclude our agreement with one
good, sweet kiss."

And she again embraced and took to kissing Tamara
hard; who, with her downcast eyes and naive, tender face,
seemed now altogether a little girl. But, having freed
herself, finally, from the proprietress, she asked in Russian:

"You see, Emma Edwardovna, that I agree in everything with you, but for that I beg you to fulfill one request
of mine. It will not cost you anything. Namely, I hope
that you will allow me and the other girls to escort the late
Jennie to the cemetery."

Emma Edwardovna made a wry face.

"Oh, if you want to, my darling Tamara, I have nothing
against your whim. Only what for? This will not help

the dead person and will not make her alive. Only senti-
mentalism alone will come out of it... But very well!
Only, however, you know yourself that in accordance
with your law suicides are not buried, or—I don't know
with certainty—it seems they throw them into some dirty
hole beyond the cemetery.''

"No, do allow me to do as I want to myself. Let it be
my whim, but concede it to me, my darling, dear, bewitching Emma Edwardovna! But then, I promise you that
this will be my last whim. After this I will be like a wise
and obedient soldier at the disposal of a talented general.''

"*Is` gut!*" Emma Edwardovna gave in with a sigh. "I
can not deny you in anything, my child. Let me press
your hand. Let us toil and labour together for the common
good.''

And, having opened the door, she called out across the
drawing room into the entrance-hall: "Simeon!" And
when Simeon appeared in the room, she ordered him
weightily and triumphantly:

"Bring us a bottle of champagne here, but the real
thing—*Rederer demi sec*, and as cool as possible. Step
lively!" she ordered the porter, who was gaping at her
with popping eyes. "We will drink with you, Tamara, to
the new business, to our brilliant and beautiful future.''

They say that dead people bring luck. If there is any
foundation at all in this superstition, then on this Saturday
it could not have told plainer: the influx of visitors was out
of the ordinary, even for a Saturday night. True, the
girls, passing through the corridor or past the room that
had been Jennka's, increased their steps; timorously
glanced at it sidelong, out of the corner of the eye; while
others even crossed themselves. But late in the night the
fear of death somehow subsided, grew bearable. All the
rooms were occupied, while in the drawing room a new
violinist was trilling without cease—a free-and-easy, clean-
shaven young man, whom the pianist with the cataract
had searched out somewhere and brought with him.

The appointment of Tamara as housekeeper was received with cold perplexity, with taciturn dryness. But, having bided her time, Tamara managed to whisper to Little White Manka:

"Listen, Manya! You tell them all that they shouldn't pay any attention to the fact that I've been chosen housekeeper. It's got to be so. But let them do as they wish, only don't let them trip me up. I am as before—their friend and intercessor... And further on we'll see."

CHAPTER VII.

On the next day, on Sunday, Tamara had a multitude of cares. She had become possessed by a firm and unde-viating thought to bury her friend despite all circum-stances, in the way that nearest friends are buried—in a Christian manner, with all the sad solemnity of the burial of secular persons.

She belonged to the number of those strange persons who underneath an external indolent calmness, careless taciturnity, egoistical withdrawal into one's self, conceal within them unusual energy; always as though slumbering with half an eye, guarding itself from unnecessary expend-iture; but ready in one moment to become animated and to rush forward without reckoning the obstacles.

At twelve o'clock she descended in a cab into the old town; rode through it into a little narrow street giving out upon a square where fairs were held; and stopped near a rather dirty tea-room, having ordered the cabby to wait. In the room she made inquiries of a boy, red-haired, with hair cut high in the back, and with a buttered parting, if Senka the Depot had not come here? The serving lad, who, judging by his refined and gallant readiness, had already known Tamara for a long time, answered that "Nohow, ma'am; they—Semen Ignatich—had not been in yet, and probably would not be here soon seein' as how yesterday they had the pleasure of going on a spree at the Transvaal, and had played at billiards until six in the morning; and that now they, in all probabilities, are at home, in the Half Way House rooms, and if the young lady will give the word, then it's possible to hop over to them this here minute."

Tamara asked for paper and pencil, and wrote a few words right on the spot. Then she gave the note to the waiter together with a half-rouble piece for a tip, and rode away.

The following visit was to the artiste Rovinskaya, living, as Tamara had known even before, in the city's most aristocratic hotel—Europe—where she occupied several rooms in a consecutive suite. To obtain an interview with the singer was not very easy: the doorman below said that it looked as if Ellena Victorovna was not at home; while her own personal maid, who came out in answer to Tamara's knocking, declared that madam had a headache, and that she was not receiving any one. Again Tamara was compelled to write on a piece of paper:

"I come to you from her who once, in a house which is not spoken of loudly, cried, standing before you on her knees, after you had sung the ballad of Dragomyzhsky. Your kind treatment of her was so splendid. Do you remember? Do not fear—she has no need of any one's help now: yesterday she died. But you can do one very important deed in her memory, which will be almost no trouble to you at all. While I—am that very person who permitted herself to say a few bitter truths to the baroness T—, who was then with you; for which truths I am remorseful and apologize up to now."

"Hand this over!" she ordered the chambermaid.

She returned after two minutes.

"The madam requests you. They apologize very much that they will receive you not fully dressed."

She escorted Tamara, opened a door before her and quietly shut it.

The great artiste was lying upon an enormous ottoman, covered with a beautiful Tekin rug and a multitude of little silk pillows, and soft cylindrical bolsters of tapestry. Her feet were wrapped up in silvery, soft fur. Her fingers, as usual, were adorned by a multiplicity of rings with emeralds, attracting the eyes by their deep and tender green.

The artiste was having one of her evil, black days to-day. Yesterday morning some misunderstandings with the management had arisen; while in the evening the public had received her not as triumphantly as she would have desired, or, perhaps, this had simply appeared so to her; while to-day in the newspapers the fool of a reviewer, who understood just as much of art as a cow does of astronomy, had praised up her rival, Titanova, in a big article. And so Ellena Victorovna had persuaded herself that her head was aching; that there was a nervous tic in her temples; and that her heart, time and again, seemed suddenly to fall through somewheres.

"How do you do, my dear!" she said, a trifle nasally, in a weak, pale voice, with pauses; as heroines on the stage speak when dying from love and from consumption. "Sit down here... I am glad to see you... Only don't be angry—I am almost dying from migraine, and from my miserable heart. Pardon my speaking with difficulty. I think I sang too much and tired my voice..."

Rovinskaya, of course, had recalled both the mad escapade of that evening; and the striking, unforgettable face of Tamara; but now, in a bad mood, in the wearisome, prosaic light of an autumn day, this adventure appeared to her as unnecessary bravado; something artificial, imagined, and poignantly shameful. But she was equally sincere on that strange, night-marish evening when she, through the night of talent, had prostrated the proud Jennka at her feet, as well as now, when she recalled it with fatigue, indolence, and artistic disdain. She, as well as many distinguished artists, was always playing a role; was always not her own self, and always regarded her words, movements, actions, as though looking at herself from a distance with the eyes and feelings of the spectators.

She languidly raised from the pillow her narrow, slender, beautiful hand, and applied it to her forehead; and the mysterious, deep emeralds stirred as though alive and began to flash with a warm, deep sparkle.

"I just read in your note that this poor...pardon me, her name has vanished out of my head..."

"Jennie."

"Yes, yes, thank you! I recall it now. She died? But from what?"

"She hanged herself...yesterday morning, during the doctor's inspection..."

The eyes of the artiste, so listless, seemingly faded, suddenly opened, and, as through a miracle, grew animated and became shining and green, just like her emeralds; and in them were reflected curiosity, fear and aversion.

"Oh, my God! Such a dear, so original, handsome, so fiery... Oh, the poor, poor soul!.. And the reason for this was?.."

"You know...the disease. She told you."

"Yes, yes... I remember, I remember... But to hang one's self!.. What horror!.. Why, I advised her to treat herself then. Medicine works miracles now. I myself know several people, who absolutely...well, absolutely cured themselves. Everybody in society knows this and receives them... Ah, the poor little thing, the poor little thing!.."

"And so I've come to you, Ellena Victorovna. I wouldn't have dared to disturb you, but I seem to be in a forest, and have no one to turn to. You were so kind then, so touchingly attentive, so tender to us... I need only your advice and, perhaps, a little of your influence, your protection..."

"Oh, please, my dear!.. All I can do, I will... Oh, my poor head! And then this horrible news. Tell me, in what way can I be of assistance to you?"

"To confess, I don't know even myself yet," answered Tamara. "You see, they carried her away to an anatomical theatre... But until they had made the protocol, until they made the journey—then the time for receiving had gone by also—in general I think that they have not had a chance to dissect her yet... I'd like, if it's only possible, that she should not be touched. To-day is Sunday; perhaps they'll postpone it until to-morrow, and in the meanwhile something may be done for her..."

"I can't tell you, dear... Wait!.. Haven't I some friend among the professors, in the medical world?.. I will look later in my memo-books. Perhaps we will succeed in doing something."

"Besides that," continued Tamara, "I want to bury her... At my expense... I was attached to her with all my heart during her life."

"I will help you with pleasure in this, materially..."

"No, no!.. A thousand thanks!.. I'll do everything myself. I would not hesitate to have recourse to your kind heart, but this...—you will understand me...—this is something in the nature of a vow, that a person gives to one's self and to the memory of a friend. The main difficulty is in how we may manage to bury her with Christian rites. She was, it seems, an unbeliever, or believed altogether poorly. And it's only by chance that I, also, will cross my forehead. But I don't want them to bury her just like a dog, somewheres beyond the enclosure of the cemetery; in silence, without words, without singing ...I don't know, will they permit burying her properly—with choristers, with priests? For that reason I'm asking you to assist me with your advice. Or, perhaps, you will direct me somewhere?..."

Now the artiste had little by little become interested and was already beginning to forget about her fatigue, and migraine, and the consumptive heroine dying in the fourth act. She was already picturing the role of an intercessor, the beautiful figure of genius merciful to a fallen woman. This was original, extravagant, and at the same time so theatrically touching! Rovinskaya, like many of her *confrères*, did not let one day pass by—and, if it were possible, she would not have let pass even one hour—without standing out from the crowd, without compelling people to talk about her: to-day she would participate in a pseudo-patriotic manifestation, while to-morrow she would read from a platform, for the benefit of revolutionaries exiled to Siberia, inciting verses, full of fire and vengeance. She loved to sell flowers at carnivals, in

riding academies; and to sell champagne at large balls.
She would think up her little *bon mots* beforehand, which
on the morrow would be caught up by the whole town.
She desired that everywhere and always the crowd should
look only at her, repeat her name, love her Egyptian,
green eyes, her rapacious and sensuous mouth; her emeralds on the slender and nervous hands.

"I can't grasp it all properly at once," said she after a
silence. "But if a person wants anything hard, he will
attain it, and I want to fulfill your wish with all my soul.
Stay, stay!.. I think a glorious thought is coming into
my head... For then, on that evening, if I mistake not,
there was with us, beside the baroness and me..."

"I don't know them... One of them walked out of the
cabinet later than all of you. He kissed Jennie's hand and
said, that if she should ever need him, he was always at her
service; and gave her his card, but asked her not to show
it to any strangers. But later all this passed off somehow
and was forgotten. In some way I never found the time to
ask Jennie who this man was; while yesterday I searched
for the card but couldn't find it..."

"Allow me, allow me!.. I have recalled it!" the artiste
suddenly became animated. "Aha!" exclaimed she,
rapidly getting off the ottoman. "It was Ryazanov...
Yes, yes, yes... The advocate Ernst Andreievich Ryazanov. We will arrange everything right away. That's a
splendid thought!"

She turned to the little table upon which the telephone
apparatus was standing, and rang:

"Central—18-35 please... Thank you... Hello!..
Ask Ernst Andreievich to the telephone... The artiste
Rovinskaya... Thank you... Hello!.. Is this you,
Ernst Andreievich? Very well, very well, but now it isn't
a matter of little hands. Are you free?.. Drop the nonsense!.. The matter is serious. Couldn't you come up to
me for a quarter of an hour?.. No, no... Yes... Only
as a kind and a clever man. You slander yourself...
Well, that's splendid, really... Well, I am not especially

well-dressed, but I have a justification—a fearful headache. No, a lady, a girl... You will see for yourself, come as soon as possible... Thanks! *Au revoir!...*"

"He will come right away," said Rovinskaya, hanging up the receiver. "He is a charming and an awfully clever man. Everything is possible to him, even the almost impossible to man... But in the meantime...pardon me—your name?"

Tamara was abashed, but then smiled at herself:

"Oh, it isn't worth your disturbing yourself, Ellena Victorovna! *Mon nomme de guerre* Tamara, but just so—Anastasia Nikolaevna. It's all the same—call me even Tamara... I am more used to it..."

"Tamara!.. That is so beautiful!.. So now, Mlle. Tamara, perhaps you will not refuse to breakfast with me? Perhaps Ryazanov will also do so with us..."

"I have no time, forgive me."

"That's a great pity!.. I hope, some other time... But, perhaps you smoke," and she moved toward her a gold cigar-case, adorned with an enormous letter E out of the same emeralds she adored.

Ryazanov came very soon.

Tamara, who had not examined him properly on that evening, was struck by his appearance. Tall of stature, almost of an athletic build, with a broad brow, like Beethoven's, tangled with artistically negligent black, grizzled hair; with the large fleshy mouth of the passionate orator; with clear, expressive, clever, mocking eyes—he had such an appearance as catches one's eyes among thousands—the appearance of a vanquisher of souls and a conqueror of hearts; deeply ambitious, not yet oversated with life; still fiery in love and never retreating before a beautiful indiscretion... "If fate had not broken me up so," reflected Tamara, watching his movements with enjoyment, "then here's a man to whom I'd throw my life; jestingly, with delight, with a smile, as a plucked rose is thrown to the beloved..."

Ryazanov kissed Rovinskaya's hand, then with unconstrained simplicity exchanged greetings with Tamara and
said:

"We are acquainted even from that mad evening, when
you dumfounded all of us with your knowledge of the
French language, and when you spoke. That which you
said was, between us, paradoxical; but then, how it was
said!.. To this day I remember the tone of your voice, so
warm, expressive... And so, Ellena Victorovna," he
turned to Rovinskaya again, sitting down on a small, low
chair without a back, "in what can I be of use to you?
I am at your disposal."

Rovinskaya, with a languid air, again applied the tips
of her fingers to her temples.

"Ah, really, I am so upset, my dear Ryazanov," said
she, intentionally extinguishing the sparkle of her magnificent eyes, "and then, my miserable head... May I
trouble you to pass me the pyramidon what-not from that
table... Let Mlle. Tamara tell you everything... I can
not, I am not able to... This is so horrible!.."

Tamara briefly, lucidly, narrated to Ryazanov all the
sad history of Jennka's death; recalled also about the card
left with Jennie; and also how the deceased had reverently
preserved this card; and—in passing—about his promise
to help in case of need.

"Of course, of course!" exclaimed Ryazanov, when she
had finished; and at once began pacing the room back and
forth with big steps, ruffling and tossing back his picturesque hair through habit. "You are performing a magnificent, sincere, comradely action! That is good!..
That is very good!.. I am yours... You say—a permit
for the funeral... Hm!.. God grant me memory!.."

He rubbed his forehead with his palm.

"Hm...hm...If I'm not mistaken—Monocanon, rule
one hundred seventy...one hundred seventy...eighth...
Pardon me, I think I remember it by heart... Pardon
me!.. Yes, so! 'If a man slayeth himself, he shall not
be chanted over, nor shall a mass be said for him, unless

he were greatly astonied, that is, to wit, out of his mind'...
Hm... See St. Timothy Alexandrine... And so, my
dear miss, the first thing... You say, that she was taken
down from the noose by your doctor—*i. e.*, the official city
doctor... His name?.."

"Klimenko."

"It seems I've met him somewheres... All right...
Who is the district inspector in your precinct station?"

"Kerbesh."

"Aha, I know... Such a strong, virile fellow, with a
red beard in a fan... Yes?"

"Yes, that is he."

"I know him very well! There, now, is somebody that
a sentence to hard labour is hankering after... Some ten
times he fell into my hands; and always, the skunk, gave
me the slip somehow. Slippery, just like an eel-pout...
We will have to slip him a little present. Well, now! And
then the anatomical theatre... When do you want to
bury her?"

"Really, I don't know... I would like to do it as soon
as possible...if possible, to-day."

"Hm... To-day... I don't vouch for it—we will
hardly manage it... But here is my memorandum book.
Well, take even this page, where are my friends under the
letter T—just write the very same way: Tamara, and
your address. In two hours I will give you an answer.
Does that suit you? But I repeat again, that probably
you will have to postpone the burial till to-morrow...
Then—pardon my unceremoniousness—is money needed,
perhaps?"

"No, thank you!" refused Tamara. "I have money.
Thanks for your interest!.. It's time for me to be going.
I thank you with all my heart, Ellena Victorovna!.."

"Then expect it in two hours," repeated Ryazanov,
escorting her to the door.

Tamara did not at once ride away to the house. She
turned into a little coffee-house on Catholicheskaya Street
on the way. There Senka the Depot was waiting for her—

a gay fellow with the appearance of a handsome Tzigan; not black but blue-haired; black-eyed, with yellow whites; resolute and daring in his work; the pride of local thieves—a great celebrity in their world, the first leader of experience and a constant, all-night gamester.

He stretched out his hand to her, without getting up. But in the way in which he so carefully, with a certain force, seated her in her place could be seen a broad, good-natured endearment.

"How do you do, Tamarochka! Haven't seen you in a long time—I grew weary... Do you want coffee?"

"No! Business first... To-morrow we bury Jennka... She hanged herself..."

"Yes, I read it in a newspaper," carelessly drawled out Senka through his teeth. "What's the odds!.."

"Get fifty roubles for me at once."

"Tamarochka, my sweetheart—I haven't a kopeck!..."

"I'm telling you—get them!" ordered Tamara, imperiously, but without getting angry.

"Oh, my Lord!.. Yours, now, I didn't touch, like I promised; but then, it's Sunday... The savings banks are closed..."

"Let them!.. Hock the savings book! In general, it's up to you!"

"Why do you need this, my dearie?"

"Isn't it all the same to you, you fool?.. For the funeral."

"Oh! Well, all right then!" sighed Senka. "Then I'd best bring it to you myself in the evening... Right, Tamarochka?.. It's so very hard for me to stand it without you! Oh, my dearie, how I'd kiss and kiss you; I wouldn't let you close your eyes!.. Shan't I come?.."

"No, no!.. You do as I ask you, Senechka... Give in to me. But you mustn't come—I'm housekeeper now."

"Well, what d'you know about that!.." drawled out the astonished Senka and even whistled.

"Yes. And don't you come to me in the meantime. But afterwards, afterwards, sweetheart, whatever you desire... There will be an end to everything soon!"

"Oh, if you wouldn't make me suffer so! Wind things up as soon as you can!"

"And I will wind 'em up! Wait one little week more, dearie! Did you get the powders?"

"The powders are a trifle!" discontentedly answered Senka. "And it isn't powders at all, but pills."

"And you're sure when you say that they'll dissolve at once in water?"

"Sure, I saw it myself."

"But he won't die? Listen, Senya: he won't die? Is that right?.."

"Nothing will happen to him... He'll only snooze for a while... Oh, Tamarka!" exclaimed he in a passionate whisper; and even suddenly stretched himself hard from an unbearable emotion, so that his joints cracked. "Finish it, for God's sake, as soon as possible!.. Let's do the trick and—bye-bye! Wherever you want to go to, sweetheart! I am all at your will: if you want to, we start off for Odessa; if you want to—abroad. Finish it up as soon as possible!.."

"Soon, soon...."

"You just wink at me, and I'm all ready... with powders, with instruments, with passports... And then—choo-choo! The machine is off! Tamarochka! My angel!.. My precious, my sparkler!.."

And he, always restrained, having forgotten that he could be seen by strangers, already wanted to embrace and squeeze Tamara to himself.

"Now, now!.." rapidly and deftly, like a cat, Tamara jumped off the chair. "Afterwards... afterwards, Senechka, afterwards, little dearie!.. I'll be all yours—there won't be any denial, nor forbiddance. I'll myself make you weary of me... Good-bye, my little silly!"

And with a quick movement of her hand having rumpled up his black curls, she hastily went out of the coffee-house.

CHAPTER VIII.

On the next day, on Monday, toward ten o'clock in the morning, almost all the inmates of the house—formerly Madam Shaibes', but now Emma Edwardovna Titzner's—rode off in cabs to the centre of the city, to the anatomical theatre—all, except the far-sighted, much-experienced Henrietta; the cowardly and insensible Ninka; and the feeble-minded Pashka, who for two days now had not gotten up from her bed, kept silent, and to questions directed at her answered by a beatific, idiotical smile and with some sort of inarticulate animal lowing. If she were not given to eat, she would not even ask; but if food were brought, she would eat with greediness, right with her hands. She became so slovenly and forgetful, that it was necessary to remind her of certain necessary functions in order to avoid unpleasantnesses. Emma Edwardovna did not send out Pashka to her steady guests, who asked for Pashka every day. Even before, she had had such periods of a detriment of consciousness; however, they had not lasted long, and Emma Edwardovna in any case determined to tide it over: Pashka was a veritable treasure for the establishment, and its truly horrible victim.

The anatomical theatre represented a long, one-storied, dark-gray building, with white frames around the windows and doors. There was in its very exterior something low, pressed down, receding into the ground, almost weird. The girls one after the other stopped near the gates and timidly passed through the yard into the chapel; nestled down at the other end of the yard, in a corner; painted over in the same dark gray colour, with white frame-work.

The door was locked. It was necessary to go after the watchman. Tamara with difficulty sought out a bald, ancient old man, grown over as though with bog moss by entangled gray bristles; with little rheumy eyes and an enormous, reddish, dark-blue granulous nose, on the manner of a cookie.

He unlocked the enormous hanging lock, pushed away the bolt and opened the rusty, singing door. The cold, damp air together with the mixed smell of the dampness of stones, frankincense, and dead flesh breathed upon the girls. They fell back, huddling closely into a timorous flock. Tamara alone went after the watchman without wavering.

It was almost dark in the chapel. The autumn light penetrated scantily through the little, narrow prison-like window, barred with an iron grating. Two or three images without chasubles, dark and without visages, hung upon the walls. Several common board coffins were standing right on the floor, upon wooden carrying shafts. One in the middle was empty, and the taken-off lid was lying alongside.

"What sort is yours, now?" asked the watchman hoarsely and took some snuff. "Do you know her face or not?"

"I know her."

"Well, then, look! I'll show them all to you. Maybe this one?.."

And he took the lid off one of the coffins, not yet fastened down with nails. A wrinkled old woman, dressed any old way in her tatters, with a swollen blue face, was lying there. Her left eye was closed; while the right was staring and gazing immovably and frightfully, having already lost its sparkle and resembling mica that had lain for a long time.

"Not this one, you say? Well, look... Here s more for you!" said the watchman; and one after the other, opening the lids, exhibited the decedents—all, probably, the poorest of the poor: picked up on the streets, intoxicated, crushed, maimed and mutilated, beginning to decompose. Certain ones had already begun to show on their hands and faces bluish-green spots, resembling mould

—signs of putrefaction. One man, without a nose, with an upper hare-lip cloven in two, had worms, like little white dots, swarming upon his sore-eaten face. A woman, who had died from hydropsy, reared like a whole mountain from her board couch, bulging out the lid.

All of them had been hastily sewn up after autopsy, repaired, and washed by the moss-covered watchman and his mates. What affair was it of theirs if, at times, the brain got into the stomach; while the skull was stuffed with the liver and rudely joined with the help of sticking plaster to the head?! The watchmen had grown used to everything during their night-marish, unlikely, drunken life; and, by the bye, almost never did their voiceless clients prove to have either relatives or acquaintances...

A heavy odour of carrion—thick, cloying, and so viscid that to Tamara it seemed as though it was covering all the living pores of her body just like glue—stood in the chapel.

"Listen, watchman," asked Tamara, "what's this crackling under my feet all the time?"

"Crack-ling?" the watchman questioned her over again, and scratched himself, "why, lice, it must be," he said indifferently. "It's fierce how these beasties do multiply on the corpseses!.. But who you lookin' for—man or woman?"

"A woman," answered Tamara.

"And that means that all these ain't yours?"

"No, they're all strangers."

"There, now!.. That means I have to go to the morgue. When did they bring her, now?"

"On Saturday, grandpa," and Tamara at this got out her purse. "Saturday, in the daytime. There's something for tobacco for you, my dear sir!"

"That's the way! Saturday, you say, in the daytime? And what did she have on?"

"Well, almost nothing; a little night blouse, an under-skirt... both the one and the other white."

"So-o! That must be number two hundred and seventeen... How is she called, now?.."

"Susannah Raitzina."

"I'll go and see—maybe she's there. Well, now, mam'selles," he turned to the young ladies, who were dully huddling in the doorway, obstructing the light. "Which of you are the braver? If your friend came the day before yesterday, then that means that she's now lying in the manner that the Lord God has created all mankind—that is, without anything... Well, who of you will be the bolder? Which two of you will come? She's got to be dressed..."

. "Well, now, you go, Manka," Tamara ordered her mate, who, grown chill and pale from horror and aversion, was staring at the dead with widely open, limpid eyes. "Don't be afraid, you fool—I'll go with you! Who's to go, if not you?!"

"Well, am I...well, am I?.." babbled out Little White Manka with barely moving lips. "Let's go. It's all the same to me..."

The morgue was right here, behind the chapel—a low, already entirely dark basement, into which one had to descend by six steps.

The watchman ran off somewhere, and returned with a candle-end and a tattered book. When he had lit the candle, the girls saw a score of corpses that were lying directly on the stone floor in regular rows—extended, yellow, with faces distorted by pre-mortal convulsions, with skulls split open, with clots of blood on the faces, with grinning teeth.

"Right away...right away..." the watchman was saying, guiding his finger over the headings. "The day before yesterday...that means, on Saturday...on Saturday... What did you say her name was, now?"

"Raitzina, Susannah," answered Tamara.

"Rai-tzina Susannah..." said the watchman, just as though he were singing, "Raitzina, Susannah. Just as I said. Two hundred seventeen."

Bending over the dead and illuminating them with the guttered and dripping candle-end, he passed from one to another. Finally he stopped before a corpse, upon whose foot was written in ink, in large black figures: 217.

"Here's the very same one! Let me, I'll carry her out into the little corridor and run after her stuff... Wait a while!..."

Grunting, but still with an ease amazing in one of his age, he lifted up the corpse of Jennka by the feet, and threw it upon his back with the head down, as though it were a carcass of meat, or a bag of potatoes.

It was a trifle lighter in the corridor; and, when the watchman had lowered his horrible burden to the floor, Tamara for a moment covered her face with her hands, while Manka turned away and began to cry.

"If you need anything, you say so," the watchman was instructing them. "If you want to dress the deceased as is fitting, then we can get everything that's required—cloth of gold, a little wreath, a little image, a shroud, gauze—we keep everything... You can buy a thing or two in clothing... Slippers, too, now..."

Tamara gave him money and went out into the air, letting Manka go in front of her.

*   *   *

After some time two wreaths were brought; one from Tamara, of asters and georginas with an inscription in black letters upon a white ribbon: "To Jennie from a friend;" the other was from Ryazanov, all of red flowers; upon its red ribbon stood in gold characters: "Through suffering shall we be purified." He also sent a short little note, expressing commiseration and apologizing for not being able to come, as he was occupied with an undeferrable business meeting.

Then came the singers who had been invited by Tamara —fifteen men from the very best choir in the city.

The precentor, in a gray overcoat and a gray hat, all gray, somehow, as though covered with dust, but with long, straight moustaches, like a military person's, recognized Verka; opened his eyes wide in astonishment, smiled slightly and winked at her. Two or three times a month, and sometimes even oftener, he visited Yamskaya Street with ecclesiastical academicians of his acquaintance, just the same precentors as he, and some psalmists; and having usually made a full review of all the establishments, always wound up with the house of Anna Markovna, where he invariably chose Verka.

He was a merry and a sprightly man; danced in a lively manner, in a frenzy; and executed such figures during the dances that all those present just melted from laughter.

Following the singers came the two-horsed catafalque, that Tamara had hired; black, with white plumes, and seven torch-bearers along with it. They also brought a white, glazed brocade coffin; and a pedestal for it, stretched over with black calico. Without hurrying, with habitually deft movements, they put away the deceased into the coffin; covered her face with gauze; curtained off the corpse with cloth of gold, and lit the candles—one at the head and two at the feet.

Now, in the yellow, trembling light of the candles, the face of Jennka became more clearly visible. The lividness had almost gone off it, remaining only here and there on the temples, on the nose, and between the eyes, in party-coloured, uneven, serpentine spots. Between the parted dark lips slightly glimmered the whiteness of the teeth, and the tip of the bitten tongue was still visible. Out of the open collar of the neck, which had taken on the colour of old parchment, showed two stripes: one dark—the mark of the rope; another red—the sign of the scratch, inflicted by Simeon during the encounter—just like two fearful necklaces. Tamara approached and with a safety pin pinned together the lace of the collar, at the very chin.

The clergy came: a little gray priest in gold spectacles, in a skull-cap; a lanky, tall, thin-haired deacon with a sickly, strangely dark and yellow face, as though of terracotta; and a sprightly, long-skirted psalmist, animatedly

exchanging on his way some gay, mysterious signs with
his friends among the singers.

Tamara walked up to the priest:

"Father," she asked, "how will you perform the funeral
service; all together or each one separate?"

"We perform the funeral service for all of them con-
jointly," answered the priest, kissing the stole, and extri-
cating his beard and hair out of its slits. "Usually, that
is. But by special request, and by special agreement, it's
also possible to do it separately. What death did the
deceased undergo?"

"She's a suicide, father."

"Hm...a suicide?.. But do you know, young person,
that by the canons of the church there isn't supposed to
be any funeral service...there ought not to be any? Of
course, there are exceptions—by special intercession...."

"Right here, father, I have certificates from the police
and from the doctor... She wasn't in her right mind...
in a fit of insanity..."

Tamara extended to the priest two papers, sent her the
evening before by Ryazanov, and on top of them three
bank-notes of ten roubles each. "I would beg you, father,
to do everything fitting—Christian like. She was a splendid being, and suffered a very great deal. And won't you
be so kind—go along with her to the cemetery, and there
hold one more little mass..."

"It's all right for me to go along with her to the cemetery, but in the cemetery itself I have no right to hold
service—there is a clergy of their own... And also here's
how, young person; in view of the fact that I'll have to
return once more after the rest, won't you, now...add
another little ten-spot."

And having taken the money from Tamara's hands, the
priest blessed the thurible, which had been brought up
by the psalmist, and began to walk around the body of the
deceased with thurification. Then, having stopped at her
head, he in a meek, wontedly sad voice, uttered:

"Blessed is our God. As it was in the beginning, is now, and ever shall be, world without end!"

The psalmist began pattering: *Holy God, Most Holy Trinity* and *Our Father* poured out like peas.

Quietly, as though confiding some deep, sad, occult mystery, the singers began in a rapid, sweet recitative: "With Thy blessed saints in glory everlasting, the soul of this Thy servant save, set at rest; preserving her in the blessed life, as Thou hast loving kindness for man."

The psalmist distributed the candles; and they with warm, soft, living little flames, one after the other, were lit in the heavy, murky air, tenderly and transparently illuminating the faces of the women.

Harmoniously the mournful melody flowed forth, and like the sighs of aggrieved angels sounded the great words: "Rest, oh God, this Thy servant and establish her in Heaven, wherein the faces of the just and the saints of the Lord shine like unto lights; set at rest this Thy servant who hath fallen asleep, contemning all her trespa-a-asses."

Tamara was listening intently to the long familiar, but now long unheard words, and was smiling bitterly. The passionate, mad words of Jennka came back to her, full of such inescapable despair and unbelief... Would the all-merciful, all-gracious Lord forgive or would He not forgive her foul, fumy, embittered, unclean life? All-Knowing—can it be that Thou wouldst repulse her—the pitiful rebel, the involuntary libertine; a child that had uttered blasphemies against Thy radiant, holy name? Thou—Benevolence, Thou—our Consolation!

A dull, restrained wailing, suddenly passing into a scream, resounded in the chapel. "Oh, Jennechka!" This was Little White Manka, standing on her knees and stuffing her mouth with her handkerchief, beating about in tears. And the remaining mates, following her, also got down upon their knees; and the chapel was filled with sighs, stifled lamentations and sobbings...

"Thou alone art deathless, Who hast created and made man; out of the dust of the earth were we made, and unto the same dust shall we return; as Thou hast ordained me, creating me and saying unto me, dust thou art and unto dust shalt thou return."

Tamara was standing motionless and with an austere face that seemed turned to stone. The light of the candle in thin gold spirals shone in her bronze-chestnut hair; while she could not tear her eyes away from the lines of Jennka's moist, yellow forehead and the tip of her nose, which were visible to Tamara from her place.

"Dust thou art and unto dust shalt thou return..." she was mentally repeating the words of the canticles. "Could it be that that would be all; only earth alone and nothing more? And which is better: nothing, or even anything at all—even the most execrable—but merely to be existing?"

And the choir, as though affirming her thoughts, as though taking away from her the last consolation, was uttering forlornly:

"And all mankind may go..."

They sang *Eternal Memory* through, blew out the candles, and the little blue streams spread in the air, blue from frankincense. The priest read through the farewell prayer; and afterwards, in the general silence, scooped up some sand with the little shovel handed to him by the psalmist, and cast it cross-wise upon the corpse, on top of the gauze. And at this he was uttering great words, filled with the austere, sad inevitability of a mysterious universal law: "The world is the Lord's, and its fulfillment the universe, and all that dwelleth therein."

The girls escorted their dead mate to the very cemetery. The road thither intersected the very entrance to Yamskaya Street. It would have been possible to turn to the left through it, and that would have been almost twice as short; but dead people were not usually carried through Yamskaya.

Nevertheless, out of almost all the doors their inmates poured out towards the cross-roads, in whatever they had on: in slippers upon bare feet, in night gowns, with kerchiefs upon their heads; they crossed themselves, sighed, wiped their eyes with their handkerchiefs and the edges of their jackets.

The weather cleared up... The cold sun shone brightly from a cold sky of radiant blue enamel; the last grass showed its green, the withered leaves on the trees glowed, showing their pink and gold... And in the crystal clear, cold air solemnly, and mournfully reverberated the sonorous sounds: "Holy God, Holy Almighty, Holy Everliving, have mercy upon us!" And with what flaming thirst for life, not to be satiated by aught; with what longing for the momentary—transient like unto a dream—joy and beauty of being; with what horror before the eternal silence of death, sounded the ancient refrain of John Damascene!

Then a brief requiem at the grave, the dull thud of the earth against the lid of the coffin... a small fresh hillock...

"And here's the end!" said Tamara to her comrades, when they were left alone. "Oh well, girls—an hour earlier, an hour later!.. I'm sorry for Jennka!.. Horribly sorry!.. We won't ever find such another. And yet, my children, it's far better for her in her pit than for us in ours... Well, let's cross ourselves for the last time—and home!.."

And when they all were already nearing their house, Tamara suddenly uttered pensively the strange, ominous words:

"And we won't be long together without her: soon we will be scattered by the wind far and wide. Life is good!.. Look: there's the sun, the blue sky... How pure the air is... Cobwebs are floating—it's Indian summer... How good it is in this world!.. Only we alone—we wenches—are wayside rubbish."

The girls started off on their journey. But suddenly from somewhere on the side, from behind a monument, a tall, sturdy student detached himself. He caught up with Liubka and softly touched her sleeve. She turned around and beheld Soloviev. Her face instantaneously turned pale, her eyes opened wide and her lips began to tremble.

"Go away!" she said quietly, with infinite hatred.

"Liuba... Liubochka..." Soloviev began to mumble. "I searched...searched for you... I... Honest to God, I'm not like that one... like Lichonin...I'm in earnest... even right now, even to-day..."

"Go away!" still more quietly pronounced Liubka.

"I'm serious... I'm serious... I'm not trifling, I want to marry..."

"Oh, you creature!" suddenly squealed out Liubka, and quickly, hard, peasant-like, hit Soloviev on the cheek with her palm.

Soloviev stood a little while, slightly swaying. His eyes were like those of a martyr... The mouth half-open, with mournful creases at the sides.

"Go away! Go away! I can't bear to look at all of you!" Liubka was screaming with rage. "Hangmen, swine!"

Soloviev unexpectedly covered his face with his palms and went back, without knowing his way, with uncertain steps, like one drunk.

CHAPTER IX.

And in reality, the words of Tamara proved to be prophetic: since the funeral of Jennie not more than two weeks had passed, but during this brief space of time so many events burst over the house of Emma Edwardovna as do not befall sometimes even in half a decade.

On the very next day they had to send off to a charitable institution—into a lunatic asylum—the unfortunate Pashka, who had fallen completely into feeble-mindedness. The doctors said that there was no hope of her ever improving. And in reality, as they had placed her in the hospital on the floor, upon a straw mattress, so did she remain upon it without getting up from it to her very death; submerging more and more into the black, bottomless abyss of quiet feeble-mindedness; but she died only half a year later, from bed-sores and infection of the blood.

The next turn was Tamara's.

For about half a month she fulfilled the duties of a housekeeper, was all the time unusually active, energetic; and somehow unwontedly wound up with that inner something of her own, which was so strongly fomenting within her. On a certain evening she vanished, and did not return at all to the establishment...

The matter of fact was, that in the city she had carried on a protracted romance with a certain notary—an elderly man, sufficiently rich, but exceedingly niggardly. Their acquaintance had been scraped up yet a year back, when they had been by chance travelling together on the same steamer to a suburban monastery, and had begun a conversation. The clever, handsome Tamara; her enigmatic, depraved smile; her entertaining conversation; her modest manner of deporting herself, had captivated the notary. She had even then marked down for herself this elderly man with picturesque gray hair, with seigniorial manners; an erstwhile jurisconsult and a man of good family. She did not tell him about her profession—it pleased her rather to mystify him. She only hazily, in a few words, hinted at the fact that she was a married lady of the middle class; that she was unfortunate in domestic life, since her husband was a gambler and a despot; and that even by fate she was denied such a consolation as children. At parting she refused to pass an evening with the notary, and did not want to meet him; but then she allowed him to write to her—general delivery, under a fictitious name. A correspondence commenced between them, in which the notary flaunted his style and the ardency of his feelings, worthy of the heroes of Paul Bourget. She maintained the same withdrawn, mysterious tone.

Then, being touched by the entreaties of the notary for a meeting, she made an appointment in Prince Park; was charming, witty, and languishing; but refused to go with him anywhere.

So she tortured her adorer and skillfully inflamed within him the last passion, which at times is stronger and more dangerous than first love. Finally, this summer, when the family of the notary had gone abroad, she decided to visit his rooms; and here for the first time gave herself up to him with tears, with twinges of her conscience, and at the same time with such ardour and tenderness, that the poor secretary lost his head completely—was plunged entirely into that senile love, which no longer knows either reason or retrospect; which compels a man to lose the last thing— the fear of appearing ridiculous.

Tamara was very sparing of her meetings. This inflamed her impatient friend still more. She consented to receiving from him bouquets of flowers, a modest breakfast in a suburban restaurant; but indignantly refused all expensive presents, and bore herself so skillfully and subtly, that the notary never got up the courage to offer her money. When he once stammered out something about a separate apartment and other conveniences, she looked him in the eyes so intently, haughtily, and sternly, that he, like a boy, turned red in his picturesque gray hairs, and kissed her hands, babbling incoherent apologies.

So did Tamara play with him, and feel the ground more and more under her. She already knew now on what days the notary kept in his fireproof iron safe especially large sums. However, she did not hurry, fearing to spoil the business through clumsiness or prematurity.

And so right now this long expected day arrived; a great contractors' fair had just ended, and all the notaries' offices were transacting deals for enormous sums every day. Tamara knew that the notary usually carried off the money to the bank on Saturdays, in order to be perfectly free on Sunday. And for that reason on Friday the notary received the following letter:

"My dear, my adored King Solomon! Thy Shulamite, thy girl of the vineyard, greets thee with burning kisses... Dear, to-day is a holiday for me, and I am infinitely happy. To-day I am free, as well as you. *He* has gone away to Homel for twenty-four hours on business matters, and I want to pass all the evening and ALL the night in your place. Ah, my beloved! All my life I am ready to pass on my knees before thee. I do not want to go anywhere. The suburban road-houses and cabarets have bored me long ago. I want you, only you...you...you alone. Await me, then, in the evening, my joy, about ten— eleven—o'clock! Prepare a great quantity of cold white wine, a canteloupe, and sugared chestnuts. I am burning, I am dying from desire! It seems to me, I will tire you out! I can not wait! My head is spinning around, my face burning, and my hands as cold as ice. I embrace you. Thy Valentina."

That very same evening, about eleven o'clock, she artfully, through conversation, led the notary into showing her his fireproof safe; playing upon his odd, pecuniary vanity. Rapidly gliding with her glance over the shelves and the movable boxes, Tamara turned away with a skillfully executed yawn and said:

"Fie, what a bore!"

And, having embraced the notary's neck, she whispered with her lips at his very ears, burning him with her hot breath:

"Lock up this nastiness, my treasure! Let's go!.. Let's go!.."

And she was the first to go out into the dining room.

"Come here, now, Volodya!" she cried out from there. "Come quicker! I want wine and after that love, love, love without end!.. No! Drink it all, to the very bottom! Just as we will drain our love to the very bottom to-day!"

The notary clinked glasses with her and at one gulp drank off his glass. Then he drew in his lips and remarked:

"Strange... The wine seems to be sort of bitter to-day.'

"Yes!" agreed Tamara and looked attentively at her lover. "This wine is always the least bit bitter. For such is the nature of Rhine wines..."

"But to-day it's especially strong," said the notary. "No, thanks, my dear—I don't want any more!"

After five minutes he fell asleep, sitting in his chair; his head thrown back against its back, and his lower jaw hanging down. Tamara waited for some time and started to awaken him. He was without motion. Then she took the lit candle, and, having placed it on the window sill giving out upon the street, went out into the entrance hall and began to listen, until she heard light steps on the stairs. Almost without a sound she opened the door and let in Senka, dressed like a real gentleman, with a brand new leather hand-bag in his hands.

"Ready?" asked the thief in a whisper.

"He's sleeping," answered Tamara, just as quietly. "Look, and here are the keys."

They passed together into the study with the fireproof safe. Having looked over the lock with the aid of a flash-light, Senka swore in a low voice:

"The devil take him, the old animal!.. I just knew that it would be a lock with a combination. Here you've got to know the letters... It's got to be melted with electricity, and the devil knows how much time it'll take."

"It's not necessary," retorted Tamara hurriedly. "I know the word... Pick it out: m-o-r-t-g-a-g-. Without the e."

After ten minutes they descended the steps together; went in purposely broken lines through several streets, hiring a cab to the depot only in the old city; and rode out of the city with irreproachable passports of citizens and landed proprietors—the Stavnitzkys, man and wife. For a long time nothing was heard of them until, a year later, Senka was caught in Moscow in a large theft, and gave Tamara away during the interrogation. They were both tried and sentenced to imprisonment.

Following Tamara came the turn of the naive, trusting, and amorous Verka. For a long time already she had been in love with a semi-military man, who called himself a civic clerk in the military department. His name was Dilectorsky. In their relations Verka was the adoring party; while he, like an important idol, condescendingly received the worship and the proffered gifts. Even from the end of summer Verka noticed that her beloved was becoming more and more cold and negligent; and, talking with her, was dwelling in thought somewhere far, far away. She tortured herself, was jealous, questioned him, but always received in answer some indeterminate phrases, some ominous hints at a near misfortune, at a premature grave...

In the beginning of September he finally confessed to her, that he had embezzled official money, big money, something around three thousand; and that after five days he would be checked up, and that he, Dilectorsky, was threatened with disgrace, the court, and, finally, hard labour... Here the civic clerk of the military department burst into sobs, clasping his head, and exclaimed·

"My poor mother!.. What will become of her? She will not be able to sustain this degradation... No!

Death is a thousand times better than these hellish tortures of a being guilty of naught.''

Although he was expressing himself, as always, in the style of the dime novels (in which way he had mainly enticed the trusting Verka), still, the theatrical thought of suicide, once arisen, no longer forsook him.

Somehow one day he was promenading for a long time with Verka in Prince Park. Already greatly devastated by autumn, this wonderful ancient park glistened and played with the magnificent tones of the foliage, blossoming out into colours: crimson, purple, lemon, orange and the deep cherry colour of old, settled wine; and it seemed that the cold air was diffusing sweet odours, like precious wine. And yet, a fine impress, a tender aroma of death, was wafted from the bushes, from the grass, from the trees.

Dilectorsky waxed tender; gave his feelings a free rein, was moved over himself, and began to weep. Verka wept a bit with him, too.

''To-day I will kill myself!'' said Dilectorsky finally. ''All is over!..''

''My own, don't!.. My precious, don't!..''

''It's impossible,'' answered Dilectorsky sombrely. ''The cursed money!.. Which is dearer—honour or life?!''

''My dear...''

''Don't speak, don't speak, Annetta!'' (He, for some reason, preferred to the common name of Verka the aristocratic Annetta, thought up by himself.) ''Don't speak. This is decided!''

''Oh, if only I could help you!'' exclaimed Verka woefully. ''Why, I'd give my life away... Every drop of blood!..''

''What is life?'' Dilectorsky shook his head with an actor's despondence. ''Farewell, Annetta!.. Farewell!..''

The girl desperately began to shake her head:

''I don't want it!.. I don't want it!.. I don't want it!.. Take me!.. I'll go with you too!..''

Late in the evening Dilectorsky took a room in an expensive hotel. He knew, that within a few hours, perhaps minutes, he and Verka would be corpses; and for that reason, although he had in his pocket only eleven kopecks, all in all, he gave orders sweepingly, like a habitual, downright prodigal; he ordered sturgeon stew, double snipes, and fruits; and, in addition to all this, coffee, liqueurs and two bottles of frosted champagne. And he was in reality convinced that he would shoot himself; but thought of it somehow affectedly, as though admiring, a trifle from the side, his tragic role; and enjoying beforehand the despair of his relatives and the amazement of his fellow clerks. While Verka, when she had suddenly said that she would commit suicide with her beloved, had been immediately strengthened in this thought. And there was nothing fearful to Verka in this impending death. "Well, now, is it better to croak just so, under a fence? But here it's together with your dearie! At least a sweet death!.." And she frantically kissed her clerk, laughed, and with dishevelled, curly hair, with sparkling eyes, was prettier than she had ever been.

The final triumphal moment arrived at last.

"You and I have both enjoyed ourselves, Annetta... We have drained the cup to the bottom and now, to use an expression of Pushkin's, must shatter the goblet!" said Dilectorsky. "You do not repent, oh, my dear?.."

"No, no!.."

"Are you ready?"

"Yes!" whispered she and smiled.

"Then turn away to the wall and shut your eyes!"

"No, no, my dearest, I don't want it so!.. I don't want it! Come to me! There, so! Nearer, nearer!.. Give me your eyes, I will be gazing into them. Give me your lips—I will be kissing you, while you... I am not afraid!.. Be braver!.. Kiss me harder!.."

He killed her; and when he looked upon the horrible deed of his hands, he then suddenly felt a loathsome,

abominable, abject fear. The half-naked body of Verka
was still quivering on the bed. The legs of Dilectorsky
gave in from horror; but the reason of a hypocrite, coward
and blackguard kept vigil: he did still have spirit sufficient
to stretch away at his side the skin over his ribs, and to
shoot through it. And when he was falling, frantically
crying out from pain, from fright, and from the thunder
of the shot, the last convulsion was running through the
body of Verka.

While two weeks after the death of Verka, the naive,
sportful, meek, brawling Little White Manka perished as
well. During one of the general, clamourous brawls, usual
in the Yamkas, in an enormous affray, some one killed her,
hitting her with a heavy empty bottle over the head. And
the murderer remained undiscovered to the last.

So rapidly did events take place in the Yamkas, in the
house of Emma Edwardovna; and well nigh not a one of
its inmates escaped a bloody, foul or disgraceful doom.

The final, most grandiose, and at the same time most
bloody calamity was the devastation committed on the
Yamkas by soldiers.

Two dragoons had been short-changed in a rouble establishment, beaten up, and thrown out at night into the
street. Torn to pieces, in blood, they returned to the
barracks, where their comrades, having begun in the
morning, were still finishing up their regimental holiday.
And so, not half an hour passed, when a hundred soldiers
burst into the Yamkas and began to wreck house after
house. They were joined by an innumerable mob that
gathered on the run—men of the golden squad,* ragamuffins, tramps, crooks, souteneurs. The panes were
broken in all the houses, and the grand pianos smashed to
smithereens. The feather beds were ripped open and the
down thrown out into the street; and yet for a long while
after—for some two days—the countless bits of down flew

Zolotorotzi—a subtle euphemism for cleaners of cesspools and
carters of the wealth contained therein.—*Trans.*

and whirled over the Yamkas, like flakes of snow. The wenches, bare-headed, perfectly naked, were driven out into the street. Three porters were beaten to death. The rabble shattered, befouled, and rent into pieces all the silk and plush furniture of Treppel. They also smashed up all the neighbouring taverns and drink-shops, while they were at it.

The drunken, bloody, hideous slaughter continued for some three hours; until the arrayed military authorities, together with the fire company, finally succeeded in repulsing and scattering the infuriated mob. Two half-rouble establishments were set on fire, but the fire was soon put out. However, on the next day the tumult again flared up; this time already over the whole city and its environs. Altogether unexpectedly it took on the character of a Jewish pogrom, which lasted for three days, with all its horrors and miseries.

And a week after followed the order of the governor-general about the immediate shutting down of houses of prostitution, on the Yamkas as well as other streets of the city. The proprietresses were given only a week's time for the settlement of matters in connection with their property.

Annihilated, crushed, plundered; having lost all the glamour of their former grandeur; ludicrous and pitiful, the aged, faded proprietresses and fat-faced, hoarse house-keepers were hastily packing up their things. And a month after only the name reminded one of merry Yamskaya Street; of the riotous, scandalous, horrible Yamkas.

However, even the name of the street was soon replaced by another, more respectable one, in order to efface even the memory of the former unpardonable times.

And all these Henriettas-Horses, Fat Kitties, Lelkas-Polecats and other women—always naive and foolish, often touching and amusing, in the majority of cases deceived and perverted children,—spread through the big city, were dissolved within it. Out of them was born a new stratum of society—a stratum of the strolling, street prostitutes-solitaries. And about their life, just as pitiful and incongruous, but tinged by other interests and customs, the author of this novel—which he still dedicates to youths and mothers—will some time tell.

THE END